Praise for Jo Nesbø and *Nemesis*

"A superb novel. . . . There is no shortage of Scandinavian crime writers available in translation, but Nesbø is in a class of his own. Bravo!—as they say in Norway." *The Evening Standard*

"Nesbø is one of Norway's hottest crime novelists, and [*Nemesis*] is as good as police procedurals get." *The Globe and Mail*

"A spiky police rivalry and terrific pace make this a cracking read, and a thrilling writer to seek out." *Financial Times*

"Nesbø has been one of Norway's leading crime fiction authors for ten years. . . . He has a terrific feel for character, and Hole, while sharing characteristics with so many similarly melancholic modern cops (including, of course, Mankell's Kurt Wallander), carves a place of distinction for himself in a crowded field." *Booklist*

"This take of revenge—with the U.S. bombing of Afghanistan pounding in the grim background—has twists galore, and enough humanity in it to keep it grounded. A master at work." *Time Out*

"This is how a truly hair-raising crime novel should be: full of surprises. . . . A skillfully written drama that never really lets you go."
Västerviks-Tidningen (Sweden)

"If you like Michael Connelly, you're going to like Jo Nesbø." *ELLE*

Jo Nesbø

Nemesis

TRANSLATED
FROM THE NORWEGIAN
BY
Don Bartlett

Vintage Canada

VINTAGE CANADA EDITION, 2009

Published in Canada by Vintage Canada, a division of Random House of Canada Limited,
Toronto, in 2009. Originally published in hardcover in Canada by Random House Canada, a
division of Random House of Canada Limited, Toronto, in 2008, and simultaneously in the
United Kingdom by Harvill Secker. Distributed by Random House of Canada Limited, Toronto.

Vintage Canada and colophon are registered trademarks of Random House of Canada Limited.

www.randomhouse.ca

Lyrics from 'Sing' by Travis
Lyrics by Fran Healy © Sony/ATV Music Publishing
All rights reserved. Used by permission.
Hávamál poem translated by Olive Bray (The Viking Club, London, 1908)

First published with the title Sorgenfri in 2002
by Aschehoug & Co. (W. Nygaard), Oslo

LIBRARY AND ARCHIVES CANADA CATALOGUING IN PUBLICATION

Nesbø, Jo, 1960–
Nemesis / Jo Nesbø ; translated from the Norwegian by Don Bartlett.

(The Harry Hole series : #4)
Translation of: Sorgenfri.
ISBN 978-0-307-35575-1

I. Bartlett, Don II. Title. III. Series: Nesbø, Jo, 1960–   . Harry Hole series ; 4

PT8951.24.E83S6713 2009   839.82'38   C2008-903681-6

This book was published with the financial assistance of NORLA
Map drawn by Reginald Piggott
Typeset by SX Composing DTP, Rayleigh, Essex

Printed and bound in the United States of America

6 8 9 7 5

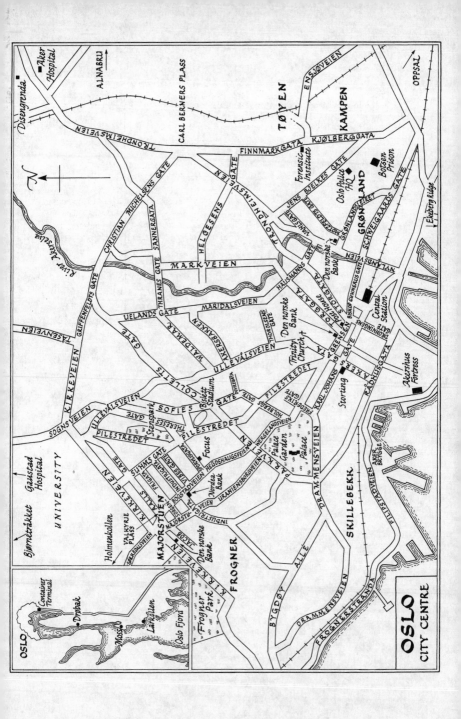

OSLO
CITY CENTRE

Part I

1

The Plan

I'M GOING TO DIE. AND IT MAKES NO SENSE. THAT WASN'T THE *plan, not my plan, anyway. I may have been heading this way all the time without realising. It wasn't my plan. My plan was better. My plan made sense.*

I'm staring down the muzzle of a gun and I know that's where it will come from. The messenger of death. The ferryman. Time for a last laugh. If you can see light at the end of the tunnel, it may be a spit of flame. Time for a last tear. We could have turned this life into something good, you and I. If we had followed the plan. One last thought. Everyone asks what the meaning of life is, but no one asks about the meaning of death.

2

The Astronaut

THE OLD MAN REMINDED HARRY OF AN ASTRONAUT. THE comical short steps, the stiff movements, the dead, black eyes and the shoes shuffling along the parquet floor. As if he were frightened to lose contact with the ground and float away into space.

Harry looked at the clock on the white wall above the exit. 15.16. Outside the window, in Bogstadveien, the Friday crowds hurry past. The low October sun is reflected in the wing mirror of a car driving away in the rush hour.

Harry concentrated on the old man. Hat plus elegant grey overcoat in dire need of a clean. Beneath it: tweed jacket, tie and worn grey trousers with a needle-sharp crease. Polished shoes, down at the heel. One of those pensioners of whom Majorstuen seems to be full. This wasn't conjecture. Harry knew that August Schulz was eighty-one years old and an ex-clothes retailer who had lived all his life in Majorstuen, apart from a period he spent in Auschwitz during the War. And the stiff knees were the result of a fall from a Ringveien footbridge which he used on his daily visits to his daughter. The impression of a mechanical doll was reinforced by the fact that his arms were bent perpendicularly at the elbow and thrust forward.

A brown walking stick hung over his right forearm and his left hand gripped a bank giro he was holding out for the short-haired young man at position number 2. Harry couldn't see the face of the cashier, but he knew he was staring at the old man with a mixture of sympathy and irritation.

It was 15.17 now, and finally it was August Schulz's turn.

Stine Grette sat at position number 1, counting out 730 Norwegian kroner for a boy in a blue woollen hat who had just given her a money order. The diamond on the ring finger of her left hand glistened as she placed each note on the counter.

Harry couldn't see, but he knew that in front of position number 3 there was a woman with a pram, which she was rocking, probably to distract herself, as the child was asleep. The woman was waiting to be served by fru Brænne, who was loudly explaining to a man on the telephone that he couldn't charge someone else's account unless the account holder had signed an agreement to that effect. She also informed him that she worked in the bank, and he didn't, so on that note perhaps they should bring the discussion to a close.

At that moment the door opened and two men, one tall, the other short, wearing the same overalls, strode into the bank. Stine Grette looked up. Harry checked his watch and began to count. The men ran over to the corner where Stine was sitting. The tall man moved as if he were stepping over puddles, while the little one had the rolling gait of someone who has acquired more muscle than he can accommodate. The boy in the blue hat turned slowly and began to walk towards the exit, so preoccupied with counting money that he didn't see the two men.

'Hello,' the tall man said to Stine, banging down a black case on the counter. The little one pushed his reflector sunglasses in place, walked forward and deposited an identical case beside it. 'Money!' he said in a high-pitched squeak. 'Open the door!'

*

It was like pressing the pause button: all movement in the bank froze. The only indication that time hadn't stood still was the traffic outside the window. And the second hand on the clock, which now showed that ten seconds had passed. Stine pressed a button under her desk. There was a hum of electronics, and the little man pressed the counter door against the wall with his knee.

'Who's got the key?' he asked. 'Quick, we haven't got all day!'

'Helge!' Stine shouted over her shoulder.

'What?' The voice came from inside the open door of the only office in the bank.

'We've got visitors, Helge!'

A man with a bow tie and reading glasses appeared.

'These gentlemen want you to open the ATM, Helge,' Stine said.

Helge Klementsen stared vacantly at the two men dressed in overalls, who were now on his side of the counter. The tall one glanced nervously at the front door while the little one had his eyes fixed on the branch manager.

'Oh, right. Of course,' Helge gasped, as if he had just remembered a missed appointment, and burst into a peal of frenetic laughter.

Harry didn't move a muscle; he simply let his eyes absorb every detail of their movements and gestures. Twenty-five seconds. He continued to look at the clock above the door, but from the corner of his eye he could see the branch manager unlocking the ATM from the inside, taking out two oblong metal dispensers and handing them over to the two men. The whole thing took place at high speed and in silence. Fifty seconds.

'These are for you, pop!' The little man had taken two similar metal dispensers from his case and held them out for Helge. The branch manager swallowed, nodded, took them and slotted them into the ATM.

'Have a good weekend!' the little one said, straightening his back and grabbing the case. One and a half minutes.

'Not so fast,' Helge said.

The little one stiffened.

Harry sucked in his cheeks and tried to concentrate.

'The receipt . . .' Helge said.

For one protracted moment the two men stared at the small, grey-haired branch manager. Then the little one began to laugh. Loud, reedy laughter with a piercing, hysterical overtone, the way people on speed laugh. 'You don't think we were going to leave here without a signature, do you? Hand over two million without a receipt!'

'Well,' Helge said. 'One of you almost forgot last week.'

'There are so many new bods on deliveries at the moment,' the little one said, as he and Helge signed and exchanged yellow and pink forms.

Harry waited for the front door to close again before looking at the clock once more. Two minutes and ten seconds.

Through the glass in the door he could see the white Nordea security van drive away.

Conversations between the people in the bank resumed. Harry didn't need to count, but he still did. Seven. Three behind the counter and four in front, including the baby and the man in overalls who had just come in and was standing by the table in the middle of the room, writing his account number on a payment slip. Harry knew it was for Sunshine Tours.

'Good afternoon,' August Schulz said and began to shuffle in the direction of the front door.

The time was exactly 15.21.10, and that was the moment the whole thing started.

When the door opened, Harry saw Stine Grette's head bob up from her papers and drop down. Then she raised her head again, slowly this time. Harry's attention moved to the front door. The man who had come in had already pulled down the zip of his boiler suit and whipped out a black-and-olive-green AG3. A navy blue balaclava completely covered his face, apart from his eyes. Harry started to count from zero.

The balaclava began to move where the mouth would have been, like a Bigfoot doll: 'This is a hold-up. Nobody move!'

He hadn't raised his voice, but in the small, compact bank building it was as if a cannon had gone off. Harry studied Stine. Above the distant drone of traffic he could hear the smooth click of greased metal as the man cocked the gun. Her left shoulder sank, almost imperceptibly.

Brave girl, Harry thought. Or maybe just frightened out of her wits. Aune, the psychology lecturer at Oslo Police College, had told them that when people are frightened enough they stop thinking and act the way they have been programmed. Most bank employees press the silent robbery alarm almost in shock, Aune maintained, citing post-robbery debriefings where many could not remember whether they had activated the alarm or not. They had been on autopilot. In just the same way as a bank robber has programmed himself to shoot anyone trying to stop him, Aune said. The more frightened the bank robber is, the less chance anyone has of making him change his mind. Harry was rigid as he tried to fix on the bank robber's eyes. Blue.

The robber unhitched a black holdall and threw it over the counter. The man in black took six paces to the counter door, perched on the top edge and swung his legs over to stand directly behind Stine, who was sitting still with a vacant expression. Good, Harry thought. She knows her instructions; she is not provoking a reaction by staring at the robber.

The man pointed the barrel of the gun at Stine's neck, leaned forward and whispered in her ear.

She hadn't panicked yet, but Harry could see Stine's chest heaving; her fragile frame seemed to be struggling for air under the now very taut white blouse. Fifteen seconds.

She cleared her throat. Once. Twice. Finally her vocal cords came to life:

'Helge. Keys for the ATM.' The voice was low and hoarse, completely unrecognisable from the one which had articulated almost the same words three minutes earlier.

Harry couldn't see him, but he knew that Helge had heard what the robber had said and was already standing in the office doorway.

'Quick, or else . . .' Her voice was hardly audible and in the following pause all that could be heard in the bank were the soles of August Schulz's shoes on the parquet flooring, like a couple of brushes swishing against the drum skin in an immeasurably slow shuffle.

'. . . he'll shoot me.'

Harry looked out of the window. There was often a car outside, engine running, but he couldn't see one. Only a blur of passing cars and people.

'Helge . . .' Her voice was imploring.

Come on, Helge, Harry urged. He knew quite a bit about the ageing bank manager, too. Harry knew that he had two standard poodles, a wife and a recently jilted pregnant daughter waiting for him at home. They had packed and were ready to drive to their mountain chalet as soon as Helge returned. At precisely this moment Helge felt he was submerged in water, in the kind of dream where all your movements slow down however much you try to hurry. Then he came into Harry's field of vision. The bank robber had swung Stine's chair round so that he was behind her, but now faced Helge. Like a frightened child who has to feed a horse, Helge stood back and held out the bunch of keys, his arm stretched to the limit. The masked man whispered in Stine's ear as he turned the machine gun on Helge, who took two unsteady steps backwards.

Stine cleared her throat: 'He says open the ATM and put the money in the black holdall.'

In a daze, Helge stared at the gun pointing at him.

'You've got twenty-five seconds before he shoots. Not you. Me.'

Helge's mouth opened and closed as though he wanted to say something.

'Now, Helge,' Stine said.

Thirty seconds had passed since the hold-up began. August Schulz had almost reached the front door. The branch manager fell to his knees in front of the ATM and contemplated the bunch of keys. There were four of them.

'Twenty seconds left,' Stine's voice rang out.

Majorstuen police station, Harry thought. The patrol cars are on their way. Eight blocks away. Friday rush hour.

With trembling fingers, Helge took one key and inserted it in the lock. It got stuck halfway. He pressed harder.

'Seventeen.'

'But . . .' he began.

'Fifteen.'

Helge pulled out the key and tried one of the others. It went in, but wouldn't turn.

'My God . . .'

'Thirteen. Use the one with the bit of green tape, Helge.'

Klementsen stared at the bunch of keys as though seeing them for the first time.

'Eleven.'

The third key went in. And round. He pulled open the door and turned towards Stine and the man.

'There is one more lock to open . . .'

'Nine!' Stine yelled.

Helge sobbed as he ran his fingers across the jagged edges of the keys, no longer able to see, using the edges as Braille to tell him which key was the right one.

'Seven.'

Harry listened carefully. No police sirens yet. August Schulz grasped the handle of the front door.

There was a metallic clunk as the bunch of keys hit the floor.

'Five,' Stine whispered.

The door opened and the sounds from the street flooded into the bank. Harry thought he could hear the familiar dying lament in the distance. It rose again. Police sirens. Then the door closed.

'Two, Helge!'

Harry closed his eyes and counted to two.

'There we are!' It was Helge shouting. He had opened the second lock and now he was half-standing, pulling at the jammed dispensers. 'Let me just get the money out! I—'

He was interrupted by a piercing shriek. Harry peered towards the other end of the bank where a woman stood staring in horror at the motionless bank robber pressing the gun into Stine's neck. She blinked twice and mutely nodded her head in the direction of the pram as the child's scream rose in pitch.

Helge almost fell backwards as the first dispenser came free. He pulled over the black holdall. Within six seconds all the money was in. Klementsen zipped up the holdall as instructed and stood by the counter. Everything had been communicated via Stine; her voice sounded surprisingly steady and calm now.

One minute and three seconds. The robbery was complete. The money was in a holdall. In a few moments the first police car will arrive. In four minutes other police cars will close off the immediate escape routes around the bank. Every cell in the robber's body must have been screaming it was time to get the hell out. And then something happened which Harry didn't understand. It simply didn't make any sense. Instead of running, the robber spun Stine's chair round until she was facing him. He leaned forward and whispered something to her. Harry squinted. He would have to go and get his eyes checked one of these days. But he saw what he saw. She was focused on her faceless tormentor; her own face went through a slow, gradual transformation as the significance of the words he whispered to her appeared to sink in. Her thin, well-tended eyebrows formed two 's's above eyes which now seemed to be popping out of her head; her top lip twisted upwards and the corners of her mouth were drawn down into a grotesque grin. The child stopped crying as suddenly as it had begun. Harry inhaled sharply. Because he knew. It was a freeze-frame, a masterly image. Two people caught for a split-second as one informed the other of the death sentence; the masked face two hands' widths away from its helpless counterpart. The Expeditor and his victim. The gun is

11

pointed at her throat and a small golden heart hanging from a thin chain. Harry cannot see, but nevertheless he can sense her pulse pounding beneath the thin skin.

A muffled wail. Harry pricks up his ears. It is not police sirens, though, just the telephone ringing in the next room.

The masked man turns and peers up at the surveillance camera hanging from the ceiling behind the counters. He holds up one hand and shows five black gloved fingers, then closes his hand and extends his forefinger. Six fingers. Six seconds too long. He turns towards Stine again, grasps the gun with both hands, holds it at hip height and raises the muzzle towards her head, standing with his legs slightly apart to withstand the recoil. The telephone keeps ringing. One minute and twelve seconds. The diamond ring flashes as Stine half-raises her hand, as though waving goodbye to someone.

It is exactly 15.22.22 when he pulls the trigger. The report is sharp and hollow. Stine's chair is forced backwards as her head dances on her neck like a mangled rag doll. Then the chair topples backwards. There is a thud as her head hits the edge of a desk and Harry can no longer see her. Nor can he see the poster advertising Nordea's new pension scheme glued to the outside of the glass partition above the counter, which now has a red background. All he can hear is the angry, insistent ringing of the telephone. The masked robber picks up the holdall. Harry has to make up his mind. The robber vaults the counter. Harry makes up his mind. In one quick movement he is out of the chair. Six strides. He is there. And picks up the phone:

'Speak!'

In the pause which follows he can hear the sound of the police siren on the TV in the sitting room, a Pakistani pop song from the neighbours and heavy steps up the stairwell sounding like fru Madsen's. Then there is a gentle laugh at the other end of the line. It is laughter from a long-distant encounter. Not in time, but just as distant. Like seventy per cent of Harry's past, which returns to him now and again in the form of vague rumours or total fabrications. But this was a story he could confirm.

'Do you really still use that macho line, Harry?'

'Anna?'

'Gosh, well done, Harry.'

Harry could feel the sweet warmth surging through his stomach, almost like whisky. Almost. In the mirror he saw a picture he had pinned up on the opposite wall. Of himself and Sis one summer holiday a long time ago in Hvitsten when they were small. They were smiling in the way that children do when they still believe nothing nasty can happen to them.

'And what do you do of a Sunday evening then, Harry?'

'Well.' Harry could hear his voice automatically mimicking hers. Slightly too deep, slightly too lingering. He didn't mean to do that. Not now. He coughed and found a more neutral pitch: 'What people usually do.'

'And that is?'

'Watch videos.'

3

The House of Pain

'Seen the video?'

The battered office chair screamed in protest as Police Officer Halvorsen leaned back and looked at his nine-years-senior colleague, Inspector Harry Hole, with an expression of disbelief on his innocent young face.

'Absolutely,' Harry said, running thumb and first finger down the bridge of his nose to show the bags under his bloodshot eyes.

'The whole weekend?'

'From Saturday morning to Sunday evening.'

'Well, at least you had a good time on Friday night,' Halvorsen said.

'Yes.' Harry took a blue folder out of his coat pocket and placed it on the desk facing Halvorsen's. 'I read the transcripts of the interviews.'

From the other pocket Harry took a grey packet of French Colonial coffee. He and Halvorsen shared an office at almost the furthest end of the corridor in the red zone on the sixth floor of Police Headquarters in Grønland. Two months ago they had gone to buy a Rancilio Silvia espresso coffee machine, which had taken pride of place on the filing cabinet beneath a framed photograph of a girl sitting with her legs up on a desk. Her freckled face seemed to be grimacing, but in fact she was helpless with laughter. The background was the same office wall on which the picture was hanging.

'Did you know that three out of four policemen can't spell "uninteresting" properly?' Harry said, hanging his coat on the stand. 'They either leave out the "e" between the "t" and the "r", or—'

'Interesting.'

'What did you do at the weekend?'

'On Friday, thanks to some anonymous nutter's phone call warning us about a car bomb, I sat in a car outside the American ambassador's residence. False alarm, of course, but things are so sensitive right now that we had to sit there all evening. On Saturday, I made another attempt to find the woman of my life. On Sunday, I concluded that she doesn't exist. What did you get on the robber from the interviews?' Halvorsen measured the coffee into a double-cup filter.

'*Nada*,' Harry said, taking off his sweater. Underneath, he was wearing a charcoal-grey T-shirt – it had once been black and now bore the faded letters *Violent Femmes*. He collapsed into the office chair with a groan. 'No one has reported seeing the wanted man near the bank before the robbery. Someone came out of a 7-Eleven on the other side of Bogstadveien and saw the man running up Industrigata. It was the balaclava that caught his attention. The surveillance camera outside the bank shows both of them as the robber passes the witness in front of a skip outside the 7-Eleven. The only interesting thing he could tell us which wasn't on the video was that the robber crossed the road twice further up Industrigata.'

'Someone who can't make up his mind which pavement to walk on. That sounds pretty uninteresting to me.' Halvorsen put the double-cup filter in the portafilter handle. 'With two "e"s, one "r" and one "s".'

'You don't know much about bank robberies, do you, Halvorsen.'

'Why should I? We're supposed to catch murderers. The guys from Hedmark can take care of the robbers.'

'Hedmark?'

'Haven't you noticed as you walk around the Robberies Unit? The rural dialect, the knitted cardigans. But what's the point you're making?'

'The point is Victor.'

'The dog handler?'

'As a rule, the dogs are the first on the scene, and an experienced bank robber knows that. A good dog can follow a robber on foot, but if he crosses the street and cars pass, the dog loses the scent.'

'So?' Halvorsen compressed the coffee with the tamper and finished off by smoothing the surface with a twist, which he maintained was what distinguished the professionals from the amateurs.

'It corroborates the suspicion that we are dealing with an experienced bank robber. And that fact alone means we can concentrate on a dramatically smaller number of people than we might otherwise have done. The Head of Robberies told me—'

'Ivarsson? Thought you weren't exactly on speaking terms?'

'We aren't. He was talking to the whole of the investigation team. He said there are under a hundred bank robbers in Oslo. Fifty of them are so stupid, doped up or mental that we nail them almost every time. Half of *them* are in prison, so we can ignore them. Forty are skilled craftsmen who manage to slip through so long as someone helps them with the planning. And then there are ten pros, the ones who attack security vans and cash-processing centres. To get them we need a lucky break, and we try to keep tabs on them at all times. They're being asked to give alibis right now.' Harry cast a glance at Silvia, who was gurgling away on the filing cabinet. 'And I had a word with Weber from Forensics on Saturday.'

'Thought Weber was retiring this month.'

'Someone slipped up. He won't be stopping until the summer.'

Halvorsen chuckled. 'He must be even grumpier than usual then.'

'He is, but that's not the reason,' Harry said. 'His lot found sod all.'

'Nothing?'

'Not one fingerprint. Not one strand of hair. Not even clothing fibres. And, of course, you could see from the footprint that he was wearing brand new shoes.'

'So they can't check the patterns of wear against other shoes?'

'Cor-rect,' Harry said, with a long 'o'.

'And the bank robber's weapon?' said Halvorsen, taking one of the cups of coffee over to Harry's desk. On looking up, he noticed that Harry's left eyebrow was almost into his cropped blond hair. 'Sorry. The murder weapon.'

'Thank you. It wasn't found.'

Halvorsen sat on his side of the two desks sipping at his coffee. 'So, in a nutshell, a man walked into a crowded bank in broad daylight, took two million kroner, murdered a woman, strolled out, up a relatively unpopulated but heavily trafficked street in the centre of the capital of Norway, a few hundred metres from a police station and we, the salaried police professionals, do not have a thing to go on?'

Harry nodded slowly. 'Almost nothing. We have the video.'

'Which you can visualise every second of, if I know you.'

'No, every tenth of a second, I would say.'

'And you can quote the witnesses' statements verbatim?'

'Only August Schulz's. He told me a lot of interesting things about the War. Reeled off the names of competitors in the clothing industry; so-called good Norwegians who had supported the confiscation of his family's property during the War. He knew precisely what these people are doing nowadays. Yet he didn't realise that a bank robbery had been committed.'

They drank their coffee in silence. The rain beat against the window.

'You like this life, don't you,' Halvorsen said suddenly. 'Sitting alone all weekend chasing ghosts.'

Harry smiled, but didn't answer.

'I thought that now you had family obligations you'd given up the solitary lifestyle.'

Harry sent his younger colleague an admonitory grimace. 'Don't know if I see it like that,' he said slowly. 'We don't even live together, you know.'

'No, but Rakel has a little boy and that makes things different, doesn't it?'

'Oleg,' Harry said, edging his way towards the filing cabinet. 'They flew to Moscow on Friday.'

'Oh?'

'Court case. Father wants custody.'

'Ah, that's right. What's he like?'

'Hm.' Harry straightened the crooked picture above the coffee machine. 'He's a professor Rakel met and married while she was working there. He comes from a wealthy, traditional family with loads of political influence, Rakel says.'

'So they know a few judges, eh?'

'Bound to, but we think it'll be alright. The father's a wacko, and everyone knows that. Bright alcoholic with poor self-control, you know the type.'

'I think I do.'

Harry looked up smartly, just in time to see Halvorsen wipe away a smile.

At Police HQ it was fairly well known that Harry had alcohol problems. Nowadays, alcoholism is not in itself grounds for dismissing a civil servant, but to be drunk during working hours is. The last time Harry had had a relapse, there were people higher up in the building who had advocated having him removed from the force, but *Politiavdelingssjef*, PAS for short, Bjarne Møller, head of Crime Squad, had spread a protective wing over Harry pleading extenuating circumstances. The circumstances had been the woman in the picture above the espresso machine – Ellen Gjelten, Harry's partner and close friend – who had been beaten to death with a baseball bat on a path down by the river Akerselva. Harry had struggled to his feet again, but the wound still stung. Particularly because, in Harry's opinion, the case had never been cleared up satisfactorily. When Harry and Halvorsen had found forensic evidence incriminating the neo-Nazi Sverre Olsen, Inspector Tom Waaler had wasted no time in going to Olsen's home to arrest him. Olsen had apparently fired a shot at Waaler, who had returned fire in self-defence and killed him. According to Waaler's report, that is. Neither the investigations at the scene of the shooting, nor the inquiry by SEFO, the independent police authority, suggested otherwise. On the other hand, Olsen's motive for killing Ellen had never been explained, beyond indications that he had been involved in the illegal arms trafficking which had caused Oslo to be flooded with handguns over recent years, and Ellen had stumbled onto his trail. Olsen was just an errand boy, though; the police still didn't have any leads on those behind the liquidation.

After a brief guest appearance with *Politiets Overvåkningstjeneste*, or POT, the Security Service, on the top floor, Harry had applied to rejoin Crime Squad to work on the Ellen Gjelten case. They had been all too happy to get rid of him. Møller was pleased to have him back on the sixth floor.

'I'll just nip upstairs to give Ivarsson this,' Harry muttered, waving the VHS cassette. 'He wanted to take a look with a new wunderkind they have up there.'

'Oh? Who's that?'

'Someone who left Police College this summer and has apparently solved three robberies simply by studying the videos.'

'Wow. Good-looking?'

Harry sighed. 'You young ones are so boringly predictable. I hope she's competent. I don't care about the rest.'

'Sure it's a woman?'

'Herr and fru Lønn might have called their son Beate for a joke, I suppose.'

'I have an inkling she's good-looking.'

'Hope not,' Harry said, ducking, out of ingrained habit, to allow his 192 centimetres to pass under the door frame.

'Oh?'

The answer was shouted from the corridor: 'Good police officers are ugly.'

At first sight, Beate Lønn's appearance didn't give any firm indicators either way. She wasn't ugly; some would even call her doll-like. But that might have been mostly because she was small: her face, nose, ears – and her body. Her most prominent feature was her pallor. Her skin and hair were so colourless that she reminded Harry of a corpse Ellen and he had once fished out of Bunnefjord. Unlike with the woman's body, however, Harry had a feeling that if he just turned away for a second he would forget what Beate Lønn looked like. Which, it seemed, she wouldn't have minded as she mumbled her name and allowed Harry to shake her small, moist hand before she quickly retrieved it.

'Inspector Hole is a kind of legend here in the building, you know,' PAS Rune Ivarsson said, standing with his back to them and fiddling with a bunch of keys. At the top of the grey iron door in front of them a sign said, in Gothic letters: THE HOUSE OF PAIN. And underneath: CONFERENCE ROOM 508. 'Isn't that right, Hole?'

Harry didn't answer. He had absolutely no doubt about the kind of legendary status Ivarsson had in mind; he had never made the slightest attempt to hide his view that Harry was a blot on the force and should have been removed years ago.

Ivarsson finally unlocked the door and they went in. The House of Pain was the Robberies Unit's dedicated room for studying, editing and copying video recordings. There was a large table in the middle with three workplaces; no windows. The walls were covered with shelving packed with video tapes, a dozen posters of wanted robbers, a large screen on one wall, a map of Oslo and various trophies from successful arrests: for example beside the door, where two cut-off woollen sleeves with holes for eyes and mouth hung from the wall. Otherwise the room contained grey PCs, black TV monitors, video and DVD players as well as a number of other machines which Harry could not have identified.

'What has Criiime Squad got out of the video?' Ivarsson asked, flopping down onto one of the chairs. He drawled the diphthong in an exaggerated fashion.

'Something,' Harry said, walking over to a shelf of video cassettes.

'Something?'

'Not very much.'

'Shame you lot didn't come to the lecture I gave in the canteen last September. All the units were represented except yours, if I'm not very much mistaken.'

Ivarsson was tall, long-limbed, with a fringe of undulating blond hair above two blue eyes. His face had those masculine characteristics which models for German brands like Boss tend to have, and was still tanned after many summer afternoons on the tennis court and perhaps the odd solarium session in a fitness centre. In short, Rune Ivarsson was what most would regard as a good-looking man, and as such he underpinned Harry's theory about the link between looks and competence in police work. However, what Rune Ivarsson lacked in investigative talent, he made up for with a nose for politics and the ability to form alliances within the Police HQ hierarchy. Furthermore, Ivarsson had the natural self-confidence that many misinterpret as a leadership quality. In his case, this confidence was based solely on being blessed with a total blindness to his own shortcomings, a quality which would inevitably take him to the top and one day make him – in one way or another – Harry's superior. Initially, Harry saw no reason to complain about mediocrity being kicked upwards, out of the way of investigations, but the danger with people like Ivarsson was that they could easily get it into their heads that they should intervene and dictate to those who really understood detection work.

'Did we miss anything?' Harry asked, running a finger along the small handwritten labels on the videos.

'Maybe not,' Ivarsson said. 'Unless you're interested in those minute details which solve crime cases.'

Harry successfully resisted the temptation to say he hadn't gone to the lecture because he had been told by others, who had attended earlier talks, that the sole purpose of his grandstanding was to announce to all and sundry that after he had taken over as Head of the Robberies Unit the clear-up rate for bank robberies rose from thirty-five per cent to fifty per cent. Not a word about the fact that his appointment coincided with a doubling of manpower in his unit, a general extension of their investigative powers and the simultaneous departure of their worst investigator – Rune Ivarsson.

'I regard myself as reasonably interested,' Harry said. 'So, tell me how you solved this one.' He took out one of the cassettes and read aloud what was written on the label: '20.11.94, NOR Savings Bank, Manglerud.'

Ivarsson laughed. 'Gladly. We caught them the old-fashioned way. They switched getaway cars at a waste site in Alnabru and set fire to the one they dumped. But it didn't burn out. We found the gloves of one of the robbers and traces of DNA. We matched them with those of known robbers our investigators had highlighted as potential suspects after having seen the video, and one of them fitted the bill. The idiot had fired a shot into a ceiling and got four years. Anything else you were wondering about, Hole?'

'Mm.' Harry fidgeted with the cassette. 'What sort of DNA was it?'

'I told you, DNA that matched.' The corner of Ivarsson's left eye began to twitch.

'Right, but what was it? Dead skin? A nail? Blood?'

'Is that important?' Ivarsson's voice had become sharp and impatient.

Harry told himself he should keep his mouth shut. He should give up these Don Quixote-like offensives. People like Ivarsson would never learn, anyway.

'Maybe not,' Harry heard himself say. 'Unless you're interested in those minute details which solve crime cases.'

Ivarsson looked daggers at Harry. In the specially insulated room the silence felt like physical pressure on everyone's ears. Ivarsson opened his mouth to speak.

'Knuckle hair.'

Both men in the room turned to Beate Lønn. Harry had almost forgotten she was there. She looked from one to the other and repeated in a near-whisper: 'Knuckle hair. The hair on your fingers . . . isn't that what it's called . . . ?'

Ivarsson cleared his throat. 'You're right, it was a hair. But I think it was – although we don't need to go into this any deeper – a hair from the back of the hand. Isn't that right, Beate?' Without waiting for an answer he tapped on the glass of his large wristwatch. 'Have to be off. Enjoy the video.'

As the door slammed behind Ivarsson, Beate took the video cassette out of Harry's hand and the next moment the video player sucked it in with a hum.

'Two hairs,' she said. 'In the left-hand glove. From the knuckle. And the rubbish tip was in Karihaugen, not Alnabru. But the bit about four years is right.'

Harry gave her an astonished look. 'Wasn't that a little before your time?'

She shrugged as she pressed PLAY on the remote control. 'It's only a matter of reading reports.'

'Mm,' Harry said and studied her profile. Then he made himself comfortable in the chair. 'Let's see if this one left behind a few knuckle hairs.'

The video player groaned and Beate switched off the light. In the moments that followed, while the blue lead-in picture illuminated them, another film unravelled in Harry's head. It was short, lasting barely a couple of seconds, a scene bathed in the blue strobe light from Waterfront, a long-defunct club in Aker Brygge. He didn't know her name, the woman with the smiling brown eyes who was trying to shout something to him above the music. They were playing cow-punk. Green on Red. Jason and the Scorchers. He poured Jim Beam into his Coke and didn't give a stuff what her name was. The next night, though, he knew. When they were in the bed adorned with a ship's figurehead, a headless horse, had cast off all the moorings and set out on their maiden voyage. Harry felt the warmth in his belly from the evening before when he had heard her voice on the telephone.

Then the other film took over.

The old man had begun his trek across the floor towards the counter, filmed from a different camera every five seconds.

'Thorkildsen at TV2,' Beate Lønn said.

'No, it's August Schulz,' Harry said.

'I mean the editing,' she said. 'It looks like Thorkildsen's handiwork at TV2. There are a few tenths missing here and there . . .'

'Missing? How can you see . . . ?'

'Number of things. Follow the background. The red Mazda you can make out in the street outside was in the centre of the picture on two cameras when the picture shifted. An object can't be in two places at the same time.'

'Do you mean someone has bodged the recording?'

'Not at all. Everything on the six cameras inside and the one outside is recorded on the same tape. On the original tape the picture jumps quickly from one camera to another and all you see is a flicker. So the film has to be edited to get longer coherent sequences. Occasionally we call in people from the TV stations when we don't have the capacity. TV editors like Thorkildsen fiddle with the time code to improve the quality of the recording, not as jagged. Professional neurosis, I guess.'

'Professional neurosis,' Harry repeated. It struck him that was a strangely middle-aged thing for a young girl to say. Or perhaps she wasn't as young as he had first thought? Something had happened to her as soon as the lights were off. The silhouetted body language was more relaxed, her voice firmer.

The robber entered the bank and shouted in English. His voice sounded distant and muffled, it seemed to be wrapped in a duvet.

'What do you think about this?' Harry asked.

'Norwegian. He speaks English so that we won't recognise his dialect, accent or any characteristic words we might be able to link to earlier robberies. He's wearing smooth clothes which don't leave fibres we might be able to trace in getaway cars, bolt-holes or his house.'

'Mm. Any more?'

'All the openings in his clothes are taped over so he won't leave any traces of DNA. Like hair or sweat. You can see his trouser legs are taped round his boots, and the sleeves round his gloves. I would guess he has tape round his head and wax on his eyebrows.'

'A pro then?'

She shrugged. 'Eighty per cent of bank raids are planned less than a week in advance and are carried out by people under the influence of alcohol or drugs. This one was thought through and the robber doesn't appear to be on anything.'

'How can you make that out?'

'If we'd had better light and cameras, we'd have been able to magnify the pictures and see his pupils. But we don't, so I go by his body language. Calm, considered movements, can you see that? If he was on anything, it wasn't speed or any kind of amphetamine. Rohypnol, perhaps. That's the popular one.'

'Why's that?'

'Robbing a bank is an extreme experience. You don't need speed, just the opposite. Last year someone went into Den norske Bank in Solli plass with an automatic weapon, peppered the ceiling and walls and ran out again without any money. He told the judge that he'd popped so much amphetamine that he just had to get it out of his system. I prefer criminals who take Rohypnol, if I may put it like that.'

Harry motioned with his head to the screen. 'Look at Stine Grette's shoulder at position number 1; she's pressing the alarm. And the sound on the recording is suddenly much better. Why?'

'The alarm is connected to the recording device, and when it is activated the film begins to run much faster. That gives us better pictures and better sound. Good enough for us to analyse the robber's voice. And, then, speaking English doesn't help him.'

'Is it really as reliable as they say?'

'The sound of our vocal cords is like a fingerprint. If we can give our voice analyst, at the university in Trondheim, ten words on tape, he can match two voices with ninety-five per cent reliability.'

'Mm. But not with the sound quality we had before the alarm went, I take it?'

'It's less reliable.'

'So that's why he shouts in English first, and then when he reckons the alarm has been activated, he uses Stine Grette as his mouthpiece.'

'Exactly.'

In silence they observed the black-clad man manoeuvring himself over the counter, putting the gun barrel to Stine Grette's neck and whispering into her ear.

'What do you think about her reaction?' Harry asked.

'What do you mean?'

'Her facial expression. She seems relatively calm, don't you think?'

'I don't think anything. Generally, you can't get much information from a facial expression. I would think her pulse is close on 180.'

They watched Helge Klementsen floundering on the floor in front of the cash dispenser.

'Hope he gets proper post-trauma treatment,' Beate said sotto voce and shook her head. 'I've seen people become psychological wrecks after being exposed to robberies like this one.'

Harry said nothing, but thought that statement had to be something she had picked up from older colleagues.

The robber turned and displayed six fingers.

'Interesting,' Beate mumbled and, without looking down, made a note on the pad in front of her. Harry followed the young police-woman out of the corner of his eye and watched her jump when the shot was fired. While the robber on the screen swept up the holdall, sprang over the counter, and ran out of the door, Beate's little chin rose and her pen fell out of her hand.

'We haven't put the last part on the Net, or passed it on to any of the TV stations,' Harry said. 'Look, now he's on the camera outside the bank.'

They watched the robber walk across the pedestrian crossing – on green – in Bogstadveien before making his way up Industrigata. Then he was outside the frame.

'And the police?' Beate asked.

'The closest police station is in Sørkedalsveien just after the toll station, only eight hundred metres from the bank. Nevertheless, it took just over three minutes from the time the alarm went off until they arrived. So the robber had less than two minutes to make his escape.'

Beate looked at the screen thoughtfully, at the people and cars passing by as though nothing had happened.

'The escape was as meticulously planned as the hold-up. The getaway car was probably parked around the corner so that it wouldn't be caught by the cameras outside the bank. He's been lucky.'

'Perhaps,' Harry said. 'On the other hand, he doesn't strike you as someone who relies on good fortune, does he?'

Beate shrugged. 'Most bank robberies seem well planned if they're successful.'

'OK, but here it was odds on that the police would be delayed. On Friday at this time all the patrol cars in the area were busy somewhere else, at—'

'—the American ambassador's residence!' Beate exclaimed, slapping her forehead. 'The anonymous phone call about the car bomb. I had Friday off, but I saw it on the TV news. And if you think how hysterical people are nowadays, it's obvious everyone there would have been.'

'There was no bomb.'

'Of course not. It's the classic ruse to keep the police busy somewhere else before a hold-up.'

They sat watching the last part of the recording in thoughtful

27

silence. August Schulz standing waiting at the pedestrian crossing. Green changes to red and back again without him moving. What's he waiting for? Harry wondered. An irregularity? An extra-long sequence on green? A kind of hundred-year green wave? Alright. Should come soon. In the distance he heard the police sirens.

'There's something not quite right.'

Beate Lønn answered with the weary sigh of an old man: 'There's always something not quite right.'

Then the film was over and the snowstorm swept across the screen.

4

The Echo

'Snow?'

Harry shouted into his mobile phone as he hurried along the pavement.

'Yes, really,' Rakel said over a bad line from Moscow. This was followed by a hissy echo: '. . . eally.'

'Hello?'

'It's freezing here . . . ere. Inside and outside . . . ide.'

'And in the court?'

'Well below freezing there, too. When we lived here, his mother even said I should take Oleg away. Now she's sitting with the others and sending me such hateful scowls . . . owls.'

'How's the case going?'

'How should I know?'

'Well. First of all, you studied law. Secondly, you speak Russian.'

'Harry. In common with 150 million Russians I don't understand a thing about the legal system here, OK? . . . kay?'

'OK. How's Oleg taking it?'

Harry repeated his question without getting an answer and held up the display to see if he had lost the connection, but the seconds on the conversation timer were ticking away. He put the phone to his ear again.

'Hello?'

'Hello, Harry, I can hear you . . . oooh. I miss you so . . . ohh. What's with the ha ha? . . . aah.'

'There's an echo on the line. Lots of oohs, ohs and aahs.'

Harry had reached the main door, pulled out a key and unlocked the hall entrance.

'Do you think I'm too pushy, Harry?'

'Of course not.'

Harry nodded to Ali, who was trying to manoeuvre a kicksled through the cellar door. 'I love you. Are you there? I love you! Hello?'

Harry looked up from the dead phone in bewilderment and noticed his Pakistani neighbour's beaming smile.

'Yes, yes, you, too, Ali,' he mumbled as he laboriously tapped in Rakel's number again.

'Call register,' Ali said.

'Hey?'

'Nothing. Tell me if you want to let your cellar room. You don't use it much, do you?'

'Have I got a storeroom in the cellar?'

Ali rolled his eyes. 'How long have you lived here, Harry?'

'I said . . . I love you.'

Ali gave Harry a searching look. Harry waved goodbye to Ali and gestured that he had got through. He jogged upstairs with the key in front of him like a divining rod.

'That's it, we can talk now,' Harry said as he went through the doorway into his sparsely furnished yet tidy two-room flat, bought for a song some time in the nineties when the housing market was rock bottom. Every so often he thought the flat had used up his share of luck for the rest of his life.

'I wish you were here with us, Harry. Oleg misses you, too.'

'Did he say that?'

'He doesn't need to say it. In that respect, you're very similar.'

'You, I've just told you I love you. Three times. With the neighbour listening. Do you know what that sort of thing does to a man?'

Rakel laughed. Harry loved her laugh, had done so from the very first moment he heard it. Instinctively, he knew he would do anything to hear it more often. Every day for preference.

He kicked off his shoes and smiled when he saw the answerphone in the corridor blinking to tell him there was a message. He didn't need to be psychic to know it was from Rakel earlier in the day. No one else phoned Harry Hole at home.

'How do you know you love me then?' Rakel cooed. The echo was gone.

'I can feel myself getting hot in the . . . what's it called?'

'Heart?'

'No, it's back a bit and under the heart. Kidneys? Liver? Spleen? Yes, that's the one. I can feel my spleen heating up.'

Harry wasn't sure if it was sobbing or laughing he could hear at the other end. He pressed PLAY on the answerphone.

'I hope to be home in two weeks,' Rakel said on the mobile before being drowned out by the answerphone:

'Hi, it's me again . . .'

Harry felt his heart skip a beat and he reacted before thinking. He pressed STOP. But it was as if the echo of the words spoken in the charming, slightly husky woman's voice continued to wash back and forth between the walls.

'What was that?' Rakel asked.

Harry took a deep breath. One thought struggled to reach him before he answered, but it arrived too late: 'Just the radio.' He cleared his throat. 'When you're sure, let me know which flight you'll be on and I'll pick you up.'

'Of course I will,' she said with surprise in her voice.

There was a strained pause.

'I have to hang up now,' Rakel said. 'Shall we talk at eight tonight?'

31

'Yes. I mean, no. I'll be busy then.'

'Oh? I hope it's something nice for a change.'

'Well,' Harry said with a sharp intake of breath. 'I'm going out with a woman anyway.'

'Who's the lucky person?'

'Beate Lønn. New officer in the Robberies Unit.'

'And what is the occasion?'

'A chat with Stine Grette's husband. She was shot during the Bogstadveien hold-up I told you about. And with the branch manager.'

'Enjoy yourself. We'll talk tomorrow. Oleg wants to say goodnight first.'

Harry heard small feet running and then excited breathing on the line.

After they had finished speaking, Harry stood in the hall staring at the mirror above the telephone table. If his theory held true, he was now looking at a competent policeman. Two bloodshot eyes, one on each side of a large nose with a network of fine blue veins in a pale, bony face with deep pores. His wrinkles looked like random knife slashes across a wooden beam. How had it happened? In the mirror he saw behind him the wall with the photograph of the suntanned, smiling face of the boy with his sister. But it wasn't lost good looks or lost youth Harry's mind was occupied with, because the thought had finally made its way through now. He was searching his own features for the deceit, the evasion, the cowardice which had just made him break one of the few promises he had made to himself: that he would never, ever, come what may, lie to Rakel. Of all the skerries in the sea for their relationship to founder on, and there were many, lies would not be one. So why had he told a lie? It was true he and Beate were going to meet Stine Grette's husband, but why had he not told her he was going to meet Anna afterwards? An old flame, but so what? It had been a brief stormy affair which had left scars, though no lasting injuries. They were only going to chat over a cup of coffee and tell each other the what-they-did-afterwards stories. And then each go their separate ways.

Harry pressed PLAY on the answerphone to hear the rest of the message. Anna's voice filled the hall: '. . . look forward to seeing you at M this evening. Just two things. Could you pop into the locksmith's in Vibes gate on the way and pick up the keys I ordered? They're open till seven and I've told them to keep them in your name. And would you mind wearing the jeans you know I like so much?'

Deep, husky laugh. The room seemed to vibrate to the same rhythm. No doubt about it, she had not changed.

5

Nemesis

THE RAIN WAS MAKING SPEED LINES AGAINST THE PRE-
maturely darkened October sky in the light from the outside
lamp. From the ceramic sign beneath, Harry read that Espen, Stine
and Trond Grette lived here, 'here' being a yellow terraced house
in Disengrenda. He pressed the bell and surveyed the locality.
Disengrenda was four long rows of terraced houses at the centre of a
large flat field encircled by blocks of flats, which reminded Harry of
pioneers on the prairie taking up a defensive position against Indian
attacks. Perhaps that was how it was. The terraced houses were built
in the sixties for the burgeoning middle classes and perhaps the
dwindling local population of workers in the blocks in Disenveien
and Traverveien already knew that these were the new conquerors;
that they would have hegemony over the new country.

'Doesn't seem to be at home,' Harry said, pressing the button
once more. 'Are you sure he understood we were coming this
afternoon?'

'No.'

'No?' Harry turned and looked down at Beate Lønn shivering
under the umbrella. She was wearing a skirt and high-heeled shoes,

and when she picked him up outside Schrøder's it had crossed his mind that she seemed to be dressed for a coffee morning.

'Grette confirmed the meeting twice when I rang,' she said. 'But he seemed completely . . . out of it.'

Harry leaned across the step and flattened his nose against the kitchen window. It was dark inside and all he could see was a white Nordea Bank calendar on the wall.

'Let's go back,' he said.

At that moment the neighbour's kitchen window opened with a bang. 'Are you looking for Trond?'

The words were articulated in *bokmål*, standard Norwegian, but in a Bergen accent with such strong trilled 'r's that it sounded like a medium-sized train being derailed. Harry turned round and gazed into a woman's brown, wrinkled face caught in an attempt to smile and appear grave at the same time.

'We are,' Harry confirmed.

'Family?'

'Police.'

'Right,' the woman said and dropped the funereal expression. 'I thought you had come to express your sympathy. He's on the tennis court, poor thing.'

'Tennis court?'

She pointed. 'On the other side of the field. He's been there since four o'clock.'

'But it's dark,' Beate said. 'And it's raining.'

The woman rolled her shoulders. 'Must be the grief, I suppose.' She trilled her 'r's so much that Harry began to think about when he was growing up in Oppsal and about the bits of cardboard they used to insert in cycle wheels so they flapped against the spokes.

'You grew up in East Oslo, too, I can hear,' Harry said as he and Beate walked towards where the woman had indicated. 'Or am I mistaken?'

'No,' Beate said, unwilling to expatiate.

The tennis court was positioned halfway between the blocks and the terraced houses. They could hear the dull thud of racquet strings on wet tennis ball. Inside the high wire-mesh fence they could make out a figure standing and serving in the quickly gathering autumn gloom.

'Hello!' Harry shouted when they reached the fence, but the man didn't answer. It was only now that they saw he was wearing a jacket, shirt and tie.

'Trond Grette?'

A ball hit a black puddle of water, bounced up, hit the fence and sprayed them with a fine shower of rainwater, which Beate fended off with her umbrella.

Beate pulled at the gate. 'He's locked himself in,' she whispered.

'Police! Officers Hole and Lønn!' Harry yelled. 'We were due to meet. Can we . . . Christ!' Harry hadn't seen the ball until it lodged itself in the wire fence with a smack a few centimetres from his face. He wiped the water from his eyes and looked down: he had been spray-painted with dirty, reddish-brown water. Harry automatically turned his back when he saw the man toss up the next ball.

'Trond Grette!' Harry's shout echoed between the blocks. They watched a tennis ball curve in an arc towards the lights in the blocks before being swallowed by the dark and landing somewhere in the field. Harry faced the tennis court again, only to hear a wild roar and see a figure rushing towards him out of the dark. The metal fence squealed as it checked the charging tennis player. He fell onto the shale on all fours, picked himself up, took a run-up and charged the fence again. Fell, got up and charged.

'My God, he's gone nuts,' Harry mumbled. He instinctively took a step back as a white face with staring eyes loomed up in front of him. Beate had managed to switch on a torch and shone it at Grette, who was hanging on the fence. With wet, black hair stuck to his white forehead, he seemed to be searching for something to focus on as he slid down the fence like sleet on a car windscreen, until he lay lifeless on the ground.

'What do we do now?' Beate breathed.

Harry felt his teeth crunching and spat into his hand. From the light of the torch he saw red grit.

'You ring for an ambulance while I get the wirecutters from the car,' he said.

'Then he was given sedatives, was he?' Anna asked.

Harry nodded and sipped his Coke.

The young West End clientele perched on bar stools around them drinking wine, shiny drinks and Diet Coke. M was like most cafés in Oslo – urban in a provincial and naive but, as far as it went, pleasant way, which made Harry think about Kebab, the bright, well-behaved boy in his class at school who, they discovered, kept a book of all the slang expressions the 'in' kids used.

'They took the poor guy to hospital. Then we chatted to the neighbour again and she told us he had been out there hitting tennis balls every evening since his wife had been killed.'

'Goodness. Why?'

Harry hunched his shoulders. 'It's not so unusual for people to become psychotic when they lose someone in those circumstances. Some repress it and act as if the deceased were still alive. The neighbour said Stine and Trond Grette were a fantastic mixed-doubles pair, that they practised on the court almost every afternoon in the summer.'

'So he was kind of expecting his wife to return the serve?'

'Maybe.'

'Jeesus! Will you get me a beer while I go to the loo?'

Anna swung her legs off the stool and wiggled her way across the room. Harry tried not to follow her movements. He didn't need to, he had seen as much as he wanted. She had a few wrinkles around the eyes, a couple of grey strands in her raven-black hair; otherwise she was exactly the same. The same black eyes with the slightly hunted expression under the fused eyebrows, the same high, narrow nose above the indecently full lips and the hollow cheeks which tended to give her a hungry look. She might not have qualified for the epithet 'beautiful' – for that her features were too hard and stark – but her slim body was curvaceous enough for Harry to spot at least two men at tables in the dining area lose their thread as she passed.

Harry lit another cigarette. After Grette, they had paid a visit to Helge Klementsen, the branch manager, but that hadn't given them much to work on, either. He was still in a state of shock, sitting in a chair in his duplex in Kjelsåsveien and staring alternately at the poodle scurrying between his legs and his wife scurrying between kitchen and sitting room with coffee and the driest cream horn Harry had ever tasted. Beate's choice of clothes had suited the Klementsen family's bourgeois home better than Harry's faded Levi's and Doc Martens. Nevertheless, it was mostly Harry who maintained conversation with the nervously tripping fru Klementsen about the unusually high precipitation this autumn and the art of making cream horns, to the interruptions above of stamping feet and loud sobbing. Fru Klementsen explained that her daughter Ina, the poor thing, was seven months pregnant to a man who had just given her the heave-ho. Well, in fact, he *was* a sailor and had set sail for the Mediterranean. Harry had almost spattered the cream horn across the table. It was then that Beate took charge and asked Helge, who had given up pursuing the dog with his eyes as it had padded out through the living-room door, 'How tall would you say the robber was?'

Helge had observed her, then picked up the coffee cup and lifted it to his mouth where, of necessity, it had to wait because he couldn't drink and talk at the same time: 'Tall? Two metres perhaps. She was always so accurate, Stine was.'

'He wasn't that tall, herr Klementsen.'

'Alright, one ninety. And always so well turned out.'

'What was he wearing?'

'Something black, like rubber. This summer she took a proper holiday for the first time. In Greece.'

Fru Klementsen sniffled.

'Like rubber?' Beate asked.

'Yes. And a balaclava.'

'What colour, herr Klementsen?'

'Red.'

At this point Beate had stopped taking notes and soon after they were in the car on their way back to town.

'If judges and juries only knew how little of what witnesses said about bank robberies was reliable, they would refuse to let us use it as evidence,' Beate had said. 'What people's brains recreate is almost fascinatingly wrong. As if fear gives them glasses which make all robbers grow in stature and blackness, makes guns proliferate and seconds become longer. The robber took a little over one minute, but fru Brænne, the cashier nearest the entrance, said he had been there for close on five minutes. And he isn't two metres tall, but 1.79. Unless he wore insoles, which is not so unusual for professionals.'

'How can you be so precise about his height?'

'The video. You measure the height against the door frame where the robber enters. I was in the bank this morning chalking up, taking new photos and measuring.'

'Mm. In Crime Squad we leave that kind of measuring job to the Crime Scene Unit.'

'Measuring height from a video is a bit more complicated than it sounds. The Crime Scene Unit's measurements were out by three centimetres, for example, in the case of the Den norske Bank robber in Kaldbakken in 1989. So I prefer to use my own.'

Harry had squinted at her and wondered whether he should ask her why she had joined the police. Instead, he had asked her if she could drop him off outside the locksmith's in Vibes gate. Before getting out, he had also asked her if she had noticed that Helge hadn't spilt a drop of coffee from the brimming cup he had been holding during their questioning. She hadn't.

'Do you like this place?' Anna asked, sinking back on her stool.

'Well.' Harry cast his eyes around. 'It's not my taste.'

'Not mine, either,' Anna said, grabbing her bag and standing up. 'Let's go to my flat.'

'I've just bought you a beer.' Harry nodded towards the frothy glass.

'It's so boring drinking alone,' she said and pulled a face. 'Relax, Harry. Come on.'

It had stopped raining outside and the cold, freshly washed air tasted good.

'Do you remember the day, one autumn, we drove to Maridalen?' Anna asked, slipping her hand inside his arm and starting to walk.

'No,' Harry said.

'Of course you do! In that dreadful Ford Escort of yours, with the seats that don't fold down.'

Harry smiled wryly.

'You're blushing,' she exclaimed with glee. 'Well, I'm sure you also remember that we parked and went for a walk in the forest. With all the yellow leaves it was like . . .' She squeezed his arm. 'Like a bed, an enormous bed of gold.' She laughed and nudged him. 'And afterwards I had to help you push-start that wreck of a car. I hope you've got rid of it by now?'

'Well,' Harry said, 'it's at the garage. We'll have to see.'

'Dear, oh dear. Now you make it sound like an old friend who's been taken to hospital with a tumour or something.' And she added – softly: 'You shouldn't have been so quick to let go, Harry.'

He didn't answer.

'Here it is,' she said. 'You can't have forgotten that, anyway, can you?' They had stopped outside a blue door in Sorgenfrigata.

Harry gently detached himself. 'Listen, Anna,' he began and tried to ignore her warning stare. 'I've got a meeting with Crime Squad investigators at the crack of dawn tomorrow.'

'I didn't say a word,' she said, opening the door.

Harry suddenly remembered something. He put his hand inside his coat and passed her a yellow envelope. 'From the locksmith.'

'Ah, the key. Was everything alright?'

'The person behind the counter scrutinised my ID very closely.

40

And I had to sign. Odd person.' Harry glanced at his watch and yawned.

'They're strict about handing out system keys,' Anna said hastily. 'It fits the whole block, the main entrance, the cellar, flat, everything.' She gave a nervous, perfunctory laugh. 'They have to have a written application from our housing co-op just to make this one spare key.'

'I understand,' Harry said, rocking on his heels. He drew breath to say goodnight.

She beat him to it. Her voice was almost imploring: 'Just a cup of coffee, Harry.'

There was the same chandelier hanging from the ceiling high above the same table and chairs in the large sitting room. Harry thought the walls had been light – white or maybe yellow – but he wasn't sure. Now they were blue and the room seemed smaller. Perhaps Anna had wanted to reduce the space. It is not easy for one person living alone to fill a flat with three reception rooms, two big bedrooms and a ceiling height of three and a half metres. Harry remembered that Anna had told him her grandmother had also lived in the flat on her own, but she hadn't spent so much time here, as she had been a famous soprano and had travelled the world for as long as she was able to sing.

Anna disappeared into the kitchen and Harry looked around the sitting room. It was bare, empty, apart from a vaulting horse the size of an Icelandic pony, which stood in the middle on four splayed wooden legs with two rings protruding from its back. Harry went over and stroked the smooth, brown leather.

'Have you taken up gymnastics?' Harry called out.

'You mean the horse?' Anna shouted back from the kitchen.

'It's for men, isn't it?'

'Yes. Sure you won't have a beer, Harry?'

'Quite sure,' he shouted. 'Seriously, though, why have you got it here?'

Harry jumped when he heard her voice behind his back: 'Because I like to do things that men do.'

Harry turned. She had taken off her sweater and was standing in the doorway. One hand resting on her hip, the other up against the door frame. At the very last minute Harry resisted the temptation to let his eyes wander from top to toe.

'I bought it from Oslo Gym Club. It's going to be a work of art. An installation. Much like "Contact", which I am sure you haven't forgotten.'

'You mean the box on the table with the curtain you could stick your hand in? And inside there were loads of false hands you could shake?'

'Or stroke. Or flirt with. Or reject. They had heating elements in so they could maintain body temperature and were such a great hit, weren't they. People thought there was someone hiding under the table. Come with me and I'll show you something else.'

He followed her to the furthest room, where she opened sliding doors. Then she took his hand and pulled him into the dark with her. When the light was switched on, at first Harry stood staring at the lamp. It was a gilt standard lamp formed into the shape of a woman holding scales in one hand and a sword in the other. Three bulbs were located on the outside edge of the sword, the scales and the woman's head, and when Harry turned, he could see each illuminated its own oil painting. Two of them were hanging on the wall while the third, which clearly wasn't finished yet, was on an easel with a yellow-and-brown-stained palette fastened to the left-hand corner.

'What sort of pictures are they?' Harry asked.

'They're portraits. Can't you see that?'

'Right. Those are eyes?' He pointed. 'And that's a mouth?'

Anna tilted her head. 'If you like. There are three men.'

'Anyone I know?'

Anna gazed at Harry pensively for a long time before answering. 'No. I don't think you know any of them, Harry, but you could get to know them if you really wanted.'

Harry studied the pictures more closely.

'Tell me what you can see.'

'I can see my neighbour with a kicksled. I can see a man coming out of the backroom at the locksmith's as I'm leaving. And I can see the waiter in M. And that TV celeb, Per Ståle Lønning.'

She laughed. 'Did you know that the retina reverses everything so your brain receives a mirror image first? If you want to see things as they really are, you have to see them in a mirror. Then you would have seen some quite different people in the pictures.' Her eyes were radiant and Harry couldn't bring himself to object that the retina didn't reverse images, it turned them upside down. 'This will be my final masterpiece, Harry. This is what I will be remembered for.'

'These portraits?'

'No, they're merely a part of the whole work of art. It's not finished yet. Just wait.'

'Mm, has it got a name?'

' "Nemesis",' she said in a low voice.

He gazed enquiringly at her and their eyes locked.

'After the goddess, you know.'

The shadow fell over one side of her face. Harry looked away. He had seen enough. The curve of her back begging for a dancing partner, one foot in front of the other as if unsure whether to move forwards or backwards, her heaving bosom and the slim neck with the veins he imagined he could see throbbing. He felt hot and a tiny bit faint. What was it she said? 'You shouldn't have been so quick to let go.' Had he been?

'Harry . . .'

'I have to go,' he said.

He pulled her dress over her head, and she fell back laughing against the white sheet. She loosened his belt as the turquoise light, which shone through the swaying palm trees of the laptop's screensaver, flickered over the imps and open-mouthed demons snarling from

43

the carvings on the bedhead. Anna had told him it was her grandmother's bed and it had been there for almost eighty years. She nibbled at his ear and whispered sweet nothings in an unfamiliar language. Then she stopped whispering and rode him as she yelled, laughed, entreated and invoked external forces and he just wished it would go on and on. He was about to come when she suddenly held back, took his face between her hands and whispered: 'Mine for ever?'

'Not bloody likely,' he laughed and turned her so that he was on top. The wooden demons grinned at him.

'Mine for ever?'

'Yes,' he groaned and came.

When the laughter had died down and they lay there sweating, but still tightly entwined on the bedcovers, Anna told him that the bed had been given to her grandmother by a Spanish nobleman.

'After a concert she gave in Seville in 1911,' she said, raising her head slightly so that Harry could place the lit cigarette between her lips.

The bed arrived in Oslo three months later on SS *Elenora*. Chance, among other things, would have it that the Danish captain, Jesper something-or-other, would be her grandmother's first lover – though not her first ever – in this bed. Jesper had obviously been a passionate man, and according to the grandmother, that was why the horse adorning the bed had lost its head. Captain Jesper, in his ecstasy, bit it off.

Anna laughed and Harry smiled. Then the cigarette was finished and they made love to the creaking and groaning of the Spanish Manila wood, which made Harry think he was in a boat with no one at the helm, but that it didn't matter.

That was a long time ago and it was the first and last night he had slept sober in Anna's grandmother's bed.

Harry twisted in the narrow iron bed. The display of the radio alarm clock on the bedside table glowed 3.21. He cursed. He closed his eyes and his thoughts slowly glided back to Anna and the summer on the white sheets of her grandmother's bed. More often than not he had been drunk, but he could recall the nights, pink and wonderful like erotic picture postcards. Even the final line he had delivered when the summer was over had been a hackneyed, but a passionately felt cliché: 'You deserve someone better than me.'

At this stage he was drinking so hard that everything pointed in only one direction. In one of his clearer moments he had made up his mind he would not drag her down with him. She had cursed him in her foreign tongue and sworn that one day she would do the same to him: take the thing he loved most from him.

That was seven years ago, and the relationship had only lasted six weeks. After that he had only met her twice. Once in a bar when she had gone over to him with tears in her eyes and asked him to go somewhere else, which he had done. And once at an exhibition where Harry had taken his younger sister. He had promised to call her, but he never did.

Harry rolled over to look at the clock again. 3.22. He had kissed her. At the end of the evening. Once he was safely outside the door of her flat with the wavy glass, he had leaned over to give her a goodnight hug and it had become a kiss. Easy and great. Easy, at any rate. 3.33. Christ, when had he become so sensitive that he felt pangs of guilt for giving an old flame a goodnight kiss? Harry tried to take deep, regular breaths to concentrate his mind on possible escape routes from Bogstadveien via Industrigata. In. Out. In again. He could still smell her fragrance. Feel the sweet pressure of her body. The rough insistence of her tongue.

6

Chilli

THE DAY'S FIRST RAYS HAD JUST RISEN OVER THE EDGE OF Ekeberg Ridge, peeped under the half-drawn blind in the Crime Squad conference room and wedged themselves between the folds of skin around Harry's pinched eyes. Rune Ivarsson stood at the end of the long table, legs apart, rocking up and down on the soles of his feet, his hands behind his back. A flip chart with WELCOME in big red letters at his rear. Harry presumed this was something Ivarsson had picked up at a seminar on presentations and made a half-hearted attempt to stifle a yawn as the Head of the Robberies Unit began to speak.

'Good morning, everyone. The eight of us sitting around the table constitute the team assembled to investigate the bank robbery committed in Bogstadveien on Friday.'

'Murder,' Harry mumbled.

'I beg your pardon?'

Harry straightened up in his chair. The damned sun was blinding him whichever way he turned. 'I suppose it would be correct to base the investigation on the fact that it was a murder.'

Ivarsson gave a wry smile. Not to Harry, but to the others sitting around the table whom he took in with one fleeting glance. 'I thought I should start by introducing you to each other, but our friend from Crime Squad has already made a start. Inspector Harry Hole has been kindly loaned by his superior, Bjarne Møller, as his speciality is murder.'

'Serious Crime,' Harry said.

'Serious Crime. On the left of Hole, we have Torleif Weber from Forensics who led the inquiry at the crime scene. As many of you know, Weber is our most experienced forensic investigator. Famous for his analytical powers and unerring intuition. The Chief Superintendent once said that he would have liked to have Weber with him as a tracker dog in his hunting parties.'

Laughter around the table. Harry didn't need to look at Weber to know that he wasn't smiling. Weber almost never smiled, at least not for people he didn't like, and he liked almost no one. Especially among the younger stratum of bosses which, in Weber's opinion, was comprised exclusively of incompetent careerists with no feeling for the profession or the force, but who had stronger instincts for the administrative power and influence which could be attained through brief appearances at Police HQ.

Ivarsson smiled and swayed up and down like the skipper of a sea-going vessel as he waited for the laughter to die down.

'Beate Lønn is quite new in this context and our video recording specialist.'

Beate's face went as red as a beetroot.

'Beate is the daughter of Jørgen Lønn who served for over twenty years in what was then called the Robberies and Serious Crime Unit. So far she seems to be following in her legendary father's footsteps. She has already contributed vital evidence which has helped solve a number of cases. I don't know if I have mentioned it before, but over the last year in the Robberies Unit we have had a conviction rate bordering on fifty per cent, which in an international context is reckoned to be—'

'You have mentioned it before, Ivarsson.'

'Thank you.'

This time Ivarsson eyed Harry directly when he smiled. A stiff, reptilian smile baring his teeth far beyond the jawbone on both sides. And he continued to smile that smile for the rest of the introductions. Harry knew two of them. Magnus Rian, a young detective from Tomrefjord who had been in Crime Squad for six months and made a solid impression. The other was Didrik Gudmundson, the most experienced investigator around the table and the second-in-command of the Robberies Unit. A quiet, methodical policeman with whom Harry had never had any problems. The last two were also from the Robberies Unit, both with Li as a surname, but Harry immediately established that they were not identical twins. Toril Li was a tall blonde woman with a narrow mouth and a closed face, while Ola Li was a squat, red-haired man with a rounded face and laughing eyes. Harry had seen them enough times in the corridor for many to think it would be natural to say hello, but it had never occurred to him.

'As for myself, I should be familiar to you from other contexts,' Ivarsson concluded the round by saying. 'But just for formality's sake, I am the PAS of the Robberies Unit and have been appointed to lead this investigation. And to come back to what you said initially, Hole, this is not the first time we have had to investigate a robbery with a fatal outcome for the innocent parties.'

Harry tried not to rise to the bait. He really did, but the crocodile grin made it impossible.

'Also with a conviction rate of just under fifty per cent?'

Only one person at the table laughed, but his laughter was loud. Weber.

'My apologies, I obviously omitted to mention something about Hole,' Ivarsson said without smiling. 'He is said to have a talent for comedy. A real wit, I've heard say.'

There was a second's embarrassed silence. Then Ivarsson gave a brief honk of laughter and a low chuckle spread around the table.

'OK, let's start with a summary.' Ivarsson flipped over the front sheet. The next bore the title FORENSIC EVIDENCE. He took the top off a marker and prepared himself. 'It's all yours, Weber.'

Karl Torleif Weber stood up. He was a short man with a lion's mane of grey hair and a beard. His voice was an ominous, low-frequency rumble, but, for all that, clear. 'I'll be brief.'

'By all means,' Ivarsson said, putting the pen to paper. 'But take all the time you need, Karl.'

'I'll be brief because I don't need much time,' Weber growled. 'We haven't got a thing.'

'Right,' Ivarsson said, lowering the pen. 'You haven't got a thing. Exactly what do you mean by that?'

'We have a print of a brand new Nike shoe, size 45. Most things about this robbery have such a professional ring about them that the only information I can infer is that it is unlikely to be the size he normally takes. The bullet has been analysed by the ballistics boys. It is standard 7.62 millimetre ammo for the AG3, the most common ammunition to be found in the kingdom of Norway since it is in every military barracks, arms store and home of a reserve officer or volunteer around the country. In other words, impossible to trace. Apart from that, you would think he had never been in the bank. Or outside it. We've searched for evidence there, too.'

Weber sat down.

'Thank you, Weber, that was . . . erm, informative.' Ivarsson turned over the next sheet. WITNESSES.

'Hole?'

Harry slumped even further into his chair. 'Everyone who was in the bank was questioned immediately afterwards, and no one can tell us anything we can't see on the video. That is to say, they remember a few things which we know to be incorrect. One witness saw the robber heading up Industrigata. No one else has called in.'

'Which brings us to the next point – getaway cars,' Ivarsson said. 'Toril?'

Toril Li stepped forward, switched on the overhead projector, where there was already a transparency with a summary of private vehicles stolen over the past three months. In her strong Sunnmørsk dialect she explained which four cars she considered to be the most probable getaway cars, basing her judgement on the fact that they were run-of-the-mill brands and models, neutral, light colours and new enough for the robber to feel confident that they wouldn't let him down. One particular car, a Volkswagen GTI parked in Maridalsveien was of interest as it had been stolen the night before the bank raid.

'Bank robbers tend to steal cars as near the time to the robbery as possible so they don't appear on patrol-car lists,' Toril Li elucidated. She switched off the overhead projector and picked up the transparency on her way back to her seat.

Ivarsson nodded. 'Thanks.'

'For nothing,' Harry whispered to Weber.

The title on the next sheet was VIDEO ANALYSIS. Ivarsson had put the top back on the marker. Beate swallowed, cleared her throat, took a sip of water from the glass in front of her and coughed again before beginning, her eyes firmly fixed on the table. 'I've measured the height—'

'Speak a little louder, would you please, Beate.' Reptilian smile. Beate cleared her throat several times.

'I've measured the height of the robber from the video. He's 1.79. I checked this out with Weber, who agrees.'

Weber nodded.

'Brilliant!' Ivarsson called out with laboured enthusiasm in his voice. He snatched the top off the marker and wrote: HEIGHT 1.79 m.

Beate continued talking to the table: 'I've just spoken to Aslaksen from the university, our voice analyst. He's had a look at the five words the robber says in English. He . . .' Beate peered nervously up at Ivarsson, who was standing with his back to her, ready to take notes. '. . . said the recording quality was too poor to do anything with. It was unusable.'

Ivarsson dropped his arm at the same time as the low sun disappeared behind a cloud and the large rectangle of light on the wall behind them faded away. There was a deafening silence in the room. Ivarsson inhaled and moved forward onto the balls of his feet.

'Fortunately, we have saved our trump for last.'

The Head of the Robberies Unit flipped over the last sheet of paper.

SURVEILLANCE.

'For those of you who do not work in the Robberies Unit we should perhaps explain that we always bring in the surveillance section first when we have a video recording of a bank raid. In seven out of ten cases a good video recording will reveal the identity of the robber, if he's one of our old friends.'

'Even if he's masked?' Weber asked.

Ivarsson nodded. 'A good undercover investigator will identify an old lag by his build, body language, the way he speaks during the robbery, all the small details you cannot hide behind a mask.'

'But it's not enough knowing who it is,' Ivarsson's second-in-command Didrik Gudmundson interposed. 'We have to—'

'That's right,' Ivarsson broke in. 'We have to have proof. A robber can spell his name out to the camera, but so long as he's masked and does not leave tangible evidence, in the eyes of the law we have nothing.'

'So, how many of the seven you recognise end up being convicted?' Weber asked.

'A few,' Gudmundson said. 'It's still better to know who has committed a robbery, even if they go free. Then we learn something about the pattern and their methods. And we get them the next time.'

'And if there's no next time?' Harry asked. He noticed how the thick veins over Ivarsson's ears expanded when he laughed.

'Dear murder expert,' Ivarsson said, still in jocular mood. 'If you look around you, you'll see that most people are smiling in their beards at what you just asked. That's because a bank robber who has pulled off a successful raid will always – always – strike again. That's a law of gravity with bank robbers.' Ivarsson peered out of the window and allowed himself another chuckle before spinning round on his heel. 'If that's the end of adult education for today, perhaps we can see if we have any suspects.'

Ola Li looked at Ivarsson, uncertain whether he should get up or not, but decided in the end to remain seated. 'Well, I was on duty last weekend. We had an edited video ready by eight on Friday evening, and I got the surveillance folk in to view the video in the House of Pain. Those not on duty were called in on Saturday. In all, thirteen surveillance officers were here, the first at eight o'clock on Friday and the last . . .'

'That's fine, Ola,' Ivarsson said. 'Just tell us what you found.'

Ola laughed nervously. It sounded like the tentative cry of a seagull. 'Well?'

'Espen Vaaland is off sick,' Ola said. 'He knows bank robber turf pretty well. I'll try to get him here tomorrow.'

'What you're trying to say is . . . ?'

Ola's eyes did a racing jig around the table. 'Not a great deal,' he said softly.

'Ola is still relatively new here,' Ivarsson said and Harry noticed how his jaw muscles were beginning to grind. 'Ola demands a hundred per cent certainty when identifying people, and that's laudable, but it's a bit too much to expect when the robber—'

'The killer.'

'—is covered from top to toe, average height, keeps his mouth shut, moves atypically and wears shoes too big for him.' Ivarsson raised his voice. 'So give us the whole list, Ola. Who's in the running?'

'No one.'

'There must be some names!'

'No,' Ola said with a gulp.

'Are you trying to tell us that no one had any suggestions, that all of our volunteer slum rats, zealous undercover boys that they are, who take pride in their daily dealings with the worst scum in Oslo, who in nine out of ten cases hear rumblings about the getaway driver, the man carrying the swag, the lookout, are suddenly unwilling even to hazard a guess?'

'They guessed alright,' Ola said. 'Six names were mentioned.'

'Well, spit them out then, man.'

'I've checked all the names. Three are in the nick. One was seen in Plata market square when the robbery was being committed. One is in Pattaya in Thailand. I've checked that. And there was one all the undercover officers mentioned because he has a similar build and the robbery was so professional, and that is Bjørn Johansen from the Tveita gang.'

'Oh yes?'

Ola looked as if he wanted to slide off his chair and disappear under the table.

'He's in Ullevål hospital, and last Friday he was being operated on for *aures alatae*.'

'*Aures alatae*?'

'Sticky-out ears,' Harry groaned, flicking a drop of sweat off his eyebrow. 'Ivarsson almost exploded. How many have you done?'

'I've just passed twenty-one.' Halvorsen's voice resounded around the walls. As it was early afternoon they had the fitness centre in the basement of the police station almost to themselves.

'Have you taken a short cut or what?' Harry clenched his teeth and managed to increase the rate a little. There was already a pool of sweat around his ergometer bike while Halvorsen's forehead was barely moist.

'So, you haven't got a bean then?' Halvorsen asked, breathing regularly and calmly.

'Unless there's something in what Beate Lønn said at the end, we haven't got a lot, no.'

'And what did she say?'

'She's working on a program which can make a 3-D image of the robber's head and face from the video pictures.'

'Plus mask?'

'The program uses the information it gets from the pictures. Light,

53

shadow, recesses, protrusions. The tighter the mask, the easier it is to make an image which resembles the person underneath. Nevertheless, it's only a sketch, but Beate says she can use it to match pictures of suspects.'

'Is it the FBI identification program?' Halvorsen turned to Harry and with a certain fascination verified that the sweat stain which had started at the dating agency logo on Harry's chest had now spread to cover the whole of the T-shirt.

'No, she has a better program,' Harry said. 'How far?'

'Twenty-two. Which one?'

'*Fusiform gyrus*.'

'Microsoft? Apple Mac?'

Harry tapped his forefinger on a bright red forehead. 'Software common to all. Sits in the temporal lobe in the brain and its sole function is to recognise people. That's all it does. It's the bit that makes sure we can distinguish between hundreds and thousands of human faces, but scarcely a dozen rhinos.'

'Rhinos?'

Harry pinched his eyes and tried to blink away the smarting sweat. 'That was an example, Halvorsen, but there's no doubt that Beate Lønn is a special case. Her *fusiform* can do a couple of extra turns which, so to speak, allow her to remember all the faces she has seen in her life. And I don't just mean people she knows or has spoken to, but faces behind sunglasses she passed in a crowded street fifteen years ago.'

'You're kidding.'

'Nope.' Harry tucked in his head as he regained enough breath to continue: 'There are only about a hundred known cases like hers. Didrik Gudmundson said that she took a test at Police College and beat several well-known identification programs. The woman is a walking archive of faces. If she asks you *Haven't I seen you somewhere before?* you can take it from me, it's not just a chat-up line.'

'Jeez. What's she doing in the police? With talent like that, I mean.'

Harry shrugged. 'Do you remember the officer who was shot during a bank raid in the eighties in Ryen?'

'Before my time.'

'He happened to be close by when the call went out and as he was the first to arrive on the scene, he went into the bank to negotiate unarmed. He was mown down by automatic gunfire and the robbers were never caught. It was later used at Police College as an example of what you *shouldn't* do when you surprise bank robbers.'

'You should wait for reinforcements. You must not confront robbers or expose yourself, bank employees or the robbers to unnecessary danger.'

'Right, that's what the manual says. The odd thing is that he was one of the best and most experienced investigators they had. Jørgen Lønn. Beate's father.'

'Right. And you think that's why she joined the police? Because of her father?'

'Possibly.'

'Is she good-looking?'

'She's good. How far?'

'Just passed twenty-four, six left. And you?'

'Twenty-two. I'll catch you up, you know.'

'Not this time,' Halvorsen said, increasing his speed.

'Yes, I will, because here come the hills. And here I come. And you'll be psyched out and get cramp. As usual.'

'Not this time,' Halvorsen said, pedalling harder. A bead of sweat became visible in his thick hairline. Harry smiled and leaned over the handlebars.

Bjarne Møller stared alternately at the shopping list he had received from his wife and at the shelf, at what he thought might be coriander. Margrete had fallen in love with Thai food after their holiday in Phuket last winter, but the Crime Squad head was still not completely at ease with the various vegetables which were flown daily from Bangkok to the Pakistani grocer's store in Grønlandsleiret.

'That's green chilli, boss,' a voice by his ear said and Bjarne Møller spun round and looked into Harry's flushed, sweat-stained face. 'Couple of those and a few slices of ginger and you can make tom yam soup. There'll be steam coming out of your ears, but you'll have sweated out a fair bit of crap.'

'Looks like you've had a foretaste, Harry.'

'Just a little cycle race with Halvorsen.'

'Oh yes? And what's that in your hand?'

'Japone pepper. A small red chilli.'

'Didn't know you cooked.'

Harry gazed with wonderment at the bag containing the chilli, as if it was new to him, too. 'By the way, lucky I met you, boss. We have a problem.'

Møller could feel his scalp chafing.

'I don't know who decided Ivarsson should lead the investigation into the killing in Bogstadveien, but it's not working.'

Møller put the list in the shopping basket. 'How long have you worked together now? Two whole days?'

'That's not the point, boss.'

'Can't you just do your job for once in your life, Harry? And let others decide how it's organised? Having a go at not being against everyone won't inflict permanent damage, you know.'

'I just want the case to be solved as quickly as possible, boss, so that I can get on with the other one, you know.'

'Yes, I know, but you've been working on that case for a good deal longer than the two months I promised you, and I cannot defend the commitment of time and resources with personal considerations and emotions, Harry.'

'She was a colleague, boss.'

'I know!' Møller barked. He paused, looked around, then continued in more muted tones: 'What's your problem, Harry?'

'They're used to working on robberies, and Ivarsson is not in the slightest bit interested in constructive input.'

Bjarne Møller was unable to suppress a grin at the thought of Harry's 'constructive input'.

Harry leaned forward. He spoke quickly and intensely: 'What's the first thing we ask ourselves when a murder has been committed, boss? Why? What's the motive? That's what we ask. In the Robberies Unit they automatically take it for granted money is the motive and don't ask the question.'

'So what do you think the motive is?'

'I don't think anything. The point is that they use completely the wrong methodology.'

'A different methodology, Harry, *different*. I have to get these vegetable things bought and go home, so tell me what it is you want.'

'I want you to talk to the people you have to talk to so that I can have one person to work solo with.'

'Step down from the investigation team?'

'Parallel investigation.'

'Harry—'

'That was how we caught the Redbreast, do you remember?'

'Harry, I can't interfere—'

'I want to work with Beate Lønn, so that she and I can start afresh. Ivarsson is already getting bogged down—'

'Harry!'

'Yes?'

'What's the real reason?'

Harry shifted weight. 'I can't work with the smiling croc.'

'Ivarsson?'

'I'll go and do something extremely stupid.'

Bjarne Møller's eyebrows met across the bridge of his nose in a black V: 'Is that supposed to be a threat?'

Harry placed a hand on Møller's shoulder. 'Just this one favour, boss. I'll never ask for anything else again. Ever.'

Møller growled. Over the years, how many times had he put his head on the block for Harry, instead of heeding the well-meant career advice from older colleagues? Keep him at arm's length, they said. A loose cannon, he is. The only thing that was certain about Harry Hole was that one day something was going to go disastrously wrong. However, because, in some mysterious way, he and Harry had so far always landed on their feet, no one had been able to implement any drastic measures. So far. The most interesting question of all, though, was: Why did he put up with it? He looked across at Harry. The alcoholic. The troublemaker. The ever-unbearable, arrogant bullhead. And the best investigator he had, apart from Waaler.

'You keep your nose clean, Harry. Otherwise I'll shove you behind a desk and lock the door. Have you got that?'

'Received loud and clear, boss.'

Møller sighed. 'I have a meeting with the Chief Superintendent and Ivarsson tomorrow. We'll have to wait and see. I'm not promising anything, do you hear?'

'Aye, aye, boss. Regards to your wife.' Harry craned his head round on the way out. 'Coriander's on the far left, bottom shelf.'

Bjarne Møller stood staring into his shopping basket. He remembered the reason now. He liked the alcoholic, obstreperous, stubborn bastard.

7

White King

Harry nodded to one of the regulars and sat down at a table under the narrow, wavy window panes looking out onto Waldemar Thranes gate. On the wall behind him hung a large painting of a sunny day in Youngstorget with women holding parasols and being cheerily greeted by men promenading in top hats. The contrast with the forever autumnally gloomy light and the almost devout afternoon quiet in Restaurant Schrøder could not have been greater.

'Nice that you could come,' Harry said to the corpulent man already sitting at the table. It was easy to see he was not one of the regulars. Not by the elegant tweed jacket, nor by the bow tie with red dots, but because he was stirring a white mug of tea on a cloth smelling of beer and perforated with blackened cigarette burns. The unlikely customer was Ståle Aune, a psychologist, one of the country's finest in his field and an expert to whom the police had had frequent recourse. Sometimes with pleasure and sometimes regret, as Aune was a thoroughly upright man who preserved his integrity and in a court of law never pronounced on matters which he could not support to the hilt with scientific evidence. However, since there is

59

little evidence for anything in psychology, it often happened that the prosecution witness became the defence's best friend, the doubts he sowed generally working in favour of the accused. Harry, in his capacity as a police officer, had used Aune's expertise in murder cases for so long that he regarded him as a colleague. In his capacity as an alcoholic, Harry had put himself so totally in the hands of this warm-hearted, clever and becomingly arrogant man that – if cornered – he would have called him a friend.

'So this is your refuge?' Aune said.

'Yes,' Harry said, raising an eyebrow to Maja at the counter, who responded at once by scuttling through the swing doors into the kitchen.

'And what have you got there?'

'Japone. Chilli.'

A bead of sweat rolled down Harry's nose, clung for a second to the tip, then fell onto the tablecloth. Aune studied the wet stain with amazement.

'Sluggish thermostat,' Harry said. 'I've been in the gym.'

Aune screwed up his nose. 'As a man of science, I ought to applaud you, I suppose, but as a philosopher I would question putting your body through that kind of unpleasantness.'

A steel coffee jug and a mug landed in front of Harry. 'Thanks, Maja.'

'Pangs of guilt,' Aune said. 'Some people can only deal with it by punishing themselves. Like when you go to pieces, Harry. In your case alcohol isn't a refuge but the ultimate way to punish yourself.'

'Thank you. I've heard you put forward that diagnosis before.'

'Is that why you train so hard? Bad conscience?'

Harry shrugged.

Aune lowered his voice: 'Is Ellen playing on your mind?'

Harry's eyes shot up to meet Aune's. He put the mug of coffee to his lips slowly and took a long drink before putting it down again with a grimace. 'No, it's not the Ellen Gjelten case. We're getting nowhere, but it's not because we've done a bad job. That I do know. Something will turn up. We just have to bide our time.'

'Good,' Aune said. 'It's not your fault Ellen was killed. Keep that uppermost in your mind. And don't forget: all your colleagues consider that the right man was arrested.'

'Maybe, maybe not. He's dead and can't answer.'

'Don't let it become an *idée fixe*, Harry.' Aune poked two fingers into the pocket of his tweed waistcoat, pulled out a silver pocket watch and cast a rapid glance at it. 'But I scarcely imagine you wanted to speak about guilt?'

'No, I didn't.' Harry took a wad of photographs from his inside pocket. 'I'd like to know what you think about these.'

Aune held out his hand and began to leaf through the pile. 'Looks like a bank raid. My understanding is this is not a Crime Squad matter.'

'You'll understand when you see the next picture.'

'Indeed? He's holding up one finger to the camera.'

'Sorry, the next one.'

'Ooh. Does she . . . ?'

'Yes, you can hardly see the flame as it's an AG3, but he has just fired. Look there, the bullet has just entered the woman's forehead. In the next picture it exits the back of her head and bores into the woodwork beside the glass partition.'

Aune put down the photos. 'Why do you always have to show me grisly pictures, Harry?'

'So that you know what we're talking about. Look at the next one.'

Aune sighed.

'The robber's got his money there,' Harry said, pointing. 'All he has to do now is escape. He's a pro, calm, precise, and there's no reason to intimidate anyone or force anyone to do anything. Yet he opts to delay his escape for a few seconds to shoot the bank cashier. Simply because the branch manager was six seconds too slow emptying the ATM.'

Aune formed slow figures of eight in his tea with the spoon. 'And now you're wondering what his motive is?'

'Well, there's always a motive, but it's difficult to know which side of rationality to look. First reactions?'

'Serious personality disorder.'

'But everything else he does seems so rational.'

'A personality disorder doesn't mean he is stupid. Sufferers are just as good, frequently better, at achieving their aims. What distinguishes them from us is that they want different things.'

'What about drugs? Is there a drug which can make an otherwise normal person so aggressive that he wants to kill?'

Aune shook his head. 'Drugs will only emphasise or weaken latent tendencies. A drunk who kills his wife also has a propensity to beat her when sober. Wilful murders like this one are almost always committed by people with a particular predisposition.'

'So what you're saying is that this guy is barking?'

'Or pre-programmed.'

'Pre-programmed?'

Aune nodded in assent. 'Do you remember the robber who was never caught, Raskol Baxhet?'

Harry shook his head.

'Gypsy,' Aune said. 'There were rumours going round about this mysterious figure for a number of years. He was supposed to be the real brains behind all the major robberies of security vans and financial institutions in Oslo in the eighties. It took a number of years for the police to accept that he actually existed and even then they never managed to produce any evidence against him.'

'Now I have a vague recollection,' Harry said. 'But I thought he'd been arrested.'

'False. The closest they got was two robbers who pledged they would give evidence against Raskol, but they disappeared under curious circumstances.'

'Not unusual,' Harry said, taking out a packet of Camel cigarettes.

'It's unusual when they're in prison.'

Harry gave a low whistle. 'I still think that's where he ended up.'

'That is true,' Aune said. 'But he wasn't arrested. Raskol gave himself up. One day he appears at the Police HQ reception desk, saying he wants to confess to a string of old bank robberies. Naturally, this creates a tremendous commotion. No one understands a thing, and Raskol refuses to explain why he is giving himself up. Before the case comes to court, they ring me up to check he is of sound mind and that his confessions will stand up. Raskol agrees to talk to me on two conditions. One, that we play a game of chess – don't ask me how he knew I was an active player. And, two, that I take a French translation of *The Art of War* with me, an ancient Chinese book about military strategy.'

Aune opened a box of Nobel Petit cigarillos.

'I had the book sent from Paris and took a chess set along. I was let into his cell and greeted a man with all the outward appearance of a monk. He asked if he could borrow my pen, flicked through the book and with a jerk of his head indicated that I could set out the board. I put the pieces in position and led with Réti's opening – you don't attack your opponent until you control the centre, frequently effective against medium-calibre players. Now it's impossible to see from a single move that this is what I'm thinking, but this gypsy peers over the book at the board, strokes his goatee, looks at me with a knowing smile, makes a note in the book . . .'

A silver lighter bursts into flame at the end of the cigarillo.

'. . . and continues to read. So I say: *Aren't you going to make a move?* I watch his hand scribbling away with my pen as he answers: *I don't need to. I'm writing down how this game will finish, move for move. You will knock over your king.* I explain that it is impossible for him to know how the game will develop after just one move. *Shall we have a bet?* he says. I try to laugh it off, but he is insistent. So I agree to bet a hundred to put him into a benevolent frame of mind for my interview. He demands to see the note and I have to place it beside the board where he can see it. He raises his hand as if to make his move, then things happen very fast.'

'Lightning chess?'

Aune smiled and, deep in thought, exhaled a ring of smoke

towards the ceiling. 'The next moment I was held in a vice-like grip with my head forced backwards so that I was looking up at the ceiling, and a voice whispered into my ear: *Can you feel the blade, Gadjo?* Of course I could feel it, the sharp, razor-thin steel pressed against my larynx, straining to cut through the skin. Have you ever experienced that feeling, Harry?'

Harry's brain raced through the register of related experiences, but failed to find anything altogether identical. He shook his head.

'It felt, to quote a number of my patients, rank. I was so frightened I was on the point of urinating in my trousers. Then he whispered in my ear: *Knock over the king, Aune.* He slackened his grip a little so that I could raise my arm and I sent my pieces flying. Then, equally abruptly, he let me go. He returned to his side of the table and waited for me to get on my feet and regain control of my breathing. *What the hell was that?* I groaned. *That was a bank robbery,* he answered. *First the plan and then the execution.* Then he showed me what he had written in the book. All I could see was my solitary move and *White king capitulates.* Then he asked: *Does that answer your questions, Aune?*'

'What did you say?'

'Nothing. I yelled for the guard to come. However, before he came, I asked Raskol one last question because I knew I would drive myself crazy thinking about it if I didn't get an answer there and then. I said: *Would you have done it? Would you have cut my throat if I hadn't capitulated? Just to win an idiotic bet?*'

'And what did he answer?'

'He smiled and asked if I knew what pre-programming was.'

'Yes?'

'That was all. The door opened and I left.'

'But what did he mean by pre-programming?'

Aune pushed his mug away. 'You can pre-programme your brain to follow a particular pattern of behaviour. The brain will overrule other impulses and follow the predetermined rules, come what may. Useful in situations when the brain's natural impulse is to panic.

64

Such as when the parachute doesn't open. Then, I hope, parachutists have pre-programmed emergency procedures.'

'Or soldiers fighting.'

'Precisely. There are, however, methods which can programme humans to such a degree that they go into a kind of trance, unaffected by even extreme external influences, and they become living robots. The fact is that this is every general's wet dream, frighteningly easy, provided you know the necessary techniques.'

'Are you talking about hypnosis?'

'I like to call it pre-programming. There is less mystification. It is a matter of opening and closing routes for impulses. If you're clever, you can easily pre-programme yourself, so-called self-hypnosis. If Raskol had pre-programmed himself to kill me if I hadn't capitulated, he would have prevented himself from changing his mind.'

'But he didn't kill you, did he.'

'All programs have an escape button, a password which brings you out of the trance. In this case, it may have been knocking down the white king.'

'Mm. Fascinating.'

'And now I've come to my point . . .'

'I think I know it,' Harry said. 'The bank robber in the photo may have pre-programmed himself to shoot if the branch manager didn't keep to the time limit.'

'The rules of pre-programming have to be simple,' Aune said, dropping the cigarillo in the mug and putting the saucer on top. 'In order for you to fall into a trance they have to form a small yet logical closed system which rejects other thoughts.'

Harry put a fifty-kroner note beside the coffee mug and stood up. Aune watched in silence as Harry gathered up all the photographs before saying: 'You don't believe a word I've said, do you.'

'No.'

Aune stood up and buttoned up his jacket over his stomach. 'So, what do you believe?'

'I believe what experience has taught me,' Harry said. 'That villains by and large are as stupid as I am, go for easy options and have uncomplicated motives. In a nutshell, that things are very much what they seem to be. I would bet this robber was either out of his skull or panic-stricken. What he did was senseless and from that I conclude he is stupid. Take the gypsy whom you clearly consider to be very smart. How much time did he get in the slammer for attacking you with a knife?'

'Nothing,' Aune said with a sardonic smile.

'Eh?'

'They never found a knife.'

'I thought you said you were locked in his cell.'

'Have you ever been lying on your stomach on the beach and your chums tell you to lie still because they are holding red hot coals over your back? And then you hear someone say whoops and the next second you can feel the coals burning your back?'

Harry's brain sorted through his holiday memories. It didn't take long. 'No.'

'And it turned out it was a trick; it was just ice cubes?'

'And?'

Aune sighed. 'Now and then I wonder how you've spent the thirty-five years you maintain you've been alive, Harry.'

Harry ran a hand across his face. He was tired. 'OK, Aune, what's your point?'

'My point is that a good manipulator can make you believe that the edge of a hundred-kroner note is the edge of a knife.'

The blonde looked Harry straight in the eye and promised him sun although it would cloud over in the course of the day. Harry pressed the OFF button and the picture shrank into a small luminous dot in the centre of the 14-inch screen. When he closed his eyes, however, it was the image of Stine Grette which remained on his retina, and he heard the echo of the reporter's '. . . the police have no suspects in the case so far'.

He opened his eyes again and studied the reflection in the dead screen. Himself, the old green wing chair from Elevator and the bare coffee table, embellished with glass and bottle rings. Everything was the same. The portable TV had stood on the shelf between the Lonely Planet guide to Thailand and a Norwegian road atlas for as long as he had lived here, and it hadn't travelled one metre for several years. He had read about the Seven Year Itch and how people typically began to long for somewhere new to live. Or a new job. Or a new partner. He hadn't noticed anything, and he had had the same job for almost ten years. Harry looked at his watch. Eight o'clock, Anna had said.

As far as partners were concerned, his relationships had never lasted long enough for him to test the theory. Apart from the two which might have lasted that long, Harry's romances had terminated because of what he called the Six Week Itch. Whether his reluctance to get involved was due to his being rewarded with tragedies on the two occasions he had loved a woman, he didn't know. Or should his two unswerving loves – murder investigations and alcohol – bear the blame? At any rate, before he met Rakel two years ago, he had begun to lean towards the view that he wasn't cut out for long-term relationships. He thought of her large, cool bedroom in Holmenkollen. The coded grunts they made at the breakfast table. Oleg's drawing on the refrigerator door, three people holding hands, one of whom was a towering figure, as high as the yellow sun in the clear blue sky, with HARY written underneath.

Harry got up from the chair, found the slip of paper with her telephone number on beside the answerphone and tapped the number into his mobile. It rang four times before there was an answer at the other end.

'Hi, Harry.'

'Hi. How did you know it was me?'

A low, deep laugh. 'Where have you been these last years, Harry?'

'Here. And there. Why's that? Have I said something stupid again?'

She laughed even louder.

'Aha, you can see my number on the display. How stupid I am.'

Harry could hear how lame he sounded, but it didn't matter. The most important thing was to say what he had to and ring off. End of story. 'Listen, Anna, about that date of ours this evening . . .'

'Don't be childish, Harry!'

'Childish?'

'I'm in the process of making the curry of the millennium. And if you're frightened I'm going to seduce you, I have to disappoint you. I just think we owe each other a couple of hours over a dinner to chat. Remember old times. Clear up a few misunderstandings. Or perhaps not. Maybe have a laugh. Can you remember japone chilli?'

'Well, yes.'

'Great. Eight sharp then, OK?'

'Well . . .'

'Good.'

Harry stood staring at the phone.

8

Jalalabad

'I'M GOING TO KILL YOU SOON,' HARRY SAID, SQUEEZING harder on the cold steel of the gun. 'I just want you to know first. Let you think about it. Mouth open!'

Harry was talking to wax dolls. Immobile, soulless, dehumanised. Harry was sweating inside the mask now and the blood was throbbing in his temples, each throb leaving a dull pain. He didn't want to see people around him, didn't want to meet their accusatory eyes.

'Put the money in a bag,' he said to the faceless person in front of him. 'And put the bag above your head.'

The faceless one began to laugh, and Harry turned the gun round to hit him over the head with the butt, but missed. Now the others in the bank started to laugh and Harry observed them through the unevenly cut holes in the mask. They suddenly seemed familiar. The girl by the second counter resembled Birgitta. And he would swear the coloured man by the ticket dispenser was Andrew. And the white-haired lady with the pram ...

'Mother,' he whispered.

'Do you want the money or not?' the faceless one said. 'Twenty-five seconds to go.'

'*I* decide how long this takes!' Harry roared, jabbing the barrel into his open black mouth. 'It was you. I knew it was all the time. You're going to die in six seconds. Fear for your life!'

A tooth hung on a thread from the gum and blood ran from the faceless one's mouth, but he spoke as if he were unaware: *I cannot defend the commitment of time and resources with personal considerations and emotions.* Somewhere the frenetic tones of a telephone sounded.

'Fear for your life! Fear for your life as she did!'

'Don't let it become an *idée fixe*, Harry.' Harry felt the mouth chewing the gun barrel.

'She was a colleague, you bastard! She was my best . . .' The mask stuck to Harry's mouth and made it difficult to breathe. But the voice of the faceless one went on regardless: 'Gave her the heave-ho.'

'. . . friend.' Harry squeezed the trigger. Nothing happened. He opened his eyes.

Harry's first thought was that he had just dropped off. He was sitting in the same green chair looking into the lifeless TV screen. The coat was new though. It lay over him, covering half his face; he could taste the wet material in his mouth. And daylight filled the room. Then he felt the sledgehammer. It hit a nerve behind his eyes, time and time again, with merciless precision. The result was both a dramatic and a familiar pain. He tried to rewind the tape. Did he end up at Schrøder's? Had he started drinking at Anna's? But it was all as he dreaded: a void. He remembered sitting in the sitting room after talking to Anna on the phone, but after that it was a blank. At that moment the contents of his stomach rose. Harry leaned over the edge of the chair and heard the vomit splashing on the parquet floor. He groaned, closed his eyes and tried to shut out the sound of the telephone ringing and ringing. When the answerphone cut in, he had fallen asleep.

It was as if someone had been snipping away at his time and had discarded the scraps. Harry woke up again, but delayed opening his eyes to find out if there was any improvement. None that he could detect. The only differences were that the sledgehammers were now spread over a wider area, he stank of vomit and he knew he wouldn't be able to go back to sleep. He counted to three, got up, staggered the eight steps into the bathroom with his head down by his knees and emptied his stomach. He stood clutching the toilet bowl as he struggled to regain his breath. To his surprise, he saw that the yellow matter running down the white porcelain contained microscopic red and green particles. He managed to catch one of the red bits between his forefinger and thumb, took it over to the tap where he washed it and held it up to the light. Then he cautiously placed it between his teeth and chewed. He pulled a face as he tasted the burning juices of japone chilli. He washed his face and stood up straight. And caught sight of the huge black eye in the mirror. The light in the sitting room stung his eyes as he played back the message on the answerphone.

'This is Beate Lønn. Hope I'm not disturbing, but Ivarsson said I should ring everyone immediately. There's been another bank robbery. Den norske Bank in Kirkeveien, between Frogner park and the Majorstuen crossroads.'

9

The Fog

THE SUN HAD DISAPPEARED BEHIND A LAYER OF STEEL-GREY clouds which had crept in very low over Oslo fjord, and the southerly wind was gusting near to gale force, like an overture to the rain that had been forecast. Roof gutters whistled and awnings flapped all along Kirkeveien. The trees were completely stripped now; it was as though the last colours had been sucked out of the town and Oslo had been left in black and white. Harry bent into the wind and put his hands in his pockets to hold onto his coat. He noted that the bottom button had decamped, probably during the evening or night, and it wasn't the only thing to have gone missing. When he went to call Anna for some help reconstructing the night, he discovered he had lost his mobile phone, too. And on ringing her from a fixed line, he heard a voice which vaguely reminded him of an announcer from the past. It said the person he was trying to contact was unavailable at the moment, but he could leave his number or a message. He hadn't bothered.

Harry was soon on the mend and found it surprisingly easy to resist the urge to continue drinking, to take the all too short walk to Vinmonopolet or Schrøder's. Instead he took a shower, dressed and walked from Sofies gate past Bislett stadium, via Pilestredet, past Stenspark and across Majorstuen. He wondered what he had been drinking. In the absence of the obligatory abdominal pains autographed by Jim Beam, a fog lay over him coating all his senses, and even the fresh blasts of wind were unable to lift it.

Two police patrol cars with rotating blue lights stood outside the branch of Den norske Bank. Harry flashed his ID to one of the uniformed officers, ducked under the police tape and went to the entrance where Weber was talking to one of his men from *Krimteknisk*, the forensics department.

'Good afternoon, Inspector,' Weber said, emphasising the 'afternoon'. He raised an eyebrow when he saw Harry's shiner. 'Missus started beating you?'

Harry couldn't come up with any repartee, so he flipped a cigarette out of the packet instead: 'What have we got here then?'

'Masked man with an AG3.'

'And the bird has flown?'

'Very much flown.'

'Anyone talked to witnesses?'

'Yes, indeed. Li and Li are busy down at HQ.'

'Any details about what happened yet?'

'The robber gave the female branch manager twenty-five seconds to unlock the ATM while he held the gun to the head of one of the women behind the counter.'

'And he made her do the talking?'

'Yup. And when he came into the bank, he used the same English words.'

'This is a hold-up. Nobody move!' a voice behind them said, followed by a short, staccato laugh. 'So nice you were able to come, Hole. Oh dear, slipped in the bath?'

Harry lit his cigarette with one hand while passing the pack to Ivarsson, who shook his head. 'Filthy habit, Hole.'

'You're right.' Harry put the pack of Camel in his inside pocket.

73

'You should never offer your cigarettes but assume that a gentleman buys his own. Benjamin Franklin.'

'Really?' Ivarsson said, ignoring Weber's grin. 'You're very knowledgeable, Hole. Perhaps you know our bank robber has struck again – just as we said he would?'

'How do you know it was him?'

'As you've probably heard, it's a carbon copy of the Nordea robbery in Bogstadveien.'

'Oh?' Harry said, inhaling deeply. 'Where's the body?'

Ivarsson and Harry eyeballed each other. The reptilian teeth glinted. Weber interposed: 'The branch manager was fast. She emptied the cash machine in twenty-three seconds.'

'No murder victims,' Ivarsson said. 'Disappointed?'

'No,' Harry said, releasing the smoke through his nostrils. A gust of wind dispersed the smoke. But the fog in his head refused to let go.

Halvorsen looked up from Silvia as the door opened.

'Can you fix me a high-octane espresso pronto?' Harry said, collapsing in his office chair.

'Good morning to you, too,' Halvorsen said. 'You look bloody awful.'

Harry put his face in his hands: 'I can't remember diddly-squat about what happened last night. I have no idea what I was drinking, but I'll never let a drop pass my lips ever again.'

He peeped out between his fingers and saw his colleague with a deep frown of concern etched in his brow.

'Relax, Halvorsen, it was just one of those things. I'm as sober as this desk now.'

'What happened?'

Harry gave a hollow laugh. 'Stomach contents suggest I had dinner with an old friend. I've rung several times to have that confirmed, but she won't answer.'

'She?'

'Yes, she.'

'Not a very clever policeman, then, eh?' Halvorsen said circumspectly.

'You concentrate on the coffee,' Harry growled. 'An old flame, that was all. Quite innocent.'

'How do you know if you can't remember anything?'

Harry rubbed the palm of his hand over his unshaven chin, reflecting on what Aune had said about drugs simply emphasising latent tendencies. He didn't know if he found that reassuring. Isolated details were beginning to emerge. A black dress. Anna had been wearing a black dress. And he was lying on the stairs. And a woman helped him up. With half a face. Like one of Anna's portraits.

'I always have blackouts,' Harry said. 'This is no worse than any of the others.'

'And your eye?'

'Probably bumped into a kitchen cupboard when I came home or some such thing.'

'I don't want to worry you, Harry, but it looks like something more serious than a kitchen cupboard.'

'Well,' Harry said, taking the cup of coffee with both hands. 'Do I look bothered? The times I ended up in a drunken free-for-all, it was with people I didn't like when I was sober, either.'

'Message from Møller, incidentally. He asked me to tell you it was fine, but didn't say what.'

Harry rolled the espresso round in his mouth before swallowing it. 'You'll find out, Halvorsen, you'll find out.'

The bank robbery was discussed in detail at the briefing by the investigation team at Police HQ that afternoon. Didrik Gudmundson informed them that three minutes passed from the moment the alarm sounded until the police appeared, but by then the robber had already fled the crime scene. In addition to surrounding and blocking off the closest streets immediately with patrol cars, within the subsequent ten minutes they had set up an outer cordon covering the main traffic arteries: the E18 by Fornebu, Ring 3 by Ullevål, Trondheimsveien by Aker hospital, Griniveien above Bærum and the intersection by Carl Berners plass. 'I wish we could call this an iron cordon, but you know what it's like with staffing nowadays.'

Toril Li had interviewed a witness who reported having seen a man with a balaclava over his head jumping into the passenger side of a waiting white Opel Ascona in Majorstuveien. The car had promptly turned left up Jacob Aalls gate. Magnus Rian mentioned that another witness had seen a white car, possibly an Opel, driving into a garage in Vindern and that straight afterwards a blue Volvo had left. Ivarsson studied the map hanging on the whiteboard.

'Doesn't sound unreasonable. Put out an alert for blue Volvos too, Ola. Weber?'

'Textile fibres,' Weber said. 'Two behind the counter he leapt over and one by the door.'

'Yesss!' Ivarsson punched a fist in the air. He had taken to strutting around the table behind them, which Harry found extremely irritating. 'So all we have to do is find a few candidates. We'll put the video of the burglary out on the Net as soon as Beate is finished with the editing.'

'Is that wise?' Harry asked, rocking his chair back against the wall to cut off Ivarsson's passage.

The PAS looked at him in surprise. 'Wise? We wouldn't exactly object to anyone ringing in to give us the name of the person in the video.'

Ola interrupted. 'Do you remember the time a mother rang in to say she had seen her son on a burglary video on the Net? And it turned out he was already inside for another robbery?'

Loud laughter. Ivarsson smiled. 'We never turn away new witnesses, Hole.'

'Or new copycats?' Harry put his hands behind his head.

'An imitator? Now get a grip, Hole.'

'Hm. If I were going to rob a bank today, I would obviously copy the most sought-after bank robber in Norway at this moment and divert suspicion towards him. All the details of the Bogstadveien robbery were available on the Net.'

Ivarsson shook his head. 'I'm afraid your average bank robber these days is not so sophisticated, Hole. Would someone else like to explain to Crime Squad what the typical hallmark of an inveterate robber is? No? Well, he always – with painful precision – repeats what he did on the previously successful occasion. It is only when he fails – if he doesn't get the money or he is arrested – that he changes the pattern.'

'That substantiates your theory, but it doesn't exclude mine,' Harry said.

Ivarsson cast a desperate look around the table, as if begging for help. 'Fine, Hole. You will have the chance to test your theories. In fact, I've just decided to experiment with a new approach. The gist is that a small party will work independently of, but in parallel with, the investigation team. The idea originates with the FBI and the aim is to avoid getting into a rut, having only one view of the case, which does often happen with large groups of officers when, consciously or unconsciously, a consensus is formed about the principal features of an investigation. The small party can bring a new and fresh focus because they are working separately and are not influenced by the other group. This method has proved to be effective in tricky cases. Most of us here, I am sure, will agree that Harry Hole has the natural qualifications to be a member of such a party.'

Scattered chuckles. Ivarsson came to a halt behind Beate's chair. 'Beate, you will join Harry.'

Beate blushed. Ivarsson placed a paternal hand on her shoulder: 'If it doesn't work, all you have to do is say.'

'I will,' Harry said.

Harry was about to unlock the front door to his apartment building when he changed his mind and walked back ten metres to the little grocery shop, where Ali was carrying in boxes of fruit and vegetables from the pavement.

'Hi, Harry! Are you better now?' Ali had a broad grin on his face and Harry closed his eyes for a second. It was as he feared.

'Did you help me, Ali?'

'Just up the stairs. When we opened your door, you said you could manage.'

'How did I get home? On foot or . . . ?'

'Taxi. You owe me a hundred and twenty.'

Harry groaned and followed Ali into the shop. 'I apologise, Ali. Really. Can you give me an abridged version, without too many embarrassing details?'

'You and the driver were arguing in the street. And our bedrooms face that way.' He added with a winning smile: 'Bloody awful to have the window there.'

'And when was that?'

'In the middle of the night.'

'You get up at five o'clock, Ali. I don't know what people like you mean by the middle of the night.'

'Half past eleven. At least.'

Harry promised it would never happen again. Ali kept nodding in the way that people do when listening to stories they know off by heart. Harry asked how he could thank Ali, who answered that Harry could rent him his unused cellar storage space. Harry said he would give the matter more thought and paid Ali the money for the taxi, a bottle of Coke, a bag of pasta and meatballs.

'We're quits then,' Harry said.

Ali shook his head. 'Quarterly rates,' said the chairman, treasurer and Mr Fix-it of the housing co-op committee.

'Oh shit, I'd forgotten.'

'Eriksen.' Ali smiled.

'Who's that?'

'Someone I got a letter from last summer. He asked me to send the account number so that he could pay his rates for May and June 1972.

He reckoned that was why he hadn't been able to sleep for the last thirty years. I wrote back saying no one in the block remembered him, so he didn't need to pay.' Ali pointed a finger at Harry. 'But I'm not going to do that with you.'

Harry raised both arms in surrender: 'I'll transfer the money tomorrow.'

The first thing Harry did when he was in his flat was to call Anna's number again. The same ex-presenter as the previous time. But he had barely emptied the bag of pasta and meatballs into the frying pan when he heard the telephone ringing above the sizzling noises. He ran into the hall and snatched at the phone.

'Hello!' he yelled.

'Hello,' said the familiar woman's voice at the other end, somewhat taken aback.

'Oh, it's you.'

'Yes, who did you think it was?'

Harry squeezed his eyes shut. 'Work. There's been another robbery.' The words tasted like bile and chilli. The numb ache behind his eyes was back.

'I tried to catch you on your mobile,' Rakel said.

'I've lost it.'

'Lost it?'

'Left it somewhere, or it's been stolen. I don't know, Rakel.'

'Is something wrong, Harry?'

'Wrong?'

'You sound so . . . stressed.'

'I . . .'

'Mm?'

Harry breathed in. 'How's the court case going?'

Harry was listening, but was unable to order the words into sentences which made sense. He picked up 'financial status', 'the best for the child' and 'arbitration' and gathered that there wasn't much news. The next meeting with the lawyers had been postponed until Friday; Oleg was fine, but was sick of living in a hotel.

'Tell him I'm looking forward to having you back,' he said.

When they had rung off, Harry stood wondering if he should ring back. But what for? To tell her he had been invited to dinner by an old flame and he had no idea what had taken place? Harry rested his hand on the telephone, but then the smoke alarm in the kitchen went off. And when he had taken the frying pan off the hob and opened the window, the telephone rang again. Later Harry was to reflect that a lot would have been different, if Bjarne Møller had not chosen to ring him that evening.

'I know you've just gone off duty,' Møller said, 'but we're a bit short-staffed and a woman has been found dead in her flat. Appears she shot herself. Could you take a look?'

'Of course, boss. I owe you one for today. By the way, Ivarsson presented the parallel-investigation approach as his idea.'

'What would you have done, if you were boss and had received such an order from above?'

'The idea of me as a boss is mind-boggling, boss. How do I get to this flat?'

'Stay where you are. You'll be picked up.'

Twenty minutes later there was a harsh buzzing sound that Harry heard so seldom it made him jump. The voice, metallic and distorted by the intercom, said the taxi had arrived, but Harry could feel the hairs on his neck rising. When he got downstairs and saw the low-slung, red sports car, a Toyota MR2, his suspicions were confirmed.

'Good evening, Hole.' The voice came from the open car window, but it was so close to the tarmac that Harry couldn't see who was speaking. Harry opened the car door and was welcomed by a funky bass, an organ as synthetic as a blue boiled sweet and a familiar falsetto: 'You sexy motherfucka!'

With difficulty, Harry heaped himself into a narrow bucket seat.

'It's us two tonight then,' Inspector Tom Waaler said, opening a Teutonic jaw and revealing an impressive row of impeccable teeth in the centre of his suntanned face. But the arctic-blue eyes remained cold. There were many at Police HQ who disliked Harry, but as far as he knew there was only one person who actually nourished a hatred of him. In Waaler's eyes, Harry knew he was an unworthy representative of the police force and therefore a personal affront. On several occasions, Harry had made it clear he didn't share Waaler's and some other colleagues' crypto-fascist views on homos, commies, dole cheats, Pakis, chinks, niggers, gyppos and dagos, while Waaler, for his part, had called Harry a 'pissed-up rock journo'. However, Harry suspected that the real reason for his hatred was that Harry drank. Tom Waaler could not tolerate weakness. Harry assumed that was why he spent so many hours in the fitness studio practising high kicks and punches against sacks of sand and a stream of new sparring partners. In the canteen, Harry had overheard one of the younger officers, with admiration in his voice, describing how Waaler had broken both arms of a karate kid in a Vietnamese gang by Oslo Central station. Given Waaler's view on skin colour, it was a paradox for Harry that his colleague spent so much time in the solarium, but perhaps it was true what one wag had said: Waaler wasn't actually a racist. He was just as happy beating up neo-Nazis as blacks.

Over and above what was common knowledge, there were some matters no one knew as such, but a few had a gut feeling about nevertheless. It was more than a year ago now since Sverre Olsen – the only person who could have told them why Ellen Gjelten was murdered – was found lying on his bed with a warm gun in his hand and a bullet from Waaler's Smith & Wesson between his eyes.

'Be careful, Waaler.'

'I beg your pardon?'

Harry reached out and turned down the love-making groans. 'It's icy tonight.'

The engine purred like a sewing machine, but the sound was deceptive; as the car accelerated Harry experienced for himself how hard the back of the seat was. They raced up the hill by Stenspark along Suhms gate.

'Where are we going?' Harry asked.

'Here,' Waaler said, swinging abruptly to the left in front of an oncoming car. The window was still open and Harry could hear the sound of wet leaves sucking at the tyres.

'Welcome back to Crime Squad,' Harry said. 'Didn't they want you in POT?'

'Restructuring,' Waaler said. 'Besides, the Chief Super and Møller wanted me back. I achieved some pretty useful results in Crime Squad, if you remember.'

'How could I forget.'

'Well, one hears so much about the long-term effects of drinking.'

Harry had just managed to put his arm against the dashboard before the sudden braking sent him into the windscreen. The glove compartment sprang open and something heavy hit Harry on the knee on its way to the floor.

'What the fuck was that?' he groaned.

'A Jericho 941, Israeli police issue,' Waaler said, switching off the engine. 'Not loaded. Leave it where it is. We've arrived.'

'Here?' Harry asked in amazement and bent down to look up at the yellow block of flats in front of him.

'Why not?' Waaler said, already halfway out of the car.

Harry felt his heart beginning to pound. As he searched for the door handle, out of all the thoughts racing through his mind one took hold: he should have made the call to Rakel.

The fog was back. It seeped in through the streets, from the cracks around the closed windows behind the trees in the avenue, out of the blue door which opened after they had heard Weber's abrupt bark over the intercom, and out through the keyholes in the doors they passed on the way upstairs. It lay like a duvet of cotton wool around Harry, and as they entered the flat, Harry had the sensation of walking on clouds. Everything around him – the people, the voices, the crackle of the walkie-talkies, the light from the camera flashes –

had taken on a dreamlike sheen, a coating of detachment because this was not, could not be, real. But, standing in front of the bed where the deceased lay with a pistol in her right hand and a black hole in her temple, he found himself unable to look at the blood on the pillow or meet her vacant, accusatory gaze. Instead he focused on the bedhead, on the horse with the bitten-off head, hoping the fog would soon lift and he would wake up.

10

Sorgenfrigata

Voices came and went around him.

'I'm Inspector Waaler. Can anyone give me a quick recap?'

'We got here three quarters of an hour ago. The electrician here found her.'

'When?'

'At five. He immediately rang the police. His name is . . . let me see . . . René Jensen. I've got his National Insurance number here and his address too.'

'Good. Ring in and check his record.'

'OK.'

'René Jensen?'

'That's me.'

'Can you come over here? My name's Waaler. How did you get in?'

'As I said to the other officer, with this spare key. She popped it down to my shop on Tuesday because she wasn't going to be at home when I came.'

'Because she was working?'

'No idea. Don't think she had a job. Well, not the normal kind. She said she was putting on an exhibition of some stuff.'

'She was an artist then. Anyone here heard of her?'

Silence.

'What were you doing in the bedroom, Jensen?'

'Looking for the bathroom.'

Another voice: 'The bathroom's behind that door.'

'OK. Anything suspicious strike you when you came into the flat, Jensen?'

'Er . . . how do you mean *suspicious*?'

'Was the door locked? Any windows left open? A particular smell or sound? Anything.'

'The door was locked. Didn't see windows open, but I wasn't looking. The only smell was that solvent . . .'

'Turpentine?'

Another voice: 'There are some painting materials in one of the bigger rooms.'

'Thanks. Anything else you noticed, Jensen?'

'What was the last one again?'

'Sound.'

'Sound, yeah! No, not a lot of sound, quiet as the grave it was. That is . . . ha ha . . . I didn't mean . . .'

'That's fine, Jensen. Had you met the deceased before?'

'Never seen her before she came to the shop. Seemed pretty perky then.'

'What did she want you to do?'

'Fix the thermostat for the underfloor heating in the bathroom.'

'Could you do us a favour and check if there's really a problem with the cables? See if she had any heater cables even.'

'What for? Oh, I see, she might have set the whole thing up and we were kind of supposed to find her?'

'Something like that.'

'Yeah, well, the thermostat was fried.'

'Fried?'

'Not functional.'

'How do you know?'

Pause.

'You must have been told not to touch anything, Jensen, weren't you?'

'Ye-es, but you took such a bloody long time to come, and I got a bit twitchy, so I had to find something to do.'

'So, now, the deceased has a fully functional thermostat?'

'Er . . . ha ha . . . yes.'

Harry tried to move off the bed, but his feet wouldn't obey. The doctor had closed Anna's eyes and now she seemed to be sleeping. Tom Waaler had sent the electrician home and told him to make himself available for the next few days. He had also dismissed the uniformed patrolmen who had responded to the call. Harry would never have believed he would feel this way, but in fact he was pleased that Waaler had been there. Without his experienced colleague's presence, not one single intelligent question would have been asked, and even fewer intelligent decisions taken.

Waaler asked the doctor if he could give them some provisional conclusions.

'The bullet has obviously passed through the skull, destroyed the brain and thus arrested all vital bodily functions. On the assumption that the room temperature has been constant, body temperature suggests that she has been dead for at least sixteen hours. No signs of violence. No injection marks or external indications of medicinal use. However . . .' The doctor paused for effect. 'The scars on the wrists suggest that she has tried this before. A purely speculative but educated guess is that she was manic depressive, or simply depressive, and suicidal. I wouldn't mind betting we will find a psychologist's case file on her.'

Harry tried to say something, but his tongue wouldn't obey, either.

'I'll know more when I've undertaken a closer examination.'

'Thank you, Doctor. Anything to tell us, Weber?'

'The weapon is a Beretta M92F, a highly unusual gun. We can only find one set of fingerprints on the gunstock, and they are obviously hers. The bullet was lodged in one of the bed boards and the ammo matches the weapon, so the ballistics report will show it was fired by this pistol. You'll get a full report tomorrow.'

'Good, Weber. One more thing. The door was locked when the electrician arrived. I noticed the door was fitted with a standard lock and not a latch, so no one can have been here and then left the flat, unless they took the deceased's key and locked the door after them, of course. In other words, if we find her key, we can wrap this one up.'

Weber nodded and lifted a yellow pencil, dangling from which was a ring and a key. 'It was on the chest of drawers in the hall. It's the kind of system key that opens the main door to the block and all the rooms for common use. I checked and it fits the lock on the flat door.'

'Excellent. All we're missing then is basically a signed suicide letter. Any objections to calling this one an open and shut case?'

Waaler looked at Weber, the doctor and Harry. 'OK. Family can be given the sad news and come to identify her.'

He went into the hall while Harry stood by the bed. Soon after, Waaler stuck his head in again.

'Isn't it great when all the cards just fall into place, Hole?'

Harry's brain sent a message to the head to nod, but he had no idea if it obeyed.

11

The Illusion

I'm watching the first video. When I take it frame by *frame I can see the spurt of flame. Particles of powder which as yet have not been converted into pure energy, like a glowing swarm of asteroids following the large comet into the atmosphere to burn up while the comet continues serenely on its course. And there is nothing anyone can do because this is the course that was predestined millions of years ago, before mankind, before emotions, before hatred and mercy were born. The bullet enters the head, truncates mental activity and revokes dreams. In the core of the cranium the last thought, a neural impulse from the pain centre, is shattered. It is a last contradictory SOS to itself before everything is silenced. I click onto the second video title. I stare out of the window while the computer grinds away scouring the Internet night. There are stars in the sky and I think that each of them is proof of the ineluctability of fate. They make no sense; they are elevated above the human need for logic and context. And that is why, I think, they are so beautiful.*

Then the second video is ready. I click on PLAY. *Play a play. It is like a travelling theatre which stages the same performance, but in a different place. The same dialogues and actions, the same costumes, the* same scenery. Only the extras have changed. And the final scene. There was no tragedy this evening.

I am pleased with myself. I have found the nucleus of the character I play – the cold professional adversary who knows exactly what he wants and kills if he has to. No one tries to drag out the time; no one dares after Bogstadveien. And that is why I am God for the two minutes, the one hundred and twenty seconds I have allowed myself. The illusion works. The thick clothes under the boiler suit, the double insoles, the coloured contact lenses and the rehearsed movements.

I log off and the room goes dark. All that reaches me from outside is the distant rumble of the town. I met the Prince today. An odd person. He gives me the ambivalent feeling of being a Pluvianus aegyptius, *the little bird which lives by cleaning the crocodile's mouth.* He told me everything was under control, that the Robberies Unit had not found any clues. He got his share and I got the Jew-gun he had promised me.

Perhaps I ought to be happy, but nothing can ever make me whole again.

Afterwards I rang Police HQ from a public telephone box, but they didn't want to divulge anything unless I said I was family. They told me it was suicide; that Anna had shot herself. The case was closed. I only just managed to put the receiver down before I started laughing.

Part II

12

Freitod

'ALBERT CAMUS SAID THAT FREITOD, SUICIDE, WAS THE ONE truly serious problem philosophy had,' said Aune, sticking his nose up towards the grey sky above Bogstadveien. 'Because the decision about whether life was worth living or not was the answer to philosophy's fundamental question. Everything else – whether or not the world had three dimensions or the mind nine or twelve categories – comes later.'

'Mm,' Harry said.

'Many of my colleagues have undertaken research into why people commit suicide. Do you know what they found the most common cause was?'

'That was the sort of thing I was hoping you could answer.' Harry had to slalom between people on the narrow pavement to keep up with the tubby psychologist.

'That they didn't want to live any longer,' Aune said.

'Sounds like someone deserves a Nobel Prize.' Harry had rung Aune the evening before and arranged to pick him up at his office in Sporveisgata at nine. They passed the branch of Nordea Bank and Harry noticed that the green skip was still outside the 7-Eleven on the other side of the street.

'We often forget that the decision to commit suicide tends to be taken by rationally thinking, sane people who no longer consider that life has anything to offer,' Aune said. 'Old people who have lost their life's companion or whose health is failing, for example.'

'This woman was young and energetic. What rational grounds could she have had?'

'First of all, you have to define the meaning of rational. When someone who is depressed opts to escape from pain by taking their own life, you have to assume the distressed party has weighed up both sides. On the other hand, it is difficult to see suicide as rational in the typical scenario where the sufferer is on their way out of the trough, and only then finds the energy to perform the active deed which suicide is.'

'Can suicide be a completely spontaneous act?'

'Of course it can. It is more usual, however, for there to be attempts first, especially among women. In the USA there are calculated to be ten pseudo-suicide attempts among women for every one suicide.'

'Pseudo?'

'Taking five sleeping tablets is a cry for help, serious enough it's true, but I don't include it as a suicide attempt when a half-full bottle of pills is still on the bedside table.'

'This one shot herself.'

'A masculine suicide then.'

'Masculine?'

'One of the reasons men are more successful is that they choose more aggressive, lethal methods than women. Guns and tall buildings, instead of cutting their wrists or taking an overdose. It is very unusual for a woman to shoot herself.'

'Suspiciously unusual?'

Aune regarded Harry closely. 'Have you any reason to believe this wasn't suicide?'

Harry shook his head. 'I just want to be quite sure. We have to turn right here. Her flat is a little way up the street.'

'Sorgenfrigata?' Aune chuckled and squinted up at the ominous clouds moving across the sky. 'Naturally.'

'Naturally?'

'Sorgenfri was the name of the palace belonging to Christophe, the Haitian king who committed suicide when he was taken prisoner by the French, or as they called it Sans Souci. So, carefree. Carefree Street. Sorgenfrigata. He pointed the cannons at the heavens to avenge himself on God, you know.'

'Well . . .'

'And I suppose you know what the writer, Ola Bauer, said about this street? *I moved to Sorgenfrigata, but that didn't help much, either.*' Aune was laughing so much his double chin was wobbling.

Halvorsen stood outside the door waiting. 'I met Bjarne Møller as I was leaving the station,' he said. 'He was under the impression this case was done and dusted.'

'We just need to tie up a few loose ends,' Harry said, unlocking the door with the key the electrician had given him.

The police tape in front of the door had been removed and the body taken away; otherwise nothing had been touched since the evening before. They went into the bedroom. The white sheet on the large bed shone in the half-light.

'What are we looking for then?' Halvorsen asked as Harry drew the curtains.

'A spare key for the flat,' Harry answered.

'Why's that?'

'We presumed she had a spare key, the one she gave to the electrician. I've been doing a bit of checking. System keys can't be cut at any locksmith; they have to be ordered from the manufacturer via an authorised locksmith. Since the key fits the main door and the cellar door, the housing committee with responsibility for the block of flats wants control of them. Therefore flat residents have to apply for written permission from the committee when they order new keys, don't they. According to an agreement with the committee, it is the authorised locksmith's duty to keep a list of the keys issued to every single flat. I rang Låsesmeden, the locksmith in Vibes gate, last night. Anna Bethsen was issued two spare keys, thus making three in all. We found one in the flat and the electrician had one. But where is the third? Until it has been found, we cannot rule out the possibility that someone was here when she died and locked the door on their way out.'

Halvorsen nodded slowly: 'The third key, mm.'

'The third key. Can you start over here, Halvorsen, and I'll show Aune something in the meantime?'

'OK.'

'Right, and one more thing. Don't be surprised if you find my mobile phone. I think I left it here yesterday afternoon.'

'I thought you said you lost it the day before.'

'I found it again. And lost it again. You know . . .'

Halvorsen shook his head. Harry led Aune into the corridor towards the reception rooms. 'I asked you because you're the only person I know who paints.'

'Unfortunately, that is a slight exaggeration.' Aune was still out of breath from the stairs.

'Yes, but you know a little about art, so I hope you can make something of this.'

Harry opened the sliding doors to the furthest room, switched on the light and pointed. Instead of looking at the three paintings, Aune sucked in his breath and walked over to the three-headed standard lamp. He took his glasses from the inside pocket of his tweed jacket, bent down and read the heavy plinth.

'I say!' he exclaimed with enthusiasm. 'A genuine Grimmer lamp.'

'Grimmer?'

'Bertol Grimmer. World-famous German designer. Among other things, he designed the victory monument which Hitler had erected in Paris in 1941. He could have been one of the greatest artists of our time, but at the zenith of his career it came out that he was three-quarters Romany. He was sent to a concentration camp and his name was erased from several buildings and works of art he had worked on.

Grimmer survived, but both his hands had been shattered in the quarry where the gypsies worked. He continued to work after the War although he never attained the same magnificent heights because of his injuries. This must be from the post-War years, though, I would wager.' Aune took off the lampshade.

Harry coughed: 'I was actually thinking more about these portraits.'

'Amateur,' Aune snorted. 'You would do better to concentrate on this elegant statue of a woman. The goddess Nemesis, Bertol Grimmer's favourite motif after the War. The goddess of revenge. Incidentally, revenge is a frequent motive in suicides, you know. They feel it is someone's fault their lives have been unsuccessful, and they want to inflict this guilt on others by committing suicide. Bertol Grimmer also took his own life, after his wife's, because she had a lover. Revenge, revenge, revenge. Did you know that humans are the only living creatures to practise revenge? The interesting thing about revenge—'

'Aune?'

'Oh yes, these pictures, you wanted me to interpret them, didn't you? Hm, they look not too dissimilar to the Rorschach blot.'

'The pictures you give to patients to prompt associations?'

'Correct. The problem here is that if I interpret these pictures, it will probably say more about my inner life than hers. Except that no one believes in the Rorschach blot any more, so why not? Let me see . . . These pictures are very dark, possibly more angry than depressed. One of them clearly isn't finished, though.'

'Perhaps it's supposed to be like that, perhaps it forms a whole?'

'What makes you say that?'

'I don't know, perhaps because the light from the three individual lamps falls perfectly on its own picture?'

'Hm.' Aune placed an arm over his chest and rested a forefinger on his lips. 'You're right. Of course you're right. And do you know what, Harry?'

'No. What?'

'They mean nothing to me at all – please excuse the expression – absolutely bugger all. Have we finished?'

'Yes. Oh, by the way, there is just one minor detail, since you paint. As you can see, the palette is on the left of the easel. Isn't that extremely impractical?'

'Yes, unless you're left-handed.'

'I see. I'll have to help Halvorsen. I don't know how I can thank you.'

'I know. I'll add an hour to my next invoice.'

Halvorsen had finished in the bedroom.

'She didn't have many possessions,' he said. 'It's a bit like searching a hotel room. Just clothes, toiletries, an iron, towels, bed linen and so on. No picture of the family, no letters or personal papers.'

An hour later, Harry knew exactly what Halvorsen meant. They had gone through the whole flat and were back in the bedroom without having turned up so much as a telephone bill or a bank statement.

'That's the strangest thing I've ever experienced,' Halvorsen said, sitting down opposite Harry at the writing desk. 'She must have cleaned up. Perhaps she wanted to take everything with her, her whole person, when she went, if you know what I mean.'

'I do. You didn't see any signs of a laptop?'

'Laptop?'

'Portable PC.'

'What are you talking about?'

'Can't you see the faded square on the wood here?' Harry pointed to the desk between them. 'Looks like there's been a laptop here and it's been moved.'

'Does it?'

Harry could feel Halvorsen's probing eyes.

In the street, they stood staring up at her windows in the pale yellow facade while Harry smoked a stray concertinaed cigarette he had found lying in the inside pocket of his coat.

'That family business was strange, wasn't it,' Halvorsen said.

'The what?'

'Didn't Møller tell you? They couldn't find the addresses of her parents, brothers, sisters or anyone, just an uncle in prison. Møller had to ring the undertaker's himself to have the poor girl taken away. As if dying wasn't lonely enough.'

'Mm. Which undertaker?'

'Sandemann,' Halvorsen said. 'The uncle wanted her to be cremated.'

Harry pulled at his cigarette and watched the smoke rise and disperse. The end of a process which had started when a peasant sowed tobacco seeds in a field in Mexico. The seed became a tobacco plant as tall as a man within four months, and two months later it was harvested, shaken, dried, graded, packed and sent to RJ Reynolds factories in Florida or Texas where it became a filter cigarette in a vacuum-packed, yellow Camel packet in a carton and was shipped to Europe. Eight months after being a leaf on a green sprouting plant under the sun in Mexico, it falls out of a drunken man's coat pocket as he falls down steps or out of a taxi or spreads his coat over himself as a blanket because he cannot or dare not open the door to his bedroom with all the monsters under the bed. And then, when he finally finds the cigarette, crumpled and covered in pocket fluff, he puts one end in his malodorous mouth and lights the other. After the dried, sliced tobacco leaf has been inside this body for a brief moment of enjoyment, it is blown out and is at long last free. Free to dissolve, to turn to nothing. To be forgotten.

Halvorsen cleared his throat twice: 'How did you know she had ordered the keys from the locksmith in Vibes gate?'

Harry threw the end of the cigarette onto the ground and pulled his coat tighter around him. 'Looks like Aune was right,' he said. 'It's going to rain. If you're heading straight to Police HQ, I could use a lift.'

'There must be hundreds of locksmiths in Oslo, Harry.'

'Mm. I rang the deputy chairman of the housing committee, Knut

Arne Ringnes. Nice man. They've used the same locksmith for twenty years. Shall we go?'

'Good you've come,' Beate Lønn said as Harry walked in the House of Pain. 'I discovered something last night. Look at this.' She rewound the video and pressed the PAUSE button. A quivering still of Stine Grette's face turned towards the robber's balaclava filled the screen. 'I've magnified one portion of the video frame. I wanted to have Stine's face as large as possible.'

'Why was that?' Harry asked, flinging himself onto a chair.

'If you look at the counter, you'll see that this is eight seconds before the Expeditor shoots . . .'

'The Expeditor?'

She smiled bashfully. 'It's just something I've started calling him in private. My grandfather had a farm, so I . . . yes.'

'Where was that?'

'Valle in the Sete valley.'

'And you saw animals being slaughtered there?'

'Yes.' The intonation didn't invite further questions. Beate pressed the SLOW button and Stine Grette's face became animated. Harry saw her blinking and her lips moving in slow motion. He had begun to dread seeing the shot when Beate suddenly stopped the video.

'Did you see that?' she asked excitedly.

A few seconds passed before Harry clicked.

'She was speaking!' he said. 'She says something seconds before she is shot, but you can't hear anything on the sound recording.'

'That's because she's whispering.'

'How did I miss that? But why? And what does she say?'

'I hope we'll soon find out. I've got hold of a lip-reading specialist from the Institute for the Deaf and Dumb. He's on his way now.'

'Great.'

Beate glanced at her watch. Harry bit his bottom lip, breathed in and said quietly: 'Beate, I once . . .'

He saw her stiffen when he used her first name. 'I had a colleague called Ellen Gjelten.'

'I know,' she said in a rush. 'She was killed next to the river.'

'Yes. When she and I ground to a halt in a case we had several techniques for activating information trapped in the subconscious. Association games. We wrote down words on scraps of paper, that kind of thing.' Harry, ill at ease, smiled. 'It may sound a bit vague, but occasionally it produced results. I wondered if we could have a go.'

'If you like.' Again it struck Harry how much more confident Beate seemed when they focused on a video or a computer screen. Now she was eyeing him as if he had just suggested playing strip poker.

'I want to know what you *feel* about this particular case,' he said.

She laughed nervously. 'Feelings, hm.'

'Forget cold facts for a while.' Harry leaned forward in his chair. 'Don't be the clever girl. You don't need to back up what you say. Just say what your gut instinct tells you.'

She stared at the table. Harry waited. Then she raised her gaze and looked him straight in the eyes: 'My money's on a two.'

'Two?'

'Football pools. Away team wins. It's one of the fifty per cent we never solve.'

'Right. And why's that?'

'Simple arithmetic. When you think of all the idiots we *don't* catch, a man like the Expeditor, who has thought things through and knows a bit about how we work, has pretty good odds.'

'Mm.' Harry rubbed his face. 'So your gut instincts do mental arithmetic?'

'Not exclusively. There's something about the way he functions. So determined. He seems to be driven . . .'

'What's driving him, Beate? Money?'

'I don't know. According to statistics, the prime motive for robberies is money and the second excitement and—'

'Forget statistics, Beate. You're a detective now. You're analysing

101

not only video images now, but your own subconscious interpretations of what you've seen. Trust me, that's the most important lead a detective has.'

Beate looked at him. Harry was aware he was trying to coax her out of herself. 'Come on!' he urged. 'What drives the Expeditor?'

'Feelings.'

'What kind of feelings?'

'Strong feelings.'

'What kind of strong feelings, Beate?'

She closed her eyes. 'Love or hatred. Hatred. No, love. I don't know.'

'Why does he shoot her?'

'Because he . . . no.'

'Come on. Why does he shoot her?' Harry had inched his chair towards hers.

'Because he has to. Because it is predetermined . . .'

'Good! Why is it predetermined?'

There was a knock at the door.

Harry would have preferred it if Fritz Bjelke from the Institute for the Deaf and Dumb had not cycled quite as mercurially through the city to assist them, but now he was standing in the doorway – a gentle, rotund man with round glasses and a pink cycle helmet. Bjelke was not deaf, and definitely not dumb. In order that he could learn as much as possible about Stine Grette's lip positions, they played the first part of the video tape where they could hear what she said. While the tape was running, Bjelke talked non-stop.

'I'm a specialist, but actually we're all lip-readers even though we can hear what people say. That's why it's such an uncomfortable feeling when the dubbing on films is just hundredths of a second out.'

'Really,' Harry said. 'Personally, I can't make anything out of her lip movements.'

'The problem is that only thirty to forty per cent of all words can be read directly from the lips. To understand the rest you have to study the face and body language, and use your own linguistic instincts and logic to insert the missing words. Thinking is as important as seeing.'

'She starts whispering here,' Beate said.

Bjelke immediately shut up and concentrated intently on the minimalist lip movements on the screen. Beate stopped the recording before the shot was fired.

'Right,' Bjelke said. 'Once more.'

And afterwards: 'Again.'

Then: 'One more time please.'

After seven times, he nodded that he had seen enough.

'I don't understand what she means,' Bjelke said. Harry and Beate exchanged glances. 'But I think I know what she says.'

Beate half-ran down the corridor to keep up with Harry.

'He's reckoned to be the country's foremost expert in the field,' she said.

'That doesn't help,' Harry said. 'He said himself he wasn't sure.'

'But what if she did say what Bjelke thought?'

'It doesn't make sense. He must have missed a negative.'

'I don't agree.'

Harry came to a halt and Beate almost ran into him. With an alarmed expression, she looked up at one wide-open eye.

'Good,' he said.

Beate was perplexed. 'What do you mean?'

'Disagreeing is good. Disagreeing means that you've seen or understood something even though you're not exactly sure what. And there's something I haven't understood.' He set off again. 'Let's assume you're right. Then we can consider where this takes us.' He stopped in front of the lift and pressed the button.

'Where are you going now?' Beate asked.

'To check some details. I'll be back in less than an hour.'

The lift doors opened and PAS Ivarsson stepped out.

'Aha!' He beamed. 'The master sleuths on the trail. Anything new to report?'

'The point about parallel groups is that we don't have to report in so often. Isn't it?' Harry said, sidestepping him and walking into the lift. 'If I understood you and the FBI correctly, that is.'

Ivarsson's broad smile and gaze held. 'We obviously have to share key information.'

Harry pressed the button for the first floor, but Ivarsson placed himself between the doors: 'Well?'

Harry shrugged. 'Stine Grette whispers something to the robber before she is shot.'

'Uhuh?'

'We believe she whispers: *It's my fault*.'

'It's my fault?'

'Yes.'

Ivarsson's brow furrowed. 'That can't be right, can it? It would make more sense if she had said *It's* not *my fault*. I mean, it isn't her fault the branch manager took six seconds too long putting the money in the holdall.'

'I don't agree,' Harry said, looking conspicuously at his watch. 'We've received assistance from one of the country's leading experts in the field. Beate can fill you in on the details.'

Ivarsson was leaning against one lift door, which was impatiently pushing at his back. 'So she forgets a negative in her confusion then. Is that all you have? Beate?'

Beate flushed. 'I've just started studying the video of the bank robbery in Kirkeveien.'

'Any conclusions?'

Her eyes wandered from Ivarsson to Harry and back again. 'Not for the time being.'

'Nothing then,' Ivarsson said. 'Perhaps you would be pleased to know that we have identified nine suspects we've brought in for questioning. And we have a strategy for finally getting something out of Raskol.'

'Raskol?' Harry asked.

'Raskol Baxhet, the king of the sewer rats himself,' Ivarsson said, hooking his fingers into his belt loops. He breathed in and hitched his trousers up with a cheery grin: 'But Beate can probably fill you in on the details later.'

13

Marble

HARRY WAS AWARE THAT, ON CERTAIN MATTERS, HE WAS small-minded. Take Bogstadveien, for example. He didn't like Bogstadveien. He didn't know why; perhaps it was because in this street, paved with gold and oil, the Mount Happy of Happyland, no one smiled. Harry didn't smile himself, but he lived in Bislett, wasn't paid to smile and right now had a few good reasons for not smiling. However, that didn't mean that Harry, in common with most Norwegians, didn't appreciate being smiled *at*.

Inwardly, Harry tried to excuse the boy behind the counter in the 7-Eleven. He probably hated his job, he probably lived in Bislett, too, and it had started to piss down with rain again.

The pale face with the fiery red pimples cast a bored eye over his police ID card: 'How should I know how long the skip's been outside?'

'Because it's green and it covers half of your view of Bogstadveien,' Harry said.

The boy groaned and put his hands on hips which barely held up his trousers. 'A week. Sort of. Hey, queue of people waiting behind you, you know.'

'Mm. I had a look inside. It's almost empty apart from a few bottles and newspapers. Do you know who ordered it?'

'No.'

'I see you have a surveillance camera over the counter. Looks as if it might just catch the skip?'

'If you say so.'

'If you still have the film from last Friday I would like to see it.'

'Ring tomorrow. Tobben's here.'

'Tobben?'

'Shop manager.'

'I suggest you ring Tobben now and get permission to give me the tape, then I won't detain you any longer.'

'You have a look for it,' he said and the spots went redder. 'I haven't got time to start searching for some video now.'

'Oh,' Harry said without making a move. 'What about after closing time?'

'We're open twenty-four hours,' the boy said, rolling his eyes.

'That was a joke,' Harry said.

'Right. Ha ha,' said the boy with the somnambulant voice. 'You going to buy sumfin or what?'

Harry shook his head and the boy looked past him: 'Till's free.'

Harry sighed and turned to the queue crowding towards the counter. 'The till is not free. I am from Oslo Police.' He held up his ID. 'And this person is arrested for being unable to pronounce *th*.'

Harry could be small-minded on certain matters. At this particular moment, though, he was extremely pleased with the response. He appreciated being smiled at.

But he didn't like the smile which appeared to be part of the professional training of preachers, politicians and undertakers. They smile with their *eyes* while speaking and it gave herr Sandemann of Sandemann Funeral Directors a sincerity which together with the temperature in the coffin storeroom under Majorstuen church made

Harry shudder. He surveyed the locale. Two coffins, a chair, a wreath, a funeral director, a black suit and a comb-over.

'She looks wonderful,' Sandemann said. 'Peaceful. Restful. Dignified. Are you a member of the family?'

'Not exactly.' Harry showed his police card in the hope that sincerity was reserved for closest family. It wasn't.

'Tragic that such a young life should pass on in this way.' Sandemann smiled, pressing his palms together. The funeral director's fingers were unusually thin and crooked.

'I would like to have a look at the clothes the deceased was wearing when she was found,' Harry said. 'At the office they said you had brought them here.'

Sandemann nodded, fetched a white plastic bag and explained that he had done this in case parents or siblings turned up, and he could dispose of them. Harry searched in vain for pockets in the black dress.

'Was there anything specific you were after?' Sandemann asked in an innocent tone of voice as he peered over Harry's shoulder.

'A house key,' Harry said. 'You didn't find anything when you . . .' He stared at Sandemann's crooked fingers. '. . . undressed her?'

Sandemann closed his eyes and shook his head. 'The only thing under the skirt was herself. Apart from the picture in the shoe, of course.'

'The picture?'

'Yes. Curious, isn't it? What customs they have. It's still in her shoe.'

Harry lifted a black, high-heeled shoe out of the bag and caught a flash of her in the doorway when he arrived: black dress, black shoes, red mouth.

The picture was a dog-eared photograph of a woman and three children on a beach. It looked like a holiday snap from somewhere in Norway with large, smooth rocks in the water and tall pine trees on the hills in the background.

'Has anyone from her family been here?' Harry asked.

'Only her uncle. Together with one of your colleagues, naturally.'

'Naturally?'

'Yes, I understood he was serving a sentence.'

Harry didn't answer. Sandemann leaned forward and bent his back in such a way that the little head withdrew between his shoulders making him resemble a vulture: 'I wondered what for.' The whisper sounded like a hoarse birdcall: 'Since he won't even be allowed to attend the funeral, I mean.'

Harry cleared his throat. 'May I see her?'

Sandemann seemed disappointed, but gestured civilly with his hand to one of the coffins.

As usual, it struck Harry how a professional job could enhance a corpse. Anna really did seem at peace. He touched her forehead. It was like touching marble.

'What is the necklace?' Harry asked.

'Gold coins,' Sandemann said. 'Her uncle brought it.'

'And what's this?' Harry lifted up a wad of paper held together by a thick, brown elastic band. It was a stack of hundred-kroner notes.

'A custom they have,' Sandemann said.

'Who are these *they* you keep talking about?'

'Didn't you know?' Sandemann formed his thin, wet lips into a smile. 'She was a gypsy.'

All the tables in the canteen at Police HQ were occupied by colleagues in animated conversation. Except for one. Harry walked over to it.

'You'll get to know people by and by,' he said. Beate looked up at him with incomprehension, and he realised they might have more in common than he had thought. He sat down and placed a video cassette in front of him. 'This is taken from the 7-Eleven shop diagonally opposite the bank on the day of the robbery. Plus a recording of the Thursday before. Could you check it for anything interesting?'

'See if the bank robber's on it, you mean?' Beate mumbled with her mouth full of bread and liver paste. Harry studied her packed lunch.

'Well, we can only hope,' he said.

'Of course,' she said and her eyes filled with water as she struggled to swallow the food. 'In 1993, the Kreditkasse in Frogner was held up. The robber had taken plastic bags with the Shell logo on to put the money in, so we checked the surveillance camera at the nearest Shell station. Turned out he had been in to buy bags ten minutes before the job. Wearing the same clothes, but without a mask. We arrested him half an hour later.'

'*We*, eight years ago?' Harry asked, not thinking.

Beate's face changed colour like traffic lights. She snatched a slice of bread and tried to hide behind it. 'My father,' she muttered.

'I apologise. I didn't mean it like that.'

'It doesn't matter,' came the swift response.

'Your father . . .'

'Was killed,' she said. 'It's a long time ago now.'

Harry sat listening to the sounds of chewing while studying his hands.

'Why did you take a tape of the week before the robbery?' Beate asked.

'The skip,' Harry said.

'What about it?'

'I rang the skip company and asked. It was ordered on a Thursday by one Stein Søbstad in Industrigata and delivered to the agreed site directly outside the 7-Eleven the day after. There are two Stein Søbstads in Oslo and both deny having ordered a skip. My theory is that the robber had it placed there to cut off the view through the window so that the camera won't film him crossing the road as he leaves the bank. If he had been scouting around the 7-Eleven the same day as he had ordered the skip, we might see someone looking into the camera and out of the window towards the bank, checking angles and so on.'

'With a bit of luck. The witness outside the 7-Eleven says the robber was still masked when he crossed the road, so why would he go to all the bother with a skip?'

'The plan might have been to take off the balaclava while crossing the road.' Harry sighed. 'I don't know, I only know there is something about that green skip. It has been there for a week and apart from the odd passer-by throwing refuse in it, no one has used it.'

'OK,' Beate said, taking the video and standing up.

'One more thing,' Harry said. 'What do you know about this Raskol Baxhet?'

'Raskol?' Beate frowned. 'He was a kind of mythical figure until he gave himself up. If the rumours are true, in one way or another he's had a hand in ninety per cent of the bank robberies in Oslo. My guess is he could finger everyone who has committed a bank robbery here over the last twenty years.'

'So that's what Ivarsson is using him for. Where's he banged up?'

Beate thrust a thumb over her shoulder. 'A-Wing over there.'

'In Botsen?'

'Yes. And he's refused to utter a word to any policeman for the duration of his sentence.'

'So what makes Ivarsson think he can succeed?'

'He's finally found something Raskol wants that he can use to negotiate. In Botsen they say it's the only thing Raskol has asked for since he arrived. Permission to go to the funeral of a relative.'

'Really?' Harry said, hoping his face didn't give anything away.

'She'll be buried in two days' time, and Raskol has lodged an urgent plea with the prison governor to be allowed to attend.'

After Beate had gone, Harry remained at the table. The lunch break was over and the canteen was thinning out. It was supposed to be light and snug and was run by a national catering company, so Harry preferred to eat in town. But he suddenly remembered this was where he had danced with Rakel at the Christmas party; it was precisely here he had decided to make a move on her. Or was it vice versa? He could still feel the curve of her back on his hand.

Rakel.

In two days Anna would be buried, and no one had the slightest doubt that she had died by her own hand. He was the only person who had been there and could have contradicted them, but he couldn't remember a thing. So why couldn't he let sleeping dogs lie? He had everything to lose and nothing to gain. If for no other reason, why couldn't he forget the case for their sake, for his and Rakel's?

Harry put his elbows on the table and cradled his face in his hands. If he had been able to contradict them, would he have done?

At the neighbouring table they turned when they heard the chair scraping on the floor and watched the close-cropped, long-legged policeman with the bad back stride quickly out of the canteen.

14

Luck

THE BELLS OVER THE DOOR RANG WILDLY IN THE DARK, cramped kiosk as the two men came running in. Elmer's Fruit&Tobacco shop was one of the last kiosks of its kind with car, hunting and fishing magazines on one wall and soft porn, cigarettes and cigars on the other, and three piles of pools coupons on the counter between sweaty liquorice bars and dry, grey marzipan pigs from the previous Christmas tied in a ribbon.

'Just made it,' said Elmer, a thin, bald man of sixty with a beard and a Nordland accent.

'Wow, that was sudden,' Halvorsen said, brushing the rain off his shoulders.

'Typical Oslo autumn,' the northerner said in his acquired *bokmål*. 'Either a drought or a deluge. Twenty Camel?'

Harry nodded and took out his wallet.

'And two scratch cards for the young officer?' Elmer held out the scratch cards to Halvorsen, who gave him a broad smile and quickly pocketed them.

'Is it alright if I light up in here, Elmer?' Harry asked, peering out into the downpour, which was lashing the now deserted pavements outside the dirty window.

'By all means,' Elmer said, giving them their change. 'Poisons and gambling are my bread and butter.'

He bent down and went out through a crooked brown curtain behind which they could hear a coffee machine gurgling.

'Here's the photo,' Harry said. 'I'd just like you to find out who the woman is.'

'Just?' Halvorsen looked at the dog-eared, grainy photograph Harry passed him.

'Start by finding out where the photo was taken,' Harry said and had a severe coughing fit when he tried to hold the smoke in his lungs. 'Looks like a holiday area. If it is, there must be a small grocer's or someone who rents out chalets, that sort of thing. If the family in the photo are regular visitors, someone working there knows who they are. When you know that, leave the rest to me.'

'All of this is because the photo was in the shoe?'

'It's not the usual place to keep photos, is it now?'

Halvorsen shrugged and walked into the street.

'It's not stopping,' Harry said.

'I know, but I have to get home.'

'What for?'

'For something called a life. Nothing that would interest you.'

Harry imitated a smile to show that he understood it was meant to be a witticism. 'Enjoy yourself.'

The bells rang and the door slammed behind Halvorsen. Harry sucked at his cigarette and, while studying Elmer's selection of reading matter, he was struck by how few interests he shared with the average Norwegian man. Was it because he no longer had any? Music, yes, but no one had done anything good in the last ten years, not even his old heroes. Films? If he came out of a cinema nowadays without feeling he had been lobotomised, he counted himself as fortunate. Nothing else. In other words, the only thing he was still interested in was finding people and locking them up. And not even that made his heart beat like before. The spooky thing was, Harry mused, laying a hand on Elmer's cold, smooth counter, that this state didn't bother him in the slightest. The fact that he had capitulated. It simply felt liberating to be older.

The bells rang furiously again.

'I forgot to tell you about the guy we pulled in for illegally possessing a weapon last night,' Halvorsen said. 'Roy Kinnsvik, one of the skinheads in Herbert's Pizza.' He stood in the doorway with the rain dancing around his wet shoes.

'Mm?'

'He was obviously frightened, so I told him to give me something I needed and I would let him off.'

'And?'

'He said he saw Sverre Olsen in Grünerløkka the night Ellen was killed.'

'So what? We've got several witnesses who can confirm that.'

'Yes, but this guy saw Olsen sitting and chatting with someone in a car.'

Harry's cigarette fell to the ground. He ignored it.

'Did he know who it was?' he asked slowly.

Halvorsen shook his head. 'No, he only recognised Olsen.'

'Did you get a description?'

'He could only remember he thought the person looked like a policeman. But he said he would probably recognise him again.'

Harry could feel himself getting warm under his coat and articulated each word with care: 'Could he say what car it was?'

'No, he had just rushed by.'

Harry nodded, running his hand up and down the counter.

Halvorsen cleared his throat: 'But he thought it was a sports car.'

Harry noticed the cigarette smoking on the ground. 'Colour?'

Halvorsen showed one upturned palm in apology.

'Was it red?' Harry asked in a low, thick voice.

'What did you say?'

Harry straightened up. 'Nothing. Remember the name. And go home to your life.'

The bells jingled.

Harry stopped stroking the counter, but held his hand there. All of a sudden it felt like cold marble.

Astrid Monsen was forty-five years old and made her living by translating French literature in the study of her flat in Sorgenfrigata. She didn't have a man in her life, but she had a tape loop of a dog barking, which she put on at night. Harry heard her steps and at least three locks being released behind the door before it opened a fraction and a small, freckled face peered out from beneath black curls.

'Ugh,' it exclaimed when it saw Harry's towering frame.

The face may have been unfamiliar, but he had the immediate sensation that he had met her before. Presumably because of Anna's detailed description of her ghastly neighbour.

'Harry Hole, Crime Squad,' he said, showing his card. 'I apologise for disturbing you so late in the afternoon. I have a few questions about the evening Anna Bethsen died.'

He tried to smile reassuringly when he saw she was having problems closing her mouth. From the corner of his eye, Harry saw movement behind the glass in the neighbour's door.

'Could I come inside, fru Monsen? It won't take a minute.'

Astrid Monsen took two steps back, and Harry seized the opportunity to slip in and close the door behind him. Now he could see the whole of her Afro hairdo. She had obviously dyed it black, and it enclosed her little white head like an enormous globe.

They stood opposite each other in the frugal light of the hallway, beside dried flowers and a framed poster from the Chagall Museum in Nice.

'Have you seen me before?' Harry asked.

'What . . . do you mean?'

'Just whether you've seen me before. I'll come to the rest afterwards.'

Her mouth opened and closed. Then she shook her head firmly.

'Fine,' Harry said. 'Were you at home on Tuesday night?'

She nodded tentatively.

'Did you see or hear anything?'

'Nothing,' she said. Rather too hastily for Harry's taste.

'Take your time and think it over,' he said with an attempt at a friendly smile, not the most practised feature in his repertoire of facial expressions.

'Nothing . . .' she said, her eyes searching for the door behind Harry. 'At all.'

Back on the street, Harry lit up. He had heard Astrid Monsen apply the safety lock the second he was on the other side of her door. Poor thing. She was the last on his list and he was able to conclude that no one had either seen or heard him or anyone else on the stairway the night Anna died.

After two drags, he threw away the cigarette.

He sat in his chair at home watching the red eye of the answer machine for a long time before pressing the PLAY button. It was Rakel wishing him goodnight, and there was a journalist wanting a comment on the two bank raids. Afterwards he rewound the tape and listened to Anna's message: 'And would you mind wearing the jeans you know I like so much?'

He stroked his face. Then he took out the tape and threw it in the bin. Outside, the rain dripped and, inside, Harry zapped. Women's handball, soaps and some quiz game in which you could become a millionaire. Harry stuck with a discussion on a Swedish channel between a philosopher and a social anthropologist about the concept of revenge. One maintained that a country like the USA, which stands for certain values like freedom and democracy, has a moral responsibility to avenge attacks on its territory as they are also attacks on its values. 'Alone the desire for retaliation – and the execution of it – can protect such a vulnerable system as democracy.'

'What about if the values the democracy stands for themselves fall victim to an act of vengeance?' the other replied. 'What about if another nation's rights as laid down by international law are violated? What kind of values are you defending if you deprive innocent civilians of rights in your hunt for guilty parties? And what about the moral value of turning the other cheek?'

'The problem is that we only have two cheeks,' said the other man, with a smile. 'Isn't it?'

Harry switched off. Wondered whether he should ring Rakel, but decided it was too late. He tried to get his nose in a Jim Thompson book, but discovered that pages 24 to 38 were missing. He got up and paced up and down his room. He opened the refrigerator and stared in frustration at a white cheese and a jar of strawberry jam. He felt like something, but didn't know what. He slammed the refrigerator door shut. Who was he trying to kid? What he wanted was a drink.

At two o'clock in the morning he woke up in his chair, fully clothed. He got up, went to the bathroom and drank a glass of water.

'Fuck,' he said to himself in the mirror. He went to the bedroom and turned on his PC. He found 104 articles in Norwegian on the Net about suicide, but none about revenge, just keywords and links to motives for revenge in literature and Greek mythology. He was just going to switch it off when he realised he hadn't checked his e-mails for a couple of weeks. There were two e-mails. One was from his ISP, who warned him two weeks ago the service was going to be closed down. The other address was anna.beth@chello.no. He double-clicked and read the message: *Hi Harry. Don't forget the key. Anna.* The time showed it had been sent two hours before he was due to meet her for the last time. He read the message again. So short. So . . . simple. He assumed that was how people e-mailed each other. *Hi Harry.* To outside observers it must have seemed as if they were old friends, but they had known each other for six weeks, a long time ago, and he hadn't even realised she had his e-mail address.

When he fell asleep, he dreamed that he was standing in the bank with the gun again. The people around him were made of marble.

15

Gadjo

'WHAT FANTASTIC WEATHER IT IS TODAY,' BJARNE MØLLER said as he came sailing into Harry and Halvorsen's office the next morning.

'Well, you would know, wouldn't you. You've got a window,' Harry said without looking up from his cup of coffee. 'And a new chair,' he added as Møller dropped into Halvorsen's defective chair, which gave a scream of pain.

'Hi, sunshine,' Møller said. 'Having a bad day?'

Harry shrugged. 'I'm pushing forty and I've started to enjoy grumbling. Anything wrong with that?'

'Not at all. Good to see you in a suit, by the way.'

Harry lifted the lapels of his jacket as if he had only now discovered the dark suit.

'There was a meeting of Unit Heads yesterday,' Møller said. 'Do you want the short or the long version?'

Harry stirred his coffee with a pencil. 'We have to stop investigating Ellen's case. Is that it?'

'The case was closed ages ago, Harry. And the Head of Forensics says you're pestering them to check all sorts of old evidence.'

'We found a new witness yesterday who—'

'There's always a new witness, Harry. They just don't want any more.'

'But—'

'We've drawn a line under it, Harry. Sorry.'

Møller turned at the door. 'Go for a walk in the sun. It might be the last warm day for a while.'

'Rumours going round it's sunny,' Harry said as he entered the House of Pain and saw Beate. 'Just so you know.'

'Turn off the light,' she said. 'And I'll show you something.'

She had sounded excited on the telephone, but she didn't mention why. She picked up the remote control: 'I didn't find anything on the tape from the day the skip was ordered, but take a peek at this one from the day of the robbery.'

Harry saw the 7-Eleven on the screen. He saw the green skip outside the window, the cream buns inside the shop, the back of the head and bum-crack of the boy he had talked to the day before. He was serving a girl who was buying milk, *Cosmopolitan* and condoms.

'The recording is timed at 15.05, so about fifteen minutes before the robbery. Look now.'

The girl took her things and left, the queue moved forward and a man in a black boiler suit and a peaked cap with the earflaps pulled well down pointed at something on the counter. He held his head down so that his face couldn't be seen. Under his arm he was carrying a folded black holdall.

'What the hell,' Harry whispered.

'That's the Expeditor,' Beate said.

'Sure? Lots of people wear black boiler suits, and the robber didn't have a cap.'

'When he goes away from the counter, you'll see they're the same shoes as on the video. And notice the bulge on his left. That's the AG3.'

'He's taped it to his body. But what's he doing in a 7-Eleven?'

'He's waiting for the armoured van and he needs a lookout post where he won't be conspicuous. He's done a recce in the area and knows that the security van comes between 15.15 and 15.20. In the meantime, he can't exactly walk around wearing a balaclava and announce his intentions, so he uses a cap which covers most of his face. When he goes to the counter, if you look hard, you can see a small rectangle of light flickering on it. It's a reflection off glass. You're wearing sunglasses, aren't you, you Expeditor bastard.' Beate spoke in a low voice, but fast, with an anger Harry had not heard from her before. 'He's obviously aware of the camera in the 7-Eleven, too. He doesn't show any of his face. Look at him checking the angles! In fact, he does it really well. I've got to give him that.'

The boy behind the counter gave the man in the boiler suit a cream bun and picked up the ten-kroner coin he put down.

'Hello.'

'Right,' Beate said. 'He's not wearing gloves. But he doesn't seem to have touched anything in the shop. And there you can see the rectangle of light I was telling you about.'

Harry didn't say a word.

The man went out of the shop as the last person in the queue was being served.

'Mm. We'll have to start searching for witnesses again,' Harry said, getting up.

'I wouldn't be too optimistic,' Beate said, still staring at the screen. 'Remember only one witness reported having seen the Expeditor escape in the Friday rush hour. The robber's best hiding place is in a crowd.'

'OK, but have you got any other suggestions?'

'Sit down or you'll miss the climax.'

Mildly disconcerted, Harry shot her a look and faced the screen. The boy behind the counter had turned towards the camera with a finger jammed up his nose.

'One man's climax is another—' Harry grumbled.

'Look at the skip outside the window.'

The window pane reflected the light, but they could still see the man in the black boiler suit. He was standing on the pavement between the skip and a parked car. His back was to the camera and a hand was resting on the edge of the skip. He seemed to be keeping an eye on the bank while eating the cream bun. The holdall he was carrying was on the tarmac.

'That's his lookout post,' Beate said. 'He ordered the skip and had it placed on that precise spot. It is ingeniously simple. He can watch for the security van while hiding from the security cameras. And notice the way he stands. First of all, half of the passers-by won't even be able to see him because of the skip, and those who can will see a man in a boiler suit and cap beside a skip: a builder, a removal man or a waste-disposal worker. In short, nothing that will gain a foothold in the cerebral cortex. No wonder we didn't get any witnesses.'

'He's leaving some nice, fat fingerprints on the skip,' Harry said. 'Shame it's done nothing but rain for the last week.'

'But the cream bun—'

'He's eating his fingerprints too,' Harry sighed.

'—makes him thirsty. Watch this now.'

The man bent down, unzipped the holdall and pulled out a white plastic bag. From this he removed a bottle.

'Coca-Cola,' Beate whispered. 'I zoomed in on a still before you came. It's a Coke bottle with a cork in.'

The man held the bottle at the top while pulling out the cork. Then he threw back his head, held the bottle high in the air and poured. They could see the last dregs running out, but the cap blotted out the open mouth and face. Then he put the bottle in the plastic bag, knotted it and was about to put it in his holdall when he paused.

'Watch. Now he's thinking,' Beate whispered, and in a low monotone: 'How much room will the money take up? How much room will the money take up?'

The protagonist studied the holdall. Looked at the skip. Then he made up his mind and with a quick toss of his arm the bag, with the bottle inside, sailed in an arc through the air and landed in the open skip.

'A three-pointer!' Harry roared.

'The crowd goes wild!' Beate yelled.

'Fuck!' Harry shouted.

'Oh no,' Beate groaned and banged her forehead against the wheel in despair.

'They must have just been here,' Harry said. 'Hang on!'

He flung open the car door in front of a cyclist who swerved out of the way, and ran across the street, into the 7-Eleven and over to the counter.

'When did they take the skip?' he asked the boy who was about to wrap two Big Bite sausages for two large-bottomed girls.

'Wait your turn, for Christ's sake,' the boy said without looking up.

One of the girls let out an indignant whine as Harry leaned over, blocking access to the ketchup bottle, and grabbed hold of the boy's green shirt front.

'Hello there, it's me again,' Harry said. 'Now follow this carefully, otherwise this sausage will be going right up . . .'

The boy's terrified expression forced Harry to collect himself. He released his grip and pointed to the window, through which you could now see Nordea Bank on the other side of the street because of the gaping hole left by the skip. 'When did they take the skip? Quickly!'

The boy swallowed and stared at Harry. 'Now. Just now.'

'When is now?'

'Two minutes ago.' His eyes had glazed over.

'Where were they going?'

'How should I know? I don't know nuffin about skips.'

'Nothing.'

'Eh?'

But Harry had already gone.

*

Harry put Beate's red mobile phone to his ear.

'Oslo Waste Management? This is the police, Inspector Harry Hole. Where do you empty those skips of yours? The private ones, yes. Metodica, OK. Where are . . . Verkseier Furulands vei in Alnabru? Thank you. What? *Or* Grønmo? How do I know which one . . . ?'

'Look,' Beate said. 'A traffic jam.'

Cars formed an apparently impenetrable wall down towards the T-junction in front of Kafé Lorry in Hegdehaugsveien.

'We should have taken Uranienborgveien,' Harry said. 'Or Kirkeveien.'

'Shame you're not driving,' Beate said, forcing the front offside wheel up onto the pavement, leaning on the horn and accelerating. People jumped out of the way.

'Hello?' Harry said on the mobile phone. 'You've just collected a green skip from Bogstadveien by the Industrigata crossroads. Where is it going? Yes. I'll wait.'

'Let's take a chance on Alnabru,' Beate said and swung out into the crossroads in front of a tram. The wheels spun on the steel rails until they got a grip on the tarmac. Harry had a vague feeling of déjà vu.

They had come to Pilestredet when the man from Oslo Waste Management came back to say that they couldn't contact the driver on his mobile, but the skip was *probably* on its way to Alnabru.

'Fine,' Harry said. 'Can you ring Metodica and ask them not to empty the contents of the skip into the incinerator until we . . . Your office is closed from 11.30 to 12.00? Careful! No, I was talking to the driver. No, *my* driver.'

In the Ibsen tunnel Harry called Police HQ and asked them to send a patrol car to Metodica, but the closest available car was at least fifteen minutes away.

'Fuck!' Harry threw the mobile phone over his shoulder and smacked the dashboard.

At the roundabout between Byporten and Plaza Beate sneaked

into the space between a red bus and a Chevy van, straddling the white line. When she came down the raised intersection known as the traffic machine doing 110 km/h and performed a controlled skid on screaming tyres, into the hairpin bend on the fjord side of Oslo Central station, Harry realised that all hope was not yet lost.

'Who was the mad bastard who taught you to drive?' he asked, holding on tight as they swerved in and out between cars on the three-lane motorway leading to Ekeberg tunnel.

'Self-taught,' Beate said.

In the middle of the Vålerenga tunnel a large, ugly, diesel-vomiting lorry loomed up ahead of them. It lumbered into the right-hand lane; on the back, held in place by two yellow arms, was a green skip bearing the words OSLO WASTE MANAGEMENT.

'Yess!' Harry shouted.

Beate swung in front of the lorry, slowed down and activated the right indicator. Harry rolled down the window, stretched out a hand holding his ID and waved the lorry into the side of the road with the other.

The driver had no objection to Harry taking a look inside the skip, but wondered if they shouldn't wait until they were in the Metodica yard, where they could empty the contents onto the ground.

'I don't want the bottle to be smashed!' Harry yelled over the noise of passing traffic from the back of the lorry.

'I was thinking about your nice suit,' the driver said, but by then Harry had already scrambled up into the skip. The next moment, a rumble of thunder could be heard from inside, and the driver and Beate heard Harry roundly cursing. Then quite a bit of rooting around. And finally another 'Yess!' before he reappeared over the top of the skip with a white plastic bag held above his head like a trophy.

'Give the bottle to Weber immediately and tell him it's urgent,' Harry said as Beate started the car. 'Say hello from me.'

'Will that help?'

Harry scratched his head. 'No. Just say it's urgent.'

She laughed. Not very much, nor heartfelt, but Harry noted the laughter.

'Are you always so enthusiastic?' she asked.

'Me? What about you? You were ready to drive us into an early grave for this evidence, weren't you?'

She smiled, but didn't answer. Checked the mirror before returning to the carriageway.

Harry glanced at his watch. 'Damn!'

'Late for a meeting?'

'Do you think you could drive me to Majorstuen church?'

'Of course. Is that why you're wearing the black suit?'

'Yes. A . . . friend of mine.'

'Then perhaps you'd better try and get rid of the brown stain on your shoulder first.'

Harry craned his head. 'From the skip,' he said, brushing at it. 'Has it gone now?'

Beate passed him a handkerchief. 'Try a little spit. Was it a close friend?'

'No. Or yes . . . for a while perhaps. But you have to go to funerals, don't you.'

'*Do* you?'

'Don't *you*?'

'I've only been to one funeral all my life.'

They drove in silence.

'Your father?'

She nodded.

They passed the intersection at Sinsen. At Muselunden, the large area of grass below Haraldsheimen, a man and two boys had a kite in the air. All three stood looking at the blue sky and Harry saw the man give the string to the taller of the two boys.

'We still haven't caught the man who did it,' she said.

'No, we haven't,' Harry said. 'Not yet.'

'God giveth and God taketh away,' the priest said, peering down over the empty rows of benches and at the tall man with cropped hair who had just tiptoed in, looking for a seat at the very back. He waited as the echo of a loud, heart-rending sob died away under the arched ceiling. 'But on occasion it can seem as if He is merely taking.'

The priest stressed 'taking' and the acoustics lifted the word and carried it to the back of the church. The sobbing grew in volume again. Harry watched. He had thought that Anna, who was so extroverted and bubbly, would have had lots of friends, but Harry counted only eight people, six in the front row and two further back. Eight. Yes, well, how many would go to his funeral? Eight people was perhaps not such a bad turnout.

The sobbing came from the front row where Harry could see three heads wrapped in bright scarves and three bare-headed men. The other two were a man sitting to the left and a woman in the middle. He recognised the globe-shaped afro of Astrid Monsen.

The organ pedals creaked, then the music began. A psalm. The grace of God. Harry closed his eyes and felt how tired he was. The notes from the organ rose and sank, the high notes trickled like water from the ceiling. The frail voices sang for forgiveness and mercy. He longed to immerse himself in something which could warm and conceal him. The Lord shall come to judge the quick and the dead. God's vengeance. God as Nemesis. The low organ notes caused the unoccupied wooden benches to vibrate. The sword in one hand and the scales in the other, punishment and justice. Or no punishment and no justice. Harry opened his eyes.

Four men were carrying the coffin. Harry recognised Officer Ola Li behind two swarthy men in Armani suits, white shirts open at the neck. The fourth person was so tall he made the coffin tip. The suit hung loosely on the thin body, but he was the only one of the four who did not seem weighed down by the coffin. Harry's eye was particularly caught by the man's face. Narrow, finely formed with large, pained, brown eyes set in deep hollows in the cranium. The black hair was swept back in a long plait, leaving the high, shiny forehead bared. The sensitive, heart-shaped mouth was enwreathed by a long, well-groomed beard. It was as if Christ had stepped down from the altar behind the priest. And there was something else: there are very few faces you can say this about, but this face was *radiant*. As the four men approached Harry down the aisle, he tried to see what made it radiant. Was it grief? Not pleasure. Goodness? Evil?

Their eyes met for a brief moment as they passed. Behind them followed Astrid Monsen with eyes downcast, a middle-aged accountant-like man and three women, two older and one younger, dressed in colourful skirts. They sobbed and wailed, rolling their eyes and wringing their hands in silent accompaniment.

Harry stood as the tiny procession left the church.

'Funny, these gypsies, aren't they, Hole?' The words resounded around the church. Harry turned. It was Ivarsson, black suit, tie and smile. 'When I was growing up, we had a gypsy gardener. Ursari, they travelled round with dancing bears, you know. Josef he was called. Music and pranks all the time. But death, you see . . . These people have an even more strained relationship with death than we have. They are scared stiff of *mule* – spirits of the dead. They believe they return. Josef used to go to a woman who would chase them away. Only women can do that apparently. Come on.'

Ivarsson touched Harry's arm lightly. Harry had to grit his teeth to resist the impulse to shake it off. They walked down the church steps. The noise of the traffic in Kirkeveien drowned the peeling of the bells. A black Cadillac with the rear door open waited for the funeral procession in Schønings gate.

'They take the coffin to Vestre crematorium,' Ivarsson said. 'Burning the body, that's a Hindu custom they took with them from India. In England, they burn the deceased's caravan, but they're not allowed to lock the widow in any more.' He laughed. 'They're allowed to take personal effects. Josef told me about the gypsy family of a demolition man in Hungary. They put his dynamite in the coffin and blew the whole of the crematorium sky high.'

Harry took out a pack of Camels.

'I know why you're here, Hole,' Ivarsson said without relaxing the smile. 'You wanted to see if the occasion would throw up a chat with him, didn't you.' Ivarsson motioned with his head to the procession and the tall, thin figure stepping out slowly as the other three tripped along, trying to keep up.

'Is he the one called Raskol?' Harry asked, inserting a cigarette between his lips.

Ivarsson nodded. 'He's her uncle.'

'And the others?'

'Friends, apparently.'

'And the family?'

'They don't acknowledge the deceased person.'

'Oh?'

'That's Raskol's version. Gypsies are notorious liars, but what he says squares with Josef's stories about their thinking.'

'And it is?'

'Family honour is everything. That's why she was thrown out. According to Raskol, she had been married off to a Greek-speaking *gringo*-gypsy in Spain when she was fourteen, but before the marriage was consummated she'd hopped it with a *gadjo*.'

'*Gadjo*?'

'A non-gypsy. A Danish sailor. Worst thing you can do. Brings shame on the whole family.'

'Mm.' The unlit cigarette jumped up and down in Harry's mouth as he spoke. 'I understand you've got to know this Raskol pretty well?'

Ivarsson wafted away imaginary smoke. 'We've had the odd chat. Skirmishes. I would call them. Substantial talks will come after our part of the deal has been kept, in other words, when he has attended this funeral.'

'So, he hasn't said a lot so far?'

'Nothing of any import to the investigation, no. But the tone has been positive.'

'So positive that I see the police are helping to carry his kin to her resting place?'

'The priest asked if Li or I would be one of the bearers to make the numbers up. That's OK, we're here to keep an eye on him anyway. And we will continue. To keep an eye on him, that is.'

Harry squinted into the piercing autumn sun.

Ivarsson turned towards him. 'Let me make one thing clear, Hole. No one is allowed to speak to Raskol until we've finished with him. No one. For three years I've tried to make a deal with the man who knows everything. And now I have it. No one will be allowed to screw up. Do you understand what I'm saying?'

'Tell me, Ivarsson, since we're having a tête-à-tête here,' Harry said, plucking a flake of tobacco from his mouth. 'Has this case turned into a competition between you and me?'

Ivarsson raised his face to the sun and chuckled. 'Do you know what I would have done if I were you?' he said with closed eyes.

'What's that?' Harry said when the silence was no longer tolerable.

'I would have sent my suit to the dry cleaner's. You look as if you've been lying in a rubbish tip.' He put two fingers to his brow. 'Have a good day.'

Harry stood alone on the steps smoking as he watched the uneven passage of the white coffin along the pavement.

Halvorsen spun round on his chair when Harry came in.

'Great you're here. I've got some good news. I . . . shit, what a smell!'

Halvorsen held his nose and said with shipping forecast intonation: 'What happened to your suit?'

'Slipped in a rubbish skip. What's the news?'

'Ooh . . . yes, I thought the photo might have been of a holiday area in Sørland, so I e-mailed it to all the police stations in Aust-Agder. And, bingo, an officer from Risør rang straight away to say he knew the beach well. But do you know what?'

'Er, no, actually.'

'It wasn't in Sørland, but in Larkollen!'

Halvorsen looked at Harry with an expectant grin and added, when Harry failed to react: 'In Østfold. Outside Moss.'

'I know where Larkollen is, Halvorsen.'

'Yes, but this officer comes from—'

'People from Sørland go on holiday, too. Did you ring Larkollen?'

Halvorsen rolled his eyes in desperation. 'Yes, of course. I rang the camping site and two places where they rent chalets. And the only two grocery shops.'

'Any luck?'

'Yep.' Halvorsen beamed again. 'I faxed the photo and one of the guys running the grocery shop knew who she was. They've got one of the most fantastic chalets in the area. He drives deliveries up there now and then.'

'And the lady's name is?'

'Vigdis Albu?'

'Albu? Elbow?'

'Yep. There are just two of them in Norway. One was born in 1909. The other is forty-three years old and lives at Bjørnetråkket 12 in Slemdal with Arne Albu. And hey presto – here's the telephone number, boss.'

'Don't call me that,' Harry said, grabbing the telephone.

Halvorsen groaned. 'What's up? Are you in a bad mood or something?'

'Yes, but that's not why. Møller is the boss. I'm not a boss, OK?'

Halvorsen was about to say something when Harry imperiously held up a hand: 'Fru Albu?'

Someone had needed a lot of time, money and space to build the Albus' house. And a lot of taste. Or as Harry saw it: a lot of bad taste. It looked as if the architect – if such there were – had tried to fuse Norwegian chalet tradition with Southern US plantation style and a dash of pink suburban bliss. Harry's feet sank in the shingle drive leading past a trim garden of ornamental shrubs and a little bronze hart drinking from a fountain. On the ridge of the garage roof there was an oval copper sign emblazoned with a blue flag containing a yellow triangle on a black triangle.

The sound of a dog barking furiously came from behind the house. Harry walked up the broad steps between the pillars, rang the bell and half-expected to be met by a black mama in a white apron.

'Hello,' she twittered at roughly the same time as the door was flung open. Vigdis Albu was the image of one of those women off the fitness adverts Harry occasionally saw on TV when he came home at night. She had the same white smile, bleached Barbie hair and a firm, well-toned, upper-class body packed into running tights and a skimpy top. And she'd had a boob job, but at least she'd had the sense not to exaggerate the size.

'Harry—'

'Come in!' She smiled with the merest suggestion of wrinkles around her large, blue, discreetly made-up eyes.

Harry stepped into a large hallway populated with fat, ugly, carved wooden trolls reaching up to his hips.

'I'm just washing,' Vigdis Albu explained. She flashed a white smile and carefully wiped away the sweat with a forefinger so as not to streak her mascara.

'I'd better take off my shoes then,' Harry said and at that moment remembered the hole in his sock over his right big toe.

'No, God forbid, not the house. We've got people to do that,' she laughed. 'But I like to wash clothes myself. There have to be limits to how far we let strangers into the house, don't you think?'

'Too true,' Harry mumbled. He had to move briskly to keep up with her up the steps. They passed a classy kitchen and came into the living room. A spacious terrace lay beyond two sliding glass doors. On the main wall there was a huge brick construction, a sort of halfway house between Oslo City Hall and a cenotaph.

'Designed by Per Hummel for Arne's fortieth birthday,' Vigdis said. 'Per's a friend of ours.'

'Yes, Per has really designed one . . . a fireplace there.'

'I'm sure you know Per Hummel, the architect, don't you? The new chapel in Holmenkollen, you know.'

'I'm afraid not,' Harry said and passed her the photograph. 'Would you mind having a look at this?'

He studied the surprise spreading across her face.

'But that's the photo Arne took last year in Larkollen. How did you get hold of this?'

Harry waited to see if she could maintain her genuinely puzzled expression before he responded. She could.

'We found it in the shoe of a woman called Anna Bethsen,' he said. Harry witnessed a chain reaction of thoughts, reasoning and emotions reflected in Vigdis Albu's face, like a soap opera in fast forward. First surprise, next wonder and afterwards confusion. Then an intuition, which was at first rejected with a sceptical laugh, but took hold and seemed to grow into a dawning realisation. And finally the closed face with the subtitle: *There have to be limits to how far we let strangers into the house, don't you think?*

Harry fidgeted with the packet of cigarettes he had taken out. A large glass ashtray had pride of place in the middle of the coffee table.

'Do you know Anna Bethsen, fru Albu?'

'Certainly not. Should I?'

'I don't know,' Harry said honestly. 'She's dead. I'm left wondering what such a personal photograph is doing in her shoe. Any ideas?'

Vigdis Albu tried to put on a forbearing smile, but her mouth wouldn't obey. She contented herself with an energetic shake of her head.

Harry waited, without moving, relaxed. As his shoes had sunk into the shingle, he felt his body sinking into the deep, white sofa. Experience had taught him that silence was the most effective of all methods to make people talk. When two strangers sit facing each other, silence functions like a vacuum, sucking words out. They sat like that for ten eternal seconds. Vigdis Albu swallowed: 'Perhaps the cleaner saw it lying somewhere and took it with her. And gave it to this . . . was it Anna she was called?'

'Mm. Do you mind if I smoke, fru Albu?'

'This is a smoke-free house. Neither my husband nor I . . .' She lifted a hand quickly to her plait. 'And Alexander, our youngest, has got asthma.'

'Sorry to hear that. How does your husband spend his time?'

She gaped at him and her big, blue eyes grew even bigger.

'What's his job, I mean?' Harry put his cigarettes back in his inside pocket.

'He's an investor. He sold the company about three years ago.'

'Which company?'

'Albu AS. Importing towels and shower mats for hotels and institutions.'

'Must have been quite a lot of towels. And shower mats.'

'We had the agency for the whole of Scandinavia.'

'Congratulations. The flag on the garage, isn't that a consulate flag?'

Vigdis Albu had regained her composure and took off her hair band. It struck Harry that she had had something done to her face. Something about the proportions didn't tally. That is to say, they tallied *too* well; her face was almost artificially symmetrical.

'St Lucia. My husband was the Norwegian consul there for eleven years. We had a factory where they sew shower mats. We have a little house there, too. Have you been to—?'

'No.'

'A fantastic, wonderful, sweet island. Some of the older inhabitants still speak French. Incomprehensible French I have to say, but they are so charming you wouldn't believe it.'

'Creole French.'

'What?'

'I've read about it. Do you think your husband might know how this photo ended up in the deceased's possession?'

'Can't imagine how. Why should he?'

'Hm.' Harry smiled. 'It's perhaps just as difficult to say why one would have a photo of a stranger in one's shoe.' He got to his feet. 'Where can I find him, fru Albu?'

As Harry noted down the telephone number and address of Arne Albu's office, he happened to look down at the sofa where he had been sitting.

'Erm . . .' he said when he saw Vigdis Albu following his gaze. 'I slipped in a refuse skip. Of course, I'll—'

'It doesn't matter,' she interrupted. 'The cover's going to the dry cleaner's next week anyway.'

On the steps outside, she asked Harry if on second thoughts he could wait until five o'clock before he rang her husband.

'He'll be home then and won't be so busy.'

Harry didn't answer and watched the corners of her mouth going up and down.

'Then he and I can . . . see if we can sort out this business for you.'

'Thank you, that's nice of you, but I have my car here and it's on the way, so I'll drive to his work and see if I can find him there.'

'OK,' she said with a brave smile.

The barking followed Harry down the long drive. At the gate, he turned round. Vigdis Albu was still standing on the steps in front of the pink plantation building. Her head was bowed and the sun shone on her hair and glossy sports gear. From a distance she looked like a tiny bronze hart.

Harry could find neither a legal place to park nor Arne Albu at the address in Vika Atrium. Just a receptionist who informed him that Albu rented an office with three other investors, and that he was having lunch with 'a firm of brokers'.

On leaving the building, Harry found a parking ticket under the windscreen wiper. He took it and his bad mood with him to SS *Louise*, which was in fact not a steamship but a restaurant in Aker

Brygge. Unlike at Schrøder's, they served edible food to solvent customers with office addresses in what somewhat charitably might be called Oslo's Wall Street. Harry had never felt completely at home in Aker Brygge, but perhaps that was because he was Oslo-bred and not a tourist. He exchanged a few words with a waiter, who pointed to a window table.

'Gentlemen, I'm sorry to disturb,' Harry said.

'Ah, finally,' one of the three at the table exclaimed, flicking his fringe back. 'Would you call this wine room temperature, waiter?'

'I'd call it Norwegian red wine decanted into a Clos des Papes bottle,' Harry said.

Taken aback, the Fringe ran his eye down Harry in his dark suit.

'A joke.' Harry smiled. 'I'm a policeman.'

The surprise segued into alarm.

'Not environmental crime.'

Relief segued into question marks. Harry heard boyish laughter and breathed in. He had decided how he was going to do it, but had no idea how it would turn out. 'Arne Albu?'

'That's me,' answered the one who was laughing. He was slim with short, curly, dark hair and laughter lines around his eyes, which told Harry that he laughed a lot and was older than the thirty-five years he would have guessed initially. 'Apologies for the misunderstanding,' he continued, still with laughter in his voice. 'Can I help you, Constable?'

Harry observed him, quickly trying to form a picture of him before going on. The voice was the sonorous variety. Fixed gaze. Shiny white collar behind a tie that was not too loose and not too tight. The fact that he hadn't left it at 'That's me,' but had added an apology and 'Can I help you, Constable?' – with a slightly ironic stress on 'Constable' – suggested that Arne Albu was either very self-confident or had a lot of practice giving that impression.

Harry concentrated. Not on what he was going to say, but on how Albu would react.

'Yes, you can, Albu. Do you know Anna Bethsen?'

Albu looked at Harry with the same blue eyes as his wife's and after a moment's reflection gave a loud, clear answer: 'No.'

Albu's face revealed no more to Harry than the mouth said. Not that Harry had thought it would. He had long given up believing the myth that people whose professions brought them face to face with lies on a daily basis learn to recognise them. A policeman had once claimed during a court case that from his long experience he knew when the accused was lying. Ståle Aune, once again a tool of the defence, had answered that research showed that no one single professional group was any better than another at spotting lies; a cleaner was just as good as a psychologist or a policeman, that is to say, just as bad. The only group in the comparative study to have acquitted itself with an above-average score was that of the Secret Service agents. Harry was no Secret Service agent, though. He was an Oppsal boy pressed for time, in a bad mood and right now showing poor judgement. To confront a man with potentially compromising circumstances in the presence of others, without any grounds for suspicion, was hardly very effective and not what anyone would call fair play. So Harry knew he shouldn't be doing what he was doing: 'Any idea who could have given her this photo?'

All three men studied the photograph Harry set on the table.

'Haven't a clue,' Albu said. 'My wife? The kids maybe?'

'Mm.' Harry looked for changes in the pupils, signs of an increased pulse such as sweating or blushing.

'I don't know what this is about, Constable, but since you have taken the trouble to find me, I assume it is not a bagatelle. Perhaps we could discuss this in private after my meeting with these gentlemen from Handelsbanken is over. If you would like to wait, I can ask the waiter to give you a table down in the smoking area.'

Harry could not decide whether Albu's smile was mocking or simply obliging. Not even that.

'I haven't time,' Harry said. 'So if we could sit down—'

'I'm afraid I don't have time, either,' Albu interposed in a calm but firm voice. 'This is my working time, so we'll have to talk this afternoon. If you are still of the opinion there is something I can help you with, that is.'

Harry swallowed. He was powerless and he could see Albu knew.

'Let's say that then,' Harry said and could hear how pathetic it sounded.

'Thank you, Constable.' Albu inclined his head with a smile. 'And you're probably right about the wine.' He turned to face Handelsbanken. 'You were saying, Stein, about Opticom?'

Harry picked up the photograph and had to endure the barely concealed smile from the broker with the fringe before leaving.

At the edge of the quay, Harry lit a cigarette, but it didn't have any taste and he threw it away with a growl. The sun glinted off a window in Akershus fortress and the sea was so calm there seemed to be a thin layer of clear ice on top. Why had he done it? Why this kamikaze attempt to humiliate a man he didn't know? Just to be lifted with silk gloves and gently thrown out.

He faced the sun, closed his eyes and wondered if today he ought to do something intelligent for a change. Like dropping the whole case. Nothing seemed to make sense; it was just the usual state of chaos and bafflement. The bells in the City Hall started chiming.

Little did Harry know that Møller was to be proved right. It was the last warm day of the year.

16

Namco G-Con 45

BRAVE OLEG.

'It'll be fine,' he had said on the telephone. Again and again as if he had a secret plan. 'Mummy and I will be back soon.'

Harry stood by the window looking at the sky over the roof of the block facing him, where the evening sun was painting the underside of a thin, creased layer of cloud in orange and red. On his way home the temperature had fallen sharply and inexplicably, as though someone had opened an invisible door and all the heat had been sucked out. In the flat, the cold had begun to creep up through the floorboards. Where had he put his felt slippers? In the cellar or in the attic? Did he have any slippers? He couldn't remember. Fortunately, he had written down the name of the Playstation kit he had promised to buy Oleg if he managed to beat Harry's Tetris record on the Gameboy. Namco G-Con 45.

The news droned on the 14-inch TV behind him. Another gala to collect money for victims. Julia Roberts showing her sympathy and Sylvester Stallone receiving donors' incoming calls. And the hour of vengeance had come. Pictures showing the sides of mountains being carpet-bombed. Black pillars of smoke from the rocks and nothing growing in the desolate landscape. The telephone rang.

It was Weber. At Police HQ the general reputation of Weber was that he was a stubborn old sourpuss and difficult to work with. Harry thought the contrary. You just had to be aware that he would be intractable if you were disrespectful or hassled him.

'I know you're waiting for results,' Weber said. 'We didn't find any DNA on the bottle, but we did find a couple of faint fingerprints.'

'Good. I was afraid they might be destroyed even if they were in a plastic bag.'

'Luckily it was a glass bottle. The grease in the prints on a plastic bottle would have been absorbed after so many days.'

Harry could hear the clicking sound of swabbing in the background. 'Are you still at work, Weber?'

'Yes.'

'When will you have checked the prints against the data bank?'

'Are you hassling me?' the old forensics man growled suspiciously.

'Not at all. I've got oceans of time, Weber.'

'Tomorrow. I'm no computer whizz and the young guys have gone home for the night.'

'And you?'

'I'll just check the prints against a few possibilities in the old way. Sleep tight, Hole. Uncle Plod will keep an eye open.'

Harry put down the telephone, went into the bedroom and switched on his computer. The chirpy Windows jingle drowned the American revenge rhetoric from the sitting room for a second. He clicked his way through to the video of the robbery in Kirkeveien. Ran the jerky clip several times without becoming any the wiser, or more foolish. He clicked on the e-mail icon. The hourglass and *You have 1 message* came up. The hall telephone rang again. Harry cast a glance at his watch before lifting the receiver and saying hi with the soft voice reserved for Rakel.

'Arne Albu. I apologise for calling you in the evening, but I was given your name by my wife and thought I would clear up this matter at once. Is it convenient?'

'Fine,' Harry said sheepishly in his usual voice.

'Well, I've had a chat with my wife, and neither of us has heard of this woman or knows how she got hold of the photo. But it was developed by a professional, perhaps someone working in the shop took a copy. Also, there is a lot of coming and going in our house and so there could be many, *many* possible explanations.'

'Mm.' Harry noticed that Arne Albu's voice didn't have the same assured composure it had had earlier in the day. After a few seconds of crackly silence Albu continued: 'If you need to talk about this more, I would appreciate it if you would contact me at the office. I understood from my wife that she gave you my number.'

'And I understood that you didn't want to be disturbed during your working hours.'

'I don't want . . . my wife to be stressed. A dead woman with a photo in a shoe, my God! I would like you to deal with me.'

'I understand. But the photo is of your wife and the children!'

'She knows nothing about it, I'm telling you!' And then apparently regretting his angry tone, he added: 'I promise I will examine every possibility I can envisage to explain how this might have happened.'

'Thank you for the offer, but I still reserve the right to talk to whoever I think fit.' Harry listened to Albu's breathing before adding: 'I hope you understand.'

'Listen here—'

'I'm afraid this is not a topic for discussion. I'll contact you or your wife if there is something I need to know.'

'Wait a minute! You don't understand. My wife gets . . . very upset.'

'You're right, I don't understand. Is she ill?'

'Ill?' said Albu with surprise in his voice. 'No, but—'

'Then I suggest we conclude this conversation now.' Harry saw himself in the mirror. 'These are not my working hours. Good evening.'

He put down the telephone and looked in the mirror again. It was gone now, the little smile, the glee that Spite gives. The Small-mindedness. The Self-righteousness. The Sadism. The four 'S's of revenge. There was something else, too, though. Something looked wrong. Something was missing. He studied the reflected image. Perhaps it was just the way the light fell.

Harry sat down in front of the computer while thinking that he would have to tell Aune about the four 'S's. He collected that sort of thing. The e-mail he had received came from an address he had never seen before: <u>furie@bolde.com</u>. He clicked on it.

As he was sitting there, a chill spread through Harry Hole's body that would linger for a good year.

It happened while he was reading from the screen. The hairs on the back of his neck stood up and the skin around his body tightened like shrinking clothes.

Shall we play? Let's imagine you've been to dinner with a woman and the next day she's found dead. What do you do?
S²MN

The telephone chirruped its lament. Harry knew it was Rakel. He let it ring.

17

Arabia's Tears

HALVORSEN WAS VERY SURPRISED TO SEE HARRY AS HE entered their office.

'Here already? You are aware it's only—'

'Couldn't sleep,' Harry mumbled, sitting in front of the computer screen with crossed arms. 'These machines are so bloody slow.'

Halvorsen peered over his shoulder. 'It all depends on the data transfer rate when you're on the Net. You're using a standard ISDN line now, but, rejoice, we'll soon be on broadband. Looking for articles in *Dagens Næringsliv*?'

'Eh? . . . Yes.'

'Arne Albu? Did you talk to Vigdis Albu?'

'Yes.'

'What have they actually got to do with the bank robbery?'

Harry didn't look up. He hadn't said it was anything to do with the robbery, but he hadn't said it wasn't either, so it was quite natural for his colleague to make the assumption. Harry was spared answering him as at that moment Arne Albu's face filled the screen. By far the broadest smile Harry had seen today presided over the tightly knotted tie. Halvorsen smacked his lips and read aloud:

'*Thirty million for family business. Today Arne Albu can salt away thirty million kroner after the hotel chain* Choice *bought up all the shares in Albu AS yesterday. Albu says he wants to devote more time to his family, which was the biggest reason for him selling his successful company. "I want to see my children grow up," Albu said when interviewed. "The family is my most important investment."*'

Harry pressed PRINT.

'Don't you want the rest of the article?'

'No, I just want the picture,' Harry said.

'Thirty mill in the bank and now he's started holding up banks, too?'

'I'll explain later,' Harry said, rising from his chair. 'In the meantime, I wonder if you could explain to me how you find out who sends an e-mail.'

'The address is in the e-mail.'

'And that's in the telephone book, is it?'

'No, but you can find out which mail server sent it. That's in the address. The server has a list of which clients own which addresses. Very simple. Have you received an interesting e-mail?'

Harry shook his head.

'Give me the address and I'll find it for you in no time,' Halvorsen said.

'OK. Have you heard of a server called bolde.com?'

'No, but I'll check it out. What's the rest of the address?'

Harry hesitated. 'Forgotten,' he said.

Harry requisitioned a car from the garage and drove slowly through Grønland. A biting wind swirled the leaves which had dried on the pavement in yesterday's sun. People walked with their hands buried in their pockets and their heads drawn in between their shoulders.

In Pilestredet Harry tucked in behind a tram and found the NRK news broadcast on the radio. They didn't say anything about the Stine Grette case. There were fears that hundreds of thousands of refugee children would not survive the tough Afghan winter. An

American soldier had been killed. There was an interview with his family. They wanted revenge. Bislett was closed to traffic and there was a diversion.

'Yes?' One syllable on the door intercom was enough to establish that Astrid Monsen had a bad cold.

'Harry Hole. Thank you for your help so far. I wondered if it would be possible to ask a couple more questions. Have you got time?'

She sniffled twice before answering. 'What about?'

'I would prefer not to stand out here and ask.'

Two more sniffs.

'Is this not a convenient time?' Harry asked.

The lock buzzed and Harry shoved open the door.

Astrid Monsen was standing in the corridor with a shawl over her shoulders and her arms crossed as Harry came up the stairs.

'I saw you at the funeral,' Harry said.

'I thought at least one of her neighbours should put in an appearance,' she said. She sounded as if she was talking through a megaphone.

'I wonder if you recognise this person?'

Reluctantly she took the dog-eared photograph. 'Which one?'

'Any of them, in fact.' Harry's voice resounded up and down the stairwell.

Astrid Monsen stared at the picture. At length.

'Well?'

She shook her head.

'Sure?'

She nodded.

'Mm. Do you know if Anna had a partner?'

'One?'

Harry breathed in deeply. 'Do you mean there were many?'

She shrugged. 'You can hear every sound in this house. The stairs creaked, let's put it that way.'

'Anything serious?'

'I have no idea.'

Harry waited. She didn't pause for long: 'A note with a name on was stuck next to her post box this summer. I don't know if it was serious though . . .'

'No?'

'I think it was her handwriting on the note. It just said ERIKSEN.' There was a hint of a smile on her thin lips. 'Perhaps he had forgotten to tell her his Christian name. At any rate, the note was gone after a week.'

Harry looked down over the banisters. The stairs were steep. 'A week's better than nothing, though, isn't it?'

'For some maybe,' she said, resting her hand on the door handle. 'I have to go now. I've just received an e-mail, I can hear.'

'It's not going anywhere, is it?'

She was overpowered by another fit of sneezing. 'I have to answer it,' she said with tear-filled eyes. 'It's the author. We're discussing my translation.'

'Then I'll be quick,' Harry said. 'I just want you to look at this, too.'

He passed her a sheet of paper. She held it, cast an eye over it and looked up at Harry suspiciously.

'Just have a good look,' Harry said. 'Take all the time you need.'

'Quite unnecessary,' she said, returning the sheet.

It took Harry ten minutes to walk from Police HQ to Kjølberggata 21A. In its time the run-down brick building had been a tannery, a printing press, a forge and probably several other things too. A reminder that Oslo had once had industry. Now *Krimteknisk* had taken it over. Despite new lighting and a modern interior, the building still had an industrial feel to it. Harry found Weber in one of the large, cold rooms.

'Shit,' Harry said. 'Are you absolutely sure?'

Weber gave a tired smile. 'The fingerprint on the bottle is so good that if we had had it on our files, the computer would have found a match. Of course, we could search manually to be one hundred and ten per cent sure, but it would take weeks and we wouldn't find anything, anyway. It's definite.'

'Sorry,' Harry said. 'I was just so sure we had him. I reckoned the chances of a guy like him never having been arrested for anything were microscopic.'

'The fact that we don't have him in our archives just means we have to look elsewhere. But now at least we have tangible evidence. This fingerprint and the fibres from Kirkeveien. If you can find the man, we have conclusive proof. Helgesen!'

A young man passing by pulled up smartly.

'I was given this cap from the Akerselva in an *un*sealed bag,' Weber grumbled. 'This isn't a pigsty we're running. Have you got that?'

Helgesen nodded and sent Harry a knowing look.

'You'll have to take it like a man,' Weber said, turning to Harry again. 'At least you didn't have to put up with what Ivarsson went through today.'

'Ivarsson?'

'Haven't you heard what happened in the Culvert today?'

Harry shook his head and Weber chuckled and rubbed his hands. 'In that case, I'll tell you a good story to help you on your way, Hole.'

Weber's presentation was a lot like the police reports he wrote. Brief, rough-hewn sentences sketching out the action taken without any florid descriptions of feelings, tone of voice or facial expression. Harry had no problem filling in the gaps though. He could visualise PAS Rune Ivarsson and Weber going into one of the visitors' rooms in A-Wing and could hear the door being locked behind them. Both rooms were next to the reception desk and kitted out for families. Inmates could enjoy a few moments of peace with their nearest and dearest in a room which someone had even tried to make cosy – basic furnishings, plastic flowers and a couple of pale watercolours on the wall.

Raskol was standing when the two of them arrived. He had a thick book under his arm, and on the low table in front of them there was a chessboard with the pieces set up and ready. He didn't say a word, just beheld them with his pained brown eyes. He was wearing a white coat-like shirt hanging almost down to his knees. Ivarsson was ill at ease and brusquely told the tall, thin gypsy to take a seat. Raskol obeyed the order with a slight smile.

Ivarsson had taken Weber with him instead of the younger officers in the investigation team because he thought that the old fox would be able to help Ivarsson 'size Raskol up', as he put it. Weber placed a chair against the door and took out a notebook while Ivarsson sat face to face with the infamous prisoner.

'Please, *Politiavdelingssjef* Ivarsson,' Raskol said, displaying an open palm to invite the policeman to start the game.

'We have come here to gather information, not to play games,' Ivarsson said and placed five photographs of the robbery in Bogstadveien beside each other across the table. 'We would like to know who this is.'

Raskol picked up the photos one after the other and studied them with loud 'hm's.

'May I borrow a pen?' he asked, after looking at all of them.

Weber and Ivarsson exchanged glances.

'Take mine,' Weber said, passing him a fountain pen.

'I prefer the usual kind,' Raskol said without taking his eyes off Ivarsson.

The PAS shrugged, took out a biro from his inside pocket and gave it to him.

'First of all, I would like to explain the principle behind dye cartridges,' Raskol said, beginning to unscrew Ivarsson's white pen, which happened to bear the Den norske Bank logo. 'As you know, bank employees always add a dye cartridge to the money in case they are raided. The cartridge is attached to money dispensers in an ATM. Some cartridges are connected to a transmitter and are activated by movement, being put in a bag for example. Others are activated when they pass a portal which may be secured above the main door of a bank. The cartridge may have a micro-transmitter connected to a receiver which triggers an explosion when it is a certain distance from the receiver, say, a hundred metres. Others explode after an inbuilt time delay post-activation. The cartridge itself can have all sorts of formats, but it has to be so small that it can be hidden between notes. Some are this small.' Raskol held his thumb and forefinger two centimetres apart. 'The explosion is not dangerous to the robber; the problem is the dye, the ink.'

He held up the ink cartridge from the biro.

'My grandfather was an ink maker. He taught me that in the old days they used gum arabic to make iron gallus ink. The gum comes from the acacia tree and is called Arabia's tears because it trickles out in yellowish drops this size.'

He made a circle with his thumb and forefinger, about the size of a walnut.

'The point about the gum is that it thickens and reduces the surface tension of ink. And it keeps iron salts liquid. You also need a solvent. Long ago rainwater or white wine were recommended. Or vinegar. My grandfather said you should add vinegar to the ink when you were writing to an enemy and wine when you were writing to a friend.'

Ivarsson cleared his throat, but Raskol continued regardless.

'At first, the ink is invisible. It becomes visible when put on paper. In the dye cartridge there are red particles which perform a chemical reaction when they come into contact with the paper of banknotes and this makes it impossible to remove. The money will be forever marked as robbery money.'

'I know how a dye cartridge works,' Ivarsson said. 'I would rather know—'

'Patience, dear *Politiavdelingssjef*. The fascinating thing about this technology is that it is extremely simple. So simple that I could make a dye cartridge myself, put it wherever I liked and make it explode at a certain distance from the receiver. All the equipment required would fit into a lunch box.'

Weber had stopped taking notes.

'But the principle of the cartridge is not the technology, PAS Ivarsson. The principle is incrimination.' Raskol's face lit up into a huge smile. 'The ink also attaches itself to the clothes and skin of the robber. And the ink is so strong that once it is on your hands you will never be able to wash it off. Pontius Pilate and Judas, right? Blood on his hands. Blood money. The agony of the arbiter. The punishment of the informer.'

Raskol dropped the ink cartridge on the floor behind the table and while he bent to pick it up, Ivarsson signalled to Weber that he wanted the notebook.

'I would like you to write the name of the person in the photos,' Ivarsson said and put the pad on the table. 'As I said, we are not here to play games.'

'Not to play games, no,' Raskol said, slowly screwing the pen together. 'I promised I would give you the name of the man who took the money, didn't I?'

'That was the agreement, yes.' Ivarsson said. He leaned over as Raskol started to write.

'We Xoraxans know what an agreement is,' he said. 'I'm not just writing his name, but also the prostitute he uses regularly and the man he contacted to shatter the knee of a young man who recently broke his daughter's heart. The person in question refused the job by the way.'

'Ah . . . excellent.' Ivarsson turned quickly to Weber and gave an excited grin.

'Here.' Raskol handed the pad and pen to Ivarsson, who hurriedly read the note.

The elated smile died. 'But . . .' he stammered. 'Helge Klementsen. He's the branch manager.' A light of illumination revealed itself to him. 'Is he involved?'

'Very much so,' Raskol said. 'He took the money, didn't he?'

'And put it in the robber's holdall,' came Weber's deep growl from the door.

Ivarsson's expression slowly changed from questioning to furious. 'What is this twaddle? You promised to help me.'

Raskol studied the long, pointed nail of the little finger on his right hand. Then he nodded gravely, leaned over the table and waved Ivarsson closer. 'You're right,' he whispered. 'Here's a tip. Learn what life is about. Sit down and observe your child. It isn't easy to find the things you've lost, but it is possible.' He patted the PAS on the back and motioned towards the chessboard. 'Your turn, *Politiavdelingssjef.*'

Ivarsson was fuming with anger as he and Weber traipsed through the Culvert, a three-hundred-metre-long underground tunnel connecting Botsen prison with Police HQ.

'I trusted one of the race who discovered lying!' hissed Ivarsson. 'I trusted a bloody gypsy!' The echo ricocheted along the brick walls. Weber was racing along; he wanted to get out of the cold, damp tunnel. The Culvert was used to transport prisoners to and from questioning at Police HQ, and many were the rumours circulating about what had happened down here.

Ivarsson pulled his suit jacket tighter around him and stepped out. 'Promise me one thing, Weber: you won't breathe a word of this to anyone. Alright?' He turned towards Weber with a raised eyebrow: 'Well?'

The answer to Ivarsson's question was a qualified 'yes' inasmuch as they had just reached the point in the Culvert where the walls are painted orange and Weber heard a little 'pooff' sound. Ivarsson let out a terrified scream and fell to his knees in a pool of water, holding his chest.

Weber spun round and looked up and down the tunnel. No one. Then he turned back to the PAS, who was staring at his red-stained hand.

'I'm bleeding,' he groaned. 'I'm dying.'

Weber could see Ivarsson's eyes growing in his head.

'What is it?' Ivarsson asked, his voice tremulous with fear as he looked into Weber's open-mouthed stare.

'You'll have to go to the dry cleaner's,' Weber said.

Ivarsson cast his eyes downwards. The red dye had spread across the whole of his shirt front and parts of the lime-green jacket.

'Red ink,' Weber said.

Ivarsson pulled out the remains of the Den norske Bank pen. The micro-explosion had sheered it down the middle. He stayed on his knees with his eyes closed until his breathing was normal again. Then he fixed his eyes on Weber.

'Do you know what Hitler's greatest sin was?' he asked, stretching out his clean hand. Weber grabbed it and pulled Ivarsson to his feet. Ivarsson squinted down the tunnel the way they had come. 'Not doing a more thorough job on the gypsies.'

'*Not a word to anyone about this*,' Weber mimicked, with a chuckle. 'Ivarsson went straight to the garage and drove home. The ink will stain his skin for at least three days.'

Harry shook his head in disbelief. 'And what did you do to this Raskol?'

Weber shrugged. 'Ivarsson said he would have him put in solitary. Not that that would help in the slightest, I reckon. The man is . . . different. Talking about different, how are you and Beate getting on? Have you got any more than this fingerprint?'

Harry shook his head.

'That girl is special,' Weber said. 'I can recognise her father in her. She could be good.'

'She could. Did you know her father?'

Weber nodded. 'Good man. Loyal. Shame it all ended as it did.'

'Strange that such an experienced policeman would slip up like that.'

'I don't think it was a slip-up,' Weber said, rinsing a coffee cup in the sink.

'Oh?'

Weber mumbled.

'What did you say, Weber?'

'Nothing,' he growled. 'He must have had a reason. That's all I'm saying.'

'Bolde.com will be a server,' Halvorsen said. 'All I'm saying is that it isn't registered anywhere. It might be in a cellar in Kiev for example and have anonymous clients who send specialised porn to each other. What do I know? We mere mortals won't find people who don't want to be found in that jungle. You'll have to get hold of a bloodhound, a real specialist.'

The knock at the door was so feather-light Harry didn't hear it, but Halvorsen shouted: 'Come in.'

The door opened cautiously.

'Hi,' Halvorsen said with a smile. 'Beate, isn't it?'

She nodded and looked hastily across at Harry. 'I was trying to get hold of you. That mobile number of yours on the list . . .'

'He's lost his mobile,' Halvorsen said, getting up. 'Take a seat and I'll make you a Halvorsen espresso.'

She hesitated. 'Thank you, but there's something I have to show you in the House of Pain, Harry. Have you got time?'

'All the time in the world,' Harry said, leaning back in his chair. 'Weber had only bad news. No matching fingerprints. And Raskol tricked Ivarsson good and proper today.'

'Is that bad news?' It slipped out before Beate could stop herself. She covered her mouth in alarm. Harry and Halvorsen laughed.

'Nice to see you again, Beate,' Halvorsen said before she and Harry left. He didn't get an answer, just a searching look from Harry, and was left standing a little embarrassed in the middle of the floor.

Harry noticed a blanket rumpled up on the two-seater IKEA sofa in the House of Pain. 'Did you sleep here last night?'

'Just a nap,' she said and started the video player. 'Watch the Expeditor and Stine in this picture.'

She pointed to the screen where she had freeze-framed the robber with Stine leaning towards him. Harry could feel the hairs on his neck standing up.

'There's something about this, isn't there?' she said.

Harry scrutinised the robber. Then Stine. And he knew it was this still which had made him watch the video over and over again, searching all the time for something which was there but kept eluding him.

'What is it?' he asked. 'What is it you can see and I can't.'

'Try.'

'I've already tried.'

'Imprint the image on your retina, close your eyes and feel.'

'Honestly . . .'

'Come on, Harry.' She smiled. 'This is what investigating is, isn't it.'

He looked at her in mild surprise. Then he shrugged his shoulders and did as she said.

'What can you see, Harry?'

'The inside of my eyelids.'

'Concentrate. Tell me what jars.'

'There's something about him and her. Something . . . about the way they're standing.'

'Good. What about the way they're standing?'

'They're standing . . . I don't know. They're standing wrong somehow.'

'Wrong in what way?'

Harry had the same sinking feeling he'd had in Vigdis Albu's house. He saw Stine Grette sitting forward. As if to catch the robber's words. He was staring out of the holes of the balaclava and into the face of the person he was about to kill. What was he thinking? And what was she thinking? In this frozen moment in time, was she trying to discover who he was, this man under the balaclava?

'Wrong in what way?' Beate repeated.

'They . . . they . . .'

Gun in hand, finger on trigger. Everyone around turned to marble. She is opening her mouth. He can see her eyes over the sights. The barrel nudging her teeth.

'Wrong in what way?'

'They . . . they're too close.'

'Bravo, Harry!'

He opened his eyes. Amoeba-like specks sparkled and floated across his field of vision.

'Bravo?' he mumbled. 'What do you mean?'

'You've put words to what we've seen the whole time. You're absolutely correct, Harry. They're standing too close to each other.'

'Yes, I heard myself say that, but too close in relation to what?'

'In relation to how close two people who have never met should stand.'

'Eh?'

'Have you heard of Edward Hall?'

'Not exactly.'

'Anthropologist. He was the first to demonstrate the link between the distance people keep between each other and the relationship they have. It's fairly well documented.'

'Explain.'

'The social space between people who don't know each other is from one to three and a half metres. That's the distance you would keep if the situation allowed, but look at bus queues and toilets. In Tokyo people stand closer to each and feel comfortable, but variations from culture to culture are in fact relatively minor.'

'He can't whisper to her from more than a metre away, can he.'

'No, but he could easily have managed it within what is known as the personal space, which is from one metre to forty-five centimetres. That's the distance people keep with strangers and so-called acquaintants. But as you see, the Expeditor and Stine Grette break this boundary. I've measured the distance. It's twenty centimetres.

That means they're well inside the intimate space. Then you're so close to the other person you can't keep the other person's face in focus or avoid their aroma and body heat. It's a space reserved for partners or close family.'

'Mm,' Harry said. 'I'm impressed by your knowledge, but these two people are involved in high drama.'

'Yes, but that's what's so fascinating!' Beate burst out, holding on to the arm of the chair so that she wouldn't take off. 'If they're not supposed to, people don't cross the boundaries that Edward Hall talks about. And the Expeditor and Stine Grette are *not* supposed to.'

Harry rubbed his chin. 'OK, let's follow that line of thought.'

'I think the Expeditor knew Stine Grette,' Beate said. 'Well.'

'Good, good.' Harry rested his face on his hands and spoke through his fingers. 'So Stine knew a professional bank robber who performs a perfect heist before shooting her. You know where this reasoning is taking us, don't you.'

Beate nodded. 'I'll see what we can find out about Stine Grette right away.'

'Great. And afterwards let's have a chat with someone who's frequently been inside her intimate space.'

18

A Wonderful Day

'THIS PLACE GIVES ME THE CREEPS,' BEATE SAID.

'They had a famous patient here called Arnold Juklerød,' Harry said. 'He said this place was the brain of the sick beast known as psychiatry. So you didn't find anything about Stine Grette?'

'No. Unblemished record, and her bank accounts don't suggest financial irregularities. No shopping sprees in clothes shops or at restaurants. No payments to Bjerke trotting stadium or any other symptoms of gambling. The only extravagance I could turn up was a trip to São Paulo this summer.'

'And her husband?'

'Exactly the same. Solid and sober.'

They passed under the gateway to Gaustad hospital and came into a square surrounded by large red-brick buildings.

'Reminiscent of a prison,' Beate said.

'Heinrich Schirmer,' Harry said. 'Nineteenth-century German architect. Also designed Botsen prison.'

A carer came to pick them up from reception. He had dyed black hair and looked as though he should be playing in a band or doing design work. Which, in fact, he did.

'Trond Grette has mostly been sitting and staring out of the window,' he said as they trotted down the corridor to section G2.

'Is he ready to speak?' Harry asked.

'Yes, he can talk alright . . .' The carer had paid six hundred kroner to have his black hair look unkempt, and now he was adjusting one of the tufts and blinking at Harry through a pair of black horn-rimmed glasses, which made him look like a nerd, in exactly the right way, that is, so that the cognoscenti could see he wasn't a nerd but hip.

'My colleague is wondering if Grette is well enough to talk about his wife,' Beate said.

'You'll find out,' said the carer and put the tuft of hair back in front of his glasses. 'If he gets psychotic again, he's not ready.'

Harry didn't ask how they could tell when a person was psychotic. They came to the end of the corridor and the carer unlocked a door with a circular window.

'Does he have to be locked in?' Beate asked, looking around the bright reception room.

'No,' the carer said, without giving any further explanation, and pointed to the back of a white dressing gown on a chair which had been pulled over to the window. 'I'm in the duty office on the left on your way out.'

They walked over to the man in the chair. He was staring out of the window and the only thing that stirred was his right hand, which was slowly moving a pen over a notepad, jerkily and mechanically like a robotic arm.

'Trond Grette?' Harry asked.

He didn't recognise the person who turned round. Grette had cut off all his hair, his face was leaner and the wild expression in his eyes from the evening on the tennis court was replaced by a calm, vacant thousand-metre stare which went right through them. Harry had seen it before. They looked like that after the first weeks behind bars when they started doing their penance. Harry knew instinctively this man was doing the same. He was doing penance.

'We're police,' Harry said.

Grette shifted his stare towards them.

'It's about the bank raid and your wife.'

Grette half-closed his eyes, as if he had to concentrate to understand what Harry was saying.

'We were wondering if we could ask you some questions,' Beate said in a loud voice.

Grette nodded slowly. Beate pulled a chair closer and sat down.

'Can you tell us about her?' she asked.

'Tell you?' His voice creaked like a badly oiled door.

'Yes,' Beate said with a gentle smile. 'We would like to know who Stine was. What she did. What she liked. What plans you had. That sort of thing.'

'That sort of thing?' Grette looked at Beate. Then he put down the pen. 'We were going to have children. That was the plan. Test-tube babies. She hoped for twins. Two plus two, she always said. Two plus two. We were just about to start. Right now.' Tears welled in his eyes.

'You'd been married for a long time, hadn't you?'

'Ten years,' Grette said. 'If they hadn't played tennis, I wouldn't have minded. You can't force children to like the same things as parents, can you. Perhaps they would have preferred horse riding. Horse riding is wonderful.'

'What sort of person was she?'

'Ten years,' Grette repeated, facing the window again. 'We met in 1988. I had started at Management School in Oslo and she was in her last year at Nissen High School. She was the best-looking girl I'd ever seen. I know everyone says the good-looking one is the one you never got and have perhaps forgotten, but with Stine it was true. And I never stopped thinking she was the best-looking. We moved in together after a month and were together for every single day and night for three years. Yet I still couldn't believe that she had said yes to becoming Stine Grette. Isn't it strange? When you love someone enough, you find it incomprehensible that they can love you. It should be the opposite, shouldn't it?'

A tear fell on the arm of the chair.

'She was kind. There are not so many people who value that quality any more. She was reliable, loyal and always gentle. And brave. If she thought she heard noises downstairs and I was asleep, she got up herself and went down. I said she should wake me because what if one day burglars really were downstairs? But she just laughed and said: *Then I'll offer them waffles and the waffle smell will wake you up, because it always does*. The smell of waffles was supposed to wake me up when . . . yes.'

He snorted air through his nose. The bare branches of the birch trees outside waved to them in the gusting wind. 'You should have made waffles,' he whispered. Then he tried to laugh, but it sounded like crying.

'What were her friends like?' Beate asked.

Grette hadn't finished laughing and she had to repeat the question.

'She liked being on her own,' he said. 'Perhaps because she was an only child. She had a lot of contact with her parents. And then we had each other. We didn't need anyone else.'

'She could have had contact with others you didn't know about, couldn't she?' Beate said.

Grette looked at her. 'What do you mean?'

Beate's cheeks went a flustered red and she gave a quick smile. 'I mean that your wife may not necessarily have passed on the conversations she had with all the people she met.'

'Why not? What are you trying to say?'

Beate swallowed and exchanged glances with Harry. He took over. 'In our investigations we always have to examine all the possibilities, however unlikely they may seem. And one of them is that some of the bank employees may be in league with the robber. Sometimes there is inside help with both the planning and the execution of the job. There is little doubt, for example, that the robber knew when the ATM would be refilled.' Harry studied Grette's face for signs of how he took that. But his eyes told him that he had left them again. 'We've been through the same questions with all the other employees,' he lied.

A magpie shrieked from the tree outside. Plaintive, lonely. Grette nodded. At first slowly, then faster.

'Aha,' he said. 'I understand. You think that's why Stine was shot. You think she knew the robber. And when he had finished using her, he shot her to remove any possible leads. Isn't that right?'

'Well, at least it's a theoretical possibility,' Harry said.

Grette shook his head and laughed again: sad, hollow laughter. 'It's clear you didn't know my Stine. She could never do anything like that. And why should she? If she'd lived a little longer, she would have been a millionaire.'

'Oh?'

'Walle Bødtker, her grandfather. Eighty-five years old and owner of three blocks of flats in the city centre. He was diagnosed with lung cancer this summer and since then there has been only one way it was going to go. His grandchildren would have received a block each.'

Harry's question was purely a reflex action: 'Who will get Stine's block now?'

'The other grandchildren,' Grette answered with revulsion in his voice. 'And now you're going to check their alibis, aren't you?'

'Do you think we should?' Harry asked.

Grette was about to answer, but paused when his eyes met Harry's. He bit his lower lip.

'I apologise,' he said, running a hand across his unshaven face. 'Of course I ought to be glad that you're examining every possibility. It all just seems so hopeless. And meaningless. Even if you catch him, I'll never get back what he's taken from me. Not even the death penalty would do that. Losing your life is not the worst thing that can happen.' Harry already knew how he would continue. 'The worst thing is to lose your reason for living.'

'Yes,' Harry said, standing up. 'This is my card. Ring me if anything occurs to you. You can also ask to speak to Beate Lønn.'

Grette had turned to face the window again and didn't see Harry holding out his card, so he left it on the table. Outside, it was becoming darker and they were seeing semi-transparent reflections in the window, like ghosts.

'I have a feeling I've seen him,' Grette said. 'On Fridays I usually go straight from work to play squash at the Focus centre in Sporveisgata. I didn't have a partner and so I went into the fitness room instead. Lifted weights, cycled, that sort of thing. There are so many people at that time you often have to queue.'

'That's right,' Harry said.

'When Stine was killed, I was in there. Three hundred metres down from the bank. Looking forward to a shower and going home and starting to cook. I always cooked the meal on Fridays. I liked waiting for her. Liked . . . waiting. Not all men do.'

'What do you mean you saw him?' Beate asked.

'I saw someone walk past me into the changing room. He was wearing baggy, black clothes. Like overalls.'

'Balaclava?'

Grette shook his head.

'Cap with a peak maybe?' Harry asked.

'He was holding some headgear in his hand. It might have been a balaclava. Or a peaked cap.'

'Did you see his fa—?' Harry began, but was interrupted by Beate.

'Height?'

'Don't know,' Grette said. 'Average height. What's average though? 1.80?'

'Why didn't you tell us this before?' Harry asked.

'Because,' Grette said, pressing his fingers against the glass, 'it's just a feeling. I know it wasn't him.'

'How can you be so sure?' Harry asked.

'Because two of your colleagues were here a few days ago. They were both called Li.' He swivelled round and looked at Harry. 'Are they related?'

'No. What did they want?'

Grette took his hand away. The window had misted up around the greasy marks.

'They wanted to check if Stine might have been involved in some way with the bank robber. And they showed me photos of the robbery.'

'And?'

'The overalls were black without any markings. Those I saw at the Focus centre had large white letters on the back.'

'What letters?' Beate asked.

'P-O-L-I-T-I,' Grette said, rubbing the greasy marks off. 'When I was in the street afterwards, I could hear police sirens in Majorstuen. The first thing I thought was how strange it was that thieves could escape with such a large police presence.'

'Yes, indeed. What made you think that?'

'I don't know. Perhaps because someone had just stolen my squash racquet from the changing room while I was training. My next thought was that Stine's bank was being robbed. That's how your mind works when your imagination runs wild, isn't it. Then I went home and made lasagne. Stine loved lasagne.' Grette made an attempt at a smile. Then the tears began to flow.

Harry fixed his eyes on the piece of paper Grette had written on so as not to see the grown man crying.

'I saw from your six-monthly bank statement there had been a large withdrawal.' Beate's voice sounded harsh and metallic. 'Thirty thousand kroner in São Paulo. What did you spend it on?'

Harry looked up at her in surprise. She seemed quite untouched by the situation.

Grette smiled through his tears. 'Stine and I celebrated our tenth wedding anniversary there. She had some holiday due and went a week before me. That was the longest we had ever been apart.'

'I asked you what you spent the thirty thousand in Brazilian currency on,' Beate said.

Grette turned to the window. 'That's a private matter.'

'And this is a murder case, herr Grette.'

Grette fixed her with a long, hard look. 'You've obviously never been in love with anyone, have you.'

Beate's brow darkened.

'The German jewellers in São Paulo are reckoned to be among the best in the world,' Grette said. 'I bought the diamond ring Stine was wearing when she died.'

Two carers came for Grette. Lunch. Harry and Beate stood by the window watching him while they waited for the carer to show them the way out.

'I'm sorry,' Beate said. 'I made a fool of myself. I . . .'

'It was fine,' Harry said.

'We always check the finances of suspects in bank cases, but I probably went too far this time . . .'

'I said it was fine, Beate. Never apologise for the questions you asked; apologise for the ones you didn't ask.'

The carer arrived and unlocked the door.

'How long will he be here?' Harry asked.

'He's being sent home on Wednesday,' the carer said.

In the car on the way to the city centre Harry asked Beate why carers always 'send patients home'. After all, they didn't provide the transport, did they. And the patients decided themselves if they wanted to go home, or anywhere else, didn't they. So why couldn't they say 'were going home'? Or 'were being discharged'?

Beate didn't have a view on this, and Harry focused on the grey weather, thinking he had begun to sound like a grumpy old man. Before, he had only been grumpy.

'He's changed his hair,' Beate said. 'And he's wearing glasses.'

'Who's that?'

'The carer.'

'Oh, I didn't know you knew each other.'

'We don't. I saw him on the beach in Huk once. And in Eldorado. And in Stortingsgata. I think it was Stortingsgata . . . must be five years ago.'

Harry studied her. 'I didn't realise he was your type.'

'It's not that,' she said.

'Ah,' Harry said. 'I forgot. It's that brain defect of yours.'

She smiled. 'Oslo's a small town.'

'Oh yes? How many times had you seen me before you came to Police HQ?'

'Once. Five years ago.'

'Where was that?'

'On TV. You had solved that case in Sydney.'

'Mm. I guess that must have made an impression.'

'I only remember it irritated me that you came over as a hero even though you had failed.'

'Oh.'

'You never brought the murderer to court, you shot him dead.'

Harry closed his eyes and thought about how good the first drag of his next cigarette would be. He patted his chest to feel if the packet was in his inside pocket and pulled out the folded piece of paper to show to Beate.

'What's that?' Beate asked.

'The page Grette was scribbling on.'

'A Wonderful Day,' she read.

'He's written it thirteen times. A bit like *The Shining*, isn't it.'

'*The Shining*?'

'You know, the horror film. Stanley Kubrick.' He shot her a glance from the corner of his eye. 'The one where Jack Nicholson is sitting in a hotel writing the same sentence again and again.'

'I don't like horror films,' she said quietly.

Harry faced her. He was on the point of saying something, but then felt it was best to leave it.

'Where do you live?' she asked.

'Bislett.'

'It's on the way.'

'Hm. What to?'

'Oppsal.'

'Yes? Where in Oppsal?'

'Vetlandsveien. Right by the station. Do you know where Jørnsløkkveien is?'

'Yes, there's a big yellow timber house on the corner.'

'Exactly. That's where I live. On the first floor. My mother lives on the ground floor. I grew up in that house.'

'I grew up in Oppsal, too,' Harry said. 'Perhaps we know the same people?'

'Perhaps,' Beate said, looking out through the window.

'Have to check that out some time,' Harry said.

Neither of them said another word.

The evening came and the wind picked up. The weather report forecast storms south of Stadt and squalls in the north. Harry coughed. He took out the sweater his mother had knitted for his father and which he had given Harry as a Christmas present some years after her death. A strange thing to do, Harry mused. He heated the pasta and meatballs, and then rang Rakel and told her about the house where he had grown up.

She didn't say much, but he could tell she liked hearing him talk about his bedroom. About his games and the little dressing table. About how he had made up stories from the wallpaper pattern, as if they were fairy tales written in code. And one drawer in the dressing table which his mother and he had agreed was only his, and she would never touch.

'I kept my football cards there,' said Harry. 'Tom Lund's autograph. A letter from Sølvi, a girl I met one summer holiday in Åndalsnes. Later, my first packet of cigarettes. A packet of condoms. They lay there unopened until they had passed the sell-by date. Then, when my sister and I blew them up, they were so dry they split.'

Rakel laughed. Harry carried on, just to hear her laughing.

After the call he paced up and down restlessly. The news was a reprise of the day before. Squalls building up over Jalalabad.

He went into his bedroom and switched on the computer. As it creaked and hummed he saw that he had received another e-mail. He felt his pulse race when he saw the address. He clicked.

Hi Harry
The game has begun. The post-mortem established you could have been present when she died. Is that why you're keeping it to yourself? Probably very wise. Even if it looks like suicide. There are a couple of things that don't tally, though, aren't there? Your move.
S²MN

A bang made Harry jump and he realised he had smacked his palm down on the table with all his strength. He looked around the dark room. He was angry and frightened, but the frustrating thing was his instinct that the e-mail writer was so . . . close at hand. Harry stretched out his arm and placed his still-smarting hand against the screen. The cold glass cooled his skin, but he could feel heat, a kind of body heat, building up inside the machine.

19

The Shoes on the Wire

ELMER SCAMPERED DOWN GRØNLANDSLEIRET WITH A QUICK greeting and smile to customers and employees in neighbouring shops. He was annoyed with himself. Once again he had run out of change and been obliged to hang up a BACK SOON sign on the door while he nipped into the bank.

He pulled open the door, strode into the bank, sang out his usual 'Good morning' and hurried over to take a ticket. No one answered, but he was used to that by now – only white Norwegians worked here. There was a man who seemed to be repairing the ATM and the only customers he could see were standing by the window overlooking the street. It was unusually quiet. Was something going on he hadn't quite caught wind of?

'Twenty,' a woman's voice called out. Elmer looked at the number on his ticket. It said 51, but since all the positions were closed, he went to the till where the woman's voice came from.

'Hello, Catherine, my love,' he said, inquisitively peering through the window. 'Five rolls of fives and ones, please.'

'Twenty-one.' He looked at Catherine Schøyen in surprise and only then did he notice the man standing beside her. At first glance, he thought it was a black man, but then he saw it was a man wearing a black balaclava. The barrel of his AG3 swung away from her and stopped at Elmer.

'Twenty-two,' Catherine called out in a tin-can voice.

'Why here?' Halvorsen asked, peering down at Oslo fjord beneath them. The wind tossed his fringe hither and thither. It had taken them less than five minutes to drive up from the exhaust fumes of Grønland to Ekeberg, which protruded like a green watchtower in the south-east corner of Oslo. They had found a bench under the trees with a view of the beautiful old brick building Harry still called the Seamen's School, even though it currently ran courses for business managers.

'First of all, because it's wonderful here,' Harry said. 'Second of all, to teach a foreigner a little about the history of Oslo. The "Os" of Oslo means "ridge", the hillside we're sitting on now. Ekeberg Ridge. And "lo" is the plain you can see down there.' He pointed. 'And third of all, we sit looking up at this ridge every single day and it is important to find out what's behind it, don't you think?'

Halvorsen didn't answer.

'I didn't want to do this at the office,' Harry said. 'Or at Elmer's. There is something I have to tell you.' Although they were high above the fjord, Harry thought he could still taste salt water in the wind. 'I knew Anna Bethsen.'

Halvorsen nodded.

'You don't exactly look gobsmacked,' Harry remarked.

'I reckoned it was something like that.'

'But there is more.'

'Oh, yes?'

Harry poked an unlit cigarette between his lips. 'Before I go on, I have to warn you. What I am going to say must remain between you and me, and that could pose a dilemma for you. Do you understand?

So, if you don't want to be involved, I don't need to say any more and we'll stop there. Would you like to hear more or not?'

Halvorsen searched Harry's face. If he was reflecting, he didn't need long. He nodded.

'Someone has started sending me e-mails,' Harry said. 'About Anna's death.'

'Someone you know?'

'Haven't a clue. The address means nothing to me.'

'That's why you asked me about tracing e-mail addresses yesterday?'

'I'm not remotely computer-savvy. But you are.' Harry failed in an attempt to light his cigarette in the wind. 'I need help. I think Anna was murdered.'

As the north-west wind stripped the trees of their leaves on Ekeberg, Harry talked about the strange e-mails he had received from someone who seemed to know everything they knew, and probably more. He didn't mention that the e-mails placed Harry at the scene of the crime the night Anna died. But he did mention that the gun was in Anna's right hand even though her palette proved she was left-handed. The photograph in the shoe. And the conversation with Astrid Monsen.

'Astrid Monsen said she had never seen Vigdis Albu and the children in the photo. But when I showed her the newspaper photo of her husband, Arne Albu, she didn't need a second glance. She didn't know his name, but he visited Anna regularly. She had seen him when she went down to pick up her post. He came in the afternoon and left in the evening.'

'That's what's called working late.'

'I asked Monsen if the two of them only met during the week and she said he sometimes collected her in his car at the weekend.'

'Perhaps they liked a little variety and trips into the countryside.'

'Perhaps, apart from the trip stuff. Astrid Monsen is an observant, meticulous woman. She said he never took her out during the summer. That was what made me think.'

'Think about what? A hotel?'

'Possibly. But you can go to a hotel in the summer, too. Think, Halvorsen. Think of something nearby.'

Halvorsen stuck out his lower lip and grimaced to show he had no suggestions to make. Harry smiled and expelled a cloud of smoke: 'You were the one who found the place.'

Halvorsen, nonplussed, raised an eyebrow. 'The chalet! It's obvious!'

'Isn't it? A discreet, luxurious love nest when the family is home after the season and inquisitive neighbours have closed their shutters. Just an hour's drive from Oslo.'

'But so what?' Halvorsen said. 'That doesn't take us any further.'

'Don't say that. If we can prove that Anna has been to the chalet, at least Albu will be forced to respond. It won't take much. A little fingerprint. A hair. An observant tradesman who occasionally makes a delivery.'

Halvorsen rubbed the back of his neck. 'But why not go straight to the point and look for Albu's fingerprints in Anna's flat? It must be full of them?'

'I doubt they are still there. According to Astrid Monsen, he suddenly stopped seeing Anna a year ago. Until one Sunday last month. He came to pick her up in his car. Monsen remembers it clearly because Anna rang at her door and asked her to keep an ear open for burglars.'

'And you think they went to the chalet?'

'I think,' Harry said, throwing the smoking cigarette end into a puddle where it hissed and died, 'that's one reason Anna put the photograph in her shoe. Can you remember what you learned about forensics at Police College?'

'The little we had. Don't you?'

'No. There are metal cases with the basic equipment in three of the patrol cars. Powder, brush and plastic film for fingerprints. Measuring tape, torch, pliers, that sort of thing. I want you to book one of the cars for tomorrow.'

'Harry—'

'And call the grocer in advance to get precise directions. Try to sound honest and upright so that he doesn't suspect anything. Say you're building a chalet and the architect you're working with gave Albu's chalet as a reference point. You just want to see it.'

'Harry, we can't just—'

'Bring a crowbar, too.'

'Listen to me!'

Halvorsen's shout caused two gulls to take off for the fjord with hoarse screams. He counted on his fingers: 'We don't have a warrant. We don't have any proof which might justify one. We've got . . . nothing. And most important of all we – or should I say *I* ? – don't have all the facts. You haven't told me everything, have you, Harry?'

'What makes you think—?'

'Simple. Your motive isn't strong enough. Knowing the woman is not a good enough motive for suddenly disregarding all the rules, breaking into chalets and risking your job. *And* mine. I know you can be a bit nuts, Harry, but you're no fool.'

'Harry watched the wet dog-end floating in the puddle. 'How long have we known each other, Halvorsen?'

'Soon be two years.'

'Have I ever lied to you in that time?'

'Two years isn't a long time.'

'Have I ever lied? I'm asking you.'

'Definitely.'

'Have I ever lied about anything that *counts*?'

'Not as far as I know.'

'OK. I'm not lying to you now, either. You're right, I haven't told you everything. And, yes, you're risking your job by helping me. All I can say is you would be in even more trouble if I told you the rest. As it is, you'll have to trust me. Or back out. You can still refuse.'

They sat looking across the fjord. The gulls were two small dots in the distance.

'What would *you* have done?' Halvorsen said.

'Backed out.'

The dots became bigger. The gulls were coming back.

When they returned to Police HQ there was a message from Møller on the answerphone.

'Let's go for a walk,' he said when Harry called. 'Anywhere at all,' Møller added when they were outside.

'Elmer's,' Harry said. 'I need some smokes.'

Møller followed Harry down a muddy track across the grass between Police HQ and the cobbled drive up to Botsen prison. Harry had observed that planners never seemed to appreciate that people will always find the quickest route between two points irrespective of where the road is. At the end of the track was a sign which had been kicked over: DON'T WALK ON THE GRASS.

'Have you heard about the bank robbery in Grønlandsleiret early this morning?' Møller asked.

Harry nodded. 'Interesting that he chose to do it a hundred metres from the police station.'

'Coincidentally, the bank alarm was being repaired.'

'I don't believe in coincidences,' Harry said.

'Oh? You think it was an inside job?'

Harry shrugged. 'Or someone knew about the repairs.'

'Only the bank and the repairers knew. And us.'

'It wasn't the bank raid you wanted to talk about, was it, boss?'

'No,' Møller said, skipping around a puddle. 'The Chief Superintendent has been in discussion with the Mayor. All these robberies are bothering him.'

On the path, they stopped for a woman with three children in tow. She was telling them off in an angry, drained voice, and avoided Harry's eyes. It was visiting time at Botsen.

'Ivarsson is efficient. No one doubts that,' Møller said. 'However, this Expeditor seems to be of a different calibre from what we're used

173

to. The Chief Superintendent thinks that conventional methods may not be enough this time.'

'Perhaps not, but then what? One "two" more or less is no scandal.'

'A "two"?'

'Away team wins. Unsolved case. Standard vernacular now, boss.'

'There's more at stake than that, Harry. The media have been on our backs all day, it's been a nightmare. They're calling him the new Martin Pedersen. And on the website of *Verdens Gang* it says they have found out we call him the Expeditor.'

'Always the same old story,' Harry said, crossing the road on red with a circumspect Møller at his heels. 'The media determine what we prioritise.'

'Well, he did murder someone after all.'

'And murders which are no longer in the public eye are dropped.'

'No!' Møller snapped. 'We're not starting all that again.'

Harry shrugged and stepped over a newspaper stand which had been blown down. In the street a newspaper was flicking through its own pages at a furious tempo.

'So what do you want?'

'The Chief is, naturally enough, preoccupied with the PR side of things. An isolated bank raid is forgotten by the general public long before the case is dropped. No one notices that the man hasn't been caught. On this occasion, however, everyone's eyes are on us. And the more talk there is about raids of this kind, the more the public's curiosity is aroused. Martin Pedersen was a normal person who did what many dream about; he was a modern Jesse James escaping from the law. That sort of case creates myths, heroes, and people identify with it. Hence, further recruitment for the bank-robbing industry. The number of bank raids soared right across the country while the press were writing about Martin Pedersen.'

'You're frightened of this spreading. Fair enough. What's that got to do with me?'

'As I said, no one doubts Ivarsson's efficiency. No one doubts that. He is a correct, traditional policeman who never oversteps the line.

The Expeditor, however, is no traditional bank robber. The Chief is not happy with the results so far.' Møller nodded towards the prison. 'The episode with Raskol has reached his ears.'

'Mm.'

'I was in the Chief's office before lunch and your name was mentioned. Several times, in fact.'

'My God, should I feel honoured?'

'You are, at any rate, an investigator who has achieved results using unconventional methods.'

Harry's smile stretched into a sneer. 'A kind definition of a kamikaze pilot . . .'

'In a nutshell, the message is this, Harry. Drop everything else you're doing and tell me if you need more people. Ivarsson will continue with his team, but we're relying on you. And one more thing . . .' Møller had stepped closer to Harry. 'You have a free rein. We're willing to accept that rules can be bent. In return, this must stay within the force, of course.'

'Mm. I think I understand. And if it doesn't?'

'We'll back you up as far as we're able, but there's a limit. That goes without saying.'

Elmer turned when the bells above the door rang and nodded towards the little portable radio he was standing in front of: 'And there was me thinking Kandahar was a skiing club. Twenty Camel?'

Harry assented. Elmer turned down the volume of the radio and the news commentator's voice joined the buzz of sounds outside – cars, the wind catching the awning, the leaves being swept along the tarmac.

'Anything for your colleague?' Elmer motioned towards the door where Møller was standing.

'He'd like a kamikaze pilot,' Harry said, opening the packet.

'Really?'

'But he's forgotten to ask the price,' Harry said and could sense Møller's sweetly sardonic smile without needing to turn.

'And what is the going rate for kamikaze pilots nowadays?' the kiosk owner asked, handing over Harry's change.

'If he survives, he's allowed to take on the jobs he wants afterwards,' Harry said. 'That's the only condition he makes. And the only one he insists on.'

'Sounds reasonable,' Elmer says. 'Have a good day, gentlemen.'

On the way back Møller said he would talk to the Chief Superintendent about the possibility of Harry working on the Ellen Gjelten case for three months. Provided the Expeditor was caught, that was. Harry agreed. Møller hesitated in front of the DON'T WALK ON THE GRASS sign.

'It's the shortest route, boss.'

'Yes,' Møller said. 'But my shoes will get dirty.'

'As you wish,' Harry said, walking up the track. 'Mine are filthy already.'

The traffic eased after the turn-off to Ulvøya. It had stopped raining and the Ljan road was already dry. Soon it widened into four carriageways and it was like a starting grid for cars to accelerate and race off. Harry looked over at Halvorsen and wondered when he, too, would hear the heart-stopping screams. But Halvorsen didn't hear anything as he had taken Travis's exhortation – they were on the radio – literally:

'*Sing, sing, siiing!*'

'Halvorsen . . .'

'*For the love you bring . . .*'

Harry turned down the radio and Halvorsen gave him an uncomprehending look.

'Windscreen wipers,' Harry said. 'You can switch them off now.'

'Oh, yes, sorry.'

They drove on in silence. Passed the exit for Drøbak.

'What did you say to the grocer guy?' Harry asked.

'You won't want to know.'

'But he had delivered food to Albu's chalet one Thursday five weeks ago?'

'That was what he said, yes.'

'Before Albu arrived?'

'He only said he used to let himself in.'

'So he has a key?'

'Harry, there were limits to what I could ask for with my paper-thin pretext.'

'What pretext did you give?'

Halvorsen sighed. 'County council surveyor.'

'County council sur—?'

'—veyor.'

'What's that?'

'Don't know.'

Larkollen was just off the motorway, thirteen slow kilometres and fourteen tight bends away.

'To the right by the red house after the petrol station,' Halvorsen recited from memory and turned up into a gravel driveway.

'A *lot* of shower mats,' Harry mumbled five minutes later when Halvorsen had pulled up and pointed to the enormous log construction between the trees. It looked like an overgrown mountain chalet which following a minor misunderstanding had ended up by the sea.

'Bit deserted here, isn't it,' Halvorsen said, looking at the neighbouring chalets. 'Just seagulls. *Loads* of seagulls. Perhaps there's a rubbish dump nearby.'

'Mm.' Harry checked his watch. 'Let's just park a little further up the road anyway.'

The road ended in a turning area. Halvorsen switched off the ignition and Harry opened the car door and got out. Stretched his back and listened to the screams of the gulls and the distant roar of waves beating against the rocks by the beach.

'Ah,' Halvorsen said, filling his lungs. 'This is a bit different from Oslo air, eh?'

'No doubt about that,' Harry said, searching for his packet of cigarettes. 'Will you take the metal case?'

On the path up to the chalet Harry noticed a large yellow-and-white gull on a fencepost. The head turned slowly round on its body as they passed. Harry felt he could sense the shiny bird's eyes on his back the whole way up.

'This won't be easy,' Halvorsen declared once they had taken a closer look at the solid lock on the outside door. He had hung his cap on a wrought-iron light above the heavy oak door.

'Mm. You'll just have to get stuck in.' Harry lit a cigarette. 'I'll go and have a quick recce in the meantime.'

'Why is it you're suddenly smoking so much more than before?' Halvorsen asked, opening the case.

Harry stood still for a moment and let his eyes drift towards the forest. 'To give you a chance to beat me at cycling one day.'

Pitch-black logs, solid windows. Everything about the chalet seemed sturdy and impenetrable. Harry wondered if it would be possible to get in through the impressive stone chimney, but rejected the idea. He walked down the path. The rain of recent days had churned it up, but he could easily imagine the small feet and bare legs of children running down a sun-baked path in the summer, on their way to the beach behind the sea-smoothed rocks. He stopped and closed his eyes. Until the sounds came. The buzz of insects, the swish of the tall grass rippling in the breeze, a distant radio and a song floating to and fro on the wind and children's gleeful shouts from the beach. He had been ten years old and gingerly making his way to the shop to buy milk and bread. The small stones had buried themselves in the soles of his feet, but he had clenched his teeth because he had made up his mind to harden his feet that summer so as to run barefoot with Øystein when he returned home. As he walked back, the heavy shopping bag had seemed to press him deeper into the gravel path; it felt as if he had been walking on glowing coals. He had focused his attention on something a little way ahead – a large stone or a leaf – and told himself he only had to get there, it wasn't that far. When he finally did arrive home, one and a half hours later, the milk was off and his mother angry. Harry opened his eyes. Grey clouds were scurrying across the sky.

He found car tracks in the brown grass beside the path. The deep, rough prints suggested it had been a heavy vehicle with off-road tyres, a Land Rover or something similar. With all the rain that had fallen in recent weeks, the tracks couldn't have been that old. A couple of days at most.

He scouted around, thinking there was nothing quite as desolate as summer resorts in autumn. On his way up to the chalet again, Harry nodded to the gull.

Halvorsen was bent over the front door with an electric picklock, groaning.

'How's it going?'

'Badly.' Halvorsen straightened up and wiped away his sweat. 'This is no amateur lock. It's the crowbar or give up.'

'No crowbar.' Harry scratched his chin. 'Have you checked under the doormat?'

Halvorsen sighed. 'No, and I'm not going to, either.'

'Why's that?'

'Because this is a new millennium and you don't put chalet keys under the doormat any longer. Especially not if it's a luxury chalet. So, unless you're willing to bet a hundred, I simply can't be bothered. Alright?'

Harry nodded.

'Fine,' Halvorsen said, crouching down to pack the case.

'I meant, you're on,' Harry said.

Halvorsen looked up. 'You're kidding?'

Harry shook his head.

Halvorsen grabbed the edge of the synthetic fibre mat.

'Come seven,' he mumbled and whipped the mat away. Three

ants, two woodlice and an earwig came to life and wandered around the grey concrete. But no key.

'Now and then you're incredibly naive, Harry,' Halvorsen said, holding out his palm. 'Why would he leave a key?'

'Because,' said Harry, whose attention had been caught by the wrought-iron lamp beside the door and hadn't seen the extended hand. 'Milk goes off if it's left in the sun.' He went over to the lamp and unscrewed the top.

'What do you mean?'

'The groceries were delivered the day before Albu arrived, weren't they. They obviously had to be put in the house.'

'So? Perhaps the grocery man has a spare key?'

'I don't think so. I think Albu wanted to be absolutely sure no one came bursting in while he and Anna were here.' He whipped off the top and scoured the glass interior. 'And now I know so.'

Halvorsen withdrew his hand, muttering.

'Notice the smell,' Harry said when they entered the living room.

'Green soap,' Halvorsen said. 'Someone has thought fit to wash the floor.'

The heavy furniture, the rustic antiques and the large stone fireplace reinforced the Easter holidays impression. Harry went to a pine shelving system at the other end of the room. Old books on shelves. Harry's eyes ran across the titles on the worn spines, but still had the feeling they had never been read. Not here. They might have been bought as a job lot from one of the antiquarian bookshops in Majorstuen. Old photo albums. Drawers. In the drawers there were Cohiba and Bolivar cigar boxes. One of the drawers was locked.

'So much for the clean-up then,' Halvorsen said. Harry turned and saw his colleague pointing to wet, brown footprints running diagonally across the floor.

They took off their shoes in the hallway, found a floor cloth in the kitchen and after wiping the floor, agreed Halvorsen should take the living room while Harry took the bedrooms and the bathroom.

What Harry knew about house searches he had learned in a hot classroom at Police College one Friday after lunch when everyone was dying to go home, have a shower and hit the town. There was no manual, only a certain Inspector Røkke. And on this Friday he had given Harry the one tip he had later used as his sole guide: 'Don't think about what you are searching for. Think about what you find. Why is that there? Should it be there? What does it mean? It's like reading – if you think about an "l" while looking at a "k", you won't see the words.'

The first thing Harry saw when he came into the first bedroom was the large double bed and the photograph of herr and fru Albu on the bedside table. It wasn't large, but it was conspicuous because it was the only photograph and faced the door.

Harry opened a wardrobe. The smell of another person's clothes hit him. There was no casual clothing, only evening dresses, blouses and a couple of suits. Plus a pair of studded golf shoes.

Harry went through all three wardrobes systematically. He had been a detective for too long to feel embarrassment at going through other people's personal effects.

He sat down on the bed and studied the photograph. The background was only sea and sky, but the way the light fell made Harry think it must have been taken in southern climes. Arne Albu was brown and there was the same boyish mischievousness in his expression Harry had seen in the restaurant in Aker Brygge. He had a firm grip around his wife's waist. So firm that Vigdis's upper body seemed to be leaning towards him.

Harry rolled the bedspread and duvet to the side. If Anna had been in this bed they would definitely find hair, fragments of skin, saliva or sexual secretions. All of them, probably. But it was as he thought. He ran a hand over the starched sheet and put his face to the pillow and breathed in. Just washed. Fuck.

He opened the drawer of the bedside table. A packet of Extra chewing gum, an unopened packet of Paralgin, a keyring with a key and a brass plate with the initials A.A. on, a photograph of a naked baby curled up like a larva on a changing table, and a Swiss army knife.

He was about to pick up the knife when he heard the single,

chilling scream of a gull. Involuntarily he shivered and glanced through the window. The gull was gone. He went back to his search when he heard the sharp barking of a dog.

At that moment Halvorsen appeared in the doorway: 'Someone coming up the pathway.'

His heart pounded as if turbo-charged.

'I'll get the shoes,' Harry said. 'You bring the case with all the equipment in here.'

'But—'

'We'll jump out of the window when they're in. Quick!'

The barking outside increased in volume and intensity. Harry sprinted across the living room to the hall while Halvorsen knelt in front of the shelves and threw powder, brush and sticky paper into the case. The barking was now so close that Harry could hear the deep-throated growls between the barks. Footsteps outside. The door was not locked, it was too late to do anything, he would be caught red-handed! He breathed in and stood where he was. He might just as well face the music there and then. Perhaps Halvorsen would be able to escape. That way, he wouldn't have Halvorsen's dismissal on his conscience.

'Gregor!' came a man's shout from the other side of the door. 'Come back!'

The barking became more distant and he heard the man outside move off the doorstep.

'Gregor! Leave the deer alone!'

Harry took two steps forward and discreetly turned the lock. Then he picked up the two pairs of shoes and crept through the living room as keys were being jangled outside. He closed the bedroom door behind him as he heard the front door opening.

Halvorsen was sitting on the floor under the window and staring at Harry with dilated eyes.

'What is it?' Harry whispered.

'I was on my way out of the window when the mad dog came,' Halvorsen whispered. 'It's a large Rottweiler.'

Harry peered out of the window and down at snapping jaws. The dog had both front paws against the outside wall. The sight of Harry made it jump up the wall and bark as though possessed. Saliva dripped from its fangs. The sound of heavy footsteps in the living room. Harry slumped down on the floor next to Halvorsen.

'Seventy kilos max,' he whispered. 'No big deal.'

'Please. I've seen a Rottweiler attacking Victor, the dog handler.'

'Mm.'

'They lost control of the dog in training. The officer playing the villain had to have his hand sewn back on at Rikshospital.'

'I thought they wore thick padding.'

'They do.'

They sat listening to the barking outside. The footsteps in the living room had stopped.

'Shall we go in and say hello?' Halvorsen whispered. 'It's just a question of time before—'

'Shh.'

They heard more steps. Approaching the bedroom door. Halvorsen squeezed his eyes shut. As if to steel himself against the humiliation. On reopening them, he saw Harry holding an authoritative finger over his lips.

Then they heard a voice outside the bedroom window. 'Gregor! Come on! Let's go home!'

After a couple more barks, it was suddenly quiet. All Harry could hear was short, rapid breaths, but he didn't know if they were his or Halvorsen's.

'Really obedient, those Rottweilers,' Halvorsen whispered.

They waited until they heard the car start down on the road. Then they rushed into the living room and Harry just caught sight of the back of a navy blue Jeep Cherokee disappearing. Halvorsen fell onto the sofa and leaned back.

'My God,' he groaned. 'For a while there I imagined myself returning to Steinkjer with a dishonourable discharge. What the hell was he doing? He was barely here for two minutes.' He jumped up from the sofa again. 'Do you think he'll be back? Perhaps they were just going to the shop?'

Harry shook his head. 'They went home. People like that don't tell lies to their dogs.'

'Sure?'

'Yes, of course. One day he'll shout: "Come here, Gregor. We're going to the vet to have you put down." ' Harry scanned the room. Then he went over to the shelving and ran a finger down the spines of the books in front of him, from top to bottom shelf.

Halvorsen nodded grimly and stared into space: 'And Gregor will come wagging his tail. Really strange creatures, dogs.'

Harry stopped what he was doing and grinned. 'No regrets, Halvorsen?'

'Well, I don't regret this any more than anything else.'

'You're beginning to sound like me.'

'It *is* you. I'm quoting you. The time we bought the espresso machine. What are you after?'

'Don't know,' Harry said, pulling out a big, thick book and opening it. 'Look at this. A photo album. Interesting.'

'Oh, yes? Now you've lost me again.'

Harry pointed behind him and continued flicking through. Halvorsen stood up and saw. And understood. Wet bootprints leading from the front door via the hallway to the shelf where Harry was standing.

Harry slotted the album back in, pulled out another and began to flip through.

'Right,' he said after a while. He pressed the album to his face. 'Here we are.'

'What's that?'

Harry set the album on the table in front of Halvorsen and pointed to one of six photographs attached to the black page. A woman and three children smiled up at them from a beach.

'That's the same photo I found in Anna's shoe,' Harry said. 'Smell it.'

'I don't need to. I can smell the glue from here.'

'Right. He's just stuck the picture in. If you move the photo a little, you can feel the glue is still soft. Smell the photo.'

'OK.' Halvorsen put his nose against the smiles. 'It smells . . . of chemicals.'

'What sort of chemicals?'

'Photos always smell when they've just been developed.'

'Right again. And what can we conclude from that?'

'That, erm . . . he likes sticking in photos.'

Harry looked at his watch. If Albu drove straight home, he would be there in an hour.

'I'll explain in the car,' he said. 'We've got the evidence we need.'

It was raining when they drove out onto the E6. The lights from oncoming traffic reflected on the wet tarmac.

'Now we know where the photo Anna had in her shoe came from,' Harry said. 'At a guess, I'd say Anna saw her chance to take it out of the album when she was last at the chalet.'

'But what was she going to do with it?'

'God only knows. So that she could see what stood between her and Albu perhaps. To understand better. To have something to stick pins in.'

'And when you showed him the photo, did he know where it was from?'

'Naturally. The wheel marks of the Cherokee by the chalet are the same as those before. They show he was here a couple of days ago, possibly yesterday.'

'To wash the floor and wipe all the fingerprints?'

'And to check what he already suspected – that one photo was missing from the album. So when he got home, he found the negative and took it to a chemist.'

'Probably a shop where they develop photos in an hour. Then he went back to the chalet today to stick it where the old one had been.'

'Mm.'

The rear wheels of the lorry in front of them were sending a sheet of dirty, oily water over their windscreen, and the wipers were working overtime.

'Albu has gone to great lengths to cover the traces of his escapades,' Halvorsen said. 'But do you think he took Anna Bethsen's life?'

Harry stared at the logo on the rear doors of the lorry: AMOROMA – ETERNALLY YOURS. 'Why not?'

'He doesn't exactly strike me as a murderer. A well-educated, straight-down-the-line type of guy. Reliable father with spotless record and a business he built up himself.'

'He's been unfaithful.'

'Who hasn't?'

'Yes, who hasn't,' Harry repeated slowly. And exploded in a fit of sudden irritation: 'Are we going to stay behind this lorry and take its crap with us all the way to Oslo, or what?'

Halvorsen checked the mirror and moved into the left-hand lane. 'And what would his motive be?'

'Let's ask, shall we?' Harry said.

'What do you mean? Drive to his place and ask? Reveal that we've acquired evidence by illegal means and get fired at the same time?'

'You don't have to go. I'll do it on my own.'

'And what do you think you'll achieve by doing that? If it gets out that we entered his chalet without a warrant, there is not a judge in this land who wouldn't boot the case out of court.'

'That's precisely why.'

'Precisely . . . Sorry, these puzzles are beginning to take their toll, Harry.'

'Because we don't have anything we can use in a court of law, we have to turn up the heat to find something we can use.'

'Shouldn't we take him in for questioning, give him the good chair, serve espresso and run the tape?'

'No. We don't need a load of lies on tape when we can't use what we do know to prove he's a liar. What we need is an ally. Someone who can expose him on our behalf.'

'And that is?'

'Vigdis Albu.'

'Aha. And how . . . ?'

'If Arne Albu has been unfaithful, the chances are that Vigdis will want to dig deeper into the matter. And the chances are that she's sitting on the information we need. And we know a couple of things which could help her to find out even more.'

Halvorsen slanted the mirror so that he wouldn't be dazzled by the headlamps of the lorry right up their boot. 'Are you sure this is a smart idea, Harry?'

'No. Do you know what a palindrome is?'

'No idea.'

'Word or words that can be read forwards and backwards. Look at the lorry in your mirror. AMOROMA. It's the same word whichever way you read it.'

Halvorsen was about to say something, but thought better of it and just shook his head in despair.

'Drive me to Schrøder's,' Harry said.

The air was stiff with sweat, cigarette smoke, rain-drenched clothing and orders for beer shouted from the tables.

Beate Lønn sat at the table where Aune had been sitting. She was as difficult to spot as a zebra in a cowshed.

'Have you been waiting long?' Harry asked.

'Not long at all,' she lied.

In front of her was a large beer, untouched and already flat. She followed his gaze and dutifully raised the glass.

'There's no obligation to drink alcohol here,' Harry said, making eye contact with Maja. 'It just seems like it.'

'In fact, it's not bad,' Beate took a tiny sip. 'My father said he didn't trust people who didn't drink beer.'

The coffee pot and cup arrived in front of Harry. Beate blushed to the roots of her hair.

'I used to drink beer,' Harry said. 'I had to stop.'

Beate studied the tablecloth.

'It's the only vice I've got rid of,' Harry said. 'I smoke, lie and hold grudges.' He lifted his cup in toast. 'What do you suffer from, Lønn? Apart from being a video junkie and remembering the face of everyone you've ever seen?'

'There's not a lot more.' She raised her glass. 'Apart from the Setesdal Twitch.'

'Is it serious?'

'Fairly. Actually, it's called Huntingdon's Disease. It's hereditary and was normal for Setesdal.'

'Why there of all places?'

'It's a . . . narrow dale surrounded by high fells. And a long way from anywhere.'

'I see.'

'Both my mother and father come from Setesdal and at first my mother didn't want to marry him because she thought he had an aunt with the Setesdal Twitch. My auntie would suddenly lash out with her arms, so people used to keep their distance.'

'And now you've got it?'

Beate smiled. 'My father used to tease my mother about it when I was small. Because when Dad and I played knuckles, I was so fast and hit him so hard that he thought it had to be the Setesdal Twitch. I just found it so funny I wished . . . I had the Twitch, but one day my mother told me you can die from Huntingdon's Disease.' She sat fidgeting with her glass.

'And the same summer I learned what death meant.'

Harry nodded to an old sailor on the neighbouring table, who didn't return the greeting. He cleared his throat: 'What about grudges? Do you suffer from them, too?'

She looked up at him. 'What do you mean?'

Harry shrugged. 'Look around you. Humanity can't survive

188

without it. Revenge and retribution. That's the driving force for the midget who was bullied at school and later became a multi-millionaire, and the bank robber who thinks he has been short-changed by society. And look at us. Society's burning revenge disguised as cold, rational retribution – that's our profession, isn't it.'

'That's the way it has to be,' she said, avoiding his gaze. 'Society wouldn't work without punishment.'

'Yes, of course, but there's more to it than that, isn't there. Catharsis. Revenge cleanses. Aristotle wrote that the human soul is purged by the fear and compassion that tragedy evokes. It's a frightening thought that we fulfil the soul's innermost desire through the tragedy of revenge, isn't it.'

'I haven't read a lot of philosophy.' She raised her glass and took a long swig.

Harry bent his head. 'I haven't, either. I'm just trying to impress you. Down to brass tacks?'

'First some bad news,' she said. 'The reconstruction of the face behind the mask failed. Just a nose and the outline of a head.'

'And the good news?'

'The woman who was used as a hostage in the Grønlandsleiret hold-up reckons she would recognise the robber's voice. She said it was unusually high, she'd almost thought it was a woman's.'

'Mm. Anything else?'

'Yes, I've been talking to the staff at Focus and doing some check-ing. Trond Grette arrived at half past two and left at around four.'

'How can you be so sure of that?'

'Because he paid for the squash court with a card when he arrived. The payment was registered at 14.34. And do you remember the stolen squash racquet? Naturally he told the staff. The person who was working the Friday shift noted down the time Grette was there. He left the centre at 16.02.

'And that was the good news?'

'No, I'm coming to it now. Do you remember the overalls Grette saw going past the fitness room?'

'With POLITI on the back?'

'I've been watching the video. It looks like there is Velcro on the front and back of the Expeditor's boiler suit.'

'Meaning?'

'If the Expeditor is the person Grette saw, he could have put the sign on the boiler suit with Velcro when he was out of range of the cameras.'

'Mm.' Harry slurped out loud.

'It might explain why no one reported seeing someone in a plain black boiler suit in the area. There were black police uniforms everywhere right after the hold-up.'

'What did they say at Focus?'

'That's the interesting part. The woman on duty in fact remembers a man in a boiler suit she took for a policeman. He raced past so she assumed he had booked a squash court or something like that.'

'So they didn't have a name?'

'No.'

'That's not exactly sexy . . .'

'No, but the best is to come. The reason she remembered the guy was that she thought he had to be in a special unit, or something similar, because the rest of his outfit was so Dirty Harry. He . . .' She paused and gave him a horrified look. 'I didn't mean to . . .'

'That's fine,' Harry said. 'Go on.'

Beate moved her glass, and Harry thought he detected a tiny, triumphant smile around her little mouth.

'He was wearing a half-rolled-up balaclava. And a pair of large sunglasses hiding the rest of his face. She said he was carrying a black holdall which seemed very heavy.'

Harry's coffee went down the wrong way.

A pair of old shoes hung by their laces from the wire stretched between the houses in Dovregata. The lights on the wire did what they could to illuminate the cobbled pavement, but it was as if the dark autumn evening had already sucked all the light out of the town.

That didn't bother Harry; he could find the way between Sofies gate and Schrøder's in the pitch dark. He had done it many times.

Beate had a list of the names of people who had booked squash or aerobics at Focus at the time the man in the boiler suit had been there, and she was going to start ringing round tomorrow. If she didn't find the man, there was still a good chance that someone had been in the room when he was changing and could give a description.

Harry walked beneath the shoes on the wire. He had seen them hanging there for years and had long reconciled himself to never finding an answer to the question of how they got there.

Ali was washing the steps as Harry came to the house entrance.

'You must hate Norwegian autumns,' Harry said, wiping his feet. 'Just grime and muddy water.'

'In my hometown in Pakistan visibility was down to fifty metres because of pollution.' Ali smiled. 'All year round.'

Harry could hear a distant yet familiar sound. It was the law which states that telephones start ringing when you hear them, but you can never get to them in time. He looked at his watch. Ten. Rakel had said she would ring him at nine.

'That cellar room . . .' Ali began, but Harry had already taken off at full speed, leaving a Doc Martens bootprint on every fourth step.

The telephone stopped ringing as he opened the door.

He kicked off his boots. Covered his face in his hands. Went to the telephone and lifted the receiver. The number of the hotel was on a yellow Post-it on the mirror. He took the note and caught sight of the reflection of the first e-mail from S²MN. He had printed it out and pinned it on the wall. Old habit. In Crime Squad they always decorated the wall with pictures, letters and other leads which might help them to see a connection or trigger the subconscious in some way. Harry couldn't read the mirror reflection, but he didn't need to:

Shall we play? Let's imagine you've been to dinner with a woman and the next day she's found dead. What do you do?
S²MN

191

He changed his mind, went into the sitting room, switched on the TV and slumped in the wing chair. Then he got up with a jerk, went into the hallway and dialled the number.

Rakel sounded careworn.

'At Schrøder's,' Harry said. 'I've just this minute come in.'

'I must have rung ten times.'

'Anything the matter?'

'I'm frightened, Harry.'

'Mm. Very frightened?'

Harry was standing in the doorway to the sitting room, the receiver squeezed between shoulder and ear while turning down the volume on the TV with the remote control.

'Not very,' she said. 'A little.'

'A little frightened can't hurt. You become stronger by being a little frightened.'

'But what if I become very frightened?'

'You know I'll be there instantly. You just have to say the word.'

'I've already said you can't come, Harry.'

'You are hereby granted the right to change your mind.'

Harry watched the man in the turban and camouflage uniform on TV. There was something strangely familiar about his face, a close resemblance to someone.

'My world is caving in,' she said. 'I just had to know someone was there.'

'There's someone here.'

'But you sound so distant.'

Harry turned away from the TV and leaned against the door frame. 'I'm sorry, but I'm here and I'm thinking about you. Even if I sound distant.'

She started to cry. 'Sorry, Harry. You must think I'm a terrible blubberer. Of course I know you're there.' She whispered: 'I know I can rely on you.'

Harry took a deep breath. The headache came on slowly but surely. Like an iron hoop slowly being tightened around his

192

forehead. When they finished their conversation, he could already feel every throbbing pulse in his temple.

He switched off the TV and put on a Radiohead record, but he couldn't tolerate Thom Yorke's voice. Instead he went to the bathroom and washed his face. Stood in the kitchen and stared into the refrigerator without knowing what he was looking for. Finally, it could not be postponed any longer and he went to the bedroom. The computer came to life, casting its cold, blue light into the room. He had contact with the world around him. Which informed him that he had one e-mail. Now he felt it. The thirst. It rattled the chains like a pack of hounds straining to be set free. He clicked the e-mail icon.

> *I ought to have checked her shoes. The photo must have been on the bedside table and she took it while I was loading the gun. Nevertheless, it makes the game a little more exciting. A little.*
> S²MN
>
> *PS She was frightened. I just wanted you to know that.*

Harry felt deep in his pocket and pulled out the keyring. Attached was a brass plate bearing the initials AA.

PART III

20

The Landing

WHEN SOMEONE STARES DOWN A BARREL, WHAT GOES *through their mind? Sometimes I wonder if they think at all. Like the woman I met today. 'Don't shoot me,' she said. Did she really believe that a plea of that kind would make the slightest difference one way or the other? Her name badge said* DEN NORSKE BANK *and* CATHERINE SCHØYEN, *and when I asked why there were so many 'c's and 'h's in her name, she just looked at me with a stupid cow face and repeated the words: 'Don't shoot me.' I almost lost control, mooed at her and shot her between the horns.*

The traffic in front of me isn't moving. I can feel the seat against my back, clammy and sweaty. The radio is on NRK 24-Hour News, not a peep yet. I look at my watch. Normally I would have been safely in the chalet within half an hour. The car in front has a catalytic converter, and I switch off the fan. The afternoon rush hour has started, but this is much slower than normal. Has there been an accident up ahead? Or have the police set up roadblocks? Impossible. The bag containing the money is under a jacket on the back seat. Next to the loaded AG3. The car in front revs up, slips the clutch and moves two metres. Then we are at a standstill again. I am considering whether I should be bored, nervous or irritated when I see them. Two officers walking along the white line between the lines of cars. One is a woman in uniform and the other a tall man in a grey coat. They cast a vigilant eye over the cars to the left and right. One of them stops and exchanges a few words and a smile with a driver who obviously hasn't fastened his seat belt. Perhaps just a routine check. They are getting closer. A nasal voice on NRK 24-Hour News says in English that the ground temperature is over forty degrees and precautions should be taken against sunstroke. Automatically I start sweating even though I know that outside it is dull and cold. They are standing in front of my car. It is the policeman, Harry Hole. The woman looks like Stine. She looks down at me as they pass. I breathe out in relief. I'm on the point of laughing out loud when there is a tap on the window. Slowly I crane my neck around. Incredibly slowly. She smiles and I discover the window is already rolled down. Strange. She says something which is drowned out by the revving engine in front.

'What?' I ask, opening my eyes again.

'Could you please put the back of your seat into an upright position?'

'The back of my seat?' I ask, perplexed.

'We'll be landing shortly, sir.' She smiles again and disappears.

I rub the sleep out of my eyes and everything comes back to me. The hold-up. The escape. The suitcase with the plane ticket ready at the chalet. The text message from the Prince that the coast was clear. But still the little prickles of nervousness as I showed my passport while checking in at Gardemoen. Take-off. Everything had gone according to plan.

I look out of the window. I am obviously still not quite out of dreamland. For a brief moment I seem to be flying above the stars. Then I realise it is the lights from the town and start thinking about the hire car I have booked. Should I sleep in a hotel in the huge, steaming, stinking town and drive south tomorrow? No, tomorrow I will be just as tired, from jet lag. Best to get there as soon as possible. The place I'm going is better than its reputation. There are even a couple of Norwegians there to talk to. Waking up to sun, sea and a better life. That's the plan. My plan anyway.

I hold onto the drink I managed to save before the stewardess folded my table. So why don't I trust the plan?

The drone of the engine rises and falls. I can feel I'm on the way down now. I close my eyes and instinctively breathe in, knowing what is to come. Her. She is wearing the same dress as when I first saw her. My God, I already long for her. The fact that the longing could not have been satisfied, even if she had lived, changes nothing. Everything about her was impossible. Virtue and passion. Hair which seemed to absorb all light, but instead shone like gold. The defiant laughter as tears rolled down her cheeks. The hate-filled eyes when I entered her. Her false declarations of love and her genuine pleasure when I went to her with threadbare excuses after broken agreements. Which were repeated as I lay beside her in bed with my head in the imprint of another. That's a long time ago now. Millions of years. I squeeze my eyes shut so as not to see the continuation. The shot I fired into her. Her pupils which widened slowly like a black rose; the blood trickling out, falling and landing with a weary sigh; the breaking of her neck and her head tipping back. And now the woman I love is dead. As simple as that. But it still doesn't make sense. That's what is so beautiful. So simple and beautiful you can hardly live with it. The pressure in the cabin falls and tensions increase. From the inside. An invisible force pressing on my eardrums and the soft brain. Something tells me this is how it will happen. No one will find me, no one will wrest my secret from me, but the plan will explode anyway. From inside.

21

Monopoly

HARRY WAS AWOKEN BY THE RADIO ALARM CLOCK AND THE news. The bombing had been intensified. It sounded like a reprise.

He tried to find a reason for getting up.

The voice on the radio said that since 1975 the average weight of a Norwegian man and woman had increased by thirteen and nine kilos respectively. Harry closed his eyes and was reminded of something Aune had said. Escapism has an undeservedly bad reputation. Sleep came. The same warm, sweet feeling as when he was small and lay in bed with the door open, listening to his father walking around the house switching off all the lights – one by one – and for every light that was switched off the darkness outside his door deepened.

'After the violent robberies in Oslo over recent weeks bank employees have called for armed guards in the city centre's most vulnerable banks. Yesterday's hold-up of the Den norske Bank branch in Grønlandsleiret is the latest in a series of armed robberies, for which police suspect the man dubbed the Expeditor to be responsible. It is the same person who shot and killed . . .'

Harry placed his feet on the cold linoleum. The face in the bathroom mirror was late Picasso.

Beate was talking on the telephone. She shook her head when she saw Harry in the office doorway. He nodded and was about to go, but she waved him back.

'Thank you for your help anyway,' she said and put down the receiver.

'Am I disturbing?' Harry asked, putting a cup of coffee in front of her.

'No, I shook my head to say there was no luck with Focus. He was the last name on the list. Of all the men we know were at Focus at the time in question, only one vaguely remembers seeing a man in a boiler suit. And he wasn't even sure whether he had seen him in the changing room or not.'

'Mm.' Harry took a seat and looked around. Her office was just as tidy as he had expected. Apart from a familiar potted plant he couldn't name on the windowsill, her room was as free of ornaments as his own. On her desk he noticed the back of a framed photograph. He had an idea who it might be.

'Have you only talked to men?' he asked.

'The theory is that he went into the men's changing room to change, isn't it?'

'Then he walked the streets of Morristown like any normal person, yes. Anything new on yesterday's hold-up in Grønlandsleiret?'

'Depends on what you mean by new. It's more a carbon copy, I would say. Same clothes and AG3. Used a hostage to speak. Took money from the ATM, all over in one minute and fifty seconds. No clues. In short . . .'

'The Expeditor,' Harry said.

'What's this?' Beate raised the cup and peered into it.

'Cappuccino. Regards from Halvorsen.'

'Coffee with milk?' She wrinkled her nose.

'Let me guess. Your dad said he never trusted anyone who didn't drink black coffee?'

He regretted it immediately he saw Beate's expression of surprise.

'Sorry,' he mumbled. 'I didn't mean to . . . that was stupid of me.'

'So what do we do now?' Beate hastened to ask while fidgeting with the coffee-cup handle. 'We're back to square one.'

Harry collapsed in the chair and contemplated the toes of his boots. 'Go to prison.'

'What?'

'Go straight to prison.' He sat up. 'Do not pass GO. Do not collect two thousand kroner.'

'What are you talking about?'

'Monopoly cards. That's what we have left. Trying our luck. In prison. Have you got the number of Botsen prison?'

'This is a waste of time,' Beate said.

Her voice echoed between the walls of the Culvert as she jogged along beside Harry.

'Maybe,' he said. 'Like ninety per cent of all investigation work.'

'I've read all the reports and the interview tapescripts that have ever been done. He never says anything. Except for a load of irrelevant philosophical rubbish.'

Harry pressed the intercom button beside the grey iron door at the end of the tunnel.

'Have you heard the old adage about looking for what you've lost in the light? I suppose it is meant to illustrate human foolishness. To me it makes good sense.'

'Hold your IDs up to the camera,' said the loudspeaker.

'What's the point of me coming if you're going to talk to him on your own?' Beate asked, nipping in behind Harry.

'It's a method Ellen and I used when we questioned suspects. One of us always ran the interview while the other just sat listening. If the interview was getting into a rut, we had a break. If I had done the talking, I would go out and Ellen would start up about other mundane things. Like giving up smoking or everything on TV was crap nowadays. Or she noticed how much she paid in rent since she had split up with her bloke. After they had chatted for a while, I would poke my head in and say something had cropped up and she would have to take over.'

'Did it work?'

'Every time.'

They went up the stairs to the barrier in front of the prison concourse. The prison officer behind the thick bulletproof glass nodded to them and pressed a button. 'Warder will be along in a minute,' came the nasal voice.

The prison warder was squat with bulging muscles and a dwarf's waddle. He led them to the cell block. A three-storey-high gallery with rows of light blue cell doors encircling a rectangular hall. Wire netting towered up between the floors. There was no one to be seen and the silence was only broken by a door being slammed shut somewhere.

Harry had been here many times before, but it always seemed absurd to him to think that behind all these doors were the people whom society thought fit to keep locked up against their will. He didn't quite know why he found the thought so monstrous, but it was something to do with seeing the physical manifestation of publicly institutionalised retribution for crime. The scales and the sword.

The warder's bunch of keys jangled as he unlocked a door inscribed with VISITORS in black letters. 'Here you are. Just knock when you're ready to leave.'

They stepped in and the door banged to behind them. In the ensuing silence Harry's attention was caught by the low intermittent hum of a neon tube and the plastic flowers on the wall, which cast pale shadows across the washed-out watercolours. A man was sitting erectly on a chair, placed exactly in the middle of the yellow wall behind a table. His forearms rested on the table on either side of a chessboard; his hair was drawn back tightly behind his ears. He was wearing a smooth overall-like uniform. The well-defined eyebrows and the shadow which fell on the straight nose formed a clear T every time the neon tube blinked. It was predominantly his expression, however, that Harry remembered from the funeral, the conflicting combination of suffering and a poker face which reminded Harry of someone.

Harry motioned to Beate to sit by the door. He took a chair to the table and sat down opposite Raskol. 'Thank you for taking the time to meet us.'

'Time is cheap here,' Raskol said in a surprisingly bright and gentle voice. He talked like an Eastern European with strong 'r's and clear diction.

'I understand. I'm Harry Hole and my colleague is—'

'Beate Lønn. You're like your father, Beate.'

Harry heard Beate's gasp and half-turned. Her face had not reddened; on the contrary, her pale skin was even whiter and her mouth had frozen into a grimace, as if she had been slapped.

Looking down at the table, Harry coughed, and noticed for the first time that the almost eerie symmetry either side of the axis dividing him from Raskol was broken by one minor detail: the king and the queen on the chessboard.

'Where have I seen you before, Hole?'

'I'm mostly to be seen in the vicinity of dead people,' Harry said.

'Aha. The funeral. You were one of Ivarsson's guard dogs.'

'No.'

'So you didn't like that, eh? Being called his guard dog. Is there bad blood between you?'

'No,' Harry reflected. 'We just don't like each other. You didn't either, I understand.'

Raskol smiled gently and the neon tube flickered into life. 'I hope he didn't take it personally. It looked like a very expensive suit.'

'I think his suit suffered most.'

'He wanted me to tell him something. So I told him something.'

'That snitches are marked for life?'

'Not bad, Inspector. But the ink will fade with time. Do you play chess?'

Harry tried not to show that Raskol had used the correct rank. He might have guessed.

'How did you manage to hide the transmitter afterwards?' Harry asked. 'I heard they turned the whole block upside down.'

'Who said I hid anything? Black or white?'

'They say you're still the brains behind most of the big bank robberies in Norway, that this is your base and your part of the proceeds is paid into a foreign account. Is that why you made sure you were put in A-Wing in Botsen? Because you can meet the short-termers who are soon out and can execute the plans you hatch here? And how do you communicate with them on the outside? Have you got mobile phones here, too? Computers?'

Raskol sighed. 'A promising start, Inspector, but you're beginning to bore me already. Shall we play or not?'

'A boring game,' Harry said. 'Unless there's something in the pot.'

'Fine by me. What shall we play for?'

'This.' Harry held up a keyring with one single key and a brass nameplate.

'And what's that?' Raskol asked.

'No one knows. Occasionally you have to take a risk that what's in the pot has some value.'

'Why should I?'

Harry leaned forward. 'Because you trust me.'

Raskol laughed out loud. 'Give me one reason why I should trust you, *Spiuni*.'

'Beate,' Harry said without taking his eyes off Raskol. 'Would you mind leaving us on our own?'

He heard the banging on the door and the rattle of keys behind him. The door was opened and there was a smooth click as the lock fell into place.

'Have a look.' Harry put the key on the table.

Without removing his eyes from Harry's, Raskol asked: 'AA?'

Harry picked up the white king from the board. It was hand-carved and a handsome piece. 'Those are the initials of a man with a delicate problem. He was rich. He had a wife and children. House and chalet. Dog and lover. Everything in the garden seemed rosy.'

Harry turned the piece on its head. 'But as time passed, the rich man changed. Events made him realise that the family was the most important thing in his life. So he sold his company, got rid of the lover and promised himself and his family that now they would live for each other. The problem was that the lover began to threaten the man with exposing their relationship. She may have blackmailed him, too. Not because she was greedy, but because she was poor. And because she was finishing off a piece of art which she thought would crown her life's work, and she needed money to launch it. She pressed him harder and harder, and one night he decided to pay her a visit. Not just any evening, but this special evening, because she had told him an old flame was coming round. Why did she tell him? Perhaps to make him jealous? Or to show there were other men who wanted her? He wasn't jealous. He was excited. This was a wonderful opportunity.' Harry looked at Raskol. He had crossed his arms and was watching Harry. 'He waited outside. Waited and waited, watching the lights in her flat. Just before midnight the visitor left. An arbitrary man who – should it ever come to that – would not have an alibi, who others presumably would confirm had spent the whole evening with Anna. Her watchful neighbour, if no one else, would have heard this man ring earlier in the evening. Our man didn't ring, though. Our man let himself in with a key. Crept up the stairs and unlocked the door to her flat.'

Harry picked up the black king and compared it with the white. If you didn't look too closely, you could be deceived into thinking they were identical.

'The weapon is not registered. It may have been Anna's; it may have been his. I don't know exactly what happened in the flat, and the world will probably never know, as she is dead. From the police point of view, it is an open and shut case: suicide.'

'*I? Police point of view?*' Raskol stroked his goatee. 'Why not *we* and *our point of view?* Are you trying to tell me you're flying solo here, Inspector?'

'What do you mean?'

'You know very well what I mean. The trick of sending your colleague out to give me the impression this was between you and me, I understand that, but . . .' He pressed his palms together. 'Although that might be possible. Does anyone else know what you know?'

Harry shook his head.

'So, what are you after? Money?'

'No.'

'I wouldn't be so quick, if I were you, Inspector. I haven't had a chance to say what this information is worth to me yet. We may be talking big bucks. If you can prove what you've said. And punishment of the guilty party may be done under – shall we say – private auspices without any interference from the state.'

'That's not the issue,' Harry said, hoping the perspiration on his forehead wasn't visible. 'The question is what is *your* information worth to *me.*'

'What are you suggesting, *Spiuni*?'

'What I'm suggesting,' Harry said, holding the two kings in the same hand, 'is a trade-off. You tell me who the Expeditor is and I'll obtain evidence against the man who took Anna's life.'

Raskol chuckled. 'There we have it. You can go now, *Spiuni.*'

'Think about it, Raskol.'

'Quite unnecessary. I trust people who chase money; I don't trust crusaders.'

They sized each other up. The neon tube crackled. Harry nodded, replaced the chess pieces, rose to his feet, went to the door and banged on it. 'You must have been fond of her,' he said with his back to Raskol. 'The flat in Sorgenfrigata was registered in your name, and I know exactly how broke Anna was.'

'Oh?'

'Since it's your flat, I've asked the housing committee to send you the key. A courier will be bringing it today. I suggest you compare it with the one you got from me.'

'Why's that?'

'There are three keys to Anna's flat. Anna had one, the electrician had the second. I found this one in the chalet of the man I've been talking about. In the drawer of the bedside table. It's the third and last key. The only one which can have been used, if Anna was murdered.'

They heard footsteps outside the door.

'And if it enhances my credibility,' Harry said, 'I'm only trying to save my own skin.'

22

America

People with a thirst drink anywhere. Take Malik's in Thereses gate, for example. It was a hamburger bar and had nothing of what gave Schrøder's, for all its failings, a certain dignity as a licensed taproom. It was true they had the hamburgers they pushed, rumoured to be a cut above the competition; with a degree of charity one might say that the slightly Indian-inspired interior with the picture of the Norwegian Royal Family did have a kind of naff charm; however, it was and always would be a fast-food outlet where those willing to pay for alcoholic credibility would never dream of imbibing their beer.

Harry had never been one of them.

He hadn't been to Malik's for a long time, but as he gave it the once-over, he was able to confirm that nothing had changed. Øystein was sitting with his male (and one female) drinking pals at the smokers' table. With a backdrop of outdated pop hits, Eurosport and sizzling fat they were enjoying a convivial conversation about lottery wins, a recent triple murder and an absent friend's moral shortcomings.

'Well, hi, Harry!' Øystein's gruff voice cut through the sound pollution. He flicked back his long, greasy hair, wiped his hand on the thigh of his trousers and held it out to Harry.

'This is the cop I was telling you about, folks. Who shot the guy in Australia. Hit him in the head, didn't you.'

'Good work,' said one of the other customers. Harry couldn't see his face because he was bent forward with his long hair hanging over his beer like a curtain. 'Exterminate the vermin.'

Harry pointed to a free table and Øystein nodded, stubbed out his cigarette, put the packet of Petterøes in the pocket of his denim shirt and concentrated on carrying the freshly drawn draught beer to the table without spilling it.

'Long time, no see,' Øystein said, rolling a new cigarette. 'Same as the rest of the boys, by the way. Never see 'em. They've all moved, got married and had kids.' Øystein laughed. A gravelly, bitter laugh. 'They've all settled down, anyroad. Who would've believed it?'

'Mm.'

'Ever been back to Oppsal? Your dad still lives in his house, doesn't he?'

'Yes, but I'm not there very often. We talk on the phone now and then.'

'And your sis? Is she any better?'

Harry smiled. 'You don't get better with Down's Syndrome, Øystein. She's doing fine, though. Has her own flat in Sogn. Got a partner.'

'Christ, more than I've got then.'

'How's the driving going?'

'Alright. Just changed taxi company. Last one thought I smelt. Tosser.'

'Still not interested in going back to computers?'

'Are you crazy!' Øystein shook off internal laughter as he ran the tip of his tongue along the paper. 'Annual salary of a million and a quiet office – of course, I could do with that, but I've missed the boat, Harry. The time for rock'n'roll guys like me in IT is over.'

'I was talking to someone in the data-protection department of

Den norske Bank. He said you were still reckoned to be a code-breaking pioneer.'

'Pioneer means past it, Harry. No one has any time for a washed-up hacker ten years behind the latest developments. You can understand that, can't you? And then there was all that bother.'

'Mm. What actually happened?'

'What happened?' Øystein rolled his eyes. 'You know me. Once a hippy, always a hippy. Needed dough. Tried a code I shouldn't have.' He lit his roll-up and looked around in vain for an ashtray. 'What about you? Stopped hitting the bottle for good, have you?'

'Trying.' Harry reached over for an ashtray from the next table. 'I'm with someone.'

He told Øystein about Rakel, Oleg and the court case in Moscow. And about life in general. It didn't take long.

Øystein talked about the others in the gang of friends who had grown up in Oppsal. About Sigge, who had moved to Harestua with a woman Øystein thought was much too refined for him, and Kristian who was in a wheelchair after being hit by a car while he was on his motorbike north of Minnesund. 'Doctors have given him a chance.'

'A chance of what?' Harry asked.

'Of humping again,' Øystein said, draining his glass.

Tore was still a teacher, but he had split up with Silje.

'His chances aren't so good,' Øystein said. 'He's put on thirty kilos. That was why she cleared off. It's true! Torkild met her out on the town and she told him she couldn't stand all the blubber.' He put down his glass. 'But I take it that wasn't why you called?'

'No, I need some help. I'm on a case.'

'To catch baddies? And you come to me? Jesus!' Øystein's laughter morphed into a coughing fit.

'It's a case I'm personally involved in,' Harry said. 'It's a bit difficult to explain everything, but I'm trying to trace someone who is sending me e-mails. I think he's using a server with anonymous clients somewhere abroad.'

Øystein nodded pensively. 'So you're in trouble?'

'Maybe. What makes you think that?'

'I'm a pisshead taxi driver who knows *nada* about the latest in IT. And everyone who knows me can tell you, I'm unreliable as far as work goes. In short, the only reason you've come to me is that I'm an old pal. Loyalty. I'll keep my mouth shut, won't I.' He took a long swig of a new beer. 'I may enjoy the odd bevvy, but I'm not stupid, Harry.' He pulled hard on his cigarette. 'So – when do we begin?'

Night had settled over Slemdal. The door opened and a man and a woman appeared on the steps. They took leave of their hosts amid laughter, walked down the drive, the shingle crunching under shiny black shoes as they commented in low voices on the food, the host and hostess and the other guests. Thus, as they left the gateway into Bjørnetråkket, they didn't notice the taxi parked a bit further down the road. Harry stubbed out his cigarette, turned up the car radio and listened to Elvis Costello droning through 'Watching the Detectives'. On P4. He had noticed that when his favourite hot sounds were old enough, they ended up on tepid radio channels. Naturally, he was all too aware that could mean only one thing – he was getting old, too. Yesterday they had played Nick Cave after Cliff Richard.

An ingratiating night-time voice introduced 'Another Day in Paradise' and Harry switched off. He rolled down the window and listened to the muted bass throb coming from Albu's house, which was the only sound to stir the silence. An adult party. Business connections, neighbours and old college friends. Not quite 'The Birdy Song' and not quite a rave, but G and Ts, Abba and the Rolling Stones. People in their late thirties who had been through higher education. In other words, not too late back to the babysitter. Harry looked at his watch. He thought about the new e-mail on his computer when he and Øystein had switched it on:

I am bored. Are you frightened or just stupid?
S^{2}MN

212

He had left the computer in Øystein's hands and borrowed his taxi, a clapped-out Mercedes from the seventies, which had shaken like an old sprung mattress over the speed bumps when he came into the residential area, but was still a dream to drive. He had decided to wait when he saw the formally dressed guests leaving Albu's house. There was no reason to make a scene. And, anyway, he needed to spend some time thinking things through before he did anything stupid. Harry had tried to be cold and rational, but this *I am bored* had got in the way.

'Now you've thought things through,' Harry muttered to himself in the rear-view mirror. '*Now* you can do something stupid.'

Vigdis opened the door. She had performed the magic trick only female illusionists master and one men will never get to the bottom of: she had become beautiful. The only specific change Harry could put his finger on was that she was wearing a turquoise evening dress matching her large blue eyes – suddenly wide open with surprise.

'I apologise for disturbing you at such a late hour, fru Albu. I would like to speak to your husband.'

'We're having a party. Can't it wait until tomorrow?' She sent him an imploring smile, and Harry could see how much she burned to slam the door.

'My apologies,' he said. 'Your husband was not telling the truth when he said he didn't know Anna Bethsen. And I don't think you were, either.' Harry didn't know whether it was the evening dress or the confrontation which made him choose a formal tone. Vigdis Albu's mouth was like a mute 'o'.

'I have a witness who saw them together,' Harry said. 'And I know where the photograph is from.'

She blinked twice.

'Why . . . ?' she stammered. 'Why . . . ?'

'Because they were lovers, fru Albu.'

'No, I mean – why are you *telling* me this? Who gave you the right?'

Harry opened his mouth, ready to answer, to say he thought she had a right to know, that it would come out anyway, and so on.

Instead he stood looking at her. She knew why he was telling her, and he hadn't known himself, not until now. He swallowed.

'The right to do what, dearest?'

Harry caught sight of Arne Albu as he came down the stairs. His forehead was glistening with sweat and his bow tie was hanging loose over his shirt front. From the living room up the stairs he could hear David Bowie erroneously insisting 'This Is Not America'.

'Shh, Arne, you'll wake the children,' Vigdis said, without taking her imploring eyes off Harry.

'They wouldn't wake up if an atomic bomb was dropped,' her husband slurred.

'I think that's what herr Hole just did,' she said softly. 'In order to inflict maximum damage, it appears.'

Harry met her eyes.

'Well?' Arne Albu grinned and put an arm around his wife's shoulders. 'Can I join in the game?' The smile was full of amusement, yet open at the same time, almost innocent. Like the irresponsible delight of a boy who has borrowed his father's car without permission.

'My apologies,' Harry said. 'The game is over. We have the proof we need. And right now an IT expert is tracking down the address you have been sending the e-mails from.'

'What is he talking about?' Arne laughed. 'Proof? E-mails?'

Harry studied him. 'The photograph in Anna's shoe. She took it from the photo album when you and she were at the chalet in Larkollen a few weeks ago.'

'Weeks?' Vigdis asked, looking at her husband.

'He knew that when I showed him the photo,' Harry said. 'He was in Larkollen yesterday and stuck a copy in its place.'

Arne Albu frowned, but continued to smile. 'Have you been drinking, Constable?'

'You shouldn't have told her she was going to die,' Harry went on and knew he was about to lose his grip. 'Or at the very least taken your eyes off her afterwards. She sneaked the photo into her shoe. And that was what gave you away, Albu.'

Harry heard a sharp intake of breath from fru Albu.

'A shoe here or there . . .' Albu said, still stroking his wife's neck. 'Do you know why Norwegian businessmen can't do business abroad? They forget their shoes. They wear shoes bought in Norway with Prada suits costing fifteen thousand kroner. Foreigners regard that with suspicion.' Albu pointed below. 'Look. Hand-sewn, Italian shoes. Eighteen hundred kroner. Cheap at the price if you're buying confidence.'

'What I'm wondering is why you were so keen to let me know you were waiting outside,' Harry said. 'Was it jealousy?'

Arne shook his head with a laugh as fru Albu freed herself from his arm.

'Did you think I was her new lover?' Harry persisted. 'And because you thought I wouldn't dare do anything in case my name might be brought up in the case, you thought you could play with me a little, torment me, drive me insane, was that how it was?'

'Come on, Arne! Christian wants to give a speech!' A man with a glass and cigar in hand stood swaying at the top of the stairs.

'Start without me,' Arne said. 'I'll just remove this nice gentleman first.'

The man furrowed his brow. 'Trouble, eh?'

'Not at all,' Vigdis hastened to say. 'Just join the others, Thomas.'

The man shrugged and left.

'The other thing which amazes me is that, even after I had confronted you with the photo, you were arrogant enough to continue sending me e-mails,' Harry said.

'I regret to have to repeat myself, Constable,' Albu slurred, 'but what are these . . . these e-mails you keep going on about?'

'Right. A lot of people think you can send an e-mail anonymously by subscribing to a server without giving your real name. That is a fallacy. My hacker friend has just told me that everything – absolutely everything – you do on the Net leaves an electronic trail which can be, and in this case will be, traced back to the machine they are sent from. It's just a question of knowing where to look.' Harry pulled out a packet of cigarettes from his inside pocket.

'I'd prefer it if you didn't . . .' Vigdis began, but broke off.

'Tell me, herr Albu,' Harry said, lighting a cigarette. 'Where were you on the Tuesday evening of last week between eleven and one o'clock?'

Arne and Vigdis Albu exchanged glances.

'We can do this here or at the police station,' Harry said.

'He was here,' Vigdis said.

'As I said.' Harry blew the smoke out through his nose. He knew he was over-playing his hand, but a half-hearted bluff would fail, and there was no way back now. 'We can do this here or at the police station. Shall I tell the guests the party's over?'

Vigdis chewed her bottom lip. 'But I'm telling you he was . . .' she started. She wasn't beautiful any longer.

'That's fine, Vigdis,' Albu said and patted her on the shoulder. 'Go and see to the guests. I'll walk herr Hole to the gates.'

Harry could hardly feel a breath of wind although higher up it was clearly gusting. Clouds were chasing across the sky and occasionally covering the moon. They ambled.

'Why here?' Albu asked.

'You asked for it.'

Albu nodded. 'Perhaps I did. Buy why did she have to find out like this?'

Harry shrugged. 'How did you want her to find out?'

The music had stopped and the odd salvo of laughter came from the house. Christian was under way.

'Can I borrow a cigarette?' Albu asked. 'Actually, I have given up.'

Harry passed him the packet.

'Thank you.' Albu placed a cigarette between his lips and bent over Harry's lighter. 'What are you after? Money?'

'Why does everyone ask that?' Harry mumbled.

'You're on your own. You have no papers to arrest me and you try to bluff me with threats of taking me to the police station. And if you've been inside the chalet in Larkollen, you're in at least as much trouble as I am.'

Harry shook his head.

'No money?' Albu leaned back. There were a few stars sparkling up above. 'Something personal then? Were you lovers?'

'I thought you knew everything about me,' Harry said.

'Anna took love very seriously. She loved love. No, *worshipped*, that's the word. She *worshipped* love. That was the only thing which had any place in her life. That and hatred. Do you know what neutron stars are?'

Harry shook his head. Albu held up his cigarette. 'They're planets with such compactness and high surface gravity that if I dropped this cigarette on one of them it would strike with the same force as an atom bomb. It was the same with Anna. Her gravitation to love – and hatred – was so strong that nothing could exist in the space between them. Every tiny detail caused an atomic explosion. Do you understand? It took me time to understand. She was like Jupiter – hidden behind an eternal cloud of sulphur. And humour. And sexuality.'

'Venus.'

'I beg your pardon.'

'Nothing.'

The moon protruded from between two clouds, and like a fictional beast the bronze hart stepped out of the shadows in the garden.

'Anna and I had arranged to meet at midnight,' Albu said. 'She said she had a couple of personal things of mine she wanted to return. I was parked in Sorgenfrigata between twelve and a quarter past. We had agreed I would phone her from the car instead of ringing the bell. Because of a nosy neighbour, she said. Anyway, she didn't answer, so I drove home.'

'So your wife was lying?'

'Of course. The day you arrived with the photo, we agreed she would give me an alibi.'

'And why are you giving up the alibi now?'

Albu laughed. 'Does it matter? We're two people talking, with the moon as a silent witness. I can deny everything afterwards. To be frank, I don't think you have anything you can use against me, anyway.'

'Why don't you tell me all the rest while you're at it then?'

'That I killed her, you mean?' He laughed, louder this time. 'It's your job to find out, isn't it?'

They had come to the gates.

'You just wanted to see how I would react, didn't you.' Albu rubbed the cigarette against the marble. 'And you wanted to exact your revenge, that was why you told my wife. You were angry. An angry little boy who hits out at whatever comes in his way. Are you happy?'

'When I find the e-mail address, I've got you,' Harry said. He wasn't angry any more. Just tired.

'You won't find any e-mail address,' Albu said. 'Sorry, old chap. We can continue this game, but you can't win.'

Harry struck out. The sound of knuckles on flesh was dull and brief. Albu staggered back a pace, holding his brow.

Harry could see his own grey breath in the darkness of the night. 'You'll have to get that sewn up,' he said.

Albu looked at his blood-stained hand and guffawed. 'My God, Harry, what a terrible loser you are. Is it OK if we use first names? I think this has brought us closer together, don't you?'

Harry didn't answer, and Albu laughed louder.

'What did she see in you, Harry? Anna didn't like losers. At least she wouldn't let them fuck her.'

The laughter rose higher and higher as Harry walked back to the taxi, and the jagged edges of the car keys cut into his skin as his hand closed tighter and tighter around them.

23

Horsehead Nebula

HARRY WOKE UP TO THE TELEPHONE RINGING AND SQUINTED at the clock. 7.30. It was Øystein. He had left Harry's flat only three hours ago. Then he had located the server in Egypt and now he had made further progress.

'I've e-mailed an old friend. He lives in Malaysia and does a bit of small-time hacking. The ISP is in El Tor, on the Sinai peninsula. They have quite a few ISPs there, it's a sort of centre. Were you asleep?'

'Kind of. How will you find our client?'

'There's only one way, I'm afraid. Go there with a thick wad of American greenbacks.'

'How much?'

'Enough to make someone tell you who to talk to. And to make the person you talk to tell you who you *really* have to talk to. And to make the person you really—'

'I've got you. How much?'

'A grand should make some headway.'

'Do you think so?'

'Off the top of my head. What the fuck do I know?'

'OK. Will you take the job?'

'Course.'

'I pay shit. You travel on the cheapest plane and stay in a crap hotel.'

'Deal.'

It was twelve o'clock and the Police HQ canteen was packed. Harry clenched his teeth and went in. He didn't dislike his colleagues on principle; he disliked them by instinct. And, as the years went by, it was getting worse.

'Completely normal paranoia,' Aune had called it. 'I feel the same myself. I think all psychologists are after me, whereas in reality it is probably no more than half of them.'

Harry scanned the room and spotted Beate with her packed lunch and the back of someone keeping her company. Harry tried not to notice the looks he received from the tables he passed. Someone mumbled a 'Hi', but Harry assumed it was meant ironically and didn't answer.

'Am I disturbing?'

Beate looked up at Harry as if he had caught her in the act.

'Not at all,' said a familiar voice, getting up. 'I was about to go anyway.'

The hairs on Harry's neck rose – not on principle, but by instinct.

'See you this evening then.' Tom Waaler smiled, a white flash to Beate's beetroot face. He took his tray, nodded to Harry and left. Beate stared down into her goat's cheese as she tried her best to assume a sensible expression while Harry took a seat.

'Well?'

'Well what?' she chirped, overdoing the failure to understand.

'You said on my answerphone you had something new,' Harry said. 'I gathered it was urgent.'

'I've worked it out.' Beate drank from the glass of milk. 'The drawings the program made of the Expeditor's face. I've been racking my brains who they reminded me of.'

'Do you mean the printouts you showed me? There's nothing even remotely like a face, it's just random lines on paper.'

'Nevertheless.'

Harry shrugged. 'You're the one with the *fusiform gyrus*. Out with it.'

'Last night it came to me who it was.' She took another mouthful of milk and wiped her milky smile on the serviette.

'Well?'

'Trond Grette.'

Harry stared at her. 'You're kidding, aren't you?'

'No,' she said. 'I just said there was a certain likeness. After all, Grette was not far from Bogstadveien at the time of the murder. But, as I said, I've worked it out.'

'And how . . . ?'

'I checked with Gaustad hospital. If it's the same person who held up the DnB branch in Kirkeveien, it can't be Grette. At that time he was sitting in the TV room with at least three carers. And I sent off a couple of boys from *Krimteknisk* to Grette's place to get a fingerprint. Weber has just compared it with the print on the Coca-Cola bottle. It is definitely not his print.'

'So you were wrong for once?'

Beate shook her head. 'We're looking for a person who has a number of identical external characteristics to Grette.'

'Sorry to have to say this, Beate, but Grette has no external or any other kind of characteristics. He's an accountant who looks like an accountant. I've already forgotten what he looks like.'

'Right,' she said, taking the greaseproof paper off her next sandwich. 'But I haven't. That's the crunch.'

'Mm. I may have some good news.'

'Oh, yes?'

'I'm on my way to Botsen. Raskol wanted to talk to me.'

'Wow. Good luck.'

'Thank you.' Harry stood up. Hesitated. Took a deep breath. 'I know I'm not your father, but may I be allowed to say one thing?'

'Be my guest.'

He peered round to make sure no one could hear them. 'I'd watch it with Waaler, if I were you.'

'Thank you.' Beate took a large bite of her sandwich. 'And the bit about yourself and my father is correct.'

'I've lived in Norway all my life,' Harry said. 'Grew up in Oppsal. My parents were teachers. My father's retired and, since Mum died, he's lived like a sleepwalker, only occasionally visiting the land of the living. My little sister misses him. I do too, I suppose. I miss them both. They thought I would be a teacher. I did, too. But it was Police College instead. And a bit of law. Were you to ask me why I became a policeman, I would be able to give you ten sensible answers, but not one I believed myself. I don't think about it any longer. It's a job, they pay me, and now and then I think I do something good – you can live off that for a long time. I was an alcoholic before I was thirty. Perhaps before I was twenty, it depends on how you look at things. They say it's in your genes. Possibly. When I grew up I found out my grandfather in Åndalsnes had been drunk every day for fifty years. We went there every summer until I was fifteen and never noticed a thing. Unfortunately I haven't inherited that talent. I've done things which have not exactly gone unnoticed. In a nutshell, it's a miracle I've still got a job in the police force.'

Harry looked up at the NO SMOKING sign and lit up.

'Anna and I were lovers for six weeks. She didn't love me. I didn't love her. When I stopped, I did her a greater favour than I did myself. She didn't see it like that.'

The other man in the room nodded.

'I've loved three women in my life,' Harry continued. 'The first was a childhood sweetheart I was going to marry until everything went pear-shaped for us both. She took her life a long time after I'd stopped seeing her, and that had nothing to do with me. The second was murdered by a man I was chasing on the other side of the globe.

The same happened to a female colleague of mine, Ellen. I don't know why but women around me die. Perhaps it's the genes.'

'What about the third woman?'

The third woman. The third key. Harry stroked the initials AA and the edges of the key Raskol had passed him over the table when he was let in. Harry had asked if it was identical to the one he had received and Raskol had nodded.

Then he had asked Harry to talk about himself.

Now Raskol was sitting with his elbows resting on the table and his fingers interlaced as if in prayer. The defective neon tube had been replaced and the light on his face was like bluish-white powder.

'The third woman is in Moscow,' Harry said. 'I think she's a survivor.'

'She's yours?'

'I wouldn't put it like that.'

'But you're together?'

'Yes.'

'And you're planning to spend the rest of your lives together?'

'Well. We don't plan. It's a little too early for that.'

Raskol gave him a doleful smile. '*You* don't plan, you mean. But women plan. Women always plan.'

'Like you?'

Raskol shook his head. 'I only know how to plan bank robberies. All men are amateurs in the capturing of hearts. We may believe we have a conquest, like a general capturing a fortress, and then we discover too late – if at all – that we have been duped. Have you heard of Sun Tzu?'

Harry nodded. 'Chinese general and military strategist. He wrote *The Art of War.*'

'They *maintain* he wrote *The Art of War*. Personally, I believe it was a woman. On the surface, *The Art of War* is a manual about tactics on the battlefield, but at its deepest level it describes how to win conflicts. Or to be more precise, the art of getting what you want at the lowest possible price. The winner of a war is not necessarily the victor. Many have won the crown, but lost so much of their army that they can only rule on their ostensibly defeated enemies' terms. With regard to power, women don't have the vanity men have. They don't need to make power visible, they only want the power to give them the other things they want. Security. Food. Enjoyment. Revenge. Peace. They are rational, power-seeking planners, who think beyond the battle, beyond the victory celebrations. And because they have an inborn capacity to see weakness in their victims, they know instinctively when and how to strike. And when to stop. You can't learn that, *Spiuni*.'

'Is that why you're in prison?'

Raskol closed his eyes and laughed without sound. 'I could easily give you an answer, but you mustn't believe a word I say. Sun Tzu says the first principle of war is *tromperie* – deception. Believe me – all gypsies lie.'

'Mm. Believe you? As in the Greek paradox?'

'Well I never, a policeman who knows about more than the penal code. If all gypsies lie and I'm a gypsy, then it is not true that all gypsies lie. So the truth is I tell the truth and then it is true that all gypsies lie. So I'm lying. A circular argument which is impossible to break. My life is like that and that is the only truth.' He laughed a gentle, almost feminine laugh.

'Now you've seen my opening move. It's your turn.'

Raskol looked at Harry. He nodded.

'My name is Raskol Baxhet. It's an Albanian name, but my father refused to accept that we were Albanians. He said Albania was Europe's anal orifice. So I and all my brothers and sisters were told we were born in Romania, baptised in Bulgaria and circumcised in Hungary.'

Raskol explained that his family were probably Meckari, the largest of the Albanian gypsy groups. The family fled from Enver Hoxha's persecution of gypsies over the mountains into Montenegro and began to work eastwards.

'We were hounded everywhere we went. They claimed we were

thieves. Of course we were, but they didn't even bother to gather evidence. The proof was we were gypsies. I'm telling you this because to recognise a gypsy you have to know he was born with a low-caste mark on his forehead. We have been persecuted by every single regime in Europe There is no difference between fascists, communists and democrats; the fascists were just a little more efficient. Gypsies make no particular fuss about the Holocaust because the difference from the persecution we were used to was not that great. You don't seem to believe me?'

Harry shrugged. Raskol crossed his arms.

'In 1589, Denmark introduced the death penalty for gypsy ringleaders,' he said. 'Fifty years later the Swedes decided all male gypsies should be hanged. In Moravia they cut the left ear off gypsy women, in Bohemia the right. The Archbishop of Mainz proclaimed that all gypsies should be executed without a conviction as their way of life was outlawed. In 1725, a law was passed in Prussia that all gypsies over eighteen should be executed without a trial, but later this law was repealed – the age limit was put down to fourteen. Four of my father's brothers died in captivity. Only one of them during the War. Shall I continue?'

Harry shook his head.

'But even that is a closed circle,' Raskol said. 'The reason we are persecuted and we survive is the same. We are – and want to be – different. Just as we are kept out in the cold, *gadjos* cannot enter our community. The gypsy is the mysterious, menacing stranger you know nothing about, but about whom there are all sorts of rumours. People of many generations believed gypsies were cannibals. Where I grew up – in Balteni, outside Bucharest – they claimed we were the descendants of Cain and doomed to eternal perdition. Our *gadjo* neighbours gave us money to stay away.'

Raskol's eyes flitted across the windowless walls.

'My father was a smith, but there was no work in Romania. We had to move out to the rubbish dump outside the town where the Kalderash gypsies were living. In Albania my father had been the *bulibas*, the local gypsy leader and arbitrator, but among the Kalderash he was just an unemployed smith.'

Raskol heaved a deep sigh.

'I'll never forget the expression in his eyes when he led home a small, tame brown bear. He had bought it with his last money from a group of Ursari. "It can dance," my father said. The communists paid to see a dancing bear. It made them feel better about themselves. Stefan, my brother, tried to feed the bear, but it wouldn't eat, and my mother asked if it was sick. He answered that they had walked all the way from Bucharest and just needed to rest. The bear died four days later.'

Raskol closed his eyes and smiled that doleful smile of his. 'The same autumn Stefan and I ran away. Two mouths fewer to feed. We went north.'

'How old were you?'

'I was eight, he was twelve. The plan was to get to West Germany. At that time they were letting in refugees from all over the world and feeding them. I suppose it was their way of compensating. Stefan thought that the younger we were, the better our chances of getting in. But we were stopped on the Polish border. We arrived in Warsaw where we slept under a bridge with a blanket each, in the enclosed area by Wschodnia, the eastern railway terminal. We knew we would be able to find a *schlepper* – a people smuggler. After several days' searching we found a Romany speaker who called himself a border guide and promised to get us into West Germany. We didn't have the money to pay, but he said there were ways and means; he knew some men who paid well for good-looking young gypsy boys. I didn't know what he was talking about, but obviously Stefan did. He took the guide to the side and they discussed in loud voices as the guide pointed to me. Stefan shook his head repeatedly and in the end the guide threw out his arms and gave in. Stefan asked me to wait until he came back in a car. I did as he said, but the hours passed. It was night and I lay down and slept. For the first two nights under the bridge I had been awoken by the screeching brakes of the goods wagons, but my young ears quickly learned that those were not the sounds I should be on my guard against. So I slept and didn't wake until I heard stealthy footsteps in the middle of the night. It was Stefan. He crept under his blanket and pressed up against the wet wall. I could hear him crying, but I squeezed my eyes shut and made no movements. Soon I could hear the trains again.' Raskol raised his head. 'Do you like trains, *Spiuni*?'

Harry nodded.

'The guide came back the next day. He needed more money. Stefan went off in the car again. Four days later I awoke at the crack of dawn and saw Stefan. He must have been up all night. He lay as he usually did with his eyes half open and I could see his breath hanging in the frosty early-morning air. There was blood on his scalp and one lip was swollen. I picked up my blanket and went to the main station where a family of Kalderash gypsies had settled outside the toilets, waiting to travel westwards. I talked to the oldest of the boys. He told me that the man we thought was a *schlepper* was a local pimp who frequented the station area; he had offered his father thirty zloty for the two youngest boys. I showed the boy my blanket. It was thick and in good condition, stolen from a washing line in Lublin. He liked it. It would soon be December. I asked to see his knife. It was inside his shirt.'

'How did you know he had a knife?'

'All gypsies have knives. To eat with. Even members of the same family don't share cutlery – they can catch *marime*, an infection. But he made a good deal. His knife was small and blunt. Fortunately, I was able to get it sharpened at the smith's in the railway workshop.'

Raskol ran the long pointed nail on the little finger of his right hand across the bridge of his nose.

'That night, after Stefan had got into the car, I asked the pimp if he had a customer for me, too. He grinned and said I should wait. When he came back, I stood in the shadow under the bridge watching the trains moving in and out of the station area. "Come here, *Sinti*," he shouted. "I've got a good customer. A rich Party man. Come now, we haven't got much time!" I answered: "We have to wait for the Krakow train." He came over to me and grabbed my arm. "You've got to come now, do you understand?" I was no higher than his chest. "There it is," I said, pointing. He let me go and looked up. A procession of black steel wagons rolled past our pale faces as we stared up. Then the moment I was waiting for arrived. The screeching of steel against steel as the brakes bit. That drowned everything.'

Harry squinted, as if to make it easier to see if Raskol was lying.

'As the last wagons rolled slowly by I saw a woman's face staring at me from one of the windows. She looked like a ghost. Like my mother. I raised the bloodstained knife and showed her. And do you know what, *Spiuni*? That's the only time in my life when I have felt complete happiness.' Raskol closed his eyes as if to relive the moment. '*Koke per koke*. A head for a head. That is the Albanian expression for blood vengeance. It's the best and the most dangerous intoxicant God gave to humanity.'

'What happened afterwards?'

Raskol opened his eyes again. 'Do you know what *baxt* is, *Spiuni*?'

'No idea.'

'Fate. Hell and karma. It's what governs our lives. When I took the pimp's wallet, there were three thousand zloty in it. Stefan returned and we carried the body across the rails and dumped it in one of the eastbound goods wagons. Then we went north. Two weeks later we sneaked onto a boat from Gdansk to Gothenburg. From there we went to Oslo and a field in Tøyen where there were four caravans, three occupied by gypsies. The fourth was old and abandoned, with a broken axle. That was our home for five years. That Christmas Eve, we celebrated my ninth birthday there, with biscuits and a glass of milk under the one blanket we had left. On Christmas Day we broke into our first kiosk, and we knew we had come to the right place.' Raskol beamed. 'It was like taking candy from a baby.'

They sat in silence for a long while.

'You still don't look as if you believe me entirely,' Raskol said finally.

'Does that matter?' Harry asked.

Raskol smiled. 'How do you know Anna didn't love you?' he asked.

Harry shrugged.

Handcuffed to each other, they walked through the Culvert.

'Don't assume that I know who the robber is,' Raskol said. 'It could be an outsider.'

'I know,' Harry said.

'Good.'

'So, if Anna is Stefan's daughter and he lives in Norway, why didn't he go to the funeral?'

'Because he's dead. He took a tumble from a roof they were doing up several years ago.'

'And Anna's mother?'

'She moved south to Romania with her sister and brother when Stefan died. I don't have her address. I doubt she has one.'

'You told Ivarsson the reason the family didn't go to the funeral was that she had brought shame on them.'

'Did I?' Harry could see the amusement in Raskol's brown eyes. 'Would you believe me if I said I was lying?'

'Yes.'

'But I wasn't lying. Anna had been disowned by the family. She no longer existed for her father. He refused to mention her name. To prevent *marime*. Do you understand?'

'Probably not.'

They walked into the police station and stood waiting for the lift. Raskol mumbled something to himself before he said aloud: 'Why do you trust me, *Spiuni*?'

'What choice do I have?'

'You always have a choice.'

'More to the point is: why do you trust me? The key you got from me may be like the one you were sent for Anna's flat, but I might not have found it in the murderer's house.'

229

Raskol shook his head. 'You misunderstand. I don't trust anyone. I only trust my own instinct. And it tells me you aren't a stupid man. Everyone has something they live for. Something which can be taken away from them. You, too. That's all there is to it.'

The lift doors slid open and they stepped inside.

Harry studied Raskol in the semi-darkness. He sat watching the video of the bank raid with his back erect and palms pressed together, not a flicker of an expression. Not even when the distorted sound of gunfire filled the House of Pain.

'Do you want to see it again?' Harry asked as they came to the final images of the Expeditor disappearing up Industrigata.

'Not necessary,' Raskol said.

'Well?' Harry said, trying not to sound excited.

'Have you got any more?'

Harry had a feeling bad news was on the way.

'Well, I have a video from the 7-Eleven diagonally opposite the bank, where he kept a lookout before the raid.'

'Put it on.'

Harry played it twice. 'Well?' he repeated as the snowstorm raged across the screen in front of them.

'I know he's supposed to be behind other raids and we could have watched them, too,' Raskol said, looking at his watch. 'But it is a waste of time.'

'I thought you said time was the only thing you had enough of.'

'An obvious lie,' he said, standing up and proffering his hand. 'Time is the only thing I haven't got. You'd better put the cuffs back on, *Spiuni*.'

Harry cursed to himself. He slapped the handcuffs on Raskol and they shuffled sideways between the table and the wall to the door. Harry grabbed the door handle.

'Most bank robbers are simple souls,' Raskol said. 'That's why they become bank robbers.'

Harry stopped.

'One of the most celebrated bank robbers in the world was the American Willie Sutton,' Raskol said. 'When he was arrested and taken to court, the judge asked him why he robbed banks. Sutton answered: *Because that's where the money is*. It's become a standing expression in everyday American English and I suppose it's meant to show us how brilliantly direct and easy language can be. To me, it just represents an idiot who got caught. Good bank robbers are neither famous nor quotable. You've never heard of them because they've never been caught. Because they are *not* direct and simple. The one you're looking for is one of them.'

Harry waited.

'Grette,' Raskol said.

'Grette?' Beate stared at Harry with her eyes popping out of her head. 'Grette?' The vein on her neck was swollen. 'Grette has an alibi! Trond Grette is an accountant with bad nerves, not a bank robber! Trond Grette . . . is . . . is . . .'

'Innocent,' Harry said. 'I know.' He had closed the office door behind him and sunk deep into the chair in front of the desk. 'But we're not talking about Trond Grette.'

Beate's mouth closed with an audible, wet click.

'Have you heard of Lev Grette?' Harry asked. 'Raskol said he had only needed the first thirty seconds to know, but he'd wanted to see the rest to be sure because no one has seen Lev Grette for several years. According to the latest rumour Raskol had heard, Grette was living somewhere abroad.'

'Lev Grette,' Beate said, and her gaze wandered into the distance. 'He was such a wonder boy. I remember my father talking about him. I've read reports of robberies he was suspected of having been involved in when he was just sixteen. He was a legend because the police never caught him, and when he disappeared for good, we didn't even have his fingerprints.' She looked at Harry. 'How could I be so stupid? Same build. Similar features. Trond Grette's brother, isn't it.'

Harry nodded.

Beate knitted her brows. 'But that means Lev Grette shot his own sister-in-law.'

'It makes a few things fall into place, doesn't it.'

She nodded slowly. 'The twenty centimetres between the faces. They knew each other.'

'And if Lev Grette knew he had been recognised . . .'

'Of course,' Beate said. 'She was a witness. He couldn't take the risk that she would give him away.'

Harry got up. 'I'll ask Halvorsen to brew up something really strong for us. Now let's have a look at the video.'

'My guess is that Lev Grette didn't know that Stine worked there,' Harry said, his eyes on the screen. 'The interesting thing is that he probably recognises her and still chooses to use her as the hostage. He must have known she would recognise him close up, by the voice, if nothing else.'

Beate shook her head in incomprehension as she absorbed the pictures of the bank concourse where everything was temporarily quiet, and August Schulz, with shambling gait, was in mid-trek. 'So why did he do it?'

'He's a pro. Doesn't leave anything to chance. Stine Grette was doomed from *this* moment on.' Harry freeze-framed the moment when the robber had come in the door and scanned the room. 'When Lev Grette saw her and knew there was a chance he could be identified, he knew she had to die. So he might just as well use her as the hostage.'

'Ice cold.'

'Minus forty. The only thing I don't quite see is why he's prepared to go as far as murder to avoid recognition when he's already wanted for other bank jobs.'

Weber came in with a tray of coffees.

'Yes, but Lev Grette is not wanted for any robberies,' he said, balancing the tray until it was on the coffee table. The room looked as if it had been decorated once in the fifties and then remained untouched by human hand. The plush chairs, the piano and the dusty plants on the windowsill radiated an eerie stillness. Even the pendulum of the grandfather clock in the corner swung soundlessly. The white-haired woman with the beaming eyes in the framed glass on the mantelpiece laughed without sound. The stillness which seemed to have entered when Weber was widowed eight years ago had silenced everything around him; it would even be difficult to get a note out of the piano. The flat was on the ground floor of an old apartment block in Tøyen, but the noise of the cars outside merely emphasised the silence. Weber sat down in one of the wing chairs, cautiously, as though it were a display item in a museum.

'We never found any concrete evidence that Grette had been involved in any of the robberies. No statement from witnesses, no grasses had anything on him, no fingerprints and no other forensic leads. The reports only confirm that he was a suspect.'

'Mm. So, provided Stine Grette didn't report him, he was a man with a clean sheet?'

'Right. Biscuit?'

Beate shook her head.

It was Weber's day off, but Harry had insisted on the telephone that they had to talk immediately. He knew Weber was reluctant to receive visitors at home, but that couldn't be helped.

'We talked to the duty officer at *Krimteknisk* to compare the prints on the Coca-Cola bottle with the prints from earlier raids Lev Grette was suspected of carrying out,' Beate said. 'Nothing.'

'As I said,' Weber said, checking the lid of the coffee pot was on properly, 'Lev Grette's prints were never found at a crime scene.'

Beate thumbed through her notes. 'Do you agree with Raskol that Lev Grette is our man?'

'Well, why not?' Weber started pouring the coffee.

'Because he never used violence in any of the raids where he was a suspect. And because she was his sister-in-law. Murdering because you might be recognised – isn't that a rather feeble motive for murder?'

Weber stopped pouring and looked at her. He glanced quizzically at Harry, who shrugged his shoulders.

'No,' he said. And continued to pour. Beate flushed a deep red.

'Weber comes from the classical school of detection,' Harry said almost apologetically. 'His opinion is that murder by definition excludes rational motives. There are just degrees of confused motives, which can at times resemble reason.'

'That's how it is,' Weber said, putting down the coffee pot.

'I wonder,' Harry said, 'why Lev Grette left the country if the police had nothing on him anyway.'

Weber brushed invisible dust off the arm of the chair. 'I don't know for sure.'

'*For sure*?'

Weber pressed the thin, fragile porcelain coffee-cup handle between a large, fat thumb and a nicotine-stained index finger. 'There was a rumour going round at the time. Nothing we had any faith in. Allegedly, he wasn't fleeing from the police. Someone had heard the last bank job hadn't gone according to plan. Grette had left his partner in the lurch.'

'In what way?' Beate asked.

'No one knew. Some thought Grette had been the getaway driver and had driven off when the police arrived, leaving the other man in the bank. Others said the raid had been a success, but Grette had cleared off abroad with all the money.' Weber took a sip and lowered the cup with care. 'The interesting side to the case we're talking about now is perhaps not the how, but the who. Who was this second person?'

Harry searched Weber's eyes. 'Do you mean it was . . .?'

The veteran forensics expert nodded. Beate and Harry exchanged glances.

'Fuck,' said Harry.

Beate kept an eye on the traffic to the left, waiting for a gap in the stream of cars from the right in Tøyengata. The rain beat down on the roof. Harry closed his eyes. He knew if he concentrated he could make the swish of passing cars become waves beating against the bows of the ferry as he stood in the breeze gazing down at the white froth, holding his grandfather's hand. But he didn't have time.

'So Raskol had unfinished business with Lev Grette,' Harry said, opening his eyes. 'And picks him out as the robber. Is it really Grette in the video or is it just Raskol getting his own back? Or yet another of Raskol's tricks to fool us?'

'Or as Weber said – just a rumour,' Beate said. The cars continued to pass from the right as she impatiently drummed her fingers on the steering wheel.

'You may be right,' Harry said. 'If Raskol wanted to get his own back on Grette, he wouldn't have needed police help. Supposing they're only rumours, why pick out Grette, if Grette didn't do it?'

'A whim?'

Harry shook his head. 'Raskol is a strategist. He doesn't pick out the wrong man without a good reason. I'm not sure the Expeditor was working solo here.'

'What do you mean?'

'Perhaps someone else planned the robberies. Part of a network importing arms. The getaway car. Undercover flat. A cleaner, who spirits away the clothes and weapons afterwards. And a launderer, who launders the money.'

'Raskol?'

'If Raskol wanted to distract our attention from the real guilty party, what better than to send us off on a search for a man whose whereabouts no one knows, who is dead and buried or who has settled abroad under a new name, a suspect we'll never eliminate from our inquiries? By selling us a long-term lemon he can have us chasing our shadows instead of his man.'

'So you think he's lying?'

'All gypsies lie.'

'Oh?'

'I'm quoting Raskol.'

'He's got a good sense of humour then. And why shouldn't he lie to you, if he's lied to everyone else?'

Harry didn't answer.

'At last a gap,' Beate said, lightly touching the accelerator.

'Wait!' Harry said. 'Turn right. To Finnmarkgata.'

'Right,' she said, dismayed, and turned into the road in front of Tøyen park. 'Where are we going?'

'We're going to pay Trond Grette a visit at home.'

The net in the tennis court had been removed. And there was no light in any of the windows in Grette's house.

'He's not at home,' Beate concluded after ringing twice.

The neighbour's window opened.

'Trond's in alright,' came the trill from the woman's wrinkled face, which Harry thought even browner than the last time they had seen it. 'He just won't open up. Keep your finger on the bell, then he'll come.'

Beate pressed the button and they could hear the terrorising ring inside the house. The neighbour's window closed and immediately afterwards they were looking into a pale face with two bluish-black bags beneath unresponsive eyes. Trond Grette was wearing a yellow dressing gown. He looked as if he had just got out of bed after sleeping for a week. And it hadn't been enough. Without a word, he raised his hand and waved them in. There was a flash of sunlight as it caught the diamond ring on the little finger of his left hand.

'Lev was different,' Trond said. 'He tried to kill a man when he was fifteen.'

He smiled into space, as though recalling a dear memory.

'We seemed to have been given a complete set of genes to share between us. What he didn't have, I had – and vice versa. We grew up here in Disengrenda, in this house. Lev was a legend in the area, but I was just Lev's little brother. One of the first things I can remember was from school when Lev was balancing on the school roof in the break. That was four floors up and none of the teachers dared to bring him down. We stood below cheering while he danced around with his arms out to the side. I can still see his body against the blue sky. I wasn't frightened for a moment; it didn't even occur to me that my brother might fall off. I think everyone felt like that. Lev was the only one who stood up to the Gausten brothers from the flats in Traverveien, even though they were at least two years older and had been in a youth detention centre. Lev took Dad's car when he was fourteen, drove to Lillestrøm and came back with a bag of Twist which he'd nicked from the station kiosk. Dad didn't know anything about it. Lev gave me the sweets.'

Trond Grette seemed to be trying to laugh. They had sat down around the table. Trond had made cocoa. He had poured the cocoa powder from a tin he had stood staring at for a long time. Someone had written COCOA on the metal tin with a felt pen. The handwriting was neat, feminine.

'The worst thing was that Lev could have done well for himself,' Trond said. 'His problem was that he tired of things so quickly. Everyone said he was the greatest football talent there had been in Skeid for many years, but when he was selected for the national boys' team he didn't even bother to turn up. When he was fifteen he borrowed a guitar and two months later he was performing his own songs at school. Afterwards he was asked by a guy called Waaktar to join a band in Grorud, but he turned him down because they weren't good enough. Lev was the type who can do everything. He could have got through school as easy as you like if he'd done his homework and hadn't skived so much.' Trond gave a crooked smile. 'He paid me in stolen goods to copy his handwriting and do his essays for him. At least his mark in Norwegian was in safe hands.' Trond laughed, but was soon serious again. 'Then he got sick of the guitar and began to hang out with a gang of older boys from Årvoll. Lev never seemed to think there was any danger in letting go of what he had. There was always something else, something better, something more exciting around the next bend.'

'This may seem a stupid thing to ask a brother, but would you say you knew him well?' Harry asked.

Trond reflected. 'No, it's not a stupid question. Yes, we grew up together. And yes, Lev was outgoing and funny, and everyone – boys as much as girls – wanted to know him. But actually Lev was a lone wolf. He once said to me he had never had any real pals, just fans and girlfriends. There was a lot I didn't know about Lev. Like when the Gausten brothers came to cause trouble. There were three of them and they were all older than Lev. I and the other local boys cleared off as soon as we saw them. But Lev stayed where he was. For five years, they beat him up. Then, one day, the oldest boy came on his own – Roger. We cleared off as usual. When I peered round the corner of the house I could see Roger lying on the ground with Lev on top. Lev had his knees on Roger's arms and was holding a stick. I went closer to see. Apart from the heavy breathing, not a sound came from either of them. That was when I saw that Lev had put the stick in Roger's eye socket.'

Beate shifted position in her chair.

'Lev was fully concentrated, as if he was doing something which required great precision and care. He seemed to be trying to prise out the eyeball. Roger was weeping blood; it ran from the eye, down his ear and dripped from the lobe onto the tarmac. It was so quiet you could hear the blood hitting the ground. Drip, drip, drip.'

'What did you do?' Beate asked.

'I threw up. I've never been able to stand the sight of blood; it makes me dizzy and feel unwell.' Trond shook his head. 'Lev let Roger go and came back home with me. Roger had his eye repaired, but we never saw the Gausten brothers on our patch again. I'll never forget the sight of Lev with the stick, though. It was at moments like that when I thought my big brother could occasionally become someone else, someone I didn't know, who dropped by on the odd unexpected visit. Unfortunately the visits became more and more frequent after that.'

'You said something about him trying to kill a man.'

'It was a Sunday morning. Lev had a screwdriver and a pencil with him, and cycled down to one of the footbridges over Ringveien. You know these bridges, don't you? They're a bit scary because you have to walk on square metal grids and look down on the tarmac seven metres below. As I said, it was Sunday morning, and there weren't many people about. He loosened the screws of one of the grids and left two screws on one side and the pencil in the corner under the grid. Then he waited. First of all, a lady came along, looking 'freshly fucked' as he put it. Well dressed, tousled hair, cursing and hobbling on a broken stiletto heel.' Trond laughed quietly. 'For a fifteen-year-old, Lev had a lot about him.' He lifted the cup to his mouth and looked out of the kitchen window in surprise; a dustbin lorry was parked in front of the rubbish bins behind the rotary driers. 'Is it Monday today?'

'No,' said Harry, who hadn't touched his cup. 'What happened to the girl?

'There are two lines of metal grids. She took the one to the left. Bad luck, Lev said. He said he would have preferred her rather than the guy. Then the man came. He walked on the right-hand side. Because of the pencil in the corner the loose grid was a bit higher than the others. Lev thought the man had seen the danger as he walked slower and slower, the nearer he came. Just as he was going to take the last step he seemed to freeze in the air.'

Trond slowly shook his head as he watched the lorry groaning and chewing up all the neighbours' refuse.

'As he put his foot down, the grid opened like a trapdoor. You know, like the ones they used in hangings. The man broke both legs as he hit the tarmac. Had it not been a Sunday morning he would have been run over straightaway. Bad luck, Lev called it.'

'Did he say that to the police, too?' Harry asked.

'The police, yes,' Trond said, gazing into his cup. 'They came two days later. I opened the door. They asked if the bike outside belonged to anyone in the house. I said yes. Turned out a witness had seen Lev cycling away from the footbridge and had given a description of the bike and a boy in a red jacket. So I showed them the quilted jacket Lev had been wearing.'

'You?' Harry said. 'You gave your own brother away?'

Trond sighed. 'I said it was my bike. And my jacket. Lev and I look very similar.'

'Why on earth did you do that?'

'I was just fourteen and too young for them to do anything. Lev would have ended up in the detention centre where Roger Gausten was.'

'But what did your mother and father say?'

'What could they say? Everyone who knew us knew that Lev had done it. He was the nutcase who pinched sweets and threw stones, while I was the good, kind little boy who did his homework and helped old ladies across the road. It was never talked about afterwards.'

Beate cleared her throat: 'Whose idea was it that you should take the blame?'

'Mine. I loved Lev more than anything on earth. But as the case has been dropped, I can say that now. And the fact is . . .' Trond put on his absent smile. 'Sometimes I wished it had been me who had dared to do it.'

Harry and Beate fidgeted with their cups in silence. Harry wondered which of them would ask. If he had had Ellen with him, they would have known intuitively.

'Where . . . ?' they began in unison. Trond blinked at them. Harry gave Beate the nod.

'Where does your brother live now?' she asked.

'Where . . . Lev is?' Trond looked at them in bewilderment.

'Yes,' she said. 'We know he's been away for a while.'

Grette turned to Harry. 'You didn't say this was about Lev.' The intonation was accusatory.

'We said we wanted to talk about this and that,' Harry said. 'We've finished with this, now we're on to that.'

Trond bolted up from his chair, grabbed the cups, went over to the sink and threw out the cocoa. 'But Lev . . . after all he's my . . . what on earth has he got to do with . . . ?'

'Perhaps nothing,' Harry said. 'If he has, we would like your help to eliminate him from our inquiries.'

'He doesn't even live in this country,' Trond groaned, turning round to face them.

Beate and Harry looked at each other.

'So where does he live?' Harry asked.

Trond hesitated exactly a tenth of a second too long before answering: 'I don't know.'

Harry watched the yellow dustbin lorry pass outside. 'You're not very good at lying, are you.'

Trond answered him with a rigid stare.

'Mm,' Harry said. 'Perhaps we can't expect you to help us find your brother. On the other hand, it was your wife who was killed. And we have a witness who fingered your brother as the murderer.' He raised his eyes towards Trond as he said the last word and saw his Adam's apple give a jump under the pale skin. In the ensuing silence they could hear a radio playing in the next-door flat.

Harry coughed. 'So if there's anything you can tell us, we would greatly appreciate it.'

Trond shook his head.

They sat for a few moments, then Harry got up. 'Fine. You know where to find us if you think of anything.'

Outside on the step, Trond didn't seem as tired as when they arrived. Red-eyed, Harry peered up into the low sun protruding between the clouds.

'I understand this isn't easy for you, but maybe it's time you took off the red jacket.'

241

Grette didn't answer, and the last they saw as they turned out of the car park was Grette standing on the doorstep and playing with the diamond ring on his little finger, and a glimpse of a wrinkly, tanned face behind the neighbour's window.

In the evening the clouds disappeared. Harry stopped at the top of Dovregata on his way home from Schrøder's and stared upwards. The stars twinkled in the moonless sky. One of the lights was a plane flying north towards Gardemoen airport. Orion's Horsehead Nebula. Horsehead Nebula. Orion. Who had told him about it? Had it been Anna, he wondered.

On returning to his flat, he switched on the TV to see the NRK news. Heroic tales about American firefighters. He switched it off. A man's voice screamed a woman's name down in the street; he sounded drunk. Harry rummaged around in his pockets to find the note he had made of Rakel's new number and discovered he still had the key engraved with AA. He put the key at the back of the drawer in the telephone table before ringing the number. No answer. When the telephone rang, he wasn't sure if it would be her; instead he had Øystein on a crackly line.

'Shit, the way they drive here!'

'You don't need to shout, Øystein.'

'They're fucking trying to kill me on the roads here! I took a taxi from Sharm el-Sheikh. Great trip, I thought – right through the desert, not much traffic, straight road. Boy, was I wrong. It's a miracle I'm alive, I can tell you. And so hot! And have you heard the grasshoppers here – the desert crickets? They make the world's highest-pitched grasshopper noises. Goes right through the cerebral cortex, absolutely terrible. The water here is just amazing. Amazing! Completely clear with a dash of green. Body temperature, so you don't even feel it. Yesterday I got out of the sea and wasn't even sure if I'd been in . . .'

'Forget the sea temperatures, Øystein. Have you found the server?'

'Yes and no.'

'What does that mean?'

Harry didn't get an answer. They had clearly been interrupted by a discussion at the other end. Harry caught fragments, like 'the boss' and 'the money'.

'Harry? Sorry, the guy here got a bit paranoid. And I am too. Bloody hot, it is! But I think I've found the right server. There's always a chance they're trying to screw me, but tomorrow I'll see the works and meet the boss in person. Three minutes on the keyboard and I'll know if it's the right one. And the rest is just a question of money. I hope. Ring you tomorrow. You should see the knives these Bedouins have here . . .'

Øystein's laugh sounded hollow.

The last thing Harry did before switching off the light was to consult the encyclopedia. Horsehead Nebula was a dark cloud. Not a lot was known about it, nor about Orion either, except that it was considered one of the most beautiful of all the constellations. Orion was a Greek mythical figure, a Titan and a great hunter. He was seduced by Eos, for which Artemis killed him in his fury. Harry went to sleep with the sensation that somebody was thinking about him.

On opening his eyes the following morning he could feel his thoughts were scattered far and wide, torn fragments and glimpses of half-forgotten scenes. It was as though someone had ransacked his brain, and the contents, which had been carefully tidied away in drawers and cupboards, lay strewn around. He must have been dreaming. The telephone in the hall rang and rang. Harry forced himself out of bed. It was Øystein again: he was in an office in El Tor.

'We've got a problem,' he said.

24

São Paulo

RASKOL'S MOUTH AND LIPS FORMED A GENTLE SMILE. IT WAS therefore impossible to say whether it was really a gentle smile or not. Harry guessed the latter.

'You have a friend in Egypt searching for a telephone number then,' Raskol said. Harry was unable to decipher whether the intonation was sarcastic or matter-of-fact.

'El Tor,' Harry said, rubbing his palm against the arm of his chair. He felt an intense discomfort. Not because he was sitting in the sterile visitors' room again, but on account of his errand. He had considered all the options. Taking a personal loan. Confiding in Bjarne Møller. Selling the Ford Escort to the garage where it was always being repaired. But this was the only realistic chance, the only logical way to go. It was madness.

'The telephone number is not simply a number,' Harry said. 'It will lead us to the client who sent me the e-mail. The e-mail which proves he knows details about Anna's death he would not have known, had he not been present just before she died.'

'And your friend says the owners of the ISP have asked for 60,000 Egyptian pounds. And that is?'

'Approximately 120,000 kroner.'

'Which you think I should give you?'

'I don't think anything. I'm just telling you what the situation is. They want money and I haven't got it.'

Raskol ran a finger along his top lip. 'Why should that be my problem, Harry? We made an agreement and I kept my part.'

'I'll keep my part, but it will take longer without money.'

Raskol shook his head, threw out his arms and mumbled something in what Harry supposed was Romany. Øystein had been desperate on the telephone. There was no doubt they had found the correct server, he had said. But he had imagined a rusty antique in a shed, wheezing but functional, and a horse trader with a turban who wanted three camels and a pack of American cigarettes. Instead he went to an air-conditioned office where the young besuited Egyptian behind a desk had gazed at him through silver-framed glasses and told him the price was 'non-negotiable', payment was to be in untraceable notes and the offer would stand for three days.

'I assume you've considered the consequences if it leaks out that you've been receiving money from someone like me while on duty?'

'I'm not on duty,' Harry said.

Raskol stroked his ears with the palms of his hands. 'Sun Tzu says if you do not control events, they will control you. You don't have any control over events, *Spiuni*. It means you've blundered. I don't like people who make blunders. Hence, I have a suggestion. We'll make this simple for both parties. You give me the name of this man and I'll sort out the rest.'

'No!' Harry slammed his hand down hard on the table. 'I don't want him roughed up by one of your gorillas. I want him behind lock and key.'

'You surprise me, *Spiuni*. If I've understood you correctly, you're already in a sensitive position. Why not let justice be meted out to the hilt as painlessly as possible?'

'No vendetta. That was our agreement.'

Raskol smiled. 'You're a tough nut, Hole. I like that. And I respect agreements. But now you're beginning to screw up. How can I be sure this is the right man?'

'You were given the opportunity to check the key I found at the chalet was identical with Anna's.'

'And now you come to me for help again. So you'll have to give me a bit more.'

Harry swallowed. 'When I found Anna, she had a photo in her shoe.'

'Go on.'

'My thinking is she managed to put it there before the murderer shot her. It's a picture of the murderer's family.'

'Is that all?'

'Yes.'

Raskol shook his head, looked at Harry and then shook his head again.

'I don't know who's the most stupid here. You, for letting your friend pull the wool over your eyes. Your friend, who thinks he can hide after stealing money from me.' He heaved a deep sigh. 'Or me, for giving you money.'

Harry thought he would feel happiness or at least relief. Instead he only felt the knot in his stomach tightening. 'So what do you need to know?'

'Just the name of your friend and the bank in Egypt where he wants to pick up the money.'

'You'll have them in an hour.' Harry got to his feet.

Raskol rubbed his wrists as if he had taken off handcuffs. 'I hope you don't think you understand me, *Spiuni*.' He said it in a low voice without looking up.

Harry came to a halt. 'What do you mean?'

'I'm a gypsy. My world can be an inverted world. Do you know what God is in Romany?'

'No.'

'*Devel*. Devil. Strange, isn't it? When you sell your soul, it's good to know who you're selling it to, *Spiuni*.'

246

Halvorsen thought Harry looked drained.

'Define "drained",' Harry said, leaning back in his office chair. 'Or, in fact, don't.'

When Halvorsen asked Harry how things were going and Harry asked him to define '*going*', Halvorsen sighed and left the office to try his luck with Elmer.

Harry dialled the number he had received from Rakel, but again got the Russian voice he assumed was telling him he was generally barking up the wrong tree. So he rang Bjarne Møller and tried to give his boss the impression he wasn't barking up the wrong tree. Møller didn't sound convinced.

'I want good news, Harry. Not reports on how you've been spending your time.'

Beate came in to say she had watched the video ten more times and she no longer had any doubt that the Expeditor and Stine Grette knew each other. 'I think the last thing he tells her is that she is going to die. You can see it in her eyes. Defiant and frightened at the same time, just like in the war films where you see resistance fighters lined up ready to be shot.'

Pause.

'Hello?' She waved a hand in front of his eyes. 'You look drained.'

He rang Aune.

'Harry here. How do people react when they know they're going to be executed?'

Aune chuckled. 'They're focused,' he said. 'On time.'

'And frightened? Panic-stricken?'

'That depends. What sort of execution are we talking about?'

'A public execution. In a bank.'

'I see. I'll ring you back in two minutes.'

Harry studied his watch as he waited. It took 120 seconds.

'The process of dying, much like the process of being born, is a very intimate affair,' Aune said. 'The reason people in such situations instinctively have a desire to hide is not just because they feel

247

physically vulnerable. Dying in the sight of others, as in a public execution, is a double punishment as it is an affront to the victim's modesty in the most brutal way conceivable. It was one of the reasons public executions were considered to have a more criminally preventative effect on the population than execution in the solitude of the cell. Some allowances were made, however, such as obliging the executioner to wear a mask. That wasn't, as many think, to conceal the executioner's identity – everyone knew it was the local butcher or rope-maker. The mask was out of consideration for the condemned man, so that he didn't feel a stranger was close to him at the moment of death.'

'Mm. The bank robber was also wearing a mask.'

'The use of masks is a whole field of psychological research. For example, the modern notion that wearing a mask deprives us of freedom can be turned on its head. Masks can depersonalise in a way which allows freedom. To what do you otherwise attribute the popularity of masked balls in Victorian times? Or the use of masks in sexual games? A bank robber, on the other hand, has more prosaic reasons for wearing a mask, of course.'

'Maybe.'

'Maybe?'

'I don't know,' Harry sighed.

'You seem . . .'

'Tired. See you.'

Harry's position on earth slowly moved away from the sun and the afternoons became dark earlier and earlier. The lemons outside Ali's shop shone like small yellow stars and a silent spray of fine rain fell as Harry walked up Sofies gate. The afternoon had been spent arranging the transfer of funds to El Tor. It hadn't been such a major job. He had chatted to Øystein, got his passport number plus the address of the bank beside the hotel where he was staying and phoned the information through to the prison inmates' newspaper the *Returning Phantom*, where Raskol was working on an article about Sun Tzu. Then it was simply a question of waiting.

Harry had arrived at the front door and was about to search for keys when he heard a padding of feet on the pavement behind him. He didn't turn.

Not until he heard the low growl.

In fact, he was not surprised. If you heat up a pressure cooker, you know that sooner or later something has to happen.

The dog's face was as black as the night and contrasted with the whiteness of the bared teeth. The feeble light from the lamp over the front door caught a trickle of saliva hanging off a large canine tooth and it sparkled.

'Sit!' said a familiar voice from the shadows beneath the garage entrance on the other side of the quiet, narrow street. The Rottweiler reluctantly lowered its broad, muscular hindquarters onto the wet tarmac, but its shiny brown eyes, the furthest thing from 'puppy-dog eyes' you could imagine, never left Harry.

The shadow from the cap fell across the approaching man's face.

'Good evening, Harry. Frightened of dogs?'

Harry looked down at the red jaws in front of him. A fragment of trivia floated to the surface. The Romans had used the Rottweiler's forefathers in the conquest of Europe. 'No, what do you want?'

'To make you an offer. An offer you . . . what's the phrase again?'

'That's fine, just make me the offer, Albu.'

'Truce.' Arne Albu flipped up the peak of his cap. He tried his boyish smile, but it didn't sit as well as the previous time. 'You keep away from me and I'll keep away from you.'

'Interesting. And what would you do to me, Albu?'

Albu nodded towards the Rottweiler, which was not sitting but on its haunches ready to pounce. 'I have my methods. And I'm not completely without resources.'

'Mm.' Harry patted his jacket pocket for cigarettes, but stopped when the growling became menacing. 'You look drained, Albu. Is all the running tiring you?'

Albu shook his head. 'It's not me who's running, Harry. It's you.'

'Oh? Vague threats against a police officer in a public place. I call that signs of fatigue. Why don't you want to play any more?'

'Play? Is that how you see it? A kind of ludo with human fate.'

Harry saw the anger in Arne Albu's eyes. Something else, too. His jaw was working and the blood vessels in the temples and forehead stood out. It was desperation.

'Do you realise what you've done?' he almost whispered, no longer making any attempt to smile. 'She's left me. She's . . . taken the children and gone. Because of a petty affair. Anna didn't mean a thing to me any more.'

Arne Albu stood close to Harry. 'Anna and I met when a friend of mine was showing me round his gallery and she happened to have a private viewing there. I bought two of her paintings, I don't really know why. I said they were for the office. Of course they were never hung up anywhere. When I went to fetch the pictures the next day, Anna and I fell into conversation and suddenly I had invited her to lunch. Then it was dinner. And two weeks later a weekend trip to Berlin. Things got out of hand. I was stuck and didn't even make an attempt to extricate myself. Not until Vigdis discovered what was going on and threatened to leave me.'

His voice had begun to tremble.

'I promised Vigdis it was just a one-off, an idiotic infatuation men of my age occasionally pursue when they meet a young woman. She reminds them what it had been like once. To be young, strong and independent. But *you* aren't any more. Independent, least of all. When you have children, you'll know . . .'

His voice gave way and he was breathing heavily. He buried his hands in his coat pockets and went on.

'Anna was an intense lover. It verged on the abnormal. It was as if she could never let go. I literally had to tear myself away; she ruined one of my jackets as I was trying to get out of the door. I think you know what I mean. She once told me about what it was like after you left. She almost went to pieces.'

Harry was too surprised to answer.

'But I probably felt sorry for her,' Albu continued. 'Otherwise I wouldn't have agreed to meet her again. I'd said quite clearly it was over between us, but she just wanted to give me back a few things, she said. I wasn't to know you would come and blow everything out of proportion. Make it look as if we had . . . taken up where we'd left off.' He bent his head. 'Vigdis doesn't believe me. She says she'll never be able to trust me again. Not another time.'

He lifted his face and Harry saw the despair in his eyes. 'You took the only thing I had, Hole. They're all I have left. I don't know if I can get them back.' His features distorted in pain.

Harry thought of the pressure cooker. Any moment now.

'The only chance I have is if you . . . if you don't . . .'

Harry reacted instinctively when he saw Albu's hand moving in his coat pocket. He kicked out and hit Albu in the side of the knee, sending him into a kneeling position on the pavement. Harry swung his forearm into the face of the Rottweiler as it attacked; he heard the sound of material being ripped and felt teeth puncturing his skin, sinking into the flesh. He hoped its jaws would lock, but the smart bastard let go. Harry aimed a foot at the black mound of naked muscle and missed. He heard its claws scratch at the tarmac as it launched itself and saw the jaws open to meet him. Someone had told him that Rottweilers know before they are three weeks old that the most effective method of killing someone is to tear open the throat, and now the seventy-kilo muscle machine was past his arms. Harry used the momentum the kick had given him to spin round. As the dog's jaws locked it was thus not around his throat, but his neck. Not that that meant his problems were over. He reached behind him and grabbed the upper jaw with one hand and the lower with the other and pulled with all his strength. Instead of opening, however, the jaws sank a few more millimetres into his neck. The sinews and muscles of the dog's jaws were like steel. Harry charged backwards and threw himself against the wall. He heard the dog's ribs crack, but the jaws didn't yield. He felt himself panicking. He had heard about jaws locking, about the hyena whose jaws were fastened onto the male lion's throat long after it had been torn to shreds by lionesses. He felt the warm blood running down his back inside the T-shirt and discovered he had fallen to his knees. Had everything begun to lose sensation? Where was everyone? Sofies gate was a quiet street, but Harry had never seen it as deserted as now, he thought. It struck him how everything had happened in silence, no shouts, no barking, just the sound of flesh against flesh and flesh being torn. He tried to shout, but couldn't force out a sound. His field of vision was beginning to darken at the margins; he knew an artery was being squeezed and he was getting tunnel vision because his brain wasn't receiving enough blood. The shiny lemons outside Ali's shop were losing their shine. Something black, flat, wet and solid came up and exploded in his face. He tasted gravel. Far away, he could hear Albu's voice: 'Let go!'

The pressure around his neck eased. Harry's position on earth moved slowly away from the sun and it was pitch dark when he heard someone say: 'Are you alive? Can you hear me?'

Then a steel click close to his ear. Gun parts. Cocking the trigger.

'Fu . . .' He heard a deep groan and the splat of vomit as it hit the tarmac. More steel clicks. Safety catch being removed . . . In a few seconds it would all be over. That was how it felt. Not despair – not fear – not even regret. Only relief. There wasn't much to leave behind. Albu was taking his time. Time for Harry to realise there was something after all. Something he was leaving behind. He filled his lungs with air. The network of arteries absorbed the oxygen and pumped it up to the brain.

'Right, now . . .' the voice began, but it stopped abruptly as Harry's fist struck the larynx.

Harry got to his knees. He didn't have much strength left. He tried to retain consciousness while waiting for the final onslaught. A second passed. Two seconds. Three. The smell of vomit burned in his nose. The streetlights above him came into focus. The street was empty. Deserted. Apart from a man lying beside him in a blue quilted jacket and what looked like a pyjama top sticking out from the neck, gurgling. The light shone on metal. It wasn't a gun; it was a lighter. Only now did Harry see that the man was not Arne Albu. It was Trond Grette.

With a scalding hot cup of tea in his hand, Harry sat at the kitchen table opposite Trond, whose breath was still laboured and wheezy, and whose panic-stricken goitre eyes bulged out of his skull. As for himself, he was dizzy and nauseous, and the pains in his neck throbbed like burns.

'Drink,' Harry said. 'There's loads of lemon in it. It numbs the muscles and relaxes them so you can breathe more easily.'

Trond obeyed. To Harry's great surprise, the drink seemed to work. After a few sips and a couple of coughing fits a hint of colour returned to Trond's pale cheeks.

'Ulkterbl,' he wheezed.

'Sorry?' Harry sank back in the other kitchen chair.

'You look terrible.'

Harry smiled and felt the towel he had tied around his neck. It was already soaked in blood. 'Was that why you threw up?'

'Can't stand the sight of blood,' Trond said. 'I go all . . .' He rolled his eyes.

'Well, it could have been worse. You saved my bacon.'

Trond shook his head. 'I was a fair distance away when I saw you. I just shouted. I'm not sure that was what made him call off the dog. Sorry I didn't get the registration number, but I did see it was a Jeep Cherokee they made off in.'

Harry dismissed this with a wave of his hand. 'I know who he is.'

'Oh?'

'He's under investigation. But perhaps you'd better tell me what you were doing around here, Grette.'

Trond fidgeted with his teacup. 'You should definitely go to casualty with that wound.'

'I'll consider it. Have you had a little think since we last talked?'

Trond nodded slowly.

'And what conclusion did you come to?'

'I can't help him any longer.' It was difficult for Harry to determine whether it was only the sore larynx which made Trond whisper the last sentence.

'So where's your brother?'

'I want you to tell him it was me who told you. He'll understand.'

'Alright.'

'Porto Seguro.'

'Uhuh.'

'It's a town in Brazil.'

Harry wrinkled his nose. 'Fine. How will we find him there?'

'He's just told me he has a house there. He refused to give me an address, only a telephone number.'

'Why? He's not a wanted man.'

'I'm not sure that is correct.' Trond took another sip. 'At any rate, he said it would be better if I didn't have his address.'

'Mm. Is it a large town?'

'About a million, according to Lev.'

'Right. You haven't got anything else? Other people who knew him and might have his address?'

Trond hesitated before shaking his head.

'Out with it,' Harry said.

'Lev and I went for a coffee last time we met in Oslo. He said it tasted even worse than usual. Said he'd taken to drinking *cafezinho* at a local *ahwa*.'

'*Ahwa*? Isn't that an Arab coffee house?'

'Correct. *Cafezinho* is a kind of strong Brazilian variant of espresso. Lev says he goes there every day. Drinks coffee, smokes a hookah and plays dominoes with the Syrian owner who has become a kind of pal. I can remember his name – Muhammed Ali. Like the boxer.'

'And fifty million other Arabs. Did your brother say which coffee bar it was?'

'Probably, but I don't remember. There can't be so many *ahwas* in a Brazilian town, can there?'

'Maybe not.' Harry thought. Definitely something concrete to work on. He was about to put a hand to his forehead, but as soon as he tried to raise his hand his neck hurt.

'One last question, Grette. What made you decide to tell me this?'

Trond's teacup did a few circuits. 'I knew he was here in Oslo.'

The towel felt like a heavy rope around Harry's neck. 'How?'

Trond scratched under his chin for a long time before answering. 'We hadn't spoken for over two years. Out of the blue he rang me and said he was in town. We met at a café and had a long chat. Hence, the coffee.'

'When was this?'

'Three days before the bank raid.'

'What did you talk about?'

'Everything. And nothing. When you've known one another for as long as we have, the big things have often grown so big it's the small things you talk about. About . . . the old man's roses, etc.'

'What sort of big things?'

'Things done that were best undone. And things said best unsaid.'

'So you talk about roses instead?'

'I tended the roses when Stine and I were left in the house. It was where Lev and I had grown up. It was where I wanted our children to grow up.' He bit his lower lip. His gaze was fixed on the brown-and-white wax cloth; the cloth was the only thing Harry had taken when his mother died.

'He didn't say anything about the robbery?'

Trond shook his head.

'You're aware the robbery must have been planned at that point. That your wife's bank was going to be hit?'

Trond let out a deep sigh. 'Had that been the case, I might have known and could have prevented it. Lev relished telling me about his bank robberies, you see. He got hold of copies of the videos, which he kept in the loft in Disengrenda, and every so often insisted we watch them together. To see what a clever big brother he was. When I married Stine and started working, I made it clear I wouldn't listen to any more of his plans. It would put me in a delicate position.'

'Mm. So he didn't know Stine worked in the bank?'

'I had told him she worked for Nordea, but not which branch, I don't think.'

'But they knew each other?'

'They had met a few times, yes. A couple of family gatherings. Lev was never a big fan of that sort of thing.'

'How did they get on?'

'Well, Lev can be a charmer when he wants to be.' Trond smiled wryly. 'As I said, we shared one set of genes. I was happy he could be bothered to show his good side to her. And since I had told her how he could behave towards people he didn't appreciate, she was flattered. The first time she came to our house he took her around our neighbourhood and showed her all the places he and I had played when we were small.'

'Not the footbridge though?'

'No, not that.' Trond lifted his hands pensively and looked at them. 'But you mustn't believe that was for his own sake. Lev was more than happy to talk about all the bad things he had done. It was because he knew I didn't want her to know I had a brother like that.'

'Mm. Are you sure you're not painting a nobler picture of your brother than he deserves?'

Trond shook his head. 'Lev has a dark and a light side. Like all of us. He would die for those he likes.'

'But not in prison?'

Trond opened his mouth, but no answer came out. His skin twitched under one eye. Harry sighed and, with difficulty, stood up. 'I have to get a taxi to A&E.'

'I've got a car,' Trond said.

*

The engine hummed quietly. Harry stared at the streetlights gliding by in the dark night sky, the dashboard and the diamond ring glinting on Trond's little finger as he held the steering wheel.

'You lied about the ring you're wearing,' Harry whispered. 'The diamond is too small to cost thirty thousand. I reckon it cost about five and you bought it for Stine at a jeweller's here in Oslo. Am I right?'

Trond nodded.

'You met Lev in São Paulo, didn't you. The money was for him.'

Trond nodded again.

'Enough money to keep him going,' Harry said. 'Enough for a plane ticket when he decided to return to Oslo to do another job.'

Trond didn't answer.

'Lev's still in Olso,' Harry whispered. 'I want his mobile number.'

'Do you know what?' Trond carefully turned right by Alexander Kiellands plass. 'Last night I dreamed that Stine came into the bedroom and talked to me. She was dressed as an angel. Not like a real angel, but the kind of outfit you wear at carnivals. She said she didn't belong up there. And when I awoke, I thought of Lev. I thought of him sitting on the edge of the school roof with his legs dangling down as we went into the next lesson. He was a small dot, but I remember what I was thinking. He belonged up there.'

25

Baksheesh

THREE PEOPLE WERE SITTING IN IVARSSON'S OFFICE: Ivarsson, behind the tidy desk, and Beate and Harry each in their – slightly lower – chairs. The trick with the low chairs is such a well-known dominance technique that one could be excused for thinking it was no longer used, but Ivarsson knew better. His experience was that basic techniques never went out of fashion.

Harry had tipped his chair back so that he could see out of the window. The view took in the Hotel Plaza. Rounded clouds swept over the glass tower and the town without releasing any rain. Harry hadn't slept, even though he had taken painkillers after the tetanus injection he had received at the hospital. The explanation he had given to his colleagues of a stray feral dog had been original enough to be credible and close enough to the truth for him to be able to carry it off with some conviction. His neck was swollen and the tight bandage chafed against his skin. Harry knew exactly how much it would hurt if he twisted his head towards Ivarsson, who was talking. He also knew he wouldn't have turned his head, even if it hadn't hurt.

'So you want air tickets to Brazil to search there?' Ivarsson said, brushing the tabletop clean and pretending to stifle a smile. 'While the Expeditor is demonstrably busy robbing banks here in Oslo?'

'We don't know where in Oslo he is,' Beate said. 'Or whether he is in Oslo. But we hope we can trace the house his brother says he has in Porto Seguro. If we find it, we'll also find his fingerprints. And if they match the prints we have on the Coca-Cola bottle, we have damning evidence. That ought to make the trip worthwhile.'

'Really? And which prints are these that no one else has?'

Beate struggled in vain to catch Harry's eye. She swallowed. 'Since the principle is that we are meant to be independent of each other, we decided to keep it to ourselves. Until further notice.'

'Dear Beate,' Ivarsson began, winking his right eye. 'You say "we" but I only hear Harry Hole. I appreciate Hole's keenness to adhere to my method, but we mustn't let principles stand in the way of results we can achieve together. So I repeat: which prints?'

Beate sent Harry a desperate look.

'Hole?' Ivarsson said.

'This is how we're running it,' Harry said. 'Until further notice.'

'As you like,' Ivarsson said. 'But forget the trip. You'll have to talk to the Brazilian police and ask them to help you to get hold of prints.'

Beate cleared her throat. 'I've checked. We have to send written applications via the Chief Constable in Bahia province and have a Brazilian district attorney go through the case, which will eventually result in a search warrant. The person I spoke to said that from experience this would take, without contacts in the Brazilian administration, somewhere between two months and two years.'

'We've got seats on the plane leaving tomorrow evening,' Harry said, studying a fingernail. 'What's the decision?'

Ivarsson laughed. 'What do you think? You come to ask me for money for plane tickets to the other side of the globe without even bothering to state the reasons for such a trip. You plan to search a house without a warrant, so that even if you found forensic evidence, the court would probably be obliged to reject it because you used illegal means to acquire it.'

'The old brick trick,' Harry said softly.

'I beg your pardon?'

'An unknown person heaves a brick through a window. The police happen to chance by and do not need a warrant to enter. They think there is a smell of marijuana in the sitting room. A subjective perception, but a justified reason for an immediate search. You secure forensic evidence, such as fingerprints, from the place. Very legal.'

'In short – we've thought about what you're saying,' Beate hastened to add. 'If we find the house, we'll collect the prints by legal means.'

'Oh, yes?'

'Hopefully without the brick.'

Ivarsson shook his head. 'Not good enough. The answer is a loud, resounding no.' He looked at his watch to signal the meeting was over and added with a thin reptilian smile: 'Until further notice.'

'Couldn't you have given him a bone?' Beate said on leaving Ivarsson's office and heading down the corridor.

'Such as what?' Harry said, carefully turning his neck. 'He'd made up his mind beforehand.'

'You didn't even give him a chance to give us tickets.'

'I gave him a chance not to be overruled.'

'What do you mean?' They stopped in front of the lift.

'What I told you. On this case we've been given certain freedoms.'

Beate turned towards him and stared. 'I think I see,' she said slowly. 'So what happens now?'

'He'll be overruled. Don't forget suncream.' The lift doors opened.

Later that day Bjarne Møller told Harry that Ivarsson had taken the Chief Constable's decision to let Harry and Beate go to Brazil and charge the travel and accommodation costs to the Robberies Unit very badly.

'Pleased with yourself now?' Beate said to Harry before he went home.

However, as Harry passed the Plaza and the heavens finally opened, strangely enough, he felt no satisfaction at all. Just embarrassment, and exhaustion from pain and lack of sleep.

*

'*Baksheesh*?' Harry screamed down the phone. 'What the hell is *baksheesh*?'

'Slush fund,' Øystein said. 'No one lifts a finger in this damned country without slush.'

'Fuck!' Harry kicked the table in front of the mirror. The telephone slid off the table and the receiver was tugged out of his hand.

'Hello? Are you there, Harry?' the phone on the floor crackled. Harry felt like leaving it where it was. Going away. Or putting on a Metallica record at full blast. One of the old ones.

'Don't go to pieces now, Harry!' the voice squeaked.

Harry bent down with a straight neck and picked up the receiver. 'Sorry, Øystein. How much did you say they wanted?'

'Twenty thousand Egyptian. Forty thousand Norwegian. Then I'll get the client served on a silver platter, they said.'

'They're screwing us, Øystein.'

'Of course they are. Do we want the client or not?'

'Money's on its way. Make sure you get a receipt, OK?'

Harry lay in bed staring at the ceiling as he waited for the triple dose of painkillers to kick in. The last thing he saw before tumbling into the darkness was a boy sitting up above, dangling his legs and looking down at him.

PART IV

26

D'Ajuda

FRED BAUGESTAD HAD A HANGOVER. HE WAS THIRTY-ONE years old, divorced and worked on Statfjord B oil rig as a roughneck. It was hard work and there was not a sniff of beer while he was on the job, but the money was great, there was a TV in your room, gourmet food and best of all: three weeks on, four weeks off. Some travelled home to their wives and gawped at the walls, some drove taxis or built houses so as not to go mad with boredom and some did what Fred did: went to a hot country and tried to drink themselves to death. Now and again, he wrote a postcard to Karmøy, his daughter, or 'the baby' as he still called her even though she was ten. Or was it eleven? Anyway, that was the only contact he still had with the Continental mainland, and that was enough. The last time he had spoken with his father, he had complained about Fred's mother being arrested for pinching biscuits from Rimi supermarket again. 'I pray for her,' his father had said and wondered if Fred had a Norwegian Bible with him where he was. 'The Book is as indispensable as breakfast, Dad,' Fred had answered. Which was true, as Fred never ate before lunch when he was in d'Ajuda. Unless you consider *caipirinhas* food. Which was a question of definition since he poured at least four spoonfuls of sugar in every cocktail. Fred Baugestad drank *caipirinhas* because they were genuinely bad. In Europe the drink had an undeservedly good reputation as it was made with rum or vodka instead of *cachaça* – the raw bitter Brazilian *aguardente* distilled from sugar cane, which made the drinking of *caipirinhas* the penitent act Fred claimed it was meant to be. Both Fred's grandfathers had been alcoholics, and with that kind of genetic make-up he thought it was best to err on the safe side and drink something which was so bad he could never become dependent on it.

Today he had dragged himself to Muhammed's at twelve and taken an espresso and brandy before slowly walking back in the quivering heat along the narrow pitted gravel track between the small, low, relatively white houses. The house he and Roger rented was one of the less white houses. The plaster was chipped, and inside, the grey untreated walls were so permeated by the damp wind blowing in off the Atlantic that you could taste the pungent wall smell by sticking out your tongue. But then, why would you do that, Fred mused. The house was good enough. Three bedrooms, two mattresses, one refrigerator and one stove. Plus a sofa and a tabletop on two Leca blocks in the room they defined as the sitting room since it had an almost square hole in the wall which they called a window. True enough, they should have cleaned up a bit more often – the kitchen was infested with yellow fire ants capable of a terrifying bite – but Fred didn't often go there after the refrigerator was moved to the sitting room. He was lying on the sofa planning his next move of the day when Roger came in.

'Where have you been?' Fred asked.

'At the chemist in Porto,' Roger said with a smile which went right the way round his broad, blotchy head. 'You won't fucking believe what they sell over the counter there. You can get things you can't even get a prescription for in Norway.' He emptied the contents of a plastic bag and began to read the labels aloud.

'Three milligrams of Benzodiazepine. Two milligrams of Flunitrazepam. Shit, we're practically talking Rohypnol!'

Fred didn't answer.

'Bad?' Roger effervesced. 'Haven't you had anything to eat yet?'

'*Não*. Just a coffee at Muhammed's. By the way, there was some mysterious guy in there asking Muhammed about Lev.'

Roger's head shot up from the pharmaceutical items. 'About Lev? What did he look like?'

'Tall. Blond. Blue eyes. Sounded Norwegian.'

'Fuck me, don't frighten me like that, Fred.' Roger resumed his reading.

'What do you mean?'

'Let me put it this way. If he'd been tall, dark and thin, it would have been time to leave d'Ajuda. And the western hemisphere for that matter. Did he look like a cop?'

'What do cops look like?'

'They . . . forget it, oil man.'

'He looked like a boozer. I know what they look like.'

'OK. May be a pal of Lev's. Shall we help him?'

Fred shook his head. 'Lev said he lives here totally in . . . incog . . . something Latin meaning secret. Muhammed pretended he'd never heard of Lev. The guy will find Lev if Lev wants him to.'

'I was kidding. Where is Lev, incidentally? I haven't seen him for several weeks.'

'Last I heard, he was going to Norway,' Fred said, slowly raising his head.

'Maybe he robbed a bank and got caught,' Roger said and smiled at the thought. Not because he wanted Lev to be caught, but because the thought of robbing banks always made him smile. He himself had done it three times, and it had given him a big kick every time. Fair enough, they were caught the first two times, but the third time they did everything right. When he described the coup, he usually omitted to mention the lucky circumstance that the surveillance cameras had been temporarily out of service, but nevertheless the rewards had allowed him to enjoy his otium – and from time to time his opium – here in d'Ajuda.

The beautiful little village lay to the south of Porto Seguro and until recently had housed the Continent's largest collection of wanted individuals south of Bogotá. It had begun in the seventies when d'Ajuda became a rallying point for hippies and travellers who lived off gambling and selling home-made jewellery and body decorations in Europe during the summer months. They meant welcome extra income for d'Ajuda and, by and large, didn't bother anyone, so the two Brazilian families who in principle owned all the trade and industry in the village came to an understanding with the local Chief of Police, as a result of which a blind eye was turned to the smoking of marijuana on the beach, in cafés, in the growing number of bars and, as time went on, in the streets and anywhere at all.

There was one problem, however: the fines given to tourists for smoking marijuana and breaking other rather unknown laws were, as in other places, an important source of income for the police, who were paid a pittance by the state. So that the lucrative tourist business and the police could coexist in harmony, the two families had to provide the police with alternative secure earnings. This started with an American sociologist and his Argentinian boyfriend, who were responsible for the local production and sale of marijuana, being forced to pay a commission to the Chief of Police for protection and a guaranteed monopoly – in other words potential competitors were promptly arrested and delivered to the federal police with all due pomp and ceremony. Money trickled into the pockets of the few local police officers and everything was hunky-dory until three Mexicans offered to pay a higher commission, and one Sunday morning the American and the Argentinian were delivered to the federal police with all due pomp and ceremony in the market square in front of the post office. Nevertheless, the efficient market-regulated system for the buying and selling of protection continued to flourish, and soon d'Ajuda was full of wanted criminals from all corners of the world who could be sure of a relatively safe existence for a price way below what they would have to pay in Pattaya or many other places. However, in the eighties this beautiful and hitherto almost untouched jewel of nature with long beaches, red sunsets and excellent marijuana was discovered by the tourist vultures – the backpackers. They streamed to d'Ajuda in large numbers, with a determination to consume, which meant that the two families in the town had to reassess the economic viability of d'Ajuda as a camp for fugitives from the law. As the snug, dark bars were converted into diving equipment hire shops, and the café where the locals had danced their lambada in the old way began to arrange 'Wild-Wild-Moon party' nights, the police had to undertake lightning raids on the small white houses with increasing frequency and drive the wildly protesting captives off to the square. But it was still safer for a lawbreaker to be in d'Ajuda than in many other places in the world, even though paranoia had crept under everyone's skin, not just Roger's.

That was why there was also room for a man like Muhammed Ali in d'Ajuda's food chain. The main justification for his existence was that he had a strategic observation post in the square where the bus from Porto Seguro had its terminus. From behind the counter in his open *ahwa* Muhammed had a full view of everything that happened in d'Ajuda's sole, sun-baked, cobblestoned *plaza*. When new buses arrived he stopped serving coffee and putting Brazilian tobacco – a poor replacement for his home-grown *m'aasil* – in the hookah, in order to check over the new arrivals and spot possible police officers or bounty hunters. If his unerring nose placed anyone in the former category, he immediately sounded the alarm. The alarm was a kind of subscription arrangement whereby those who paid the monthly charge were phoned or had a message pinned to their door by the small, fleet-footed Paulinho. Muhammed also had a personal reason for keeping an eye on incoming buses. When he and Rosalita fled from her husband and Rio, he hadn't a moment's doubt what awaited them if the spurned party found out where they were. You could have simple murders carried out for a couple of hundred dollars if you went to the *favelas* of Rio or São Paulo, but even an experienced professional hit man didn't take more than two to three thousand dollars plus expenses for a search-and-destroy job, and it had been a buyers' market for the last ten years. On top of that, there was a bulk discount for couples.

Sometimes people Muhammed had marked out as bounty hunters walked straight into his *ahwa*. For appearance's sake, they ordered a coffee, and at a suitable point down the coffee cup, they asked the inevitable question: Do-you-know-where-my-friend-such-and-such-lives? or Do-you-know-the-man-in-this-picture? I-owe-him-some-money. In such cases, Muhammed received a supplementary fee if his stock answer ('I saw him take the bus to Porto Seguro with a big suitcase two days ago, *senhor*') resulted in the bounty hunter leaving again on the first bus.

When the tall, blond man in the creased linen suit, with the white bandage around his neck, put a bag and a Playstation carrier bag on the counter, wiped the sweat off his brow and ordered a coffee in English, Muhammed could smell a few extra *reais* on top of the fixed fee. It wasn't the man who aroused his instincts, though; it was the woman with him. She might just as well have written POLICE across her forehead.

Harry scanned the bar. Apart from him, Beate and the Arab behind the counter, there were three people in the café. Two backpackers and a tourist of the more down-at-heel variety, apparently nursing a serious hangover. Harry's neck was killing him. He looked at his watch. It was twenty hours since they had left Oslo. Oleg had rung, the Tetris record was beaten and Harry had managed to buy a Namco G-Con 45 at the computer-game shop in Heathrow before flying on to Recife. They had taken a propeller plane to Porto Seguro. Outside the airport he had negotiated what was probably a crazy price with a taxi driver, who drove them to a ferry to take them to the d'Ajuda side where a bus jolted them the last few kilometres.

It was twenty-four hours since he had been sitting in the visitors' room explaining to Raskol that he needed another 40,000 kroner for the Egyptians. Raskol had explained to him that Muhammed Ali's *ahwa* wasn't in Porto Seguro but a village nearby.

'D'Ajuda,' Raskol had said with a big smile. 'I know a couple of boys living there.'

The Arab looked at Beate, who shook her head, before putting the cup of coffee in front of Harry. It was strong and bitter.

'Muhammed,' Harry said and saw the man behind the counter stiffen. 'You are Muhammed, right?'

The Arab swallowed. 'Who's asking?'

'A friend.' Harry put his right hand inside his jacket and saw the panic on the dark-skinned face. 'Lev's little brother is trying to get hold of him.' Harry pulled out one of the photographs Beate had found at Trond's and put it on the counter.

Muhammed closed his eyes for a second. His lips seemed to be mumbling a silent prayer of gratitude.

The photograph showed two boys. The taller of the two was wearing a red quilted jacket. He was laughing and had put a friendly arm around the other one, who smiled shyly at the camera.

'I don't know whether Lev has mentioned his little brother,' Harry said. 'His name's Trond.'

Muhammed picked up the photograph and studied it.

'Hm,' he said, scratching his beard. 'I've never seen either of them. And I've never heard of anyone called Lev, either. I know most people around here.'

He gave the photograph to Harry, who returned it to his inside pocket and drained the coffee cup. 'We have to find a place to stay, Muhammed. Then we'll be back. Have a little think in the meantime.'

Muhammed shook his head, tugged at the twenty-dollar bill Harry had put under the coffee cup and passed it back. 'I don't take big notes,' he said.

Harry shrugged. 'We'll be back, anyway, Muhammed.'

*

At the little hotel called Vitória, as it was the down season they each got a large room. Harry was given key number 69, even though the hotel only had two floors and twenty-odd rooms. On pulling out the drawer of the bedside table beside the red heart-shaped bed and finding two condoms with the hotel's compliments, he assumed he had the bridal suite. The whole of the bathroom door was covered with a mirror you could see yourself in from the bed. In a disproportionately large, deep wardrobe, the only furniture in the room except for the bed, hung two somewhat worn thigh-length bathrobes with oriental symbols on the back.

The receptionist smiled and shook her head when she was shown the photographs of Lev Grette. The same happened in the adjacent restaurant and at the Internet café further up the strangely quiet main street. It led, in the traditional manner, from church to cemetery, but had been given a new name: Broadway. In the tiny grocer's shop, where they sold water and Christmas tree decorations, with SUPERMARKET written above the door, they eventually found a woman behind the till. She answered 'yes' to everything they asked about, and watched them through vacant eyes until they gave up and left. On the way back they saw one solitary person, a young policeman leaning against a jeep, arms crossed and a bulging holster slung low on his hips, following their movements with a yawn.

In Muhammed's *ahwa* the thin boy behind the counter explained that the boss had suddenly decided to take the day off and go for a walk. Beate asked when he would be back, but the boy, at a loss, shook his head, pointed to the sun and said, 'Trancoso.'

The female receptionist at the hotel said the thirteen-kilometre walk along the unbroken stretch of white sand to Trancoso was d'Ajuda's greatest landmark. Apart from the Catholic church in the square, it was also the only one.

'Mm. Why are there so few people around, *senhora*?' Harry asked.

She smiled and pointed to the sea.

*

That was where they were. On the scorching hot sand stretching in both directions as far as the eye could see in the heat haze. There were sunbathers lying in state, beach pedlars trudging through the loose sand, bowed beneath the weight of cooler bags and sacks of fruit, bartenders grinning from makeshift bars where loudspeakers blasted out samba music under straw roofs, and surfers in the yellow national strip, their lips painted white with zinc oxide. And two people walking south with their shoes in their hands. One in shorts, a skimpy top and a straw hat which she had changed into at the hotel, the other still bare-headed in his creased linen suit.

'Did she say thirteen kilometres?' Harry said, blowing away the bead of sweat hanging off the tip of his nose.

'It'll be dark before we get back,' Beate said, pointing. 'Look, everyone else is coming back.'

There was a black stripe along the beach, an apparently endless caravan of people on their way home with the afternoon sun at their backs.

'Just what we ordered,' Harry said, straightening his sunglasses. 'A line-up of the whole of d'Ajuda. We'll have to keep our eyes peeled. If we don't see Muhammed, perhaps we'll be lucky and bump into Lev in person.'

Beate smiled. 'Bet you a hundred we don't.'

Faces flickered by in the heat. Black, white, young, old, beautiful, ugly, stoned, abstemious, smiling, scowling faces. The bars and the surfboard hire stalls were gone. All they could see was sand and sea to the left, and dense jungle vegetation to the right. Here and there, people were sitting in groups with the unmistakable smell of joints wafting over.

'I've been thinking more about that intimate-space stuff and our insider theory,' Harry said. 'Do you think Lev and Stine Grette could have known each other as more than brother- and sister-in-law?'

'You mean she was involved in the planning, and then he shot her to cover his tracks?' Beate peered at the sun. 'Well, why not?'

Even though it was past four o'clock, the heat had not noticeably relented. They removed their shoes to cross some rocks, and on the other side Harry found a thick, dry branch the sea had washed up. He stuck the branch in the sand and took the wallet and passport out of his jacket before hanging it on the makeshift hatstand.

They could see Trancoso in the distance now and Beate said they had just passed a man she had seen in a video. At first Harry thought she meant some semi-famous actor until she said he was called Roger Person, and that in addition to various narcotics charges, he had done time for robbing the post office in Gamlebyen and Veitvet. He was suspected of robbing the post office in Ulleval.

Fred had knocked back three *caipirinhas* at the beach restaurant in Trancoso, but still thought it had been a senseless idea to walk thirteen kilometres just – as Roger had put it – to 'air their skin before it started to go mouldy, too'.

'Your problem is you can't sit still because of those new pills,' Fred whined to his friend, who was lolloping ahead on tiptoes with his knees raised.

'So what? You need to burn off a few calories before going back to the smorgasbord in the North Sea. Tell me what Muhammed said on the phone about the two police officers.'

Roger sighed and reluctantly searched his short-term memory. 'He talked about a small woman who was so pale she was almost transparent. And a big German with a boozer's nose.'

'German?'

'Muhammed was guessing. Could have been Russian. Or an Inca Indian or . . .'

'Very funny. Was he sure they were cops?'

'What do you mean?' Roger stopped and Fred almost walked into him.

'I'm just saying I don't like it,' Roger said. 'As far as I know Lev didn't do bank jobs outside Norway. And Norwegian police don't come to Brazil to nab one stinking bank robber. Probably Russian. Fuck. We know who sent them. And it isn't Lev they're after.'

Fred groaned. 'Don't start all that gypsy shit again, please.'

'You think it's paranoia, but he's Satan himself. He doesn't think twice before plugging people who cheated him out of a krone. I never thought he would find out. I just took a couple of thousand for pocket money from one of the bags, didn't I. But it's the principle, you know. If you're the leader of the pack, you've got to have respect unless—'

'Roger! If I wanted to hear all this mafia crap, I could hire a video.'

Roger didn't answer.

'Hello? Roger?'

'Shut up,' Roger whispered. 'Don't turn round and keep going.'

'Hey?'

'If you weren't so pissed, you would have seen we just passed one transparent job and one boozer's conk.'

'Is that a fact?' Fred craned his head. 'Roger . . .'

'Yes?'

'I think you're right.' They turned round.

Roger continued to walk without looking back. 'Fuckfuckfuck!'

'What do we do?'

When he didn't get an answer, Fred looked back and discovered Roger had gone. He examined the sand in amazement – the deep footprint Roger had left – and followed the prints leading abruptly to the left. Up ahead, he saw Roger's flailing heels. Then Fred began to run towards the dense, green vegetation, too.

Harry gave up almost at once.

'There's no point,' he shouted after Beate, who faltered, then stopped.

They were only a few metres from the beach, yet it was as if they were in another world. A steamy, stagnant heat hung between the tree trunks in the pitch black beneath the leafy ceiling. What might have been the sounds of the two fleeing men were drowned by the bird screams and the roar of the sea behind them.

'The one at the back didn't exactly look like a sprinter,' Beate said.

'They know the paths better than we do,' Harry said. 'We haven't got any weapons, but maybe they have.'

'If Lev hasn't already been warned, he will be now. So what do we do?'

Harry rubbed the soaked neck bandage. The mosquitoes had already managed to sneak in a few bites. 'We switch to plan B.'

'Oh? And that is?'

Harry looked at Beate and wondered how it could be that there wasn't a drop of sweat to be seen on her forehead while he was leaking like rotten guttering.

'We're going fishing.'

The sunset was brief but it was a pageant of all the spectrum's shades of red. Plus a few, Muhammed reckoned, pointing to the sun, which had just melted into the horizon like a knob of butter on a hot frying pan.

The German in front of the counter was not interested in the sunset, however. He had just said he would give a thousand dollars to anyone who could help him to find Lev Grette or Roger Person. Would Muhammed mind passing on the offer? Interested informants could apply to room 69 at Vitória Hotel, said the German before leaving the *ahwa* with the pale woman.

The swallows ran amok when the insects came out for their brief evening dance. The sun had melted into a runny red mush on the surface of the sea and ten minutes later it was dark.

When Roger turned up an hour later, cursing, he was pale under his tan.

'Gyppo greaser,' he mumbled to Muhammed, and said he had already heard about the fat reward at Fredo's bar and had left instantly. On his way he had stuck his head into the supermarket, where Petra had told him the German and the blonde woman had been twice. The last time they had bought a fishing line; they hadn't asked any questions.

'What do they want that for?' he asked, casting cursory glances around him while Muhammed poured the coffee. 'Fishing perhaps?'

'There you are,' Muhammed said, motioning towards the cup. 'Good for paranoia.'

'Paranoia?' Roger shouted. 'This is good common sense. A thousand fucking dollars! People round here would happily sell their mothers for a tenth of that.'

'What are you going to do then?'

'What I have to do. Pre-empt the German.'

'Really? How?'

Roger tasted the coffee while pulling out a black pistol with a short red-brown butt from his waistband. 'Say hello to Taurus PT92C from São Paulo.'

'No, thank you,' Muhammed hissed. 'Take that away this minute. You're insane. Do you think you can take the German on alone?'

Roger shrugged and put the pistol back in his waistband.

'Fred is at home shaking. He said he'll never sober up again.'

'This man is a pro, Roger.'

Roger sniffed. 'And me? I've robbed a few banks, I have. And do you know what the most important thing is, Muhammed? The element of surprise. It means everything.' Roger drained his cup of coffee. 'And I doubt he's much of a fucking pro if he goes around telling every Tom, Dick and Harry which room he's in.'

Muhammed rolled his eyes and crossed himself.

'Allah can see you, Muhammed,' Roger muttered drily and got up.

Roger saw the blonde woman as soon as he entered the reception area. She was sitting with a group of men watching a football match on the TV above the counter. That was right, it was *flaflu* tonight, the traditional local derby between Flamengo and Fluminese in Rio. That was why Fredo's had been so full.

He quickly walked past them, hoping he hadn't been seen. Ran up the carpeted stairs and continued along the corridor. He knew all too well which room it was. When Petra's husband was due to be out of town on business, Roger reserved room 69.

Roger placed his ear against the door, but heard nothing. He peered through the keyhole, but it was dark inside. Either the German had gone out or he was asleep. Roger swallowed. His heart was pounding, but the broken half of the upper he had taken kept him calm. He checked the pistol was loaded and the catch was off before gently pressing down the handle. The door was open! Roger slipped into the room and quietly closed the door behind him. He stood in the dark holding his breath. Neither sight nor sound of anyone. No movements, no breathing. Just the gentle revolutions of the ceiling fan. Fortunately Roger knew the room intimately. He pointed the pistol where he knew the heart-shaped bed to be, as his eyes became used to the dark. A narrow strip of moonlight cast a pale sheen on the bed where the duvet had been thrown aside. Empty. He thought quickly. Could the German have gone out and forgotten to lock up? If so, Roger could just settle down and wait until the German returned to be a target in the doorway. It all seemed too good to be true, like a bank which had forgotten to activate the time lock. It just doesn't happen. The ceiling fan.

Enlightenment came that very second.

Roger jumped when he heard the sudden sound of flushing water from the bathroom. The guy had been sitting on the toilet! Roger grabbed the pistol with both hands and with outstretched arms pointed it at where he knew the bathroom door was. Five seconds passed. Eight. Roger couldn't hold his breath any longer. What the fuck was the guy waiting for? He had flushed. Twelve seconds. Perhaps he had heard something. Perhaps he was trying to escape. Roger remembered there was a little window in one wall. Shit! This was his chance; he couldn't let the guy get away. Roger crept past the wardrobe containing the dressing gown which looked so good on Petra, stood in front of the bathroom door and rested his hand on the handle. Took a deep breath. He was about to press when he felt a tiny draught. Not from a fan or an open window. It was something else.

'Freeze,' said a voice directly behind him. And after raising his head and looking in the mirror on the bathroom door, Roger did just that. He froze so much his teeth were chattering. The door of the wardrobe had come open and inside, between the white dressing gowns, he could make out a powerfully built figure. But this wasn't what caused the sudden bout of freezing. The psychological effect of discovering someone has a much bigger weapon trained on you than the one you are holding is not diminished by having some under-standing of weaponry. On the contrary. You know how much more efficiently large-bore bullets destroy a human body. Roger's Taurus PT92C was a peashooter compared with the large, black monster he glimpsed in the moonlight behind him. A squeaking noise made Roger look up. What seemed to be a fishing line glistened. It went from the crack over the bathroom door to the wardrobe.

'*Guten Abend*,' Roger whispered.

Six years later, when Roger happened to be waved over to a bar in Pattaya, only to discover Fred behind all the whiskers, he was at first so surprised that he stood there without reacting until Fred pulled over a chair.

Fred ordered drinks and told him he no longer worked in the North Sea. Disability allowance. Roger sat down hesitantly and explained, without going into detail, that for the last six years he had been running a courier business from Chang Rai. After a couple of drinks Fred cleared his throat and asked what had actually taken place the evening Roger suddenly upped sticks from d'Ajuda.

Roger peered into his glass, took a deep breath and said he hadn't had a choice. The German, who incidentally wasn't German, had tricked him and been on the point of dispatching him into the beyond there and then. However, at the last moment Roger had struck a deal with him. Roger would have thirty minutes to clear out of d'Ajuda, if he told him where Lev Grette lived.

'What kind of gun did you say the guy had?' Fred asked.

'Too dark to see. It wasn't a well-known make, anyway. I can promise you, though, it would have blown my head all the way down to Fredo's.' Roger threw a quick glance in the direction of the door.

'I've found a pad here,' Fred said. 'Have you got somewhere to stay?'

Roger looked at Fred as if he hadn't given the idea a moment's thought. He rubbed his stubble for a long time before replying.

'Actually, I haven't.'

27

Edvard Grieg

LEV'S HOUSE WAS AT THE END OF A CUL-DE-SAC. IT WAS LIKE most in the vicinity, a simple structure, the difference being that this house did actually have glass in the windows. One solitary streetlamp cast a yellow cone of light over an impressive variety of fauna fighting for living space as gluttonous bats dived in and out of the dark.

'Doesn't look like anyone is at home,' Beate whispered.

'Perhaps he's saving electricity,' Harry said.

They stopped in front of a low, rusty iron gate.

'How do we do this then?' Beate asked. 'Go up and knock on the door?'

'No. You switch on your mobile and wait here. When you can see I'm under the window, ring this number.' He gave her a page torn out of a notebook.

'Why?'

'If I hear a mobile phone ringing inside the house, we can assume Lev is at home.'

'Right. And how were you thinking of arresting him? With that?' She pointed to the black bulky object Harry held in his right hand.

'Why not?' Harry said. 'It worked on Roger Person.'

'He was in a dark room and only saw it in a fairground mirror, Harry.'

'Well, since we aren't allowed to carry weapons in Brazil, we have to use what we have.'

'Like fishing line tied to the loo and a toy?'

'This is not just any toy, Beate. This is a Namco G-Con 45.' He patted the super-lifesize plastic pistol.

'At least take off the Playstation sticker,' Beate said, shaking her head.

Harry undid his shoes and ran stooped across the dry, cracked ground which once had been laid as a lawn. He arrived, sat with his back to the wall under the window and signalled with his hand to Beate. He couldn't see her, but knew she could see him against the white wall. He gazed up at the sky where the universe was on display. Seconds later, the faint but distinct ringtone of a mobile phone sounded in the house. 'In the Hall of the Mountain King'. *Peer Gynt*. The man had a sense of humour.

Harry focused on one of the stars and tried to empty his head of all other thoughts than what he had to do. He couldn't. Once Aune had asked why we wonder if there is life out there, when we know there are more suns in our galaxy alone than grains of sand on the average beach? We ought to be asking ourselves if there was a chance they were peace-loving, then weigh up whether it was worth taking the risk of contacting them. Harry squeezed the handle of the gun. He was asking himself the same question now.

The telephone had stopped playing Grieg. Harry waited. Then he breathed in and tiptoed to the door. He listened but all he could hear was crickets. He wrapped his hand around the door handle, expecting it to be locked.

It was.

He cursed to himself. He had made up his mind beforehand that if it was locked and they lost the element of surprise, they should wait until the following day and buy some ironware before going back. He doubted it would be a problem buying two decent handguns in a place like this. But he also had the feeling Lev would soon be informed of the day's events and they didn't have a lot of time.

Harry jumped as a pain seared through his right foot. He automatically pulled his foot away and looked down. In the frugal light from the stars he could make out a black line down the whitewashed wall. The line ran from the door, across the stairs where his foot had been, and down the step, where he lost sight of it. He rummaged around in his pocket for a mini Maglite torch and switched it on. Ants. Large, yellow, semi-transparent ants formed into two columns – one down the steps and one in under the door. They were clearly a different order of ant from the black ants of home. It was impossible to see what they were transporting, but Harry knew enough about ants – yellow or not – to know there was something.

Harry switched off the torch. Had a think. And left. Down the steps and towards the gate. He stopped halfway, turned and began to run. The simple, rotting wooden door flew off the frame on both sides as it was struck by ninety-five kilos of Harry Hole, doing just under thirty kilometres an hour. He had one elbow tucked underneath him as he and the remains of the door smacked down on the stone floor and the pain shot up his arm and into his neck. Lying on the floor in the dark, he waited for the smooth click of a trigger. When it didn't come, he stood up and switched on his torch. The narrow path of light found the column of ants along the wall. Harry could feel from the heat beneath the bandage that he was bleeding again. He followed the glistening bodies of the ants across a filthy carpet into the next room. There the column took a sharp turn to the left and continued up the wall. The light of the torch caught a *Kama Sutra* picture on the way up. The caravan of ants forked off and continued across the ceiling. Harry leaned back. His neck hurt like never before. Now they were directly above him. He had to turn. The torch beam wandered around until it found the ants again. Was this really the shortest way for them? That was Harry's final thought before he stared into Lev Grette's face. Lev's body loomed over

Harry, who dropped the torch and reeled backwards. His brain might have told him it was too late, but his hands fumbled in a mixture of shock and stupidity for a Namco G-Con 45 to hold onto.

28

Lava Pe

BEATE COULDN'T STAND THE STENCH FOR MORE THAN A couple of minutes and had to dash out. She was bent double as Harry strolled out and sat down on the steps for a cigarette.

'Couldn't you smell it?' Beate groaned, with saliva dribbling down from her mouth and nose.

'Dysosmia.' Harry contemplated the glow of his cigarette. 'Partial loss of smell. There are some things I can't smell any more. Aune says it's because I've smelt too many bodies. Emotional trauma and so on.'

Beate retched again.

'I apologise,' she groaned. 'It was the ants. I mean, why do the disgusting creatures have to use the *nostrils* as a kind of two-lane highway?'

'Well, if you insist, I can tell you where you'll find the richest protein sources in the human body.'

'No, thank you!'

'Sorry.' Harry flicked the cigarette onto the dry ground. 'You coped very well in there, Lønn. It's not the same as videos.' He stood up and went back in.

Lev Grette was hanging from a short piece of rope tied to the lamp hook in the ceiling. He hovered a good half-metre off the floor and the overturned chair, and that was the reason the flies had enjoyed the monopoly of the corpse before the yellow ants, who continued their procession up and down the rope.

Beate had found the mobile phone with the charger on the floor beside the sofa and said she could find out when he last had a conversation. Harry went into the kitchen and switched on the light. A blue metallic cockroach stood on an A4 piece of paper, swinging its feelers towards him, and then made a rapid retreat to the cooker. Harry lifted the piece of paper. It was handwritten. He had read all sorts of suicide letters and very few had been great literature. The famous last words were usually confused babble, desperate cries for help or prosaic instructions about who would inherit the toaster and the lawnmower. One of the more meaningful ones Harry had seen was when a farmer from Maridalen had written in chalk on the barn wall: *A man has hanged himself in here. Please call the police. Apologies.* In light of this, Lev Grette's letter was, if not unique, then at least unusual.

Dear Trond,
I've always wondered how it felt when the footbridge suddenly disappeared beneath him. When the precipice opened and he knew something completely devoid of meaning was about to happen. He was going to die for no purpose. Perhaps he still had things he wanted to do. Perhaps someone was sitting and waiting for him that morning. Perhaps he thought that day would be the start of something new. In a way he was right about that …

I never told you I visited him in hospital. I took a large bunch of flowers with me and told him I had seen the whole thing from the window of my flat; I rang for the ambulance and gave the police a description of the boy and his bike. He lay there in bed, so small and grey, and he thanked me. Then I asked him a silly sports commentator question: 'How did it feel?'

He didn't answer. He just lay there with all the tubes and the drips, and watched me. Then he thanked me again and a nurse said I had to go.

So I never knew what it felt like. Until one day when the precipice opened beneath me too. It didn't happen when I was running up Industrigata after the robbery. Or while I was counting the money afterwards. Or while I was watching the news. It happened the same way it happened to the old man. One morning I was walking along happily, unaware of any danger. The sun was shining, I was safely back in d'Ajuda, I could relax and began to think. I had taken from the person I loved most what they loved most. I had two million kroner to live off, but nothing to live for. That was this morning.

I don't expect you to understand this, Trond. I robbed a bank, I saw she recognised me, I was caught in a game with its own rules, none of this has any place in your world. I don't expect you to understand what I am doing now, but perhaps you can see that it is possible to get tired of this, too. Of living.
Lev

PS It didn't strike me at the time that the old man didn't smile when he thanked me. I thought about it today, though, Trond. Perhaps he didn't have anything or anyone waiting for him after all. Perhaps he just felt relief when the precipice opened and he thought he wouldn't have to do it himself.

Beate was standing on a chair beside Lev's body when Harry came in. She was struggling to bend one of Lev's fingers so she could press it against the inside of a small shiny metal box.

'Blast,' she said. 'The ink pad has been standing in the sun at the hotel and it's dried out.'

'If you can't get a good print, we'll have to use the firemen's method.'

'And that is?'

'People caught in a fire automatically use their hands. Even on charred bodies the skin on the fingertips may be intact and you can use fingerprints to identify bodies. Sometimes, for practical reasons, firemen cut off a finger and take it to Forensics.'

'That's called desecration of a body.'

Harry shrugged. 'If you look at his other hand, you can see he's already missing one finger.'

'I can see,' she said. 'Looks like it's been cut off. What might that mean?'

Harry went closer and shone the torch. 'It means the finger was cut off long after he hanged himself. Someone may have come here and seen he'd already done the job for them.'

'Who?'

'Well, in some countries gypsies punish thieves by cutting their fingers off,' Harry said. 'If they stole from gypsies, that is.'

'I think I've got a good print,' Beate said, wiping the sweat off her brow. 'Shall we cut him down?'

'No,' Harry said. 'As soon as we've had a look around, we'll tidy up after us and clear off. I saw a phone box in the main street. I'll phone the police anonymously from there and report the death. When we get to Oslo, you can phone the Brazilian police and have the medical report sent. I have no doubt he died of asphyxiation, but I want the time of death.'

'What about the door?'

'Not much we can do about that.'

'And your neck? The bandage is all red.'

'Forget it. My arm hurts more. I landed on it when I went through the door.'

'How bad is it?'

Harry gingerly raised his arm and grimaced. 'It's fine so long as I don't move it.'

'Think yourself lucky you haven't got the Setesdal Twitch.'

Two out of three in the room laughed, but their laughter quickly subsided.

*

On the way back to the hotel, Beate asked Harry if it all made sense to him.

'From a technical point of view, yes. Beyond that, I'll never get suicide to make sense.'

He flicked his cigarette away. It described a glowing arc in the almost tangible night. 'But that's me.'

29

Room 316

THE WINDOW OPENED WITH A BANG.

'Trond is travelling,' she trilled. Her bleached hair had obviously been given another dose of chemicals since their previous visit and her scalp shone through the devitalised hair. 'Have you been down south?'

Harry raised a tanned face and peered at her.

'In a way. Do you know where he is?'

'He's packing his car,' she said, pointing to the other side of the houses. 'I think he's going to travel, the poor thing.'

'Mm.'

Beate wanted to go, but Harry stayed put. 'You've lived here a long time, have you?' he asked.

'Oh yes. Thirty-two years.'

'You can probably remember Lev and Trond from the time they were small, can you?'

'Of course. They left their mark on Disengrenda.' She smiled and leaned against the frame of the window. 'Especially Lev. A real charmer. We always knew he would be dangerous for the ladies.'

'Dangerous, yes. Maybe you know the story about the man who fell from the footbridge?'

Her face darkened and she whispered in a tragic voice: 'Oh, yes. Dreadful business. I heard he was never able to walk properly again, the poor chap. His knees stiffened up. Can you imagine a child thinking up such a wicked trick?'

'Mm. He must have been a real wild child.'

'Wild child?' She shaded her eyes. 'I wouldn't exactly say that. He was a polite, well-brought-up boy. That was what was so shocking.'

'And everybody round here knew he'd done it?'

'Everybody. I saw him from this window. A red jacket heading off on his bike. I should have known there was something wrong when he came back. The lad's face was completely drained of colour.' She shuddered in the cold gust of wind. Then she pointed across the road.

Trond was walking towards them with his arms hanging down by his sides. He slowed down more and more until, in the end, he was hardly moving.

'It's Lev, isn't it,' he said on finally reaching them.

'Yes,' Harry said.

'Is he dead?'

From the corner of his eye he saw the gaping face in the window. 'Yes, he's dead.'

'Good,' said Trond. Then he bent over and hid his face in his hands.

Bjarne Møller stood staring through the window with a concerned expression on his face when Harry peeked in through the half-open door. Harry tapped.

Møller turned and brightened up. 'Oh, hi.'

'Here's the report, boss.' Harry tossed a green Manila wallet on his desk.

Møller fell into his chair, managed after some exertion to heap his excessively long legs under the desk and put on his glasses.

'Aha,' he mumbled as he opened the wallet inscribed LIST OF DOCUMENTS. Inside there was a solitary piece of A4 paper.

'Didn't think you'd want to know all the ins and outs,' Harry said.

'If you say so, I'm sure you're right,' Møller said, running his eyes over the generously spaced lines.

Harry looked over his boss's shoulder and out of the window. There was nothing to see, just thick damp mist which lay like a used nappy over the town. Møller put down the piece of paper.

'So you just went there, someone told you where the man lived and you found the Expeditor hanging from a rope?'

'In broad outline, yes.'

Møller shrugged his shoulders. 'Fine by me so long as we have watertight evidence that this is the man we've been looking for.'

'Weber checked the fingerprints this morning.'

'And?'

Harry sat down in the chair. 'They tally with those we found on the Coke bottle the robber was holding before he went into action.'

'Can we be sure it's the same bottle . . . ?'

'Relax, boss. We've got the bottle and the man on the video. You just read in the report that we have a handwritten suicide note in which Lev Grette confesses, didn't you? We went to Disengrenda this morning and informed Trond Grette. We asked if we could borrow some of Lev's old schoolbooks from the loft and Beate took them to the *Kripos* handwriting expert. He says there's no doubt the suicide note was written by the same person.'

'Yes, yes, yes, I just wanted to be absolutely sure before we went public with this, Harry. It's front-page news, you know.'

'You should try to be a little happier, boss.' Harry got to his feet. 'We've just solved our biggest case for a good while. The place should be festooned with streamers and balloons.'

'I'm sure you're right,' Møller sighed. He paused before asking, 'Why don't you look happier then?'

'I won't be happy until we solve the other case, you know . . .' Harry went towards the door. 'Halvorsen and I are clearing our desks today and we'll make a start on the Ellen Gjelten case tomorrow.'

He stopped in the doorway when Møller cleared his throat. 'Yes, boss?'

'I was wondering how you found out Lev Grette was the Expeditor.'

'Well, the official version is that Beate recognised him on the video. Would you like to hear the unofficial one?'

Møller was massaging a stiff knee. The concerned expression was back. 'Probably not.'

'Mm,' said Harry, standing in the doorway to the House of Pain.

'Mm,' said Beate, twisting round on her chair and glancing at the pictures rolling across the screen.

'Suppose I ought to thank you for great teamwork.'

'Same to you.'

Harry stood fingering his bunch of keys. 'Anyway,' he said. 'I don't think Ivarsson will be pissed off for very long. After all, he bathed in some of the glory as it was his idea to make us a team.'

Beate smiled faintly. 'For as long as it lasted.'

'Don't forget what I said about you-know-who.'

'No.' Her eyes flashed.

Harry pushed his shoulders forward. 'He's a bastard. It would be unconscionable of me not to tell you.'

'Lovely to know you, Harry.'

Harry let the door close behind him.

Harry unlocked the door to his flat, put down his bag and the plastic Playstation carrier in the middle of the hall floor and went to bed. Three dreamless hours later he was awoken by the telephone ringing. He turned over and saw it was 19.03 on his alarm clock; he swung his legs out of bed, shuffled into the hallway, picked up the telephone and said: 'Hi, Øystein,' before the other person could even introduce himself.

'Hello, you in Oslo, I'm at the airport in Cairo,' Øystein said. 'We said we'd speak now, didn't we?'

'You're punctuality personified,' Harry said with a yawn. 'And you're drunk.'

'Not drunk, no,' Øystein slurred indignantly. 'Just had a couple of Stellas. Or was it three? Have to watch your fluids in the desert, y'know. I'm clear-headed and sober, Harry.'

'That's good to hear. I hope you have more good news.'

'As the doctor says, there's good news and bad news. I'll tell you the good news first . . .'

'Right.'

A long pause followed, during which all Harry could hear was a crackling noise over what sounded like heavy breathing.

'Øystein?'

'Yes?'

'I'm standing here, getting as excited as a child at Christmas.'

'Hey?'

'The good news?'

'Oh, yes. Um, well, I've got the client's number, Harry. No problemo, as they say here. It was a Norwegian mobile phone number.'

'Mobile? Is that possible?'

'You can send wireless e-mails all over the world. You just connect your computer to a mobile which in turn connects to the server. That's pretty damn old news, Harry.'

'OK, but has this client a name?'

'Er . . . of course. But the guys in El Tor don't have it. They just bill the Norwegian telephone operator, Telenor in this case, who in turn invoices the end client. So I rang Information in Norway and got the name.'

'Yes?' Harry was fully awake now.

'Now we've come to the not quite such good news.'

'OK?'

'Have you checked your telephone bill recently, Harry?'

It took a few seconds before it clicked. '*My* mobile phone. Is the bastard using *my* mobile phone?'

'You no longer have it, I suppose?'

'No, I lost it that evening . . . with Anna. Fuck!'

'And it never occurred to you it might be a good idea to cancel your contract?'

'Occurred to me?' Harry groaned. 'Nothing sensible has occurred to me since this shit started, Øystein. Sorry, I'm freaking out here. It's all so simple and obvious. That was why I didn't find my phone at Anna's. And that's why he's laughing.'

'Apologies for ruining your day.'

'Hang on a moment,' Harry said, suddenly in high spirits. 'If we can prove he has my phone, we can also prove he was at Anna's after I left!'

'Yippee!' screeched the receiver. And then a more cautious: 'If it means you're happy, anyway? Hello? Harry?'

'I'm still here. I'm thinking.'

'It's good to think. You keep thinking. I've got a date with Stella. Well, several actually. And if I'm going to make the Oslo flight . . .'

'All the best, Øystein.'

Harry stood with the receiver in his hand, weighing up whether to hurl it into the mirror or not. When he woke up next day, he hoped he had dreamed the conversation with Øystein. In fact he had. Six or seven versions of it.

Raskol sat with his head bowed, resting on his hands, as Harry talked. He neither moved nor interrupted while Harry described how they had found Lev Grette and how his own mobile phone was the reason they still had no evidence against Anna's murderer. When Harry had finished, Raskol folded his hands and slowly raised his head: 'You've solved your case then, but mine remains unresolved.'

'I don't see them as your case and mine, Raskol. My responsibility—'

'I do, though, *Spiuni*,' Raskol cut in. 'I run a military organisation.'

'Mm. What exactly do you mean by that?'

Raskol closed his eyes. 'Have I told you about the time King Wu invited Sun Tzu to teach the ladies of the court the arts of war, *Spiuni*?'

'Well, no.'

Raskol smiled. 'Sun Tzu was an intellectual and he began by precisely and pedagogically explaining marching instructions to the women. When the drums rolled, they didn't march, they just giggled and laughed. 'It's the general's fault if the commands are not understood,' Sun Tzu said and explained once more. But the same happened when he gave the order to march. 'It's the officer's fault if an order is understood but not obeyed,' he said and ordered two of his men to pick out two of the leaders of the courtesans. They were lined up and beheaded in front of the other terrified women. When the king heard that his two favourite concubines had been executed, he fell ill and had to take to his bed for several days. When he got up again, he put Sun Tzu in control of his armed forces.' Raskol opened his eyes again. 'What does this story teach us, *Spiuni*?'

Harry didn't answer.

'Well, it teaches us that in a military organisation the logic has to be total and absolutely consistent. If you relax your demands, you're left with a court of giggling concubines. When you came to ask for another 40,000 kroner, you got it because I believed the story of the photograph in Anna's shoe. Because Anna is a gypsy. When we gypsies travel, we leave a *patrin* at forks in the road. A red scarf tied around a branch, a chipped bone, they all have different meanings. A photograph means someone has died. Or will die. You weren't to know, so I trusted what you said.' Raskol placed his hands on the table, palms upwards. 'But the man who took the life of my brother's daughter is free and when I look at you now I see a giggling concubine, *Spiuni*. Absolute consistency. Give me his name, *Spiuni*.'

Harry breathed in. Two words. Four syllables. If he revealed Albu's name, what sentence would be passed on Albu? Premeditated murder motivated by jealousy. Nine years, out after six? And the consequences for Harry? The investigation would inevitably uncover the fact that he, a policeman, had concealed the truth to prevent the finger of suspicion pointing at him. Shot himself in the foot. Two words, four syllables. All Harry's problems would be solved. Albu would be the one to face the final consequence.

Harry's answer was one syllable.

Raskol nodded and regarded Harry with sad eyes. 'I was afraid you would say that. You don't give me any choice then, *Spiuni*. Do you remember what I answered when you asked me why I trusted you?'

Harry nodded.

'Everyone has something they live for. Isn't that true, *Spiuni*? Something which can be taken from them. Well, does room 316 ring any bells?'

Harry didn't answer.

'Let me tell you then. Three one six is the number of a room in the International Hotel in Moscow. Olga is on watch on that floor. She'll soon be retired and would like a nice, long holiday by the Black Sea. There are three stairways and a lift to the floor. As well as the staff lift. The room has twin beds.'

Harry gulped.

Raskol rested his forehead on his folded hands: 'The little one sleeps nearest the window.'

Harry got up, went to the door and hit it hard. He could hear the echo resounding down the corridor outside. He continued to beat the door until he heard the key in the lock.

30

Vibrate Mode

'Sorry, but I came as quickly as I could,' Øystein said, driving his taxi off the pavement outside Elmer's Fruit&Tobacco shop.

'Welcome back,' Harry said, wondering whether the bus coming from the right had realised that Øystein had no intention of stopping.

'We're going to Slemdal, aren't we?' Øystein ignored the furious hooting from the bus.

'Bjørnetråkket. You know you have to give way here?'

'Decided not to.'

Harry looked across at his pal. He could just discern two bloodshot eyes behind the narrow slits.

'Tired?'

'Jet lag.'

'The time difference between here and Egypt is one hour, Øystein.'

'At least.'

Since neither the shock absorbers nor the springs in his seat worked any more, Harry felt every cobbled stone and change of level in the road as they careered through the bends on their way up to

Albu's house, but right now nothing interested him less. He borrowed Øystein's mobile phone, rang the International Hotel and room 316. Oleg answered. Harry could hear the pleasure in his voice when Oleg asked him where he was.

'In a car. Where's your mum?'

'Out.'

'I didn't think she had to go to court until tomorrow.'

'All the solicitors are meeting in Kuznetski Most,' he said in an adult voice. 'She'll be back in an hour.'

'Listen, Oleg, can you give your mum a message. Tell her to change hotel. Immediately.'

'Why?'

'Because . . . I said so. Just tell her, OK? I'll ring again later.'

'Alright.'

'Good boy. I've got to go.'

'You . . .'

'What?'

'Nothing.'

'OK. Don't forget to tell your mum what I told you.'

Øystein braked and pulled onto the pavement.

'Wait here,' Harry said and jumped out. 'If I'm not back in twenty minutes, ring the ops room, the number I gave you. Tell them—'

'Inspector Hole from Crime Squad wants a patrol car with armed officers here right away. I got it, Harry.'

'Good. If you hear shots, ring immediately.'

'Right. Which film is this again?'

Harry looked up at the house. No barking to be heard. A dark blue BMW drove slowly past them and parked further down the street. Otherwise everything was quiet.

'Most of them,' Harry breathed.

Øystein grinned. 'Cool.' Then a wrinkle of concern appeared between his eyes. 'It is cool, isn't it? Not just *insanely* dangerous?'

*

Vigdis Albu opened the door. She was wearing a freshly ironed white blouse and a short skirt, but her blurred eyes seemed to have come straight from bed.

'I rang your husband's workplace,' Harry said. 'They told me he was at home today.'

'Could be,' she said. 'He doesn't live here any more, Inspector. You were the one who dragged up this whole business with . . . with . . .' She gesticulated as if she were looking for the right word, but with a smile of distaste she resigned herself to admitting there was no other word for it: '. . . the whore.'

'May I come in, fru Albu?'

She hunched her shoulders, and shuddered to register her disgust. 'Call me Vigdis or anything, but not that.'

'Vigdis.' Harry stooped. 'May I come in now?'

The thin plucked eyebrows angled. She hesitated. Then she thrust out her hand. 'Why not?'

Harry thought he could detect a faint smell of gin, but it might have been her perfume. Nothing in the house suggested anything out of the ordinary — it was clean, fragrant and tidy. There were fresh flowers in a vase on the sideboard. Harry noticed the sofa cover was a touch whiter than the off-white he had sat on last time. Low classical music was playing from speakers he couldn't see.

'Mahler?' Harry asked.

'Greatest hits,' Vigdis said. 'Arne only bought collections. He always said everything except the best was worthless.'

'Nice that he didn't take the collections with him then. Where is he, by the way?'

'First of all, he doesn't own anything you can see here. And I neither know nor wish to know where he is. Have you got a cigarette, Inspector?'

Harry passed her the packet and watched her fumbling with a large teak-and-silver table lighter. He leaned over the table with his disposable version.

'Thank you. He's abroad, I would guess. Somewhere hot. Not as hot as I would like it to be, I'm afraid.'

'Mm. What do you mean he doesn't own anything here?'

'Exactly what I say. The house, the furnishings, the car – it's all mine.' She blew out the smoke with force. 'Ask my solicitor.'

'I thought your husband had the money for—'

'Don't call him that!' Vigdis seemed to be trying to suck all the tobacco out of the cigarette. 'Yes, Arne had money. He had enough to buy this house, the furniture, the cars, the suits, the chalet and the jewellery he gave me for no other reason than to show off in front of all the so-called friends. The only thing that had any meaning for Arne was what others thought of him, you see. His family, my family, colleagues, neighbours and student friends.' The anger gave her voice a harsh metallic timbre as though she were talking through a megaphone. 'Everyone was a spectator to Arne Albu's fantastic life. They were meant to applaud when things were going well. If Arne had put as much energy into running the company as he did reaping plaudits, perhaps Albu AS would not have gone downhill the way it did.'

'According to *Dagens Næringsliv* Albu AS was a successful enterprise.'

'Albu AS was a family business, not a stock-exchange-listed company which has to publish details of its accounts. Arne made it look profitable by selling off its assets.' She crushed the half-smoked cigarette in the ashtray. 'A couple of years ago the company had an acute liquidity crisis and since Arne was personally responsible for the debt, he put the house and all our other possessions in my name and the children's.'

'Yes, but the buyers paid a tidy sum. Thirty million, the papers said.'

Vigdis gave a bitter laugh. 'So you swallowed the story of the successful businessman stepping down to spend more time with his family, did you? Arne's good at PR, I'll give him that. Let me put it this way – Arne had the choice of losing the business or going bust. Naturally, he chose the former.'

'And the thirty million?'

'Arne can put on the charm when he wants to. And people fall for it. That's why he's good at negotiating, especially in pressurised situations. That was what made the bank and the supplier keep the business alive for as long as they did. Arne negotiated two clauses in the contract with the supplier in what ought to have been an unconditional capitulation. He would be allowed to keep the chalet, which was still in his name, and he got the buyer to put the purchase figure at thirty million. That didn't mean much to them as they could write the whole sum off with the debts of Albu AS. He made a bankruptcy look like a sales coup. And that's not such a mean feat, is it.'

She threw back her head and laughed. Harry could see the little scar under the chin left by a facelift.

'What about Anna Bethsen?' he asked.

'His tart?' She crossed her slim legs, flicked her hair away from her face with a finger and stared into space with an air of indifference. 'She was just a toy. His big mistake was his keenness to show off to the boys about his authentic gypsy lover. Not everyone Arne regarded as friends felt they owed him any particular loyalty, shall we say. In short, it came to my ears.'

'And?'

'I gave him another chance. For the children's sake. I'm a reasonable woman.' She looked at Harry through heavy eyelids. 'But he didn't take it.'

'Perhaps he discovered she was more than a toy?'

She didn't answer, but the thin lips became even thinner.

'Did he have a study or anything like that?' Harry asked.

Vigdis Albu nodded.

She led the way up the stairs. 'He used to lock himself in and sit up here half the night.' She opened the door to an attic room with a view of neighbouring roofs.

'Working?'

Surfing the Net. He was utterly hooked. Said he looked at cars, but God knows what he did.'

Harry went to the desk and pulled out one of the drawers. 'Emptied?'

'He took everything he had here with him. It filled one plastic bag.'

'The computer too?'

'It was a laptop.'

'Which he attached to a mobile phone?'

She raised an eyebrow. 'I don't know anything about that.'

'I just wondered.'

'Anything else you want to see?'

Harry turned round. Vigdis was leaning against the door frame with one arm over her head and the other on her hip. The feeling of déjà vu was overwhelming.

'I have one last question, fru . . . Vigdis.'

'Oh, are you in a rush, Inspector?'

'The clock's running on a taxi outside. The question is simple. Do you think he could have killed her?'

She studied Harry in her own time as she lightly kicked at the door sill with the heel of her shoe. Harry waited.

'Do you know the first thing he said when I told him about his whore? *Promise me you won't tell anyone, Vigdis. I* shouldn't tell anyone! For Arne the notion that others considered us happy was more important than whether we really were. My answer, Inspector, is that I have no idea what he is capable of. I don't know the man.'

Harry took a card out of his inside pocket. 'I'd like you to give me a call if he contacts you or if you find out where he is. Immediately.'

Vigdis looked at his card with a tiny smile playing around her pale pink lips. 'Only then, Inspector?'

Harry didn't answer.

On the stairs outside he turned to her. 'Did you tell anyone?'

'That my husband was unfaithful? What do you think?'

'I think you're a practical woman.'

She beamed.

*

'Eighteen minutes,' Øystein said. 'Shit, my pulse was beginning to race.'

'Did you ring my old mobile number while I was in there?'

'Of course. It just rang and rang.'

'I didn't hear a thing. It's not there any more.'

'Sorry, but have you heard about vibrate?'

'What?'

Øystein simulated an epileptic fit. 'Like that. Vibrate mode. Silent phone.'

'Mine cost one krone and just rang. He's taken it with him, Øystein. What happened to the blue BMW down the street?'

'Eh?'

Harry sighed. 'Let's get going.'

31

Maglite

'ARE YOU TELLING ME SOME PSYCHO IS AFTER US BECAUSE YOU can't find the person who killed a member of his family?' Rakel's voice screeched down the phone.

Harry closed his eyes. Halvorsen had gone to Elmer's and he had the office to himself. 'In a nutshell, yes. I've come to an agreement with him. He's kept his part.'

'And that's why we're being hunted? That's why I have to leave the hotel with my son, who in a few days' time will find out whether he's allowed to stay with his mother or not? That's ... that's ...' Her voice rose into a furious, intermittent falsetto. He let her go on without interrupting. 'Why, Harry?'

'The oldest reason in the world,' he said. 'Blood revenge. Vendetta.'

'What's it got to do with us?'

'As I said: nothing. You and Oleg are not the end, only the means. This man sees it as his duty to avenge the killing.'

'Duty?' Her scream pierced Harry's eardrum. 'Vengeance is one of these territorial things you men like so much. It's not about duty, it's the Neanderthal urge!'

He waited until he thought she was finished. 'I'm sorry about this, but there's nothing I can do right now.'

She didn't answer.

'Rakel?'

'Yes.'

'Where are you?'

'If what you say is right, about how easily they found us, I'm not sure I'll risk telling you on the phone.'

'OK. Are you somewhere safe?'

'I think so.'

'Good.'

A Russian voice faded in and out, like on a short-wave radio station.

'Why can't you reassure me that we're not in any danger, Harry? Tell me it's your imagination, they're bluffing . . .' Her voice had become frayed at the edges. '. . . anything . . .'

Harry took his time to answer. Then he said in a slow, clear voice: 'You need to be frightened, Rakel. Frightened enough to do the right thing.'

'And that is?'

Harry took a deep breath. 'I'll straighten things out. I promise you. I'll straighten things out.'

Harry called Vigdis once Rakel had hung up. She answered after the first ring.

'Hole here. Are you sitting by the phone waiting for someone, fru Albu?'

'What do you think?' Harry could tell by the slurred speech that she had had at least a couple of drinks since he left.

'I've no idea, but I'd like you to report your husband missing.'

'Why? I don't miss him.' She gave a short, sad laugh.

'Well, I need a reason for setting the search machinery in motion. You can choose. Either you report him missing or I announce he's being investigated. For murder.'

A long silence followed. 'I don't understand, Constable.'

'There's not a lot to understand, fru Albu. Shall I say you've reported him missing?'

'Wait!' she shouted. Harry could hear a glass being smashed at the other end. 'What are you talking about? Arne is already being investigated.'

'By me, yes, but I haven't informed anyone yet.'

'Oh? And what about the three officers who came here after you left?'

Harry could feel a cold finger running up his spine. 'Three officers?'

'Don't you communicate in the police force? They wouldn't go. I was almost frightened.'

Harry had got out of his office chair. 'Did they arrive in a blue BMW, fru Albu?'

'Do you remember what I told you about the fru stuff, Harry?'

'What did you tell them?'

'Not much. Nothing I didn't tell you, I don't think. They had a look at some photos and . . . well, they weren't exactly impolite, but . . .'

'How did you get them to leave?'

'Leave?'

'They wouldn't have left unless they found what they were after. Believe me, fru Albu.'

'Harry, now I'm getting tired of reminding—'

'Think! This is important.'

'My God, I didn't say anything, I'm telling you. I . . . yes, I played a recorded message Arne left on the answerphone two days ago. Then they left.'

'You said you hadn't talked to him.'

'I haven't. He just said he'd picked up Gregor. And that was true. I could hear Gregor barking in the background.'

'Where was he ringing from?

'How should I know?'

'At any rate, your visitors knew. This is a matter of . . .' Harry tried to think of another way of saying it, but gave up: '. . . life or death.'

There was a lot Harry didn't know about roads and communication. He didn't know that calculations had shown that the building of two tunnels in Vinterbro and the extension of the motorway would reduce rush-hour congestion on the E6 south of Oslo. He didn't know that the crucial argument in favour of this billion-kroner investment had not been the voters who commuted between Moss and Drøbak, but traffic safety. The road authorities used a formula to calculate the social benefit, based on an evaluation of one human life at 20.4 million kroner, which included ambulances, re-routing of traffic and future loss of tax income. Heading south on the E6 in Øystein's Mercedes, bumper to bumper, Harry didn't even know what value he placed on Arne Albu's life. He certainly didn't know what could be gained by saving it. All he knew was that he couldn't afford to lose what he risked losing. Not under any circumstances. So it didn't do to think too much.

The recorded message Vigdis Albu had played him over the telephone had lasted five seconds and contained only one valuable piece of information. It was enough. There was nothing in the ten short words Arne Albu said before ringing off: *I took Gregor with me. Just so that you know.*

It wasn't Gregor's frenetic barking in the background.

It was the cold screams. The seagulls.

It was dark when the sign for the Larkollen turn-off appeared.

Outside the chalet was a Jeep Cherokee, but Harry continued up to the turnaround. No blue BMW there. He parked immediately beneath the chalet. There was no point trying to sneak in; he had already heard the barking when he rolled down the window on the way in.

Harry was conscious that he should have taken a gun with him.

Not that there was any reason to assume Arne Albu was armed; he couldn't know that someone craved his life – or to be more precise, his death. But they weren't the only actors in this drama any more.

Harry got out of the car. He couldn't see or hear any gulls now – perhaps they only make noises in daylight, he mused.

Gregor was chained to the railing by the front steps. His teeth glittered in the moonlight, sending cold shivers down Harry's still-sore neck, but he forced himself to approach the baying dog with long, slow strides.

'Do you remember me?' Harry whispered when he was so close he could touch the dog's grey breath. The taut chain quivered behind Gregor. Harry crouched down and, to his surprise, the barking subsided. The rasping sound suggested it had been going on for quite some time. Gregor pushed his front paws forward, lowered his head and completely stopped. Harry held the door handle. It was locked. Could he hear a voice inside? A light was on in the living room.

'Arne Albu!'

No answer.

Harry waited and tried again.

The key wasn't in the lamp. So he found a suitably large stone, climbed over the veranda railing, smashed one of the small panes in the veranda door, reached his hand through and opened the door.

There was no sign of a fight in the room. More a hasty departure. A book lay open on the table. Harry lifted it up. Shakespeare's *Macbeth*. One line of the text had been ringed with a blue pen. *I have no words; my voice is in my sword*. He scanned the room but he couldn't see a pen anywhere.

Only the bed in the smallest bedroom had been used. There was a copy of a men's magazine on the bedside table.

A small radio, more or less tuned in to P4 news, babbled quietly away in the kitchen. Harry switched it off. On the worktop was a thawed entrecote steak and broccoli still encased in plastic. Harry took the meat and went to the porch. The dog was scratching at the door and he opened up. A pair of brown puppy-dog eyes stared up at him. Or, to be more accurate, at the entrecote, which had hardly landed with a splat on the step before it was ripped to pieces.

Harry observed the ravenous dog while pondering what to do. *If* there was anything he could do. Arne Albu didn't read Shakespeare, that much was certain.

When the last scrap of meat was gone, Gregor began to bark with renewed vigour towards the road. Harry walked over to the railing, loosened the chain and just managed to stay on his feet on the wet surface as Gregor tore loose. The dog dragged him down the path, across the road and down the steep incline where Harry could see black waves crashing onto smooth rocks gleaming white in the light of the half-moon. They waded through tall, wet grass which clung to Harry's legs as if it didn't want to let them go, but Gregor didn't stop until pebbles and sand crunched beneath Harry's Doc Martens. Gregor's rounded stump of a tail pointed upwards. They were standing on the beach. It was high tide; the waves almost reached the rigid grass and bubbled as if there was carbon dioxide in the foam left on the sand as the water retreated. Gregor began to bark again.

'Did he take a boat?' Harry asked, half to Gregor and half to himself. 'Was he alone or did he have company?'

He didn't draw a response from either of them. Nevertheless, it was clear the trail ended here. As Harry pulled at the collar, the large Rottweiler refused to budge. So Harry switched on his Maglite and shone it at the sea. All he could see were rows of white waves, like lines of cocaine on a black mirror. There was clearly a gentle slope beneath the water. Harry pulled at the chain again, but then with a desperate howl the dog started to dig in the sand with its paws.

Harry sighed, switched off the torch and walked back to the chalet. He made himself a cup of coffee in the kitchen and listened to the distant barking. After rinsing his cup, he walked back down to the beach and found a gap between rocks to settle down and shelter from the wind. He lit a cigarette and tried to think. Then he pulled his coat tighter around him and closed his eyes.

*

One night they had been in her bed and Anna had said something. It must have been towards the end of the six weeks – and he must have been more sober than usual because he could remember it. She had said that her bed was a ship, and that she and Harry were two castaways, lonely people drifting on the sea, terrified they would sight land. Was that what had happened next? Had they sighted land? He didn't remember it like that. He felt as if he had jumped ship, jumped overboard. Perhaps his memory was playing tricks on him.

He closed his eyes and tried to conjure up an image of her. Not from the time they were castaways, but from the last time he had seen her. They had eaten together. Apparently. She had filled his glass – had it been wine? Had he tasted it? Apparently. She had given him a refill. He had lost his grip on things. Topped up his glass. She had laughed at him. Kissed him. Danced for him. Whispered her usual sweet nothings in his ear. They had piled into bed and cast off. Had that really been so easy for her? Or for him?

No, it can't have been.

But Harry didn't know for sure. He couldn't have said with any confidence that he hadn't been lying in a bed in Sorgenfrigata with a rapturous smile on his lips. He had been reunited with an ex-lover while Rakel lay staring up at a hotel ceiling in Moscow, unable to sleep for fear of losing her child.

Harry huddled up. The cold, raw wind blew right through him as if he were a ghost. These were thoughts he had managed to keep at bay, but now they crowded in on him: if he couldn't know whether he was capable of cheating on the woman he treasured most in his life, how could he know what else he had done? Aune maintained that drink and drugs merely strengthened or weakened qualities latent within us. But who knew for sure what was inside them? Humans are not robots and the chemistry of the brain changes over time. Who had a full inventory of all the things – given the right circumstances and the wrong medication – we are capable of doing?

Harry shivered and cursed. He knew now. Knew now why he had to find Arne Albu and get a confession before others silenced him. It wasn't because his profession had got into his bloodstream or law had become a personal matter; it was because he had to know. And Arne Albu was the only person who could tell him.

Harry closed his eyes again. The low whistle of the wind against the granite could be heard above the persistent, hypnotic rhythm of the waves.

When he opened his eyes, it was no longer dark. The wind had swept away the clouds and the matt stars twinkled above him. The moon had moved. Harry glanced at his watch. He had been sitting there for almost an hour. Gregor was barking madly at the sea. Stiff, he got to his feet and stumbled over to the dog. The gravitational pull of the moon had shifted, the water level had sunk and Harry plodded down what had become a broad sandy beach.

'Come on, Gregor. We won't find anything here.'

The dog snapped at him when he went to take his collar, and Harry automatically jumped back a step. He peered across the water. The moonlight glittered on the black surface, but now he could make out something he hadn't seen when the water was at its highest ebb. It looked like the tips of two mooring poles just above sea level. Harry went to the water's edge and shone the torch.

'Jesus Christ,' he whispered.

Gregor leapt out into the water and he waded after the dog. It was ten metres into the water, but it didn't even come up to his knees. He stared down at a pair of shoes. Hand-sewn, Italian. Harry shone the torch into the water where the light was reflected back from bare, bluish-white legs, sticking up like two pale tombstones.

Harry's shouts were carried on the wind and drowned instantly in the crashing of the waves. But the torch he dropped, to be swallowed up by the water, remained on the sandy bottom and shone for almost twenty-four hours. When the little boy who found it the following summer ran with it to his father, the salt water had corroded the black casing and neither of them connected a Maglite with the grotesque discovery of a corpse. The previous year it had been in all the papers, but in the summer sun that seemed an eternity away.

PART V

32

David Hasselhoff

THE MORNING LIGHT STOOD LIKE A WHITE PILLAR THROUGH A tear in the sky and cast what Tom Waaler called 'Jesus Light' onto the fjord. A number of similar pictures had hung on the walls at home. He strode over the plastic ribbon cordoning off the crime scene. Those who thought they knew him would have said it was his nature to jump over, rather than duck under. They were right about the latter, but not the former. Tom Waaler doubted that anyone knew him. And he intended it to stay that way.

He raised a digital camera to the steel-blue lenses of his Police sunglasses, of which he had a dozen pairs at home. A return favour from an appreciative customer. As indeed the camera was, too. The frame captured the hole in the ground and the body beside it. It was wearing black trousers and a shirt which had once been white, but was now brown from the clay and sand.

'Another photo for your private collection?' It was Weber.

'This was new,' Waaler said without looking up. 'I like creative murderers. Have you identified the man?'

'Arne Albu. Forty-two years old. Married, three children. Seems to have a fair bit of money. He owns a chalet just behind here.'

'Did anyone see or hear anything?'

'They're making door-to-door inquiries now. But you can see for yourself how deserted it is here.'

'Someone at the hotel over there perhaps?' Waaler pointed towards a large yellow wooden building at the end of the beach.

'Doubt it,' Weber said. 'There won't be anyone staying at this time of the year.'

'Who found the body?'

'Anonymous call from a telephone box in Moss. To the Moss police.'

'The murderer?'

'Don't think so. He said he saw a pair of legs sticking up when he was taking his dog for a walk.'

'Have they got the conversation on tape?'

Weber shook his head. 'He didn't ring the emergency number.'

'What do you make of this?' Waaler motioned towards the corpse.

'The doctors still have to send in their report, but to me it looks like he was buried alive. No external signs of violence, but blood in the nose and mouth and burst blood vessels in the eyes suggest a large accumulation of blood in the head. In addition, we found sand deep in his throat, which means he must have been breathing when he was buried.'

'I see. Anything else?'

'The dog was tied to the railing outside his chalet up there. Great big, ugly Rottweiler. In surprisingly good shape. The door wasn't locked. No signs of a struggle inside the chalet, either.'

'In other words, they marched in, threatened him with guns, tied up the dog, dug a hole for him and asked him if he would mind jumping in.'

'If there were several of them.'

'Big Rottweiler, one-and-a-half-metre-deep hole. I think we can take that as read, Weber.'

Weber didn't react. He had never had a problem working with Waaler. The man was a talented investigator, one of the few; his results spoke for themselves. But that didn't mean Weber had to like him. Although *dislike* wasn't perhaps the right word. It was something else, something which made you think of Spot the Difference pictures. You couldn't quite put your finger on what it was, but there was something that disquieted you. *Disquieted*, that was the word.

Waaler crouched down beside the body. He knew Weber didn't like him. That was fine by him. Weber was an older police officer working in Forensics, who was going nowhere, who could not conceivably affect Waaler's career or life in any way. He was, to cut a long story short, not someone he needed to like him.

'Who identified him?'

'A few of the locals popped by,' Weber answered. 'The owner of the grocery shop recognised him. We got hold of his wife in Oslo and brought her out here. She's confirmed it's Arne Albu.'

'And where is she now?'

'In the chalet.'

'Has anyone questioned her?'

Weber shrugged.

'I like being the first on the scene,' Waaler said, leaning forward and snapping a close-up of the face.

'Moss police district has the case. We've just been called in to assist.'

'We have the experience,' Waaler said. 'Has anyone politely explained that to the country clods?'

'A couple of us have in fact investigated murder before,' a voice behind them said. Waaler peered up at a smiling man in a black leather police jacket. The epaulettes bore one star and gold edges.

'No offence taken,' the inspector laughed. 'I'm Paul Sørensen. You must be Inspector Waaler.'

Waaler briefly acknowledged him and ignored Sørensen's moves to shake hands. He didn't like physical contact with men he didn't know. Nor with men he did know, for that matter. It was another matter with women. As long as he was in control, anyway. And he was.

'You haven't investigated anything like this before, Sørensen,'

Waaler said, prising open one of the dead man's eyelids and revealing a blood-red eyeball. 'This isn't a pub stabbing or a drunken misadventure. That's why you called us in, isn't it?'

'This doesn't look like anything local, no,' Sørensen said.

'I suggest you and the boys stick around here and keep watch while I go and have a word with the corpse's wife.'

Sørensen laughed as if Waaler had told a good joke, but stopped when he saw Waaler's raised eyebrows over the Police sunglasses. Tom Waaler stood up and began to walk to the police cordon. He counted slowly to three, then he shouted without turning: 'And move that police car. I see you've parked in the turnaround, Sørensen. Forensics will be looking for tyre tracks from the murderer's car. Thanking you.'

He didn't need to turn to know the smile had been wiped off Sørensen's jolly face. And that the crime scene had just been taken over by Oslo police district.

'Fru Albu?' Waaler enquired as he entered the living room. He had decided he wanted this over as quickly as possible. He had a lunch date with a promising young girl, and he intended to keep it.

Vigdis Albu looked up from the photo album she was flicking through. 'Yes?'

Waaler liked what he saw. The meticulously maintained body, the confident way she was sitting, the studied TV hostess-style casualness and the third button of her blouse undone. He also liked what he heard. The soft voice simply made for the special words he liked his women to say. And he liked the mouth he already hoped he would hear the words come out of.

'Inspector Tom Waaler,' he said, taking a seat opposite her. 'I understand what a shock this must have been for you. It is, of course, a cliché, and I doubt it has any significance for you at this time, but I would like to extend my sympathy to you. I have also lost someone very close to me.'

He waited. Until she was obliged to look up and he could catch her eyes. They were blurred, and at first Waaler thought tear-blurred. It wasn't until she answered that he realised she was drunk: 'Have you got a cigarette, Constable?'

'Call me Tom. I don't smoke. Sorry.'

'How long do I have to be here, Tom?'

'I'll arrange it so that you can leave as soon as possible. I just need to ask a few questions, OK?'

'OK.'

'Good. Have you any idea who could have wanted to take the life of your husband?'

Vigdis Albu rested her chin on her hand and gazed out of the window. 'Where's the other constable, Tom?'

'Pardon me?'

'Shouldn't he be here?'

'Which constable, fru Albu?'

'Harry. He's got this case, hasn't he?'

The main reason Tom Waaler had advanced through the ranks faster than anyone else from his intake year was that he had worked out that no one, not even defence counsels, would probe how he had obtained evidence of the accused's demonstrable guilt. The next reason was that he had sensitive antennae. Of course, on occasion, they didn't react when they should have. But they never reacted when they shouldn't have. And they were reacting now.

'Are you referring to Harry Hole, fru Albu?'

'You can stop here.'

Tom Waaler still liked the voice. He pulled into the kerb, leaned forward and looked up at the pink house towering over the hill. The morning sun glinted on an animal-like object in the garden.

'That was very nice of you,' Vigdis Albu said. 'To persuade Sørensen to let me leave, and to drive me home.'

Waaler gave her a warm smile. He knew it was warm. Many people

319

had said he looked like David Hasselhoff of *Baywatch* fame; he had the same chin, body and smile. He had seen *Baywatch* and knew what they meant.

'I should thank *you*,' he said.

It was true. During the drive from Larkollen he had learned several interesting things. Such as that Harry Hole had been trying to find evidence that her husband had murdered Anna Bethsen, who – to the best of his recollection – was the woman who had committed suicide in Sorgenfrigata a while back. The case had been closed. He himself had concluded it was suicide and written the report. So what was that idiot Hole up to? Was he trying to get even for old hostilities? Was Hole trying to prove Anna Bethsen was a victim of a criminal act to compromise him – Tom Waaler? It would be just like that crazy alkie to dig up something like that, but it didn't quite make sense to Waaler that Hole was putting so much energy into a case which, in the very worst scenario, would only demonstrate that Waaler had been a bit too quick to draw conclusions. He flatly rejected the notion that Harry's motive might simply be to clear up the case. Only police officers in films spent their free time doing that sort of thing.

The fact that Harry's suspect was dead now naturally meant that a number of alternative solutions were on the cards. Waaler wasn't sure which, but as his instincts told him Harry Hole was involved, he was interested in finding out. So when Vigdis Albu asked Waaler if he would like to come in for a cup of coffee it wasn't primarily the titillating thought of fresh widow that attracted him. This could be the chance to shake off the man who had been breathing down his neck for – how long was it now? Over a year?

Over a year, yes, indeed. Over a year since Officer Ellen Gjelten – thanks to one of Sverre Olsen's blunders – had discovered that Tom Waaler was the main man behind the organised arms smuggling in Oslo. When he gave Olsen the order to execute her before she passed on what she knew, he had been all too aware that Hole would never give up until he had found who killed her. So he had made sure Olsen's cap was found at the crime scene, so that he could shoot the murder suspect 'in self-defence' while arresting him. There was nothing to incriminate him, yet Waaler had the strangely unpleasant sensation that Hole was closing in. And he could be dangerous.

'The house is so empty when everyone is away,' Vigdis Albu said, unlocking the door.

'How long have you been . . . er . . . alone?' Waaler asked, as he followed her up the steps to the living room. He still liked what he saw.

'The children are with my parents in Nordby. The idea was they would stay there until things were back to normal.' She sighed and sank down into one of the deep armchairs. 'I must have a drink. Then I'd better call them.'

Tom Waaler stood observing her. She had ruined everything with what she had just said. The little tingle of excitement he had felt was gone. She suddenly looked much older. Perhaps it was because the effect of the alcohol was wearing off. It had smoothed out the wrinkles and softened her mouth, which hardened now into a crooked, pink fissure.

'Sit down, Tom. I'll make us some coffee.'

He dropped into the sofa as Vigdis disappeared into the kitchen. He spread his legs and noticed a faded stain on the material. It reminded him of the stain on his sofa, left by menstrual blood.

He smiled at the thought.

The thought of Beate Lønn.

Sweet, innocent Beate Lønn, who had sat on the opposite side of the coffee table and swallowed every word he had said as if they were sugar lumps in her café latte, the little girl's drink. *I think it's crucial to have the courage to be yourself. The most important thing in a relationship is honesty, don't you think?* It was difficult to know where to pitch your selection of pseudo-profound clichés with young girls, but he had obviously hit the bullseye with Beate. She had docilely followed him home after he had concocted a drink for her which was anything but a young girl's.

He had to laugh. Even the day after, Beate Lønn had thought her blackout was due to tiredness, and the fact that the drink had been stronger than she was used to. Getting the dose right was everything.

The best bit had been when he went into the living room in the morning and she was rubbing a wet cloth over the sofa where, the evening before, they had done the basics before she passed out and the real fun had started.

'I'm sorry,' she said, close to tears. 'I've only just seen it. It's so embarrassing. I didn't think I was due until next week.'

'Doesn't matter,' he had answered and patted her cheek. 'As long as you do your best to get the shit off.'

Then he had had to dart into the kitchen. He had turned on the tap and clattered the refrigerator door to drown his laughter. As Beate Lønn scrubbed at the bloodstain left by Linda. Or was it Karen?

Vigdis called from the kitchen. 'Do you have milk in your coffee, Tom?' Her voice sounded hard; there was an Oslo West End edge to it. Anyway, he had discovered what he needed.

'I've just remembered I have a meeting in town,' he said. He turned and saw her standing in the kitchen doorway with two coffee cups and large, surprised eyes. As if he had slapped her. He lingered on the thought.

'You need time to yourself,' he said, getting up. 'I know. I've recently lost a close friend, as I said.'

'I'm sorry to hear that,' Vigdis said, perplexed. 'I didn't even ask who it was.'

'Her name was Ellen. A colleague. I liked her very much.' Tom Waaler tilted his head to the side and watched Vigdis, who responded with a tentative smile.

'What are you thinking about?' she asked.

'I might pop by one day and see how you're getting on.' He sent her an extra warm smile, his best David Hasselhoff, and thought what a chaotic world it would be if people could read each others' minds.

33

Dysosmia

THE AFTERNOON RUSH-HOUR TRAFFIC HAD STARTED AND IN Grønlandsleiret car-borne wage slaves slowly trooped past Police HQ. A hedge sparrow sat on a branch and saw the last leaf let go, lift off and flutter past the window of the meeting room on the fifth floor.

'I'm no public speaker,' Bjarne Møller began, and those who had heard Møller's previous speeches nodded in assent.

A bottle of Opera sparkling wine costing seventy-nine kroner, fourteen plastic glasses – still in the packet – and everyone who had been involved in the Expeditor case waited for Møller to finish.

'First of all, I would like to pass on warm greetings from Oslo City Council, the Mayor and the Chief Constable, and thank you all for a job well done. We were, as you know, under quite a lot of pressure when we realised that what we were dealing with was a serial bank robber...'

'I didn't know there was any other type!' Ivarsson shouted and was rewarded with a ripple of laughter. He had positioned himself at the back of the room by the door from where he had an overview of the assembled officers.

'I suppose you could say that.' Møller smiled. 'What I wanted to say was that . . . erm . . . as you know . . . we're glad the whole thing is over. Before we take a glass of champagne I would like to say a special thank you to the person who should take most of the credit . . .'

Harry could feel the others looking at him. He hated this type of occasion. The boss's speech, speeches to the boss, thanks to the clowns, the theatre of triviality.

'Rune Ivarsson, who led the investigation. Congratulations, Rune.'

Round of applause.

'Would you like to say a few words, Rune?'

'No,' Harry muttered between gritted teeth.

'Yes, I would,' Ivarsson said. The assembled officers craned their heads. He cleared his throat. 'Unfortunately, I don't have the privilege to be able to say, as you did, Bjarne, that I am no public speaker. Because I am.' More laughter. 'And from my experience as a speaker at the successful conclusion of other cases, I know it is tiring to thank all and sundry. Police work is, as we all know, teamwork. Beate and Harry had the honour of scoring the goal, but the team did the groundwork.'

With disbelief, Harry watched the assembly nod in agreement.

'So, thank you, everyone.' Ivarsson passed his gaze over the officers, with the evident intention of making each individual feel noted and thanked. Then, more upbeat, he shouted: 'Let's crack open the champagne sharpish, shall we!'

Someone passed him the bottle and after giving it a good shake he started to loosen the cork.

'I can't be bothered with this,' Harry whispered to Beate. 'I'm off.'

She sent him a reproachful look.

'Watch out!' The cork popped and flew up to the ceiling. 'Everyone take a glass!'

'Sorry,' Harry said. 'See you tomorrow.'

He walked through the office and collected his jacket. In the lift on the way down, he leaned against the wall. He had only slept a couple of hours in Albu's chalet last night. At six in the morning, he had driven to the railway station in Moss, found a telephone box and the number of Moss police and reported the body in the sea. He knew they would ask Oslo police for assistance. When he arrived in Oslo at eight, he sat in Kaffebrenneriet in Ullevålsveien and drank a *cortado* until he was sure the case had been given to others and he could go to his office in peace.

The lift doors slid open and Harry went out through the swing doors. Into the cold, clear autumn air of Oslo, reported to be more polluted than the air in Bangkok. He told himself there was no rush and forced himself to slow down. He didn't want to think about anything today, just sleep and hope he wouldn't dream. Hope tomorrow all the doors would have closed behind him.

All except one. The one which would never close, the one he didn't *want* to close. He wasn't going to think about that until tomorrow, though. Then he would walk with Halvorsen along the river Akerselva. Stop by the tree where they had found her. Reconstruct what happened for the hundredth time. Not because they had forgotten anything, but to get the feeling back, the smell in your nostrils. He was dreading it already.

He took the narrow path across the lawn. The short cut. He didn't look at the grey prison building on the left. Where Raskol had presumably packed away the chess set for the time being. They would never find anything in Larkollen or anywhere else to point to the gypsy or any of his henchmen, even if Harry himself took on the case. They would have to keep going for as long as was necessary. The Expeditor was dead. Arne Albu was dead. *Justice is like water*, Ellen had once said. *It always finds a way.* They knew it wasn't true, but at least it was a lie they could find solace in every now and then.

Harry heard the sirens. He had heard them for a while. The white cars with rotating blue lights passed him and disappeared down Grønlandsleiret. He tried not to think why they had been called out. Probably nothing to do with him. If it was, it would have to wait. Until tomorrow.

*

Tom Waaler realised he was too early. Residents of the pale yellow block did other things than sit at home during the day. He had just pressed the bottom button in the row. He turned to walk away when he caught the caged, metallic sound of a voice: 'Hello?'

Waaler spun round. 'Hello, is that . . .?' He looked at the name-plate beside the button. 'Astrid Monsen?'

Twenty seconds later he was on the landing looking at a scared, freckled face peering up at him from behind a security chain.

'May I come in, frøken Monsen?' he asked, baring his teeth in a David Hasselhoff special.

'Rather you didn't,' she squeaked. She probably hadn't seen *Baywatch*.

He gave her his ID.

'I've come to ask if there is anything we ought to know about Anna Bethsen's death. We're not so sure it was a suicide any more. I understand a colleague of mine has been conducting a private investigation and I was wondering if you had spoken to him.'

Tom Waaler had heard that animals, especially predators, can smell fear. It didn't surprise him. What surprised him was that not *everyone* could smell fear. Fear had the same transitory, bitter odour that cow piss had.

'What are you frightened of, frøken Monsen?'

Her pupils dilated even further. Waaler's antennae were whirring now.

'It's very important you help us,' Waaler said. 'The most important aspect of the relationship between the police and the general public is honesty, don't you agree?'

Her eyes went walkabout and he took a risk: 'I believe my colleague may be involved in the case somehow.'

The chin dropped and she sent him a helpless look. Bingo.

They sat down in the kitchen. The brown walls were covered in children's drawings. Waaler guessed she must have been an auntie to loads of kids. He took notes as she talked.

'I heard a crashing noise in the corridor, and when I went out a man was on all fours on the landing outside my door. He had obviously had a fall so I asked him if he needed any help, but I didn't really get a proper answer. I went upstairs and rang Anna Bethsen's bell, but no answer there, either. When I went back down I helped him to stand up. All the things from his pockets were strewn everywhere. I found his wallet with his name and address. Then I helped him into the street, hailed an unoccupied taxi and gave the driver the address. That's all I know.'

'And you're sure it's the same person who visited you later? Harry Hole, that is?'

She gulped. And nodded.

'That's fine, Astrid. How did you know he'd been at Anna's?'

'I heard him arrive.'

'You *heard* him arrive and you *heard* him go into Anna's?'

'My study is right next to the corridor. You can hear everything that goes on there. This block's quiet; not much happens here.'

'Did you hear any other movements near Anna's flat?'

She hesitated. 'I thought I heard someone creeping up to Anna's after the policeman had gone. But it sounded like a woman. High heels, you see. They make a different sound. But I think it was fru Gundersen on the third.'

'Oh?'

'She usually creeps in when she's had a few at Gamle Major.'

'Did you hear any shots?'

Astrid shook her head. 'The walls *between* flats are well insulated.'

'Do you remember the number of the taxi?'

'No.'

'What was the time when you heard the crashing in the corridor?'

'A quarter past eleven.'

'Are you absolutely sure, Astrid?'

She nodded. Took a deep breath.

Waaler was surprised by the sudden firmness in her voice as she said: 'He killed her.'

He could feel his pulse quicken. A tad. 'What makes you say that, Astrid?'

'I knew something was wrong when I heard Anna was supposed to have committed suicide that night. There was that person lying dead drunk on the stairs, wasn't there, and she didn't answer the door. I considered contacting the police, but then he came here . . .' She looked at Tom Waaler as if she was drowning and he was a lifeguard. 'The first thing he asked me was if I recognised him. And of course I knew what he meant by that.'

'What did he mean by that, Astrid?'

Her voice rose half an octave. 'A murderer asking the sole witness if she recognises him? What do you think? He came to warn me what would happen if I gave him away. I did what he wanted. I told him I had never seen him.'

'But you said he came back later to ask you about Arne Albu?'

'Yes, he wanted me to foist the blame on someone else. You must understand how frightened I was. I pretended I didn't realise and played along . . .' He could hear sobs begin to catch hold of her vocal cords.

'But now you would be willing to tell us about this? In a court of law, on oath as well?'

'Yes, if you're . . . if I know I'm safe.'

The ping of an e-mail arriving sounded from another room. Waaler checked his watch. 4.30. He would have to move fast, this evening if possible.

At 4.35, Harry unlocked the door to his apartment and instantly realised he had forgotten that he and Halvorsen had arranged a bike session at the gym. He kicked off his shoes, went into the sitting room and pressed PLAY on the flashing answer machine. It was Rakel.

'Court makes its decision on Wednesday. I've booked tickets for

Thursday. We'll be in Gardemoen at eleven. Oleg asked if you could come and pick us up.'

Us. She had said the decision would have immediate effect. If they lost, there would be no *us* to pick up, just someone who had lost everything.

She hadn't left a number for him to ring back, to be told it was all over and she wouldn't need to keep looking over her shoulder any more. He sighed and slumped into the green armchair. Closed his eyes and saw her there. Rakel. The white sheet which was so cold it burned his skin, the curtains which barely moved against the open window and let in a strip of moonlight which fell on her naked arm. He ran the tips of his fingers so gently across her eyes, her hands, her narrow shoulders, her long, slim neck, her legs entangled in his. He felt her calm, warm breath against his neck, heard the breathing from the sleeping body imperceptibly change rhythm as he gently caressed the small of her back. Her hips which also imperceptibly began to move towards his as if she had only been hibernating, waiting.

At 5.00, Rune Ivarsson picked up the phone in his Østerås home to tell the caller that his family had just sat down to eat. Meals were holy in their house; would they mind ringing back later?

'Apologies for the disturbance, Ivarsson. This is Tom Waaler.'

'Hi, Tom,' Ivarsson said with a half-chewed potato in his mouth. 'Listen . . .'

'I need a warrant for the arrest of Harry Hole. Along with a warrant to search his apartment. Plus five people to do the search. I have reason to believe Hole is implicated in a murder case in a very unfortunate way.'

The potato went down the wrong way.

'It's urgent,' Waaler said. 'There's a risk that evidence will be destroyed.'

'Bjarne Møller,' was all Ivarsson could splutter between coughing fits.

'Right, I know strictly speaking this is Møller's responsibility,' Waaler said. 'But I bet you agree with me that he is prejudiced. He and Harry have worked together for ten years.'

'You've got a point. But we had another job to do last thing today, so my lads have their hands tied.'

'Rune . . .' This was Ivarsson's wife. He was reluctant to provoke her; he had arrived home twenty minutes late after the champagne celebration and then the alarm had gone off at the Grensen branch of Den norske Bank.

'I'll get back to you, Waaler. I'll ring the police solicitors and see what I can do.' He cleared his throat and added in a voice loud enough for his wife to hear: 'After we've eaten.'

Harry woke up to hear banging on the door. His brain automatically concluded that the person had been banging for a while and was sure Harry was at home. He looked at his watch. 5.55. He had been dreaming about Rakel. He stretched and rose from the chair.

More banging. Hard.

'Alright, alright,' Harry shouted, walking to the door. He could see the outline of a figure through the wavy glass in the door. It must be one of the neighbours, Harry thought, since they hadn't used the intercom.

He had just put his hand on the door handle when he felt himself pause. A prickling at the back of his neck. Spots in front of his eyes. Pulse rushing. Rubbish. He opened the door.

It was Ali. Deeply furrowed brow.

'You promised you would clean out your storeroom in the cellar by today,' he said.

Harry slapped his forehead with his hand.

'Shit! Sorry, Ali. I'm a good-for-nothing scatterbrain.'

'That's alright, Harry. I can help you if you've got time this evening.'

Harry eyed him with surprise. 'Help me? I can remove what I have in ten seconds. To be honest, I can't remember a single thing I've got down there, but fine.'

'They're valuable items, Harry.' Ali shook his head. 'You're crazy to keep stuff like that down in the cellar.'

'I don't know about that. I'm off to Schrøder's for a bite to eat. I'll pop by afterwards, Ali.'

Harry closed the door, sank back in the chair and pressed the remote control. The news in sign language. Harry had been on a case when several deaf people had been brought in for questioning and he had learned a couple of the signs. He tried to match the reporter's gesticulations with the lines that came up. All quiet on the Middle Eastern front. An American was to be court-martialled for fighting for the Taliban. Harry gave up. Schrøder's menu of the day, a coffee, a smoke, he mused. Down to the cellar and then straight to bed. He took the remote and was about to switch off when he saw the signer point outstretched fingers and raise a thumb at him. That was a sign he remembered. Someone had been shot. Harry automatically thought of Arne Albu, but he had been suffocated. His eyes moved down to the subtitles. He froze in his chair. And frantically started pressing the remote. This was bad – perhaps very bad news. Teletext didn't say a lot more than the subtitles:

Bank clerk shot in raid. Raider shot a cashier at the Grensen branch of DnB in Oslo this afternoon. Bank clerk's condition is critical.

Harry went into his bedroom and switched on the computer. The bank robbery was the headline on his home page. He double-clicked:

The branch was closing for the day when a masked raider came in brandishing a gun and ordered the female branch manager to empty the ATM. As this didn't happen in the time specified, he shot a 34-year-old bank clerk. The state of the wounded woman is said to be critical. PAS Rune Ivarsson says the police have no leads at present and would not comment on suggestions that the raid followed a similar pattern to raids carried out by the man dubbed the Expeditor. Police informed us this week he had been found dead in d'Ajuda, Brazil.

Could be a coincidence. Of course it could. But it wasn't. No chance. Harry ran his hand across his face. This was what he had been fearing the whole time. Lev Grette had only held up one bank. The following hold-up had been done by someone else. Someone who was well into their stride now. So well that he prided himself on copying the original Expeditor down to the last gory detail.

Harry tried to derail his train of thought. He didn't want to brood over any more bank raids now. Or bank staff being shot. Or the consequences of there turning out to be two Expeditors. The risk that he might have to work under Ivarsson and postpone the Ellen case again.

Stop. No more thinking today. Tomorrow.

But his legs still carried him out into the hall where his fingers dialled Weber's number all on their own. 'Harry here. Had any luck?'

'We certainly have.' Weber sounded surprisingly cheerful. 'Good boys and girls are always lucky in the end.'

'News to me,' Harry said. 'Let's have it then.'

'Beate Lønn rang me from the House of Pain while we were in the bank. She had just started looking at the tapes of the robbery when she saw something interesting. The man was standing close to the Plexiglas over the counter when he was talking. She suggested we check for spit. It was only half an hour after the raid and so there was still a realistic chance of finding something.'

'And?' Harry asked impatiently.

'No spit on the glass.'

Harry groaned.

'But a micro-drop of condensed breath.'

'Really?'

'Yes, indeed.'

'Someone must have been saying their evening prayers recently. Congratulations, Weber.'

'I reckon we'll have the DNA profile in three days. Then we can

332

start comparing. My guess is we'll have him before the week's out.'

'I hope you're right.'

'I am.'

'Well, thanks for rescuing my appetite.'

Harry switched off and put on his jacket. He was about to leave when he remembered he hadn't turned off the computer and went back to the bedroom. As he went to press the SHUT DOWN button, he saw it. His heart slowed and the blood in his veins thickened. He had an e-mail. Of course he could have shut down the computer anyway. Should have done, there was no urgency. It could be from anyone. There was only one person it could *not* be from. Harry would have loved to be on his way to Schrøder's right now. Padding down Dovregata, wondering about the old pair of shoes floating between heaven and earth, enjoying the images from his dream about Rakel. That sort of thing. It was too late now, though; his fingers had taken over again. The machine innards whirred. Then the e-mail appeared. It was a long one.

Hi Harry,

Why such a long face? Perhaps you thought you wouldn't be hearing from me again. Well, life is full of surprises, Harry. Something Arne Albu will have discovered by the time you read this. You and I, we made life unbearable for him, didn't we? If I'm not much mistaken, I bet his wife has taken the kids and left him. Brutal, isn't it? Taking a man's family away from him, especially when you know it's the most important thing in a person's life. But he only has himself to blame. Infidelity cannot be punished severely enough, don't you agree, Harry? Anyway, my little vendetta stops here.

But since you have been dragged into this as an innocent party, perhaps I owe you an explanation. The explanation is relatively simple. I loved Anna. I really did. What she was and what she gave me.

Unfortunately she didn't love what I gave her. The Big H. The Big Sleep. Did you know she was a pedigree junkie? Life is, as I said, full of surprises. I introduced her to drugs after one of her – let's not mince words – failed art exhibitions. And the two of them were made for each other; it was love at first stab. Anna was my client and secret lover for four years. It was impossible to separate the two roles, so to speak.

Confused, Harry? Because you didn't see any syringe marks when you stripped her, eh? Yes, well, 'love at first stab' was just a way of speaking. Anna couldn't stand syringes, you see. We smoked our heroin out of the silver paper off Cuban chocolate. It's more expensive than injecting it. On the other hand, Anna got it at wholesale price as long as she was with me. We were – what's the word? – inseparable. I still have tears in my eyes when I think about those times. She did everything a woman can do for a man: she fucked, fed, watered, amused and consoled me. And begged me. Basically, the only thing she didn't do was love me. How can that be so bloody difficult, Harry? After all, she loved you and you didn't do shit for her.

She even managed to love Arne Albu. And there was me thinking he was just a tosser she was milking to pay for junk at market prices, and to get away from me for a while.

But then one May evening I rang her. I'd just done three months for petty offences, and Anna and I hadn't spoken for a long time. I said we should celebrate. I had taken delivery of the purest stuff in the world from the factory in Chang Rai. I could immediately tell from her voice that something wasn't right. She said it was over. I asked whether she was referring to H or me, and she replied both. You see, she had started on this work of art which she would be remembered for, she said, and it needed a clear mind. As you know, Anna was an obstinate devil when she set her mind on something, so I would bet you never found any junk in her blood. Right?

Then she told me about this guy, Arne Albu. They had been seeing each other and planned to move in together. First, he had to sort things out with his wife. Heard that one before, Harry? Well, me, too.

Isn't it strange how your mind can focus when the world is crashing around you? I knew what was required before I put down the phone. Revenge. Primitive? Not at all. Revenge is the thinking man's reflex, a complex blend of action and consistency no other animal species has so

334

far succeeded in evolving. Evolutionally speaking, the practice of taking revenge has shown itself to be so effective that only the most vengeful of us have survived. Vengeance or death. It sounds like the title of a western, right, but remember it was the logic of retaliation that created the constitutional state. The enshrined promise of an eye for an eye, the sinner burning in hell or at least dangling from the gallows. Revenge is basically the foundation of civilisation, Harry.

So I sat down that same evening and worked out a plan.

I made it simple.

I ordered a key for Anna's flat from Trioving. I won't tell you how. After you left her flat, I went in. Anna had already gone to bed. She, a Beretta M92 and I had a long, enlightening chat. I asked her to find something she had been given by Arne Albu – a card, a letter, a business card, anything. The plan was to leave it on her body to help you connect the murder with him, but all she had was a photograph of his family at their chalet, which she had taken from his album. I guessed that might be a touch too cryptic and you might need a little more help. So I had an idea. Signor Beretta persuaded her to tell me how to get into Albu's chalet. The key was in the outside lamp.

After shooting her – I won't go into detail as it was a disappointing anticlimax (no sign of fear or regret) – I put the picture in her shoe and immediately left for Larkollen. I planted – as I am sure you have realised by now – Anna's spare key in the chalet. I thought about glueing it to the inside of the cistern in the toilet, that's my favourite place, where Michael hid the gun in The Godfather. But you probably wouldn't have had the imagination to search there and there was no point anyway. So I put it in the bedside-table drawer. Easy, wasn't it?

The stage was thus set, and you and the other marionettes could make your entrances. Hope, by the way, you weren't offended by the little nudges I gave you on the way. The intellectual level of you policemen is not exactly unnerving. Unnervingly high, that is.

I take my leave here. Thank you for the company and the help. It has been a pleasure working with you, Harry.

S^{2}MN

34

Pluvianus Aegyptius

A POLICE CAR WAS PARKED BY THE DOOR TO HARRY'S apartment building and another blocked the Dovregata entrance to Sofies gate.

Tom Waaler had given instructions not to use sirens or blue lights.

Over the walkie-talkie, he checked everyone was in position and received quick-fire, crackly confirmation by return. The word from Ivarsson was that the blue sheet – the arrest document and search warrant – from the police solicitor had arrived exactly forty minutes ago. Waaler had said quite clearly he didn't want the Delta group, he would lead the party himself and already had the people he needed on standby. Ivarsson had not made any fuss.

Tom Waaler rubbed his hands. Partly because of the icy-cold wind sweeping down the street from Bislett stadium, but mostly out of glee. Making arrests was the best part of the job. He had already realised that when he was small, and he and Joakim had lain in wait in their parents' orchard on autumn evenings for the riff-raff from the housing co-op on an apple-scrumping raid. And they came. Usually eight to ten of them in the gang. It made no difference how many there were, however, because it was total mayhem when he and

Joakim shone their torches and yelled through their home-made megaphones. They followed the same principles as wolves hunting reindeer: they picked out the smallest and weakest. But it was the arrest – the cornering of the prey – which fascinated Tom, the punishment which appealed to Joakim, whose creativity in this area had advanced so far that Tom occasionally had to stop him. Not because Tom felt any sympathy for the thieves, but because, unlike Joakim, he could keep a clear head and assess the consequences. Tom often thought it was not chance that brought him and Joakim together as it had. He was now a deputy judge on the Oslo Law Court circuit with a glittering career beckoning.

When Tom applied to join the police force, what had attracted him was the thought of *arrests*. Tom's father had wanted him to study medicine, or theology as *he* had done. Tom achieved the best grades in his school, so why a policeman? It was important for your self-esteem to have a decent education, his father had said, and told him about his elder brother who worked in an ironmonger's selling screws and hating everyone because he felt he wasn't as good as they were.

Tom had listened to the admonitions with the wry smile he knew his father loathed. What his father worried about wasn't Tom's self-esteem, it was what the neighbours and relatives thought about his only son becoming a 'mere' policeman. His father had never understood that you could hate people even though you were better than they were. *Because* you were better.

He checked his watch. Thirteen minutes past six. He pressed one of the bells on the ground floor.

'Hello,' said a woman's voice.

'It's the police,' Waaler said. 'Could you open up for us?'

'How do I know you're the police?'

A Paki, Waaler thought, and asked her to take a peep out of the window at the police cars. The lock buzzed.

'And stay indoors,' he said to the intercom.

Waaler placed one man at the back of the house by the fire escape. After looking at the drawings of the apartment block on the Intranet, he had memorised where Harry's flat was and discovered there was no back staircase to worry about.

Each armed with an MP5 across their shoulders, Waaler and two men crept up the worn, wooden stairs. On the second floor, Waaler stopped and pointed to the door that didn't have – and had hardly ever needed – a nameplate. He eyed the two others. Their chests heaved under their uniforms. And not because of the stairs.

They put on balaclavas. The keywords were speed, efficiency and resolve. The latter actually meant the resolve to be brutal, and if necessary, to kill. That was seldom necessary. On the whole, even hardened criminals were totally paralysed when masked, armed men entered without warning. In short, they used the same tactics as bank robbers.

Waaler steadied himself and nodded to one of the others, who gently touched the door with two knuckles. That was in order to be able to write in the report that they had knocked first. Waaler smashed the glass panel with the barrel of his machine gun, reached a hand through and opened the door in one movement. He yelled as they stormed the apartment. A vowel or the first letter of a word, he wasn't sure. He just knew it was the same thing he used to yell when he and Joakim switched on their torches. That was the best bit.

'Potato dumpling,' Maja said, taking his plate and giving Harry a reproachful look. 'You haven't touched it.'

'Sorry,' Harry said. 'No appetite. Pay my respects to the chef and tell him it wasn't his fault. This time.'

Maja laughed out loud and headed for the kitchen.

'Maja . . .'

She turned round slowly. There was something in Harry's voice, in his intonation which presaged what was coming.

'Bring me a beer, would you?'

She continued towards the kitchen. It's none of my business, she thought. I just serve customers. Nothing to do with me.

'What's up, Maja?' the cook asked as she emptied the plate into the bin.

'It's not my life,' she said. 'It's his. The fool.'

The telephone in Beate's office gave a reedy squeak and she took the receiver. She heard the sound of voices, laughter and the clink of glasses. Then came the voice.

'Am I disturbing?'

For a second she was uncertain. His voice sounded alien. But it couldn't be anyone else. 'Harry?'

'What are you up to?'

'I . . . I'm checking the Net for clues. Harry—'

'So you've put the video of the Grensen bank job on the Net?'

'Yes, but you—'

'There are a couple of things I have to tell you, Beate. Arne Albu—'

'Fine, but listen to me now.'

'You sound a bit stressed, Beate.'

'I am!' Her shout crackled over the telephone. Then – calmer: 'They're after you, Harry. I tried to ring and warn you after they had left, but no one was at home.'

'What are you talking about?'

'Tom Waaler. He's got a warrant out on you.'

'Eh? Am I going to be arrested?'

Now Beate knew what was different about Harry's voice. He had been drinking. She gulped. 'Tell me where you are, Harry, and I'll come and get you. Then we can say you gave yourself up. I don't know what this is all about yet, but I'll help you, Harry. I promise. Harry? Don't do anything stupid, OK? Hello?'

She sat listening to voices, laughter and clinking glasses, then footsteps and a woman's hoarse voice: 'This is Maja at Schrøder's.'

'Where . . . ?'

'He's gone.'

35

SOS

Vigdis Albu woke up to Gregor barking outside. The rain was drumming on the roof. She looked at her watch. Half past seven. She must have dropped off. The glass in front of her was empty, the house was empty, everything was empty. That wasn't how she had planned things.

She got up, went over to the patio door and watched Gregor. He was facing the gate with his ears and tail pointing directly upwards. What should she do? Give him away? Have him put to sleep? Not even the children had any strong feelings for this over-active, nervous creature. The plan, yes. She glanced at the half-empty gin bottle on the glass table. It was time to devise a new one.

Gregor's barking rent the air. *Woof, woof!* Arne had said he found the irritating noise reassuring; it gave you a vague sense that someone was alert. He said dogs could smell enemies because ill-wishers gave off a different scent from friends. She decided she would ring a vet tomorrow; she was sick of paying upkeep for a dog which barked every time she came into the room.

She inched open the patio door and listened. Through the baying of the dog and the rain she could hear the gravel crunching. She just managed to throw a brush through her hair and wipe away a streak of mascara under her left eye before the doorbell rang its three notes from Handel's *Messiah*, a house-warming present from her in-laws. She had an inkling who it might be. She was right. Almost.

'Constable?' she said, genuinely astonished. 'This is a nice surprise.'

The man on the step was soaked. Drops of water were hanging from his eyebrows. He leaned one arm against the door frame and looked at her without answering. Vigdis Albu opened the door completely and half-closed her eyes again: 'Won't you come in?'

She led the way and heard his shoes squelch behind her. She knew he liked what he saw. He sat down in an armchair without taking off his coat. She noticed the material darken as the water soaked in.

'Gin, Constable?'

'Got any Jim Beam?'

'No.'

'Gin's fine.'

She fetched the crystal glasses – a wedding present from the in-laws – and poured them both a drink. 'My condolences,' the policeman said, eyeing her with shiny, red eyes which told her this wasn't his first drink today.

'Thank you,' she said. '*Skål*.'

When she set down her glass she saw he had drunk half the contents of his. He sat fidgeting with it and suddenly said: 'I killed him.'

Vigdis instinctively put her hand to the necklace around her neck. The morning gift.

'I didn't want it to end like that,' he said. 'But I was stupid and careless. I led the murderers right to him.'

Vigdis pressed the glass to her mouth so he wouldn't see she was about to burst into laughter.

'So now you know,' he said.

'Now I know, Harry,' she whispered. She thought she saw a hint of surprise in his eyes.

'You've been talking to Tom Waaler.' It sounded more like a statement than a question.

'You mean the detective who thinks he's God's gift to . . . hm. I talked to him. Told him everything I knew, of course. Shouldn't I have done, Harry?'

He shrugged.

'Have I put you in a tight spot, Harry?' She had tucked her legs beneath her on the sofa and regarded him with a concerned expression from behind her glass.

He didn't answer.

'Another drink?'

He nodded. 'At least, I have one piece of good news for you.' He followed her hand carefully as she filled his glass. 'I received an e-mail this evening from someone confessing to the murder of Anna Bethsen. The person in question lured me into thinking it was Arne.'

'That's great,' she said. She spluttered gin onto the table. 'Oh dear, must be a bit too strong.'

'You don't seem exactly surprised.'

'Nothing surprises me any longer. To be honest, I didn't think Arne had the guts to kill anyone.'

Harry rubbed the back of his neck. 'Nevertheless. Now I have proof Anna Bethsen was murdered. I sent the confession to a colleague of mine before leaving home this evening. As well as all the other e-mails I've received. That means I've laid all my cards on the table as far as my own role is concerned. Anna was an ex-girlfriend of mine. My problem is that I was with her the evening she was killed. I should have turned down her invitation right away, but I was stupid and careless and thought I could solve the case on my own and at the same time make sure I wasn't dragged into it. I was . . .'

'Stupid and careless. You've said that.' She observed him pensively as he stroked the sofa cushion beside him. 'Of course, that explains a great deal. However, I still can't see why it should be a crime to spend time with a woman you would like to . . . spend time with. You had better explain yourself, Harry.'

342

'Well.' He gulped down the shiny liquor. 'I woke up the next day and couldn't remember a thing.'

'I see.' She rose from the sofa, went over to him and stood opposite him. 'Do you know who he is?'

He rested his head against the back of the sofa and looked up at her. 'Who said it's a "he"?' His words were slightly slurred.

She stretched out a slim hand. He shot her a quizzical look.

'The coat,' she said. 'Then go straight into the bathroom and take a hot bath. I'll make coffee and find some dry clothes for you in the meantime. I don't think he would have objected. He was a reasonable man in many ways.'

'I . . .'

'Come on. Now.'

The hot embrace sent shivers of pleasure running through him. The caresses continued up over his thighs to his hips and covered him in gooseflesh. He groaned. Then he lowered the rest of his body into the boiling water and leaned back.

He could hear the rain outside and listened to catch Vigdis Albu's movements, but she had put a record on. Police. Greatest Hits, to cap it all. He closed his eyes.

Sting was sending out an SOS. Speaking of which, he reckoned Beate must have read the e-mail by now. She would have passed on the message and the fox hunt would have been called off. The alcohol had made his eyelids heavy, but every time he closed his eyes he saw two legs and hand-sewn Italian shoes sticking out of the steaming-hot bathwater. He fumbled behind his head for the glass he had placed at the edge of the bath. When he rang Beate from Schrøder's he had only had two large beers, and that was nowhere near the anaesthetisation he required. But where was the damn glass? He wondered if Tom Waaler was hunting him down anyway. Harry knew he was desperate to make this arrest. But Harry was not going to give himself up until he had all the details safely in place. From now on, he couldn't afford to trust anyone. He would sort it out. Just some time out first. Another drink. Borrow the sofa here tonight. A clear head. Tomorrow.

His hand hit the heavy crystal glass and it landed on the tiled floor with a dull crunch.

Harry swore and stood up. He almost fell but caught the wall at the last moment. He tied a thick, plush towel around his waist and went into the living room. The gin bottle was still on the coffee table. He found a glass in the bar cabinet and filled it to the brim. He could hear the coffee machine. And Vigdis's voice from the hall. He went back into the bathroom and carefully placed the glass beside the clothes Vigdis had laid out for him, a complete Bjørn Borg collection in light blue and black. He cleaned the mirror with the towel and confronted his eyes in the condensation-free strip.

'You idiot,' he whispered.

He sat on the floor. A red rivulet crept down the grout between the tiles to the drain. He followed the rivulet back to his right foot where fresh blood was trickling between his toes. He stood up in the middle of the broken glass; he hadn't even noticed it. Hadn't noticed a thing. He looked in the mirror again and laughed.

Vigdis put down the receiver. She had been forced to improvise, although she hated improvising. It made her feel physically ill when things didn't go according to plan. Right from the time she was small, she had realised that nothing happened of its own accord. Planning was everything. She could still remember the family moving to Slemdal from Skien when she had been in the third class. In front of her new class, she had stood and introduced herself while they sat staring at her, her clothes and the strange plastic bag which had made a couple of the girls giggle and point. In the last lesson she had written a list detailing the girls in the class who would be her best friends, those who would be given the cold shoulder, which boys would fall in love with her and which teachers would choose her as their favourite pupil. She had hung the list over her bed when she came home and didn't take it down until Christmas, by which time there was a tick by every name.

But now it was different. Now she was at the mercy of others for life to slot into place.

She looked at her watch. Twenty to ten. Tom Waaler said they would be there within twelve minutes. He had promised to switch off the sirens well before Slemdal so she didn't need to worry about neighbours. She hadn't even mentioned it.

She sat in the hallway waiting. Hole had gone to sleep in the bath, she hoped. Another look at her watch. Listened to the music. Fortunately the stressful Police songs were finished and now Sting was singing songs off his solo album with his wonderful, soothing voice. About rain . . . like tears from a star. It was so beautiful she almost wanted to cry.

Then she heard Gregor's hoarse barking. Finally.

She opened the door and went out onto the step as arranged. She saw a figure running across the garden towards the patio and another going around the back of the house. Two masked men in black uniforms carrying small, snub pistols stopped in front of her.

'Still in the bath?' whispered one from behind the black balaclava. 'Left after the stairs?'

'Yes, Tom,' she whispered. 'And thanks for coming so—'

But they were already inside.

She closed her eyes and listened. Feet running up the stairs, Gregor's fierce snarls from the patio, Sting's gentle 'How Fragile We Are', the crash of the bathroom door being kicked in.

She turned and went inside. Up the stairs. Towards the shouting. Needed a drink. She saw Tom at the top of the stairs. He had taken off his balaclava, but his face was so distorted she hardly recognised him. He was pointing to something. On the carpet. She looked down. A trail of blood. Her eyes followed it across the living room to the open patio door. She couldn't hear what the idiot dressed in black was shouting at her. *The plan* was all she could think. *This isn't the plan.*

36

Waltzing Matilda

HARRY RAN. GREGOR'S STACCATO BARKING WAS LIKE AN angry metronome in the background, otherwise everything around him was still. His naked feet slapped against wet grass. He stretched his arms in front of him as he burst through another hedge hardly feeling the thorns tearing at his palms and the Bjørn Borg collection. He hadn't found his own clothes and shoes; he guessed she must have taken them downstairs to where she was sitting and waiting. While searching for another pair of shoes he had heard Gregor whining and he had had to make a run for it as he was, in trousers and shirt. The rain fell into his eyes, and houses, apple trees and bushes blurred in front of him. Another garden appeared out of the dark. He took the risk and jumped over the low fence. But lost his balance. Running with alcohol in your blood. A trim lawn rose and hit him in the face. He stayed down, listening.

He thought he could hear a number of dogs barking now. Was Victor there? So quickly? Waaler must have had them on standby. Harry got to his feet and scoured the area. He was at the top of the hill he had headed towards. Deliberately keeping away from the illuminated roads which police cars would soon be patrolling and where he could easily be spotted. Down by Bjørnetråkket he could see Albu's property. There were four cars outside the front gate, two of them with rotating blue lights. He looked down the other side of the hill. Wasn't it called Holmen, or Gressbanen? Something like that. A civilian car was parked on the pavement by the crossroads with its lights on. Harry had been quick, but Waaler had been quicker. Only the police parked like that.

He rubbed his face hard. Tried to get rid of the anaesthetisation he had longed for so recently. A blue light flashed between the trees in Stasjonsveien. He was caught in the net and it was already tightening. He wouldn't escape. Waaler was too good. But he didn't quite understand. This couldn't be a solo show. Someone must have authorised the use of these huge resources to arrest one single man. What had happened? Hadn't Beate received the e-mail he had sent her?

He listened. There were more dogs, no question. He cast his eyes around. At the illuminated detached houses scattered across the pitch-black hill. He thought of the snug, warm rooms behind the windows. Norwegians liked light. And they had electricity. They only turned it off when they were away for a fortnight on holiday down south. His gaze moved from house to house.

Tom Waaler stared up at the isolated houses decorating the landscape like Christmas lights. Large, black gardens. Scrumping. He had his feet up on the dashboard in Victor's specially converted van. They had the best communication equipment available, so he had moved control of the operation there. He was in radio contact with all the units closing the circle around the area. He looked at his watch. The dogs were out; it would soon be ten minutes since they had slipped into the darkness with their handlers, moving through gardens.

The radio crackled: 'Stasjonsveien to Victor zero one. We have a car here with one Stig Antonsen going to Revehiven 17. Returning from work, he says. Shall we . . . ?'

'Check ID, address and let him through,' Waaler said. 'The same holds for you others out there, OK? Use your heads.'

Waaler tugged a CD out of his top pocket and put it in the player. Several falsettos. Prince sang 'Thunder.' The man in the driver's seat beside him raised an eyebrow, but Waaler pretended not to notice and turned up the volume. Verse. Refrain. Verse. Refrain. Next song: 'Pop Daddy'. Waaler checked his watch again. Shit, what a long time the dogs were taking. He hit the dashboard. Earning another glance from the driver's seat.

'They have a fresh trail of blood to follow,' Waaler said. 'How difficult can that be?'

'They're dogs, not robots,' the man said. 'Relax, they'll soon have him.'

The artist to be known for ever as Prince was in the middle of 'Diamonds and Pearls' when the report came in: 'Victor zero three to Victor zero one. Think we've got him. We're outside a white house in . . . er, Erik's trying to find out what the road's called, but there's a number 16 on the wall, anyway.'

Waaler turned down the music. 'OK. Find out and wait for us. What's the ringing sound I can hear?'

'It's coming from the house.'

The radio crackled: 'Stasjonsveien to Victor one. Sorry to interrupt but there's a security vehicle here. They say they're going to Harelabben 16. Their central switchboard registered a burglar alarm going off there. Shall I—?'

'Victor zero one to all units!' Waaler yelled. 'Move in. Harelabben 16.'

Bjarne Møller was in a dreadful mood. In the middle of his favourite TV programme! He found the white house, number 16, parked outside, went through the gate and up to the open door where a police officer was standing with an Alsatian on a leash.

'Is Waaler here?' asked the PAS. The officer motioned to the door. Møller noticed that the glass in the hall window was smashed. Waaler stood in the hall inside in furious discussion with another officer.

'What the hell's going on here?' Møller asked without preamble.

Waaler turned. 'Right. What brings you here, Møller?'

'A phone call from Beate Lønn. Who authorised this idiocy?'

'Our police solicitor.'

'I'm not talking about the arrest. I'm asking who gave the go-ahead to World War Three because one of our very own colleagues may – *may!* – have a couple of things to explain.'

Waaler rocked back on his heels while eyeballing Møller. 'PAS Ivarsson. We found a couple of things at Harry's place which make him more than just someone we would like to talk to. He is under suspicion of murder. Anything else you were wondering about, Møller?'

Møller raised an eyebrow in surprise and concluded Waaler must be very worked up. That was the first time he had ever heard him talk to a superior in such a provocative manner. 'Yes. Where's Harry?'

Waaler pointed to the red footprints on the parquet floor. 'He was here. Broke in, as you can see. Beginning to be quite a lot to explain, isn't there?'

'I asked where he is now.'

Waaler and the other police officer exchanged looks. 'Harry is clearly not that keen to explain. The bird had flown when we arrived.'

'Oh? I was under the impression you had surrounded the whole area.'

'We had,' Waaler said.

'So how did he get away then?'

'Using this.' Waaler pointed to the telephone on the table. The receiver was stained with what looked like blood.

'He got away using a phone?' Møller felt an irrational – his bad mood and the seriousness of the situation taken into account – urge to smile.

'There is reason to believe,' Waaler said while Møller watched the

349

powerful musculature of the David Hasselhoff jaw straining, 'that he ordered a taxi.'

Øystein drove down the alley slowly and turned the taxi into the cobbled semicircle in front of Oslo prison. He reversed in between two cars, his rear end facing the empty park and Grønlandsleiret. He turned the ignition key to kill the engine, but the windscreen wipers kept swishing to and fro. And waited. No one was around, neither in the square nor in the park. He glanced up at Police HQ before pulling the lever under the wheel. There was a click and the boot lid sprang into the air.

'Come out!' he shouted, looking in the mirror.

The car rocked, the boot lid was opened fully and smacked shut. Then the back door opened and a man hopped in. Øystein studied the drenched, shivering passenger in the mirror.

'You look great, Harry.'

'Thanks.'

'Cool threads too.'

'Not my size, but it's Bjørn Borg. Lend me your shoes, will you.'

'Eh?'

'I could only find felt slippers in the hall. Can't go on a prison visit wearing them. And your jacket.'

Øystein rolled his eyes and struggled out of his short leather jacket.

'Did you have any trouble getting past the roadblocks?' Harry asked.

'Just on the way in. They had to check I had the name and address of the person I was delivering the package to.'

'I found the name on the door.'

'On my way back, they just looked in the car and waved me through. Thirty seconds passed and then there was a hell of a racket on the radio. Calling all units and so on. Heh, heh.'

'I thought I heard something from the back. You do know it's illegal to tune in to police radio, don't you, Øystein?'

'Well, it's not illegal to tune in. It's illegal to use it. And I almost never use it.'

Harry tied the shoelaces and threw the slippers over the seat to Øystein. 'You'll find your reward in heaven. If they took the number of the taxi and you receive a visit, you'll have to tell them what happened. You got a booking via a mobile and the passenger insisted on lying in the boot.'

'Absolutely. And that's the truth.'

'Truest thing I've heard for a long while.'

Harry took a deep breath and pressed the bell. Not much risk in the first phase, but it was difficult to know how quickly the news that he was a wanted man had spread. After all, police officers were in and out of this prison all the time.

'Yes,' a voice said from the intercom.

'Inspector Harry Hole,' Harry over-articulated, looking into the camera over the entrance with what he hoped was an unruffled expression. 'For Raskol Baxhet.'

'You're not on my list.'

'Really?' Harry said. 'I asked Beate Lønn to ring you and book me in. Last night, nine o'clock. Just ask Raskol.'

'If it's outside visiting hours, you have to be on the list, Inspector. You'll have to ring during office hours tomorrow.'

Harry shifted weight from one foot to the other. 'What's your name?'

'Bøygset. I'm afraid I can't—'

'Listen here, Bøygset. This visit concerns information for an important police case which cannot wait until tomorrow. I imagine you've heard the sirens going off all round Police HQ this evening, haven't you?'

'Yes, but—'

'Right, unless you'd like to answer the papers' questions tomorrow about how you messed up the schedule, I suggest we move on from robot mode and press the common-sense button. That's the one right in front of you, Bøygset.'

Harry stared into the lifeless camera eye. One-thousand-and-one, one-thousand-and-two. The lock buzzed.

Raskol was sitting in a chair in his cell when Harry was let in.

'Thank you for confirming the visit,' Harry said, looking around the four-by-two-metre cell. A bed, a desk, two cupboards, a few books. No radio, no magazines, no personal effects, bare walls.

'This is how I prefer it,' Raskol said in answer to Harry's thoughts. 'It focuses the mind.'

'Then feel how this focuses the mind,' Harry said, perching on the edge of the bed. 'Arne Albu didn't kill Anna after all. You got the wrong man. You have innocent blood on your hands, Raskol.'

Harry was not sure, but he seemed to detect the minutest of twitches in the gypsy's gentle, though cold, martyr's mask. Raskol lowered his head and placed his palms against his temples.

'I received an e-mail from the murderer,' Harry said. 'Turns out he was manipulating me from day one.' He ran a hand up and down the criss-cross pattern of the duvet as he summarised what the e-mail said. And followed up with a précis of the day's events.

Raskol sat motionless, listening until Harry had finished. Afterwards he raised his head. 'That means there is innocent blood on your hands, too, *Spiuni*.'

Harry nodded.

'Now you're here to tell me I was the one who stained your hands. And therefore I owe you a debt.'

Harry didn't answer.

'I agree,' Raskol said. 'Tell me what I owe.'

Harry stopped stroking the duvet. 'Three things. First of all, I need a place to hide until I've got to the bottom of this business.'

Raskol nodded.

'Secondly, I need the key to Anna's flat to check a couple of things.'

'I've already given it back.'

'Not the key with AA on, that's in a drawer in my place, and I can't go there now. And thirdly . . .'

Harry paused and Raskol scrutinised his face with curiosity.

'If I hear Rakel say anyone has so much as looked askance at them, I will give myself up, put all my cards on the table and finger you as the man behind Arne Albu's murder.'

Raskol gave him an indulgent, friendly smile. As if, on Harry's behalf, he regretted one thing they were both absolutely clear on – the fact that no one would ever succeed in finding any link whatsoever between Raskol and the murder. 'You don't need to worry about Rakel and Oleg, *Spiuni*. My contact was instructed to call off his artisans the moment we had dealt with Albu. You should be more concerned about the outcome of the trial. My contact says the prospects don't look too rosy. I understand the father's family has certain connections?'

Harry hunched his shoulders.

Raskol pulled out the desk drawer, took the shiny Trioving system key and gave it to Harry. 'Go to the metro station in Grønland. Go down the first set of stairs and you'll see a woman sitting behind a window by the toilets. You need five kroner to get in. Tell her Harry has arrived, go into the Gents and lock yourself in one of the cubicles. When you hear someone come in whistling "Waltzing Matilda" it means your transport is ready. Good luck, *Spiuni*.'

The rain was hammering down so hard there was a fine shower rebounding off the tarmac, and if anyone had taken the time, they would have seen small rainbows in the streetlamps at the bottom of the narrow one-way section of Sofies gate. However, Bjarne Møller didn't have time. He got out of the car, raised his coat over his head and ran across the street to the front door where Ivarsson, Weber and a man, apparently of Pakistani origin, stood waiting for him.

Møller shook hands and the dark-skinned man introduced himself as Ali Niazi, Harry's neighbour.

'Waaler will be here as soon as he has cleared up in Slemdal,' Møller said. 'What have you found?'

'Quite sensational things, I'm afraid,' Ivarsson said. 'The most important thing now is to work out how we're going to tell the press that one of our own police officers—'

'Whoa there,' Møller rumbled. 'Not so fast. How about a debriefing?'

Ivarsson smiled thinly. 'Come with me.'

The Head of the Robberies Unit led the other three through a low door and down a crooked staircase into the cellar. Møller contorted his long, thin body as well as he could to avoid touching the ceiling or walls. He didn't like cellars.

Ivarsson's voice was a dull echo between the brick walls. 'As you know, Beate Lønn received a number of forwarded e-mails from Hole. He maintains he was sent them by a person who confessed to murdering Anna Bethsen. I've been to Police HQ and I read the e-mails an hour ago. To put it bluntly, they are for the most part confused, incomprehensible gibberish. But they do contain information which the writer could not have possessed without intimate knowledge of what went on the night Anna Bethsen died. Even though the information puts Hole in the flat that evening, it also apparently gives him an alibi.'

'Apparently?' Møller ducked underneath another door frame. Inside, the ceiling was even lower, and he walked bent double while trying not to think that above him were four floors of building materials held together by centuries old wattle and daub. 'What do you mean, Ivarsson? Didn't you say the e-mails contained a confession?'

'First of all, we searched Hole's flat,' Ivarsson said. 'We switched on his computer and opened the mailbox and found all the e-mails he had received. Just as he had made out to Beate Lønn. In other words, an apparent alibi.'

'I heard that,' Møller said with obvious irritation. 'Can we get to the point quickly?'

'The point is, of course, the person who sent these e-mails to Harry's computer.'

Møller heard voices.

'It's round that corner,' the man who introduced himself as Harry's neighbour said.

They came to a halt in front of a storeroom. Two men were crouching behind the wire mesh. One shone a torch on the back of a laptop while reading out a number, which the other noted down. Møller saw two electric cables running from the wall socket, one to the laptop and the other to a scratched Nokia mobile phone, which in turn was connected to the laptop.

Møller straightened up as far as he was able. 'And what does that prove?'

Ivarsson placed a hand on the shoulder of Harry's neighbour. 'Ali says he was in the cellar a few days after Anna Bethsen was killed, and that was the first time he had seen this laptop with attached mobile phone in Harry's storeroom. We've already checked the phone.'

'And?'

'It's Hole's. Now we're trying to find out who bought the laptop. We've checked the sent items, anyway.'

Møller closed his eyes. His back was aching already.

'And there they are.' Ivarsson shook his head in vindication. 'All the e-mails Harry's trying to make us believe some mysterious murderer has sent him.'

'Hm,' Møller said. 'That doesn't look good.'

'Weber found the real proof in the flat.'

Møller looked at Weber for guidance, who, with a grim expression on his face, held up a small transparent plastic bag.

'A key?' Møller said. 'Bearing the initials AA?'

'Found in the drawer of the telephone table,' Weber said. 'It matches the key to Anna Bethsen's flat.'

Møller stared blankly at Weber. The harsh light from the naked bulb gave their faces the same deathly pale colour as the whitewashed walls and Møller had the feeling he was in a burial vault. 'I have to get out,' he murmured.

37

Spiuni Gjerman

HARRY OPENED HIS EYES AND LOOKED UP INTO A SMILING
girl's face and felt the first sledgehammer blow.

He closed his eyes again, but neither the girl's laughter nor the
headache disappeared.

He tried to reconstruct the night.

Raskol, the toilet in the metro station, a squat man in a worn
Armani suit whistling, an outstretched hand with gold rings, black
hairs and a long pointed nail on the little finger. 'Hi, Harry, I'm your
friend Simon.' And in sharp contrast to the shabby suit: a shiny new
Mercedes with a chauffeur who looked like Simon's brother with
the same cheery, brown eyes and the same hairy, gold-bedecked
handshake.

The two men in the front of the car had chatted away in a blend of
Norwegian and Swedish with the curious intonation of circus
people, knife-sellers, preachers and dance-band vocalists. But they
hadn't said much. 'How are you, my friend?' 'Terrible weather, eh?'
'Smart clothes, my friend. Shall we swap?' Hearty laughter and
flicking of a cigarette lighter. Did Harry smoke? Russian cigarettes.
Take one, please, a bit rough maybe, but 'good in their way, you

know'. More laughter. No one had mentioned Raskol's name or where they were going.

Which had turned out to be not too far away.

They turned off after the Munch Museum and bumped over potholes to a car park in front of a deserted, muddy football pitch. At the end of the car park were three caravans. Two large new ones and a small old one without wheels, standing on Leca blocks.

The door of one of the large caravans opened and Harry saw the silhouette of a woman. Children's heads poked out behind her. Harry counted five.

He said he wasn't hungry and sat in the corner watching them eat. The food was served by the younger of the two women in the caravan and was eaten quickly and without ceremony. The children stared at Harry as they giggled and shoved each other. Harry winked at them and tried a smile as feeling slowly returned to his stiff, numb body. Which was good news since there was two metres of it and every centimetre hurt. Afterwards Simon had given him two woollen blankets and a friendly pat on the shoulder, and nodded towards the small caravan. 'It's not the Hilton, but you're safe here, my friend.'

Any warmth Harry had left in his body disappeared immediately he entered the egg-shaped refrigerator of a caravan. He had kicked off Øystein's shoes which were at least one size too small, rubbed his feet and tried to make room for his long legs in the short bed. The last thing he remembered doing was trying to pull off his wet trousers.

'Hee-hee-hee.'

Harry opened his eyes again. The little brown face was gone and the laughter came from outside now, through the open door, where a stripe of sun was emboldened to shine in and onto the wall behind him and the photographs pinned there. Harry hauled himself up onto his elbows and looked at them. One of them showed two young boys with their arms around each other in front of the caravan he was lying in now. They looked pleased. No, more than that. They looked happy. That was perhaps why Harry hardly recognised a young Raskol.

Harry swung his legs out of the bunk and decided to ignore the headache. To make sure his stomach was alright, he sat for a few seconds. He had been through much worse ordeals than yesterday's, much worse. During the meal the evening before he had been on the point of asking if they had anything stronger to drink, but had managed to hold back. Perhaps his body would tolerate spirits better now he had been abstemious for so long?

His question was answered when he stepped outside.

The children stared with astonishment as Harry supported himself on the tow bar and vomited over the brown grass. He coughed and spat a couple of times and wiped his mouth with the back of his hand. When he turned, Simon was standing with a big smile on his face, as if emptying your stomach were the most natural start to the day.

'Food, my friend?'

Harry swallowed and nodded.

Simon lent Harry a creased suit, a clean shirt with a wide collar and a pair of large sunglasses. They got into the Mercedes and drove up Finnmarkgata. At the lights in Carl Berners plass Simon rolled down the window and shouted at a man standing outside a kiosk smoking a cigar. Harry had a vague feeling he had seen the man before. From experience he knew this feeling often meant the man had a record. The man laughed and shouted something back, which Harry didn't catch.

'An acquaintance?' he asked.

'A contact,' Simon said.

'A contact,' Harry repeated, watching the police car waiting on green at the other side of the crossing.

Simon turned west towards Ullevål hospital.

'Tell me,' Harry said. 'What sort of contacts has Raskol got in Moscow who can find one person in a city of twenty million people like that?' Harry clicked his fingers. 'Is it the Russian mafia?'

Simon laughed. 'Maybe. If you can't come up with anyone better at finding people.'

'The KGB?'

'If I remember correctly, my friend, they no longer exist.' Simon laughed even louder.

'The Russia expert in POT told me ex-KGB men are still running the show.'

Simon shrugged. 'Favours, my friend. And return favours. That's what it's all about, you know.'

Harry scanned the street. A van sped by. He had got Tess – the brown-eyed girl who had woken him up – to run down to Tøyen and buy him copies of *Dagbladet* and *Verdens Gang,* but there was nothing about a wanted police officer in either of them. That didn't mean he could show his face everywhere because, unless he was very much mistaken, there would be a photograph of him in every police car.

Harry walked quickly to the door, put Raskol's key in the lock and turned it. He tried not to make any noise in the hallway. There was a newspaper outside Astrid Monsen's door. Once inside Anna's flat, he closed the door softly behind him and breathed in.

Don't think about what you're looking for.

The flat smelt stuffy. He went into the furthest room. Nothing had been touched since he was last here. The dust danced in the sunlight flooding in through the window and brightening up the three portraits. He stood looking at them. There was something strangely familiar about the distorted heads. He went to the pictures and ran the tips of his fingers over the lumps of oil paint. If they were talking to him, he didn't understand what they were saying.

He went into the kitchen.

It smelt of refuse and rancid fat. He opened the window and went through the plates and cutlery in the kitchen sink. They had been rinsed but not washed. He prodded the hardened food remains with a fork. Loosened a small red particle from the sauce. Put it in his mouth. Japone chilli.

Two large wineglasses behind a big saucepan. One had a fine red sediment in while the other seemed unused. Harry put his nose in, but could only smell a warm glass. Beside the wineglasses were two normal drinking glasses. He found a dishcloth so he could hold the glasses up to the light without leaving fingerprints. One was clean, the other had a sticky coating. He scratched at the coating with his nail and sucked his finger. Sugar. With a coffee taste. Coca-Cola? Harry closed his eyes. Wine and Coke? No. Water and wine for one person. Coke and an unused glass for the other. He wrapped the glass in the cloth and put it in his jacket pocket. On impulse, he went to the bathroom, unscrewed the lid on the cistern and felt inside. Nothing.

Back out in the street, he saw clouds had moved in from the west and there was a nip in the air. Harry chewed his lower lip. He made a decision and started walking towards Vibes gate.

Harry immediately recognised the young man behind the counter at the locksmith's.

'Good morning, I'm from the police,' Harry said, hoping the boy wouldn't ask to see his ID, which was in his jacket in Vigdis Albu's house in Slemdal.

The boy put down his newspaper. 'I know.'

Panic caught hold of Harry for a second.

'I remember you came here to collect a key.' The boy gave a broad smile. 'I remember all my customers.'

Harry cleared his throat. 'Well, I'm not really a customer.'

'Oh?'

'No, the key wasn't for me. But that's not why—'

'It must have been,' the boy interrupted. 'It was a system key, wasn't it?'

Harry nodded. At the edge of his vision he could see a patrol car driving slowly past. 'It was system keys I wanted to ask about. I'm wondering how an outsider can get hold of a copy of a system key like this. A Trioving key, for example.'

'They can't,' the boy said with the total conviction of someone

360

who reads illustrated science magazines. 'Only Trioving can make a functional copy. So the only way is to falsify written authorisation from the housing committee. But even that would be found out when you come for the key because we will ask to see ID and check it against a list of flat-owners in the block.'

'But I collected one of these system keys. And it was a key for another person.'

The boy frowned. 'No, I remember quite clearly that you showed ID and I checked the name. Whose key was it you think you collected?'

In the reflection in the glass door behind the counter Harry saw the same police car passing in the opposite direction.

'Forget it. Is there any other way of getting a copy?'

'No. Trioving, who grind these keys, only receive orders from authorised dealers like ourselves. And, as I said, we check the documentation and keep an eye on keys ordered for all shared property and housing co-ops. The system should be pretty secure.'

'It sounds it, yes.' Harry rubbed his face with his hand in irritation. 'I rang some time back and was told a woman living in Sorgenfrigata had received three keys for her flat. One we found in her flat, the second she gave to the electrician who was supposed to be fixing something and the third we found somewhere else. The thing is, I don't believe she ordered the third key. Can you check that for me?'

The boy shrugged. 'Certainly I can, but why not ask her yourself?'

'Someone shot her through the head.'

'Ooops,' the boy said, without batting an eyelid.

Harry stood stock-still. He could sense something. The slightest of shivers. A draught from the door maybe? Enough to raise the hairs on the back of your neck. The sound of a tentative clearing of the throat. He hadn't heard anyone come in. Without turning, he tried to see who it was, but from that angle it was impossible.

'Police,' said a loud, high-pitched voice behind him. Harry swallowed hard.

'Yes?' said the boy, looking over Harry's shoulder.

'They're outside,' the voice said. 'They say the old lady down at number 14 has had a break-in. She needs a new lock right away, so they were wondering if we could send someone pronto.'

'Well, you can go with them, Alf. I'm caught up, as you can see.'

Harry listened intently until the footsteps had distanced themselves. 'Anna Bethsen.' He heard himself whispering. 'Can you check if she personally collected all the keys?'

'I don't need to. She *must* have done.'

Harry leaned over the counter. 'Can you check it anyway?'

The boy gave a deep sigh and disappeared into the back room. He returned with a file and flicked through. 'See for yourself,' he said. 'There, there and there.'

Harry recognised the delivery forms. They were identical to the ones he had signed himself when he came for Anna's key. But all the forms were signed by Anna. He was about to ask where the form with his own signature was when his eyes fell on the dates.

'It says here the last key was collected back in August,' he said. 'But that's a long time before I was here and . . .'

'Yes?'

Harry stared up into the air. 'Thank you,' he said. 'I've found what I needed.'

Outside, the wind had picked up. Harry rang from one of the telephone boxes in Valkyrie plass.

'Beate?'

Two seagulls headed into the wind above the tower of the Seamen's School and hovered there. Beneath the gulls lay Oslo fjord, which had gone an ominous green-black hue, and Ekeberg, where the two people on the bench were tiny dots.

Harry had finished talking about Anna Bethsen. About the time they met. About the last evening, some of which he recalled. About Raskol. Beate had finished telling him they had managed to trace the laptop. It had been bought three months ago from the Expert shop by the Colosseum cinema. The guarantee had been made out to Anna Bethsen. And the mobile phone connected to it was the one Harry maintained he had lost.

'I hate the scream of gulls,' Harry said.

'Is that all you've got to say?'

'At this very moment – yes.'

Beate stood up from the bench. 'I shouldn't be here, Harry. You shouldn't have rung me.'

'But you are here.' Harry gave up trying to light his cigarette in the wind. 'It means you believe me. Doesn't it?'

Beate's response was to fling out her arms angrily.

'I don't know any more than you do,' Harry said. 'Not even for certain that I didn't shoot Anna.'

The gulls peeled off and performed an elegant roll in the surge of wind.

'Tell me what you know one more time,' Beate said.

'I know this guy has somehow obtained keys to Anna's flat so he got in and out on the night of the murder. When he left, he took Anna's laptop with him and my mobile phone.'

'What was your mobile phone doing in Anna's flat?'

'It must have fallen out of my jacket pocket during the evening. I was a bit animated, as I told you.'

'And then?'

'His original plan was simple. Drive to Larkollen after the murder and plant the key he'd used in Arne Albu's chalet. Attached to a keyring with the initials AA so that no one would be in any doubt. When he found my mobile phone, though, he suddenly realised he could tweak the plan a bit. Make it look like I had first of all murdered Anna and then rigged it so the blame fell on Albu. Then he used my mobile phone to connect to a server in Egypt and started sending me e-mails in such a way that it was impossible to trace the sender.'

'And if he were traced, it would lead to . . .'

'Me. However, I wouldn't have discovered anything was wrong

until I received the next bill from Telenor. Probably not even then, since I don't read them that carefully.'

'Or stop your subscription when you lose your phone.'

'Mm.' Harry jumped up from the bench and began to pace to and fro. 'What's more difficult to understand is how he got into my cellar storeroom. You didn't find any signs of a break-in and no one in our block would have admitted an intruder. In other words, he must have had a key. In fact, all he would need is one key since we use one system key to fit the main door, loft, cellar and flat, but it's not easy to get hold of one. And the key to Anna's flat was also a system key . . .'

Harry stopped and looked south. A green freighter with two large cranes was on its way up the fjord.

'What are you wondering?' Beate asked.

'I'm wondering whether to ask you to run a check on some names for me.'

'I'd rather not, Harry. I shouldn't even be here, as I said.'

'And I'm wondering where you got the bruises from.'

Her hand went straight to her throat. 'Training. Judo. Anything else you were wondering?'

'Yes, I was wondering if you could give this to Weber.' Harry pulled out the glass wrapped in a cloth from his jacket pocket. 'Ask him to check it for fingerprints and compare them with mine.'

'Has he got yours?'

'Forensics has the fingerprints of all Crime Scene officers. And ask him to analyse what was in the glass.'

'Harry . . .' she began in an admonitory tone.

'Please?'

Beate sighed and took the bundle.

'Låsesmeden AS,' Harry said.

'And what do you mean by that?'

'If you change your mind about checking names, you can run through the staff list at Låsesmeden. It's a small company of locksmiths.'

364

She put on a resigned expression.

Harry shrugged. 'If you give Weber the glass, I'm more than happy.'

'Where do I contact you when Weber has the results?'

'Do you really want to know?' Harry smiled.

'I want to know as little as possible. You contact me, OK?'

Harry pulled his jacket tighter around him. 'Shall we go?'

Beate nodded, but didn't move. Harry raised his eyebrows.

'What he wrote,' she said. 'The bit about only the most vengeful surviving. Do you think it's true, Harry?'

Harry stretched out his legs in the short bed in the caravan. The noise of the cars in Finnmarkgata reminded Harry of his childhood in Oppsal, lying in bed and listening to the traffic. When they were with Grandpa in the silence of Åndalsnes in the summer it was the only thing he longed for: to return to the regular, soporific drone of cars, only broken by a motorbike, a noisy exhaust or a distant police siren.

There was a knock at the door. It was Simon. 'Tess would like you to tell her a goodnight story tomorrow, too,' he said, stepping inside. Harry had told her how the kangaroo had learned to jump and had been rewarded with a goodnight hug by all the children.

The two men smoked in silence. Harry pointed to the photograph on the wall. 'That's Raskol and his brother, isn't it? Stefan, Anna's father?'

Simon nodded.

'Where's Stefan now?'

Simon shrugged, not really interested, and Harry knew the subject was taboo.

'They look like good friends in the photo,' Harry said.

'They were like Siamese twins, you know. Pals. Raskol did two prison stretches for Stefan.' Simon laughed. 'I can see you're taken aback, my friend. It's the tradition. Can you understand? It's an honour to take a brother's or a father's punishment, you know.'

'The police don't exactly feel the same way.'

'They couldn't tell Raskol and Stefan apart. Gypsy brothers. Not easy for Norwegian police.' He grinned and offered Harry a cigarette. 'Especially when they were wearing masks.'

Harry took a drag on his cigarette and took a shot in the dark. 'What came between them?'

'What do you think?' Simon opened his eyes open wide in a dramatic gesture. 'A woman, of course.'

'Anna?'

Simon didn't answer, but Harry knew he was getting warm. 'Was the reason Stefan didn't want anything to do with Anna because she had met a *gadjo*?'

Simon stubbed out his cigarette and stood up. 'It wasn't Anna, but Anna had a mother. Goodnight, *Spiuni*.'

'Mm. Just one last question?'

Simon paused.

'What does *spiuni* mean?'

Simon chuckled. 'It's an abbreviation of *spiuni gjerman* – German spy. But relax, my friend, there's no offence meant. It's even used as a boy's name in some places.'

Then he closed the door and was gone.

The wind had dropped and all you could hear now was the drone of traffic in Finnmarkgata. Yet Harry was unable to fall asleep.

Beate lay in bed listening to the cars outside. As a child she had often fallen asleep to his voice. The stories he told were not in any book; they were created as he spoke. They were never quite the same even if they occasionally started in the same way and they involved the same people: two wicked thieves, a clever daddy and his brave daughter. And they always ended well with the thieves behind lock and key.

Beate could never recall seeing her father read. When she grew up, she realised her father suffered from something they called dyslexia.

366

But for that, he would have been a lawyer, her mother had said.

'Just as we want you to be.'

But the stories hadn't been about lawyers, and when Beate told her she had been accepted at Police College, her mother had cried.

Beate awoke with a start. Someone had rung the bell. She groaned and swung her legs out of bed.

'It's me,' the voice in the intercom said.

'I told you I didn't want to see you any more,' Beate said, shivering in her thin dressing gown. 'Go away.'

'I'll go when I've apologised. It wasn't me. I'm not like that. I just . . . lost control. Please, Beate. Only five minutes.'

She hesitated. Her neck was still stiff and Harry had noticed the bruises.

'I have a present with me,' the voice said.

She sighed. She would have to meet him some time whatever happened. Better to sort things out here than at work. She pressed the button, tightened her dressing gown around her and waited in the doorway listening to his footsteps coming up the stairs.

'Hi,' he said, on seeing her, and smiled. A big, white David Hasselhoff smile.

38

Fusiform Gyrus

Tom Waaler passed her the present, taking great care not to touch her since she still had the frightened body language of an antelope, which predators can smell. Instead he walked past her into the sitting room, and sat himself on the sofa. She followed and remained standing. He looked around. He found himself in young women's flats at regular intervals and they were all furnished more or less in the same way. Personal but unoriginal, snug but dull.

'Aren't you going to open it?' he asked. She did as he requested.

'A CD,' she said, puzzled.

'Not *any* CD,' he said. '*Purple Rain*. Put it on and you'll understand.'

He studied her as she switched on the pathetic all-in-one radio she and others like her called a stereo. Frøken Lønn wasn't exactly good-looking. Sweet in her way, though. Body was a bit uninspiring, not many curves to get hold of, but slim and fit. She had liked what he did with her and exhibited a healthy enthusiasm. At least the first few times when he had taken it a bit *piano*. Yes, in fact, it had lasted more than just the one time. Surprising really because she wasn't his type at all.

Then one evening he had given her the full treatment. And she – in common with most women he met – had not been entirely on the same wavelength. Which only made the whole thing even more appealing to him, but generally it meant that was the last time he heard from them. Which was no skin off his nose. Beate should be happy; it could have been a lot worse. A few evenings before, out of the blue, she had told him where she had seen him for the first time.

'In Grünerløkka,' she had said. 'It was evening and you were sitting in a red car. The streets were full of people and your window was rolled down. It was winter time. Last year.'

He had been pretty amazed. Especially since the only evening he could recall being in Grünerløkka last winter was the Saturday evening they had expedited Ellen Gjelten into the beyond.

'I remember faces,' she had said with a triumphant smile when she saw his reaction. '*Fusiform gyrus*. It's the part of your brain which recognises the shape of faces. Mine is abnormal. I should be doing turns at a fair.'

'I see,' he said. 'What else can you remember?'

'You were talking to someone.'

He had supported himself on his elbows, leaned over her and stroked her larynx with his thumb. Felt the throb of her pulse; she was like a startled leveret. Or was it his own pulse he had felt?

'I suppose you can remember the other face, too, can you?' he had asked, his brain already in overdrive. Did anyone know she was here tonight? Had she kept her mouth shut about their relationship, as he had asked? Did he have any bin bags under the sink?

She had turned to him with a puzzled smile: 'What do you mean?'

'Would you recognise the other person if you saw a photograph?'

She had given him a long look. Kissed him circumspectly.

'Well?' he had said, bringing his other hand up from under the duvet.

'Mm. Mm, no. He had his back to me.'

'But you could remember the clothes he was wearing? If you were asked to identify him, I mean?'

She had shaken her head. 'The *fusiform gyrus* only recognises faces. The rest of my brain is absolutely normal.'

'But you remember the colour of the car I was in?'

She had laughed and snuggled up to him. 'That must mean I liked what I saw, didn't I?'

He had surreptitiously removed his hand from her neck.

Two evenings later he had let her have the whole show. And she hadn't liked what she had been forced to see. Or hear. Or feel.

The opening lines of 'When Doves Cry' blasted from the speakers.

She turned down the volume.

'What do you want?' she asked, sitting down in the armchair.

'As I said. To apologise.'

'You've done that now. So let's draw a line under that, shall we?' She made a show of yawning. 'I was on my way to bed, Tom.'

He could feel his anger mounting. Not the red mist which distorted and obscured, but the white heat which glowed and brought clarity and energy. 'OK, let's get down to business. Where's Harry Hole?'

Beate laughed. Prince let out a falsetto scream.

Tom closed his eyes, felt himself feeling stronger and stronger from the fury streaming through his veins like assuaging glacial water. 'Harry rang you the evening he disappeared. He forwarded e-mails to you. You're his contact, the only person he can trust for the moment. Where is he?'

'I'm exhausted, Tom.' She stood up. 'If you have any more questions I'm unable to answer, I suggest we deal with them tomorrow.'

Tom Waaler didn't move. 'I had an interesting chat with a prison officer in Botsen today. Harry was there last night, right under our noses, while we and half of the uniformed division were out looking for him. Did you know Harry was in league with Raskol?'

'I have no idea what you're talking about or what it has to do with the case.'

'Me neither, but I suggest you take a seat, Beate. And listen to a little story I think will change your mind about Harry and his friends.'

'The answer's no, Tom. Out.'

'Not even if your father's in the story?'

He caught the twitch of her mouth and knew he had hit the mark.

'I have sources which are – how shall I put it? – inaccessible to the regular police officer, meaning I know what happened to your father when he was shot that time in Ryen. And I know who shot him.'

She stared open-mouthed.

Waaler laughed. 'You weren't ready for that, were you.'

'You're lying.'

'Your father was shot with an Uzi, six bullets in the chest. According to the report he went inside the bank to negotiate, even though he was alone, unarmed and thus had nothing to bargain with. All he could hope to achieve was to make the robbers nervous and aggressive. A huge blunder. Incomprehensible. Especially as your father was legendary for his professionalism. In fact, he had a colleague with him, a promising young officer of whom great things were expected, a prospective rising star. But he'd never experienced a *live* bank raid before and certainly not bank raiders with decent shooters.

'He's keen to keep in with his superior officers and that day he's supposed to drive your father home after work. So your father arrives in Ryen in a car which the report fails to mention is not your father's. Because it's in the garage, at home with you, Beate, and Mummy, when you receive the news, isn't it.'

He could see the veins on her neck engorging, becoming thick and blue.

'Fuck you, Tom.'

'Come here now and listen to Daddy's little story,' he said, patting the sofa cushion beside him. 'Because I'm going to speak in a very soft voice and I honestly think you should hear this.'

Reluctantly, she stepped forward a pace, but no further.

'OK,' Tom said. 'On this day in – when was it, Beate?'

'June,' she breathed.

'June, yes. They hear the report on the radio, the bank is close by, they drive there and take up positions outside, armed. The young officer and the experienced inspector. They go by the book, wait for reinforcements or for the robbers to come out of the bank. Not dreaming of entering the bank. Until one of the men appears in the doorway with a gun to the head of the female bank clerk. He calls your father's name. The man has seen them outside and recognised Inspector Lønn. He shouts he won't hurt the woman, but he needs a hostage. If Lønn takes her place, that would be fine by them. But he has to drop his gun and go into the bank alone to effect the exchange. And your father, what does he do? He thinks. He has to think quickly. The woman is in shock. People die of shock. He thinks of his own wife, your mother. A June day, Friday, soon the weekend. And the sun . . . was the sun shining, Beate?'

She nodded.

'He thinks how hot it must be in the bank. The strain. The desperation. Then he makes up his mind. What does he decide? What does he decide, Beate?'

'He goes in.' The whisper was thick with emotion.

'He goes in.' Waaler lowers his voice. 'Inspector Lønn has gone in and the young officer waits. Waits for reinforcements. Waits for the woman to come out. Waits for someone to tell him what to do, or that it is just a dream or a training exercise, and he can go home because it's Friday and the sun is shining. Instead he hears . . .' Waaler imitated the rattle of a gun with his tongue against his palate. 'Your father falls against the front door, which opens, and he is spread on the ground, half in, half out. Six shots in his chest.'

Beate collapsed into the chair.

'The young officer sees the inspector lying there and he knows now it isn't an exercise. Or a dream. They really do have automatic weapons in there and they do shoot policemen in cold blood. He's more frightened than he has ever been before or since. He's read about this, he got good grades in psychology, but something has cracked. He's gripped by the panic he wrote so well about in the exam. He gets in his car and drives. He drives and drives until he's home, and his new young wife comes to meet him and is angry because he's late for the evening meal. He takes his reprimand standing, like a schoolboy, and promises it will never happen again and they eat. After eating, they watch TV. A reporter says a policeman has been shot during a bank raid. Your father is dead.'

Beate hid her face in her hands. It had all come back to her. The whole day. A look of curious wonderment on the round sun in the meaninglessly blue sky. She had thought it was only a dream, too.

'Who could the bank raiders be? Who knows the name of your father, who knows the whole bank scene, who knows that of the two police officers standing outside, Inspector Lønn is the one to pose a threat? Who is so cold and calculating that he can place your father in a dilemma and know which choice he will make? So he can shoot him and do what he likes with the scared young officer? Who's that? Beate?'

The tears were flowing between her fingers. 'Ras . . .' she sniffled.

'I didn't hear, Beate.'

'Raskol.'

'Raskol, yes. And only him. His sidekick was furious. They were robbers, not killers, he said. He was stupid enough to threaten to give himself up and finger Raskol. Fortunately for him, he manages to leave Norway before Raskol catches him.'

Beate was sobbing. Waaler waited.

'Do you know what the funniest thing about this is? That you allowed yourself to be taken in by your father's murderer? Just like your father.'

Beate raised her head. 'What . . . what do you mean?'

Waaler shrugged. 'You ask Raskol to point out the murderer. He's after someone who threatened to testify against him in a murder trial. So what does he do? Of course, he points out this person.'

'Lev Grette?' She dried her tears.

'Why not? So you could help him to find him. I read you found

Grette hanging from a rope. That he'd committed suicide. I wouldn't put money on it. I wouldn't be surprised if someone got there before you.'

Beate cleared her throat. 'You're forgetting a couple of details. First of all, we found a suicide note. Lev didn't leave a lot in writing, but I talked to his brother, who dug up a few of Lev's old school exercise books from the loft in Disengrenda. I took them to Jean Hue, the writing expert in *Kripos*, who confirmed the note was written by Lev. Secondly, Raskol is already in prison. Of his own accord. That doesn't quite square with an intent to murder to avoid punishment.'

Waaler shook his head. 'You're a clever girl, but just like your father you lack psychological insight. You don't understand how the criminal mind works. Raskol isn't in prison; it's just a temporary posting to Botsen. A murder conviction would change all that. In the meantime you're protecting him. And his friend, Harry Hole.'

He leaned forward and placed a hand on her arm. 'I apologise if it was painful, but now you know, Beate. Your father didn't bungle anything. And Harry's working with the man who murdered him. So what do you say? Shall we look for Harry together?'

Beate screwed up her eyes, squeezed out the last tear. Then she opened her eyes again. Waaler held out a handkerchief, which she took.

'Tom,' she said. 'I have to explain something to you.'

'You don't need to.' Waaler stroked her hand. 'I understand. There's a conflict of loyalties. Imagine what your father would have done. It's called being professional, isn't it.'

Beate observed him. Then she slowly nodded her head. She breathed in. At that moment the telephone rang.

'Are you going to take it?' Waaler said, after three rings.

'It's my mother,' Beate said. 'I'll ring her back in thirty seconds.'

'Thirty seconds?'

'That's the time it'll take me to tell you that if I knew where Harry was, you'd be the last person I'd tell.' She passed him his handkerchief. 'And for you to put your shoes on and get out.'

374

Up his back and neck, Tom Waaler could feel the fury rising like a geyser. He took a moment to enjoy the feeling before grabbing her with one arm and forcing her under him. She gasped and resisted him, but he knew she could feel his erection and that the lips she was so tightly clenching would soon open.

After six rings Harry hung up and left the telephone box, so the girl behind him could slip in. He turned his back on Kjølberggata and the wind, lit a cigarette and blew the smoke towards the car park and the caravans. It was funny really. Here he was, a couple of hefty stones' throws away from Forensics in one direction, Police HQ in another and the caravan in the third. Wearing a gypsy's suit. A wanted man. You could kill yourself laughing.

Harry's teeth chattered. He half-turned when a police car swept down the traffic-laden but unpopulated thoroughfare. Harry hadn't been able to sleep. Couldn't bear to be inactive while time was ticking away. He crushed the cigarette end beneath his heel and was about to go when he saw the telephone box was free again. Checked his watch. Almost midnight, strange she wasn't at home. Perhaps she had been asleep and hadn't made it to the phone? He dialled the number again. She answered immediately: 'Beate.'

'It's Harry. Did I wake you?'

'I . . . yes.'

'Sorry. Shall I call back tomorrow?'

'No, it's convenient now.'

'Are you alone?'

Silence. 'Why do you ask?'

'You sound so . . . no, forget it. Have you found out anything?'

He heard her gulp as if she was trying to catch her breath.

'Weber checked the fingerprints on the glass. Most of them are yours. The analysis of the sediment in the glass should be finished in a couple of days.'

'Great.'

'As for the laptop in your storeroom, it turns out there was a specialised program running which allows you to set the date and time for when you want an e-mail to be sent. The last change to the e-mails was made the day Anna Bethsen died.'

Harry no longer felt the icy-cold wind.

'So the e-mails you received were ready and waiting when it was planted,' Beate said. 'That explains how your Pakistani neighbour had seen it in your storage space quite a time ago.'

'Do you mean it had been working away all on its own the whole time?'

'Connected to the mains, the laptop and mobile phone would manage just fine.'

'Hell!' Harry slapped his forehead. 'But that must mean the guy who programmed the laptop anticipated the whole course of events. The whole bloody thing was a puppet show, and we were the puppets.'

'Looks like that. Harry?'

'I'm here. Just trying to let it sink in. Well, better forget it for a while, it's too much in one go. How about the name of the company I gave you?'

'The company, yes. What makes you think I've done anything about that?'

'Nothing. Until you just said what you did.'

'I didn't say anything.'

'No, but the way you said it was full of promise.'

'Oh, yes?'

'You found something, didn't you.'

'I found something.'

'Come on!'

'I rang the accountants that the locksmith uses and got a lady to send me the national insurance numbers of the employees working there. Four full-time staff and two part-time. I ran the numbers through the Criminal and Social Security Register. Five of them have an unblemished record. But one . . .'

'Yes?'

'I had to use the scroll to get everything. Mostly drugs. Has been charged with peddling heroin and morphine, but has only been convicted of possession of a small amount of hash. Has done time for breaking and entering and two aggravated robberies.'

'Violence?'

'He used a gun in one of the robberies. It wasn't fired, but it was loaded.'

'Perfect. He's our man. You're an angel. What's his name?'

'Alf Gunnerud. Thirty years old, single. Thor Olsens gate 9. Seems to live on his own.'

'Repeat the name and address.'

Beate did.

'Mm. Incredible that Gunnerud got a job at a locksmith's with a record like that.'

'Birger Gunnerud is listed as the owner.'

'Right. I see. Sure everything's alright?'

Silence.

'Beate?'

'Everything's OK, Harry. What are you going to do?'

'I was thinking of paying a visit to his flat. See if I can find anything of interest. If I do, I'll ring you from his flat so you can send a car and impound the evidence according to regulations.'

'When are you going?'

'Why?'

Another silence.

'To be sure I'm in when you phone.'

'Eleven tomorrow. I hope he'll be at work then.'

When Harry rang off, he stood gazing at the cloudy night sky arching over the town like a yellow dome. He had heard the music in the background. Barely, but it was enough. Prince's 'Purple Rain'.

He shoved a coin in the slot and dialled 1881.

'I need the number for one Alf Gunnerud . . .'

*

377

The taxi glided like a silent black fish through the night, through the traffic lights, beneath the street lighting and the sign indicating the city centre.

'We can't keep meeting like this,' Øystein said. He looked into the mirror and watched Harry put on the black jumper he had brought him from home.

'Got the crowbar?' Harry asked.

'It's in the boot. What if the john's at home?'

'People at home generally answer the phone.'

'But what if he comes home while you're in his flat?'

'Then do what I said: two short hoots.'

'Alright, alright, but I don't know what the guy looks like.'

'About thirty, I said. See anyone like that going into number 9, you honk your horn.'

Øystein pulled over by a NO PARKING sign in the polluted, traffic-congested twisted bowel of a street which is referred to on page 265 of a dusty book called *City Fathers IV* in the neighbouring public library as 'the extremely dull, unsightly street bearing the name Thor Olsens gate'. But it suited Harry down to the ground that night. The noise, passing cars and the darkness would camouflage him and the waiting taxi.

Harry slipped the crowbar down the sleeve of his leather jacket and quickly crossed the street. To his relief he saw there were at least twenty bells outside number 9. That would give him a good many alternatives if his bluff didn't work at first. Alf Gunnerud's name was second down on the right. He looked up at the right-hand side of the building. The windows on the fourth floor were unlit. Harry rang the ground-floor bell. A woman's sleepy voice answered.

'Hi, I'm trying to contact Alf,' Harry said. 'But they're playing their music so loud they can't hear the bell. Alf Gunnerud, that is. The locksmith on the fourth. You couldn't open up for me, could you?'

'It's past midnight.'

'I apologise. I'll make sure Alf keeps the music down.'

Harry waited. The buzz came.

He took three steps at a time. On the fourth floor he stood and listened, but could only hear his pounding heart. There were two doors to choose between. A grey piece of cardboard with ANDERSEN written in felt pen had been glued to one door. The other was bare.

This was the most critical part of the plan. A single lock could probably be bent open without waking the whole block, but if Alf had used a barrage of locks from Låsesmeden AS, Harry had a problem. He scanned the door from top to bottom. No stickers from a security service or central switchboard. No drill-proof security locks. No burglar-proof twin cylinders with double pins. Just an old Yale cylinder lock. Piece of cake.

Harry lifted the sleeve of his jacket and caught the crowbar as it came out. He hesitated before inserting the tip inside the door under the lock. It was almost too easy. No time to think, though, and no choice. He didn't break open the door, he forced the door towards the hinges so that he could slip Øystein's bank card inside the latch and the deadlock slid out of the box in the door frame. He applied pressure, to push the door out a tiny bit, and put the sole of his foot against the bottom edge. The door creaked on its hinges as he gave the crowbar a nudge and pushed the card through. He slipped inside and closed the door after him. The whole operation had taken eight seconds.

The hum of a refrigerator and sitcom laughter from a neighbour's TV. Harry tried to breathe deeply and evenly as he listened to the total darkness. He could hear cars outside and felt a cold draught, indicating that the windows in the flat were old. But most important: no noises to suggest anyone was at home.

He found the light switch. The hall definitely needed a facelift, the sitting room replastering. The kitchen should have been condemned. The interior of the flat explained the poor security measures. Or to be precise – the lack of interior. Alf Gunnerud had nothing, not even a stereo Harry could have asked him to turn down. The only evidence that someone lived here was two camping chairs, a green coffee table, clothes scattered everywhere and a bed with a duvet but no cover.

Harry put on the washing-up gloves Øystein had brought along and carried one of the chairs into the hall. He put it in front of the row of wall cupboards reaching up to the three-metre-high ceiling, emptied his head of preconceived ideas and cautiously put one foot on the arm. At that moment, the telephone rang. Harry took a step to the side, the camping chair snapped shut and he fell to the floor with a crash.

Tom Waaler had a bad feeling. The situation lacked the clear structure he strove for at all times. Since his career and future prospects did not lie in his own hands, but in the hands of those he allied himself with, the human factor was always a risk he had to take into account. The bad feeling came from the fact that he didn't know if he could rely on Beate Lønn, Rune Ivarsson or – and this was crucial – the man who was his most important source of income: the Knave.

When it came to Tom's ears that the City Council had begun to put pressure on the Chief of Police to catch the Expeditor after the Grønlandsleiret bank hold-up, he had instructed the Knave to go into hiding. They had agreed on a place the Knave knew from the past. Pattaya had the biggest collection of wanted western criminals in the eastern hemisphere and was only a couple of hours' drive south of Bangkok. As a white tourist the Knave would melt into the crowds. The Knave had called Pattaya 'Asia's Sodom', so Waaler couldn't understand why he had suddenly shown up in Oslo, saying he couldn't stand it any longer.

Waaler stopped at the lights in Uelands gate and indicated left. Bad feeling. The Knave had carried out the latest bank job without clearing it with him first, and that was a serious breach of rules. Something would have to be done about it.

He had just tried to ring the Knave, but there was no answer. That might mean anything at all. It might mean, for example, that he was in his chalet in Tryvann working on the details of the heist of a security van they had talked about. Or going over the equipment – clothes, weapons, police radio, drawings. But it might also mean that he had had a relapse and was sitting in the corner nodding, with a syringe hanging from his forearm.

Waaler drove slowly along the dark, filthy little street where the Knave lived. A waiting taxi was parked opposite. Waaler looked up at the windows of the flat. Odd, the lights were on. If the Knave was on junk again, all hell would be let loose. It would be simple enough to get into the flat. There was a naff lock on his door. He looked at his watch. The visit to Beate had excited him, and he knew he wouldn't be able to sleep yet. He would have to cruise around for a bit, make a couple of calls and see what happened.

Waaler put Prince on louder, accelerated and drove up Ullevålsveien.

Harry sat in the camping chair with his head in his hands, an aching hip and not a shred of evidence that Alf Gunnerud was the man. It had only taken ten minutes to go through the few possessions in the flat, so few that the suspicion lingered that he lived somewhere else. Harry had found a toothbrush in the bathroom, an almost empty tube of toothpaste and a piece of unidentifiable soap stuck to a soap dish. Plus a towel which might once have been white. That was it. That was his chance.

Harry felt like laughing. Banging his head against the wall. Smashing the top off a bottle of Jim Beam and drinking the whiskey with the shards of glass. Because it had to be – had to be – Gunnerud. Of all incriminating evidence, statistically, one piece was head and shoulders above the others – previous charges and convictions. The case simply screamed out Gunnerud's name. He had narco and guns on his record, he worked for a locksmith, could order whatever system keys he needed, say, to Anna's flat. Or to Harry's.

He went over to the window. Wondering how he could have gone in a circle following an insane man's script down to the last letter. But now there were no more instructions, no more lines in the dialogue. The moon peeped through a break in the clouds and resembled a half-chewed fluoride tablet, but not even that could jog his memory.

He closed his eyes. Concentrated. What had he seen in the flat which might give him the next line? What had he missed? He went through the flat in his mind, piece by piece.

After three minutes he gave up. It was all over. There was nothing here.

He checked everything was as it had been when he arrived and turned the sitting-room light off. Went to the toilet, stood in front of the bowl and unbuttoned. Waited. Christ, now he couldn't even do that. Then it flowed and he released a weary sigh. He pressed the handle, the water flushed and at that moment he froze. Wasn't that a car horn he had heard over the gushing water? He went into the hall and closed the toilet door to hear better. It was. A short, firm beep from the street. Gunnerud was on his way! Harry was already standing in the doorway when it struck him. Of course it had to strike him now, when it was too late. Flushing water. *The Godfather*. The gun. *That's my favourite place.*

'Fuck, fuck, fuck!'

Harry ran back into the toilet, grabbed the knob on top of the cistern and frantically began to loosen it. The rusty, red screw came into view. 'Faster,' he whispered. His heart accelerated as he twisted the knob and the damned rod went round and round with a groan but refused to come off. He heard a door slam down in the stairwell. Then it came off and he lifted the cistern lid. The harsh sound of porcelain on porcelain resounded in the semi-dark as the water continued to rise. Harry stuck his hand inside and his fingers brushed against the slippery coating of the tank. What the fuck? Nothing? He turned over the cistern lid, and there it was. Taped to the inside. He took a deep breath. Every notch, every indentation, every jagged edge of the key under the shiny tape was an old friend. It fitted Harry's front entrance, the cellar and his flat. The picture beside it was equally well known. The missing photograph in the mirror. Sis was smiling and Harry was trying to look tough. A summer tan and blissfully ignorant. However, Harry was not familiar with the white powder in the plastic bag attached by three broad pieces of black gaffer tape, but he was willing to bet a tidy sum it was diacetyl morphine, better known as heroin. A lot of heroin. Six years' unconditional, at least. Harry didn't touch anything, just replaced the lid and began to screw it back while listening for footsteps. As Beate had pointed out, the evidence would be worth diddly if it was discovered that Harry had been in the flat without a warrant. The knob was back in position and he ran for the door. Had no choice, opened the door and stepped onto the landing. Shuffling steps were on their way up. He closed the door quietly, peeped over the railings and saw a dark, thick mop of hair. In five seconds he would see Harry. Three long strides up to the fifth floor would be enough to keep Harry out of sight.

The man stopped abruptly when he spotted Harry sitting in front of him.

'Hi, Alf,' Harry said, looking at his watch. 'I've been waiting for you.'

The man stared at him with large eyes. A pale, freckled face was framed by greasy, shoulder-length hair with a Liam Gallagher cut around his ears. He did not remind Harry of a hard-bitten killer but a young lad frightened of more beatings.

'What do you want?' the man asked in a loud, high-pitched voice.

'I want you to come with me to Police HQ.'

The man reacted spontaneously. He swivelled, grabbed the railings and jumped down to the landing beneath. 'Hey!' Harry shouted, but the man had already disappeared from view. The heavy smack of feet as they hit the fifth or sixth step echoed up the stairwell.

'Gunnerud!'

Harry heard the downstairs door slam by way of response.

He reached inside his jacket pocket and realised he didn't have any cigarettes. Now it was the cavalry's turn.

Tom Waaler turned down the music, pulled the bleeping mobile phone from his pocket, pressed the green button and put the phone to his ear. At the other end he could hear breathing coming in quick, nervous pants, and traffic.

'Hello?' said the voice. 'Are you there?' It was the Knave. He sounded terrified.

'What's up, Knave?'

'Oh, God, there you are. All hell's broken loose. You've got to help me. Quick.'

'I don't have to do anything. Answer the question.'

'They've found us. There was a cop on the stairs waiting for me to come home.'

Waaler stopped at the zebra crossing before Ringveien. An old man, with strange, miniscule steps, was making his way across. He seemed to be taking for ever.

'What did he want?' Waaler asked.

'What do *you* think? To arrest me, I suppose.'

'And why haven't you been arrested?'

'I ran like fuck. Legged it straight away. But they're after me. Three police cars have driven by already. Do you hear? They'll get me unless—'

'Don't shout on the phone. Where were the other officers?'

'I didn't see any others. I just took off.'

'And you got away so easily? Are you sure the guy was a policeman?'

'Yes, it was him, wasn't it!'

'Who?'

'Harry Hole, I suppose. He was in the shop again recently.'

'You didn't tell me.'

'It's a locksmith's. There are police there all the time!'

The lights changed to green. Waaler hooted at the car in front. 'OK, let's talk about it later. Where are you now?'

'I'm in a telephone box in front of er . . . the Law Courts.' He laughed nervously. 'And I don't like it here.'

'Is there anything in your flat that shouldn't be there?'

'It's clean. All the equipment is in the chalet.'

'And what about you? Are you clean?'

'You know very well I'm off the habit. Are you coming or what? Fuck me, my whole body's shaking.'

'Just take it easy, Knave.' Waaler calculated how long it would take him. Tryvann. Police HQ. City centre. 'Think of it as a bank job. I'll give you a pill when I get there.'

'I've told you, I've given up.' He hesitated. 'I didn't know you carried pills around with you, Prince.'

'Always.'

Silence.

'What have you got?'

'Mother's Arms. Rohypnol. Have you got the Jericho I gave you?'

'Always.'

'Good. Now listen carefully. Our meeting place is the quay to the east of the container terminal. I'm quite a distance away so you'll have to give me forty minutes.'

'What are you talking about? You've got to come here, for fuck's sake! Now!'

Waaler listened to the breathing crackling against the membrane, without answering.

'If they get me, I'll take you with me. I hope you understand that, Prince. I'll sing if I can get off. I'm not fucking taking your rap if you—'

'That sounds like panic, Knave. And we don't need panic now. What guarantee do I have that you haven't already been arrested and this isn't a trap to set me up? Do you understand now? Come on your own and stand under a streetlight so I can see you clearly when I come.'

The Knave groaned: 'Shit! Shit! Shit!'

'Well?'

'Right. Fine. Bring the pills. Shit!'

'Container terminal in forty minutes. Under a light.'

'Don't be late.'

'Hang on, there's more. I'll park down the road from you. When I say so, hold the gun in the air so I can see it clearly.'

'What for? You paranoid, or what?'

'Let's just say the situation is a little unclear at the present moment and I'm not taking any chances. Do as I say.'

Waaler pressed the red button and looked at his watch. Flicked the volume control right round. Guitars. Beautiful pure noise. Beautiful pure fury.

Bjarne Møller stepped into the flat and scanned the room with a disapproving expression.

'Cosy nook, isn't it,' Weber said.

'An old acquaintance, I heard?'

'Alf Gunnerud. At least the flat's in his name. There are loads of fingerprints here. Have to see whether they're his. Glass.' He pointed to a young man applying a thin brush to the window. 'Best prints are always on glass.'

'Since you're taking prints now, I assume you've found other things here?'

Weber pointed to a plastic bag on a floor rug with a number of other objects. Møller crouched down and poked a finger through a split in the bag. 'Hm. Tastes like heroin. Must be close on half a kilo. And what's this?'

'A photograph of two children. We still don't know who they are. And a Trioving key which certainly doesn't fit this door.'

'If it's a system key, Trioving can soon tell us who the owner is. There's something familiar about the boy in the photo.'

'I thought so, too.'

'*Fusiform gyrus*,' a woman's voice said behind them.

'Frøken Lønn,' Møller said in surprise. 'What's Robberies Unit doing here?'

'It was me who got the tip-off there was heroin here. I was asked to call you in.'

386

'So you have informers in the narco family, too?'

'Bank robbers, narco, it's all one big happy family, you know.'

'Who was the informer?'

'No idea. He rang me at home after I'd gone to bed. Wouldn't give his name or say how he knew I was in the police. But the tip-off was so specific and detailed I took action and woke one of the police solicitors.'

'Hm,' Møller said. 'Drugs. Previous conviction. Chance valuable evidence may be lost. You got the green light straight away, I imagine.'

'Yes.'

'I don't see a body, so why was I called?'

'The informer tipped me off about something else.'

'Oh, yes?'

'Alf Gunnerud is supposed to have known Anna Bethsen intimately. He was her lover and dealer. Until she dumped him for someone else while he was inside. What do you think about that, PAS Møller?'

Møller looked at her. 'I'm happy,' he said, without showing any reaction. 'Happier than you can imagine.'

He continued to look at her and, in the end, had to lower his gaze.

'Weber,' he said. 'I want you to cordon off this apartment and call in all the people you have at your disposal. We have a job to do.'

39

Glock

STEIN THOMMESEN HAD BEEN WORKING FOR TWO YEARS AS A uniformed policeman. His greatest wish was to become a detective and his dream to become a police expert with fixed hours, his own office and a better salary than an inspector. To be able to go home to Trine and tell her about an interesting problem at work he and a specialist from the Serious Crime Unit were discussing, which she would find immensely, unimaginably complicated. In the meantime he was doing shifts for a pittance, he woke up dog-tired even after sleeping for ten hours, and when Trine said she wasn't going to live like that for the rest of her life, he would try to explain what it does to you spending your working hours driving teenagers with an overdose to A&E, telling kids that he has to arrest their father because he's been beating up their mother, and taking all the shit from people who hate the uniform you're wearing. And Trine would roll her eyes. Heard it all before.

When Inspector Tom Waaler from Crime Squad came into the duty room and asked Stein Thommesen if he would go with him to bring in a wanted man, Thommesen's first thought was perhaps Waaler would give him a few tips on how to go about becoming a detective.

He mentioned it to Waaler in the car on their way down Nylandsveien towards the traffic machine and Waaler smiled. Slap a few words down on a piece of paper, that's all there was to it, he said. He, Waaler, might be able to put in a good word for him.

'That would be . . . great.' Thommesen wondered if he should say 'Thank you', or if it would sound ingratiating. After all, there wasn't a lot to thank him for as yet. He would certainly tell Trine that he had put out feelers, though. Yes, that was exactly the word he would use: 'feelers'. Then nothing, maintain the mystique, until perhaps he heard something.

'What sort of guy are we pulling in?' he asked.

'I was out patrolling and heard on the radio they had recovered a quantity of heroin in Thor Olsens gate. Alf Gunnerud.'

'Yes, I heard that. Almost half a kilo.'

'Then a guy tipped me off he'd seen Gunnerud down at the container terminal.'

'Informers must be on their toes this evening. It was an anonymous tip-off that led to the heroin seizure as well. Might be a coincidence, but it's odd that two anonymous—'

'Could be the same informer,' Waaler interrupted. 'Maybe someone's got it in for Gunnerud, been screwed or something?'

'Perhaps . . .'

'So you want to be a detective,' Waaler said and Thommesen thought he noted a touch of irritation in his voice. They turned off the traffic machine towards the docks area. 'Yes, I can see that. It's a change, isn't it? Thought about which section?'

'Crime Squad,' Thommesen said. 'Or Robberies Unit. Not Sexual Offences, I don't think.'

'No, of course not. Here we are.'

They crossed a dark, open square with containers piled up on top of each other and a large, pink building at the end.

'Guy standing under the streetlamp fits the description,' Waaler said.

'Where?' Thommesen said, peering into the dark.

'By the building over there.'

'Holy shit! You've got good eyes.'

'Are you armed?' Waaler asked, slowing down.

Thommesen looked at Waaler in surprise. 'You didn't say anything about—'

'That's fine, I am. Stay in the car so you can call for support if he gives us any trouble, OK?'

'OK. Are you sure we shouldn't call—?'

'No time.' Waaler switched his lights on full beam and came to a halt. Thommesen estimated the distance to the silhouette under the light to be fifty metres, but later measurements would show the exact distance was thirty-four.

Waaler loaded his Glock 20 – he had applied for and received a special permit to carry it – and, grabbing a large black torch from between the front seats, got out of the car. He shouted as he started to move towards the man. There would turn out to be a large discrepancy on exactly this point in the two policemen's incident reports. In Waaler's report, he had shouted: 'Police! Let's see them!' meaning: 'Put your hands above your head.' The Public Prosecutor agreed it was reasonable to assume that an ex-con with several arrests behind him would be familiar with that kind of jargon. And Inspector Waaler had clearly stated he was from the police. In Thommesen's original report, Waaler shouted: 'Hi, this is your police friend. Let's see it.' After some consultation between Waaler and Thommesen, however, Thommesen said that Waaler's version was probably closer to the truth.

There was no disagreement about what happened next. The man under the light reacted by putting his hand inside his jacket and taking out a gun which, it would transpire, was a Glock 23 with the serial number filed off and therefore impossible to trace. Waaler, who was, according to SEFO, the independent police authority, one of the best marksmen in the police force, screamed and fired three shots in quick succession. Two hit Alf Gunnerud. One in the left shoulder, the other in the hip. Neither of them was fatal, but they knocked Gunnerud backwards and he stayed on the ground. Waaler ran towards Gunnerud with his gun raised and shouting: 'Police! Don't touch the gun or I'll shoot! Don't touch the gun, I said!'

From this point on Stein Thommesen's report had little of any substance to add since he was thirty-four metres away, it was dark and, in addition, Waaler was in his line of vision. On the other hand, there was nothing in Thommesen's report – or in the evidence at the scene – which contradicted the next events as described in Waaler's report: Gunnerud grabbed the gun, pointed it at him despite the warnings and Waaler got his shot in first. The distance between the two was between three and five metres.

I'm going to die. And there's no sense in it. I'm staring down a smoking barrel. This wasn't the plan, not mine at any rate. I might have been heading this way all the time, though. But it wasn't my plan. My plan was better. My plan made sense. The cabin pressure is falling and an invisible force is pressing against my eardrums from inside. Someone leans over and asks me if I'm ready. We're landing now.

I whisper I've been a thief, liar, pusher and fornicator. But I've never killed anyone. The woman in Grensen I hurt, that was just one of those things. The stars beneath are shining through the fuselage.

'It's a sin . . .' I whisper. 'Against the woman I loved. Can it be forgiven, too?' But the stewardess has already moved away and the landing lights are ablaze on all sides.

It was the evening Anna said 'No' for the first time and I said 'Yes' and shoved the door open. It was the purest junk I had ever got my hands on and we weren't going to spoil the fun by smoking it. She protested but I said it was on the house and prepared the syringe. She had never injected heroin and I gave her the shot. It was harder to do it to others. After a couple of failures she looked at me and murmured: 'I've been drug-free for three months. I was cured.' 'Welcome back,' I said. She laughed and said: 'I'm going to kill you.' I found the vein the third time. Her pupils opened, slowly like black roses. Drops of blood

391

from her forearm landed on the carpet with weary sighs. Then her head tipped backwards. The day after she rang me and wanted more. The wheels are screaming on the tarmac.

We could have made something good out of our lives, you and I. That was the plan, it made sense. I have no idea what the sense of this is.

According to the post-mortem the 10-millimetre bullet hit and smashed Alf Gunnerud's nasal bone. Fragments of the bone followed the projectile through the thin tissue in front of the brain, and the lead and bone destroyed the thalamus, the limbic system and the cerebellum before the bullet penetrated the rear cranium. Finally, it bored a hole in the tarmac which was still porous after the road-maintenance people had repaired the car park two days before.

40

Bonnie Tyler

IT WAS A DISMAL, SHORT AND GENERALLY UNNECESSARY DAY. Leaden clouds heavy with rain swept across the city without releasing a drop and occasional gusts of wind tugged at the newspapers in the stand outside Elmer's Fruit&Tobacco kiosk. Headlines on the newspaper stand implied that people had begun to get sick of the so-called war on terror, which now had the somewhat odious connotation of an election slogan and had furthermore lost momentum since no one knew where the principal offender was. Some even thought he was dead. The newspapers had thus begun to give column space to reality-TV stars, minor foreign celebrities who had said something nice about Norwegians and the Royals' holiday plans. The only drama to break the monotony was a shooting incident by the container terminal where a wanted murderer and drug pusher had raised a gun at a policeman and been killed before firing a shot. The Head of the Narcotics Unit reported a substantial heroin seizure in the dead man's apartment while the Head of Crime Squad commented that the murder the thirty-year-old was alleged to have committed was still under investigation. The newspaper with the latest editorial deadline had, however, added that the evidence against the man, who was not of foreign origin, was compelling. And, oddly enough, the policeman involved was the same one who had shot dead the neo-Nazi Sverre Olsen in his home in a similar case over a year ago. The policeman had been suspended until the independent police authorities had finished making their inquiries, the paper wrote, and quoted the Chief Superintendent, who said this was routine procedure in such situations and had nothing to do with the Sverre Olsen case.

A chalet fire in Tryvann had also found space in a tiny paragraph because an empty petrol canister had been found close to the scene of the totally destroyed house, and therefore police could not rule out the possibility of arson. What didn't appear in print were attempts by journalists to contact Birger Gunnerud to ask him how it felt to lose his son and chalet in the same night.

It got dark early and by three o' clock streetlights were already on.

A freeze-frame of the Grensen robbery quivered on the screen in the House of Pain when Harry walked in.

'Got anywhere?' he asked with a nod to the picture showing the Expeditor in full swing.

Beate shook her head. 'We're waiting.'

'For him to strike again?'

'He's sitting somewhere and planning another hold-up right now. It'll be some time next week, I reckon.'

'You seem sure.'

She shrugged. 'Experience.'

'Yours?'

She smiled but didn't answer.

Harry sat down. 'Hope you weren't put out that I didn't do what I said on the phone.'

She frowned. 'What do you mean?'

'I said I wasn't going to search his flat until today.'

Harry studied her. She looked totally, and genuinely, perplexed. Well, Harry didn't work for the Secret Service. He was about to speak, but then changed his mind. Instead Beate said: 'There's something I have to ask you, Harry.'

'Shoot.'

'Did you know about Raskol and my father?'

'What about them?'

'That Raskol was . . . in the bank that time. He shot my father.'

Harry lowered his gaze. Examined his hands. 'No,' he said. 'I didn't.'

'But you had guessed?'

He raised his head and met Beate's eyes. 'The thought had occurred to me. That's all.'

'What made you think it?'

'Penance.'

'Penance?'

Harry took a deep breath. 'Sometimes a crime is so monstrous it clouds your vision. Externally or internally.'

'What do you mean?'

'Everyone has a need to do penance, Beate. You, too. God knows I do. And Raskol does. It's a basic need, like washing. It's about harmony, an absolutely essential inner balance. It's the balance we call morality.'

Harry saw Beate blanch. Then blush. She opened her mouth.

'No one knows why Raskol gave himself up,' Harry said. 'I'm convinced, though, that it was in order to do penance. For someone whose only freedom is the freedom to wander, prison is the ultimate self-punishment. Taking a life is different from taking money. Suppose he had committed a crime that caused him to lose his balance. So he chooses to do secret penance, for himself and God – if he has one.'

Beate finally stammered out the words: 'A . . . moral . . . murderer?'

Harry waited. But nothing was forthcoming.

'A moral person is someone who accepts the consequences of their own morality,' he said softly. 'Not those of others.'

'And what if I strapped this on?' Beate said bitterly, opening the drawer in front of her and taking out a shoulder holster. 'What if I locked myself in one of the visitors' rooms with Raskol and said afterwards he attacked me and I shot in self-defence? To avenge my father the same way you deal with vermin. Is that moral enough for you?' She slammed the shoulder holster on the table.

Harry leaned back in his chair and closed his eyes until he heard her accelerated breathing calm down. 'The question is what is moral enough for you, Beate. I don't know why you have your gun with you, and I have no intention of preventing you from doing whatever you want.'

He stood up. 'Make your father proud, Beate.'

As he grabbed the door handle he heard Beate sobbing. He turned.

'You don't understand!' she sobbed. 'I thought I could . . . I thought it was a kind of . . . a score to settle.'

Harry remained motionless. Then he pushed a chair close to her, sat down and placed a hand against her cheek. Her tears were hot and rolled over his rough hand as she spoke. 'You join the police because you have some idea that there has to be order, a balance to things, don't you. A reckoning, justice and all that. And then one day you have the chance you have always dreamed of, to even the scores. Only to find out that's not what you want after all.' She sniffled. 'My mother once said there's only one thing worse than not satisfying a desire. And that is not to feel any desire. Hatred – it's sort of all you have left when you've lost everything else. And then it's taken from you.'

She swept the shoulder holster off the table with her arm. It thudded against the wall.

It was pitch black as Harry stood in Sofies gate searching a more familiar jacket pocket for his keys. One of the first things he had done that morning at Police HQ had been to collect his clothes from *Krimteknisk*, where they had been taken from Vigdis Albu's house. But the very first thing had been to make an appearance in Bjarne Møller's office. The Head of Crime Squad had said that as far as Harry was concerned almost everything looked fine, but they would have to wait to see if anyone reported a break-in at Harelabben 16. Over the course of the day consideration would be given to whether there would be any response to Harry's withholding of information regarding his presence in Anna Bethsen's flat on the night of the murder. Harry replied that, in the event of an investigation into the case, he would be obliged to mention the free rein the Chief Superintendent and Møller had given him in the search for the Expeditor, plus their sanctioning of a trip to Brazil without informing the Brazilian police.

Bjarne Møller had grinned wryly and said he assumed they would conclude that no investigation was necessary, or indeed any response.

The entrance hall was quiet. Harry tore down the police tape in front of the door of his flat. A piece of chipboard had been fitted over the broken pane.

He stood surveying the sitting room. Weber explained that they had taken photographs of the flat before they started the search so that everything could be put back properly. Nevertheless, he couldn't escape the knowledge that alien hands and eyes had been there. It wasn't that there was so much to hide – some passionate but dated love letters, an open pack of condoms well past their sell-by date and an envelope containing photographs of Ellen Gjelten's dead body. Having them at home might possibly be considered as perverted. Apart from that: one pornographic magazine, one Bonnie Tyler record and a book by Linn Ullmann.

Harry regarded the flashing red light on the answer machine for a long time before pressing. The familiar voice of a boy filled the estranged room. 'Hi, this is us. They decided today. Mummy is crying, so she told me to say . . .'

Harry steeled himself and breathed in.

'We're leaving tomorrow.'

Harry held his breath. Had he heard correctly? *We're* leaving?

'We won. You should have seen their faces. Mummy said everyone thought we would lose. Mummy, do you want . . . no, she's just

397

crying. Now we're going to McDonald's to celebrate. Mummy says, will you pick us up? Bye.'

He heard Oleg breathing into the phone and someone blowing their nose and laughing in the background. Then Oleg's voice again, quieter: 'Great if you would, Harry.'

Harry slumped into the chair. A lump grew in his throat and the tears flowed.

PART VI

41

S²MN

THERE WASN'T A CLOUD IN THE SKY, BUT THE WIND WAS bitingly cold and the pale sun didn't give much warmth. Harry and Aune had turned up the collars of their jackets and walked next to each other down the avenue of birch trees, which had already divested themselves of their leaves for winter.

'I told my wife how happy you sounded when you told me Rakel and Oleg were coming back home,' Aune said. 'She asked if that meant you three would soon live together.'

Harry answered with a smile.

'At least she has enough room in that house of hers,' Aune prodded.

'There's enough room in the house,' Harry said. 'Say hi to Karoline and quote Ola Bauer.'

' "I moved to Carefree Street"?'

' "But that didn't help much, either." '

They both laughed.

'Anyway, my mind is pretty much on the case at the moment,' Harry said.

'The case, yes,' Aune said. 'I've read all the reports, as you asked.

Bizarre. Truly bizarre. You wake up in your flat, can't remember a thing and bang, you're caught up in this game of Alf Gunnerud's. Naturally, it is a bit tricky to establish a psychological diagnosis post-mortem, but he is truly an interesting case. Doubtless a very intelligent, creative soul. Almost artistic, even. It's a masterly plan he hatched. There are a couple of things I wondered about. I read the copies of the e-mails he sent you. He referred to the fact that you had had a blackout. That must mean he saw you leave the flat in an inebriated state and speculated that you wouldn't remember anything the following day?'

'That's how it is when a man has to be helped into a taxi. I would guess he was standing in the street outside, spying on me, just as he wrote in his e-mail Arne Albu was doing. Presumably he had been in touch with Anna and knew I would be coming that evening. My leaving the house so drunk must have been an unexpected bonus.'

'So then he unlocked the flat with a key he got from the manufacturer via Låsesmeden AS. And shot her. Using his own gun?'

'Probably. The serial number had been filed off. As was the number on the gun we found in Gunnerud's hand in the container terminal. Weber says the filing patterns suggest they come from the same supplier. Looks like someone is running an illegal arms-import business on a grand scale. The Glock we found at Sverre Olsen's – Ellen's killer – had exactly the same file marks.'

'So he puts the gun in her right hand. Even though she was left-handed.'

'Bait,' Harry said. 'Naturally enough, he knew I would get involved in the case at some point, if for no other reason than to make sure my position wouldn't be compromised. And he knew that, unlike the other officers, I would realise it was the wrong hand.'

'And then there was the photograph of fru Albu and the children.'

'To lead me to Arne Albu, her last lover.'

'And before he leaves, he takes Anna's laptop and the mobile telephone you dropped in the flat during the evening.'

'Another unexpected bonus.'

'So this brain concocted an intricate, watertight plan for how he was going to punish his faithless lover, the man with whom she deceived him while he was in prison and her resurrected mission, the blond-haired policeman. In addition, he begins to improvise. Once again he uses his job at Låsesmeden AS to gain access to your flat and cellar. He plants Anna's laptop there, connected to your mobile phone, and sets up an e-mail account via an untraceable server.'

'Almost untraceable.'

'Ah, yes, this anonymous computer nerd of yours found that out. But what he didn't find out was that the e-mails you received had been written in advance and were sent on pre-determined dates from the computer in your storeroom. In other words, the sender had set everything up well before the laptop was put in position. Correct?'

'Mm. Did you read the e-mails?'

'Indeed.' Aune nodded. 'In retrospect, you can see that while they factored in a certain unfolding of events, they were also vague. But it wouldn't seem like that to the person caught up in events; the sender would appear permanently well-informed and online. But he could do that because in many ways he was running the whole show.'

'Well, we don't know yet if it was Gunnerud who orchestrated the murder of Arne Albu. A colleague at the locksmith's says he and Gunnerud were at Gamle Major drinking beer at the time of the murder.'

Aune rubbed his hands. Harry wasn't sure if it was because of the cold wind or because he was enjoying the thought of so many logically possible or impossible outcomes. 'Let's assume Gunnerud didn't kill Albu,' the psychologist said. 'What fate had he planned for him by pointing you in his direction? That Albu would be convicted? But then you would go free. And vice versa. Two men can't be convicted of the same murder.'

'Right,' Harry said. 'You have to ask yourself what the most important thing in Albu's life was?'

'Excellent,' Aune said. 'A father of three who voluntarily, or not, scales down his professional ambitions. The family, I assume.'

'And what had Gunnerud achieved by revealing, or rather allowing me to find out, that Arne Albu was continuing to meet Anna?'

'His wife took the children and left him.'

' "Losing your life is not the worst thing that can happen. The worst thing is to lose your reason for living." '

'Good quote.' Aune gave him a nod of acknowledgement. 'Who said that?'

'Forgotten,' Harry said.

'But the next question you have to ask is what he wanted to take from you, Harry? What makes your life worth living?'

They had arrived at the house where Anna had lived. Harry fidgeted with the keys for a long time.

'Well?' Aune said.

'All Gunnerud probably knew about me was what Anna had told him. And she knew me from the time when I didn't have . . . much more than the job.'

'The job?'

'He wanted me behind bars. But, primarily, kicked out of the force.'

They talked as they went up the stairs.

Inside the flat Weber and his boys had finished the forensic examination. Weber was happy and said they had found Gunnerud's prints in several places, including the bedhead.

'He wasn't exactly careful,' Weber said.

'He was here so many times you would have found prints even if he had been,' Harry said. 'Besides, he was convinced he would never come under suspicion.'

'Incidentally, the way Albu was killed was interesting,' Aune said as Harry opened the sliding door to the room with the portraits and the Grimmer lamp. 'Buried upside down. On a beach. It looked like a rite, as if the murderer was trying to tell us something about himself. Have you given it any thought?'

'Not my case.'

'That wasn't what I asked.'

'OK. Maybe the murderer wanted to say something about the victim.'

'What do you mean?'

Harry switched on the Grimmer lamp and light fell on the three pictures. 'It reminds me of something in my law studies, the Gulathing Law of 1100. It states that everyone who dies should be buried in holy ground except for men of dishonour, traitors and murderers. They should be buried where the sea meets land. The place where Albu was buried doesn't suggest a jealousy killing, as it would have been if Gunnerud had killed him. Someone wanted to show that Albu was a criminal.'

'Interesting,' said Aune. 'Why should we look at these pictures again? They're terrible.'

'You're really sure you can't see anything in them?'

'I certainly can. I can see a pretentious young artist with an exaggerated sense of drama and no sense of art.'

'I have a colleague called Beate Lønn. She couldn't be here today because she's giving a talk at a police conference in Germany, about how it is possible to recognise masked criminals with the help of computer manipulation of images and the *fusiform gyrus*. She has a special innate talent: she can recognise all the faces she has seen in the whole of her life.'

Aune nodded. 'I am aware of this phenomenon.'

'When I showed her these pictures she recognised the people.'

'Oh?' Aune raised an eyebrow. 'Tell me more.'

Harry pointed. 'The one on the left is Arne Albu, the one in the middle is me and the last is Alf Gunnerud.'

Aune squinted, straightened his glasses and tried looking at the pictures from a variety of distances. 'Interesting,' he mumbled. 'Extremely interesting. I can only see the shapes of heads.'

'I only wanted to know if you, as an expert witness, can vouchsafe that this kind of recognition is possible. It would help us to make further links between Gunnerud and Anna.'

Aune waved his hand. 'If what you say about frøken Lønn is

true, she could have recognised a face with minimal information.'

Outside again, Aune said that he would be keen to meet this Beate Lønn professionally. 'She is a detective, I take it?'

'In the Robberies Unit. I worked with her on the Expeditor case.'

'Oh, yes. How's it going?'

'Well, there are not many leads. They had been expecting him to strike again soon, but nothing has happened. Odd, actually.'

In Bogstadveien, Harry noticed the first snowflakes swirling in the wind.

'Winter!' Ali shouted across the street to Harry, pointing up at the sky. He said something in Urdu to his brother, who immediately took over the job of carrying the fruit crates back inside the shop. Then Ali padded across the road to Harry. 'Isn't it wonderful it's over?' He smiled.

'Yes, it is,' Harry said.

'Autumn's bloody awful. Finally, a bit of snow.'

'Oh, yes. I thought you meant the case.'

'Of the laptop in your storeroom? Is it over?'

'Hasn't anyone told you? They've found the man who put it there.'

'Aha. That must be why my wife was told I didn't need to go to the police station for questioning today after all. What was it about, anyway?'

'To cut a long story short, a guy was trying to make out I was involved in a serious crime. Invite me to a meal one day and I'll give you all the details.'

'I've already invited you, Harry!'

'You didn't say when.'

Ali rolled his eyes. 'Why do you have to have a date and a time before you dare to drop by? Knock on the door and I'll open up. We've always got food.'

'Thanks, Ali. I'll knock loud and clear.' Harry opened the door.

'Did you find out who the lady was? Was she an assistant?'

'What do you mean?'

'The mysterious lady I saw in front of the cellar door that day. I told Tom somebody-or-other about it.'

Harry stood with his hand on the door handle. 'Exactly what did you say to him, Ali?'

'He asked if I had seen anything unusual in or around the cellar and then I remembered I'd seen the back of a lady I didn't recognise by the cellar door as I came in the building. I remembered because I was going to ask who she was, but then I heard the lock click so I assumed if she had a key, she had to be OK.'

'When was this and what did she look like?'

Ali opened his palms in apology. 'I was busy and only glimpsed her back. Three weeks ago? Five weeks? Blonde hair? Dark hair? No idea.'

'But you're sure it was a woman?'

'I must have thought it was a woman, anyway.'

'Alf Gunnerud was medium height, narrow-shouldered with dark, shoulder-length hair. Is that what made you think it was a woman?'

Ali pondered. 'Yes, it might have been. And it could also have been fru Melkersen's daughter visiting. For instance.'

'Bye, Ali.'

Harry decided to take a quick shower before changing and going to see Rakel and Oleg, who had invited him to pancakes and Tetris. On their return from Moscow, Rakel had brought back an attractive chess set with carved pieces and a board made of wood and mother-of-pearl. Unfortunately, Rakel hadn't liked the Namco G-Con 45 gun Harry had bought for Oleg and had immediately confiscated it. She had explained that she had told Oleg many times that he was not to play with firearms until he was twelve, at least. Harry and Oleg had both rather shamefacedly accepted this without any discussion. But they knew Rakel would take advantage of the opportunity to go jogging while Harry looked after Oleg. And Oleg had whispered to Harry that he knew where she had hidden the Namco G-Con 45 gun.

The burning-hot jets of water drove the cold out of his body as he tried to forget what Ali had said. There would always be room for doubts in any case, however cut and dried it seemed. And Harry was a born doubter. At some point, though, you had to have some faith, if life was to have any shape or make sense.

He dried himself down, shaved and put on a clean shirt. Checked himself over in the mirror and grinned. Oleg had said he had yellow teeth, and Rakel had laughed a bit too loudly. In the mirror he saw the printout of the first e-mail from S^{2}MN pinned to the opposite wall. Tomorrow he would take it down and put up the photograph of Sis and himself. Tomorrow. He studied the e-mail in the mirror. Strange he hadn't realised the evening he had been standing in front of the mirror and felt something was missing. Harry and his little sister. Must have been because when you see something so often you tend to develop a blindness to it. Blind to it. He scrutinised the e-mail in the mirror. Then he ordered a taxi, put on his shoes and waited. Looked at his watch. The taxi must have arrived by now. Should get going. He realised he had picked up the receiver again and was dialling a number.

'Aune.'

'I want you to read the e-mails one more time and tell me if you think they were written by a man or a woman.'

408

42

Kebab

THE SNOW MELTED OVERNIGHT. ASTRID MONSEN HAD JUST
come out of the apartment building and was making her way across
the wet, black tarmac towards Bogstadveien when she saw the blond
policeman on the opposite pavement. Her pulse, like her walking
speed, leapt. She stared rigidly ahead, hoping he wouldn't see her.
There had been photographs of Alf Gunnerud in the papers and for
days detectives had been trudging up and down the stairs disrupting
her quiet working routine. But now it was over, she had told herself.

She scuttled towards the pedestrian crossing. To Hansen's bakery.
If she got there, she would be safe. A cup of tea and a doughnut at the
table behind the counter, at the far end of the long, thin café. Every
day at precisely 10.30.

'Tea and a doughnut?' 'Yes, please.' 'That'll be 38 kroner.' 'Here
you are.' 'Thank you.'

Most days that was the longest conversation she had with anyone.

For the last weeks an elderly man had been sitting at her table
when she arrived, and even though there were several unoccupied
tables, this was the only table she could sit at because . . . no, she
didn't want to think about these things now. Nevertheless, she had

been forced to arrive a quarter of an hour earlier to get to the table first. Today that was perfect because otherwise she would have been at home when he rang. And she would have had to open the door. She had promised Mother. Ever since the time she had refused to answer the telephone or the doorbell for two months, and in the end the police had come and her mother had threatened to have her readmitted.

She didn't lie to Mother.

To others, yes. She lied to them all the time. On the telephone to the publishers, in shops and on Internet chat sites. Especially there. She could pretend to be someone else, one of the characters in the books she translated, or Ramona, the decadent, promiscuous but fearless woman she had been in an earlier life. Astrid had discovered Ramona when she was small. She was a dancer, had long black hair and brown almond-shaped eyes. Astrid used to draw Ramona, especially her eyes, but she had to do it clandestinely because Mother tore the drawings to shreds and said she didn't want to see hussies like her in the house. Ramona had been gone for many years, but she had returned, and Astrid had noticed how Ramona had begun to take over, in particular when she wrote to the male writers she translated. After the preamble about language and cultural references, she liked to write more informal e-mails, and after a couple of those, the French writers would beg to meet her. When they were in Oslo to launch the book. Besides, she alone was reason enough to make the trip. She would always refuse although that did not seem to deter the suitors, more the opposite. This was what constituted her writerly activities now, after waking up from the dream of publishing her own books several years ago. A publishing consultant had finally cracked on the telephone and hissed that he could no longer put up with her 'hysterical fussing'; no reader would ever pay to share her thoughts, but, for a fee, a psychologist might.

'Astrid Monsen!'

She felt her throat constrict and for a moment she panicked. She didn't want to have respiratory problems here on the street. She was about to cross when the lights changed to red. She could have made it, but she would never cross on red.

'Hello, I was on my way to see you.' Harry Hole caught up with her. He still had the same hunted expression, the same red eyes. 'Let me first say I read Inspector Waaler's report of the conversation he had with you. I understand you lied to me because you were frightened.'

She could feel she would start hyperventilating soon.

'It was extremely inept of me not to tell you about my role in the whole business straight away,' the police officer said.

She looked at him in surprise. He did sound genuinely sorry.

'And I've read in the paper that the guilty party has been apprehended,' she heard herself say.

They stood looking at each other.

'Is dead, I mean,' she added in a soft voice.

'Well,' he said with a tentative smile. 'Perhaps you wouldn't mind helping me with a couple of questions anyway?'

That was the first time she had not sat alone at her table in Hansen's bakery. The girl behind the counter had sent her a kind of knowing girlfriend's smile, as if the tall man with her were an escort. Since he looked as if he had just crawled out of bed, perhaps the girl even thought . . . no, she didn't want to entertain that idea now.

They had sat down and he had given her printouts of several e-mails he wanted her to read through. Could she, as a writer, decipher whether they had been written by a man or a woman? She had examined them. As a writer, he had said. Should she tell him the truth? She raised her teacup so that he couldn't see her smiling at the thought. Of course not. She would lie.

'Hard to say,' she said. 'Is it fiction?'

'Yes and no,' Harry said. 'We think the person who killed Anna Bethsen wrote them.'

'So it must be a man.'

Harry studied the table and she shot a quick glance at him. He wasn't good-looking, but he had something going for him. She had – as improbable as it sounded – noticed it as soon as she saw him lying on the landing outside her door. Perhaps because she had had one more Cointreau than usual, but she had thought he looked peaceful, almost handsome, as he lay there, like a sleeping prince someone had placed in front of her door. The contents of his pockets had been scattered over the staircase and she had picked them up one by one. She had even had a peep in his wallet and found his name and address.

Harry raised his eyes and hers quickly darted away. Could she have liked him? Certainly. The problem was he wouldn't have liked her. Hysterical fuss. Groundless fears. The sobbing. He wouldn't like that. He wanted women like Anna Bethsen. Like Ramona.

'Are you sure you don't recognise her?' he asked slowly.

She gave him a horrified look. It was only then she noticed he was holding up a photograph. He had shown her this photograph before. A woman and two children on the beach.

'On the night of the murder, for example.'

'Never seen her in my whole life,' Astrid Monsen said firmly.

Snow was beginning to fall again. Large, wet snowflakes, which were grey and dirty before they landed on the brown earth between Police HQ and Botsen. A message from Weber lay waiting in the office. It confirmed Harry's suspicions, the same suspicions which had made him see the e-mails in a new light. Nevertheless, Weber's concise message came as a shock. A kind of expected shock.

Harry was on the telephone for the rest of the day, between running to and from the fax machine. In the breaks, he brooded, placed one brick on top of another and tried not to think about what he was looking for. But it was all too clear. This roller coaster could climb, fall, twist and turn as much as it liked, but it was the same as all other roller coasters – it would end up where it started.

When Harry's brooding was over and most of the picture was clear, he leaned back in the office chair. He didn't feel any triumph, just a void.

Rakel didn't ask any questions when he rang to say she shouldn't wait for him. Afterwards he went up the stairs to the canteen and onto the terrace roof where some smokers were standing and shivering. The city lights twinkled beneath them in the early-afternoon gloom. Harry lit a cigarette, ran his hand along the wall and made a snowball. Rolled it up. Tighter and tighter, hit it with his palms, squeezed it until the melted ice ran between his fingers. Then he threw it down towards the city. He followed the shiny snowball with his eyes as it fell, faster and faster, until it disappeared into the grey-white background.

'There was a boy in my class called Ludwig Alexander,' Harry said out loud.

The smokers stamped their feet and looked at the inspector.

'He was linguistically inclined and was called Kebab. Because once in the English lesson he had been stupid enough to tell the teacher he liked the word "barbecue" spelt as "BBQ" because that would be kebab backwards. When the snows came, there was a snowball fight between the classes in every break. Kebab didn't want to join in, but we forced him to. It was the only thing we let him join in. As cannon fodder. He was so bad at throwing that all he managed was a few weak lobs. The other class had Roar, a fat kid who played handball for Oppsal. He used to head Kebab's snowballs away for fun and then pepper him black and blue with his underarm swings. One day Kebab put a big stone in a snowball and threw it as high as he could. Roar jumped up with a smile and headed it. The sound was like a stone hitting a stone in shallow water, hard and soft at the same time. That was the only time I saw an ambulance in the school yard.'

Harry sucked hard on his cigarette.

'In the staff room they argued for days about whether Kebab should be punished. After all, he hadn't thrown the snowball at anyone, so the question was: Should a person be punished for showing no consideration towards an idiot behaving like an idiot?'

Harry stubbed out his cigarette and went inside.

It was after half past four. The cold wind had picked up speed in the open stretch between the Akerselva and the metro station in Grønlands torv. Schoolchildren and pensioners were giving way to women and men with closed faces and ties hurrying home from their offices. Harry bumped into one of them as he ran down the stairs into the underground and a swear word echoed between the walls and followed him. He stopped in front of the window between the toilets. It was the same elderly lady who had sat there last time.

'I have to talk to Simon right now.'

Her calm, brown eyes took him in.

'He's not in Tøyen,' Harry said. 'Everyone has left.'

The woman shrugged her shoulders, bewildered.

'Say it's Harry.'

She shook her head and waved him away.

Harry leaned over to the glass separating them. 'Say it's the *spiuni gjerman*.'

Simon drove down Enebakkveien instead of taking the long Ekeberg tunnel.

'I don't like tunnels, you know,' he explained as they crept up the side of the mountain at snail's pace in the afternoon rush hour.

'So the two brothers who had run away to Norway and grown up together in a caravan fell out because they were in love with the same girl?' Harry said.

'Maria came from a very respectable Lovarra family. They lived in Sweden where her daddy was the *bulibas*. She married Stefan and moved to Oslo when she was just thirteen and he was eighteen. Stefan was so in love with her he would have died for her. At that time

Raskol was in hiding in Russia, you know. Not from the police, but from some Kosovo-Albanians in Germany who thought he had cheated them in some business.'

'Business?'

'They found an empty trailer by the autobahn near Hamburg.' Simon smiled.

'But Raskol returned?'

'One sunny May day he returned to Tøyen. That was when Maria and he saw each other for the first time.' Simon laughed. 'My God, how they stared at each other. I had to inspect the heavens to see if thunder was on its way, the air was so tense.'

'So they fell for each other?'

'In seconds. While everyone was watching. Some of the women were embarrassed.'

'But if it was so obvious, the relatives must have reacted, didn't they?'

'They didn't think it was so dangerous. You mustn't forget we marry earlier than you do, you know. We cannot stop the young ones. They fall in love. Thirteen, you can imagine . . .'

'I can.' Harry rubbed the back of his neck.

'But this was a serious business, you see. She was married to Stefan and loved Raskol from the first day she saw him. And even though she and Stefan lived in their own caravan, she met Raskol, who was there the whole time. So things took the course they had to take. When Anna was born, only Stefan and Raskol were not aware Raskol was the father.'

'Poor girl.'

'And poor Raskol. The only person who was happy was Stefan. He walked three metres tall, you know. He said Anna was as good-looking as her daddy.' Stefan smiled with sad eyes. 'Perhaps it could have gone on like that. If Stefan and Raskol hadn't decided to rob a bank.'

'And it went wrong?'

The queue of cars moved towards Ryen crossroads.

'There were three of them. Stefan was the oldest, so he was the first in and the last out. While the other two ran out with the money to fetch the getaway car, Stefan stayed inside the bank with his pistol raised so they would not set off the alarm. They were amateurs, they didn't even know that the bank had a silent alarm. When they drove up to collect Stefan, he was stretched out over the bonnet of a police car. One officer had put handcuffs on him. Raskol was driving. He was only seventeen and didn't even have a licence. He rolled down the window. With three thousand on the back seat, he slowly drove up to the police car where his brother was struggling on the bonnet. Then Raskol and the officer had eye contact. My God, the air was as thick as when he and Maria met. Their mutual staring went on for ever. I was frightened Raskol would yell, but he didn't say a word. He just drove on. That was the first time they saw each other.'

'Raskol and Jørgen Lønn?'

Simon nodded. They came off the roundabout and went into the bend in Ryen. Simon signalled then braked by a petrol station. They pulled up in front of a twelve-storey building. The DnB logo flashed from a blue neon sign over the entrance nearby.

'Stefan got four years because he had fired his gun in the air,' Simon said. 'But after the trial, you know, something odd happens. Raskol visits Stefan in Botsen and the day after one of the guards says he thinks the new prisoner has changed appearance. His superior says it's normal for first-time prisoners. He tells him about wives who haven't recognised their own husbands on their first visit. The guard is reassured, but a few days later a woman phones the prison. She says they have the wrong prisoner. Stefan Baxhet's little brother has taken his place and they have to let the prisoner go.'

'Is that really true?' Harry asks, pulling out his lighter and putting it to the end of his cigarette. 'Yes, it is,' Simon says. 'It's quite normal among gypsies in southern Europe for the younger sibling, or the son, to serve the convicted person's sentence, if he has a family to feed. As Stefan did. For us, it is a matter of honour, you know.'

'But the authorities would soon discover the mistake, wouldn't they?'

'Hah!' Simon threw out his arms. 'For you a gypsy is a gypsy. If he's in prison for something he didn't do, he's sure to have been guilty of something else.'

'Who rang in?'

'They never found out, but Maria vanished the same night. They never saw her again. The police drove Raskol to Tøyen in the middle of the night and Stefan was dragged kicking and swearing out of the caravan. Anna was two years old and lay in bed screaming for her mummy and there was no one, no man and no woman, who could stop her howling. Until Raskol went in and lifted her up.'

They stared at the entrance to the bank. Harry glanced at his watch. Only a couple of minutes until it closed. 'What happened then?'

'When Stefan had served his sentence, he immediately left the country. I talked to him on the phone now and then. He travelled a lot.'

'And Anna?'

'She grew up in the caravan, you know. Raskol sent her to school. She had *gadjo* friends. *Gadjo* habits. She didn't want to live like us; she wanted to do what her friends did – make her own decisions, earn her own money and have her own place to live. Since she inherited her grandmother's flat and moved into Sorgenfrigata, we haven't had anything to do with her. She . . . well, she chose to move. The only person she had any contact with was Raskol.'

'Do you think she knew he was her father?'

Simon shrugged. 'As far as I know, no one said anything, but I'm sure she knew.'

They sat in silence.

'This is where it happened,' Simon said.

'Just before closing time,' Harry said. 'Like now.'

'He wouldn't have shot Lønn if he hadn't been forced to,' Simon said. 'But he does what he has to do. He's a warrior, you know.'

'No giggling concubines.'

'What?'

'Nothing. Where is Stefan, Simon?'

'I don't know.'

Harry waited. They watched a bank employee lock the door from the inside. Harry continued to wait.

'The last time I talked to him, he was ringing from a town in Sweden,' Simon said. 'Gothenburg. That's all I can help you with.'

'It's not me you're helping.'

'I know,' Simon sighed. 'I know.'

Harry found the yellow house in Vetlandsveien. The lights on both floors were lit. He parked, got out and stood looking at the metro station. That was where they had met on the first dark autumn evenings to go apple scrumping. Sigge, Tore, Kristian, Torkild, Øystein and Harry. That was the fixed team line-up. They had cycled to Nordstrand because the apples were bigger there and the chances of anyone knowing your father smaller. Sigge had climbed over the fence first and Øystein had kept lookout. Harry had been the tallest and could reach the biggest apples. One evening, however, they hadn't felt like cycling so far and they had gone scrumping in their local neighbourhood.

Harry looked across at the garden on the other side of the road.

They had already filled their pockets when he had discovered the face staring down at them from the illuminated window on the first floor. Without saying a word. It was Kebab.

Harry opened the gate and went up to the door. JØRGEN AND KRISTIN LØNN was painted on the porcelain sign over the two bells. Harry rang the top one.

Beate didn't answer until he had pressed twice.

She asked if he wanted tea, but he shook his head and she went into the kitchen while he kicked off his boots in the hallway.

'Why's your father's name still on the sign?' he asked when she came into the sitting room with a cup. 'So that strangers will think a man lives in the house?'

She shrugged and settled into a deep armchair. 'We've never got round to doing anything about it. His name has probably been there so long we don't see it any more.'

'Mm.' Harry pressed his palms together. 'That's basically what I wanted to talk about.'

'The door sign?'

'No. Dysosmia. Not being able to smell bodies.'

'What do you mean?'

'I was standing in the hall yesterday looking at the first e-mail I'd received from Anna's murderer. It was the same as with your door sign. The senses registered it, but not the brain. That's what dysosmia is. The printout had been hanging there for so long I had stopped seeing it, just like the photo of Sis and me. When it was stolen, I only noticed something was different, but not what it was. Do you know why?'

Beate shook her head.

'Because nothing had happened to me which would make me see things differently. I saw only what I assumed to be there. Something happened yesterday, though. Ali said he had seen a woman's back by the cellar door. It suddenly struck me that all the time I had assumed Anna's murderer was a man, without realising it. Whenever you make the mistake of imagining what you think you're looking for, you don't see the other things you find. That made me see the e-mail with new eyes.'

Beate's eyebrows formed two quotation marks. 'Do you mean to say it wasn't Alf Gunnerud who killed Anna Bethsen?'

'You know what an anagram is, don't you,' Harry said.

'A letter game . . .'

'Anna's murderer left a *patrin* for me. A sign. I saw it in the mirror. The e-mail was signed with a woman's name. Back to front. So I sent the e-mail to Aune, who contacted a specialist in cognitive psychology and language. From a single sentence in an anonymous threatening letter he had been able to determine gender, age and origins of the person. In this case, he was able to say the e-mails were written by a person of either gender, between twenty and seventy and potentially from anywhere in the country. Not much help, in other words. Except that he thought it may have been a woman. Because of one single word. It says "you policemen" and not "you police" or some non-specific collective term. He says the sender may have chosen that word unconsciously because it makes a distinction between the gender of the receiver and the sender.'

Harry leaned back in the chair.

Beate put down her cup. 'I can't exactly say I'm convinced, Harry. An unidentified woman in the stairwell, a code which is a woman's name backwards and a psychologist who thinks Alf Gunnerud chose a female way of expressing himself.'

'Mm,' Harry nodded. 'Agreed. First of all, I want to tell you what put me onto this trail. But before I tell you who killed Anna, I would like to ask you if you can help me find a missing person.'

'Of course. But why ask me? Missing persons are not—'

'Yes, they are.' Harry smiled sadly. 'Missing persons are your field.'

43

Ramona

Harry found Vigdis Albu down by the beach. She was sitting on the same smooth rock where he had fallen asleep with his hands around his knees staring into the fjord. In the morning mist the sun resembled a pale imprint of itself. Gregor ran up to Harry wagging his tail. It was low tide and the sea smelt of seaweed and oil. Harry sat down on a small rock behind her and flipped out a cigarette.

'Did *you* find him?' she asked, without turning. Harry wondered how long she had been waiting for him.

'Many people found Arne Albu,' he answered. 'I was one of them.'

She stroked away a wisp of hair dancing in front of her face in the wind. 'Me, too. But that was a long, long time ago. You may not believe me, but I loved him once.'

Harry clicked the lighter. 'Why shouldn't I believe you?'

'You can believe what you like. Not everyone can love. We – and they – may believe that, but it is so. They learn the movements, the lines and the steps, that's all. Some of them are so good they can fool us for quite a while. What surprises me is not that they succeed, but that they can be bothered. Why go to all the effort to have a feeling reciprocated which you don't understand? Do you understand, Constable?'

Harry didn't answer.

'Perhaps they're just frightened,' she said, turning to him. 'To see themselves in the mirror and discover they're cripples.'

'Who are you talking about, fru Albu?'

She turned back to the water. 'Who knows? Anna Bethsen? Arne? Me? The me I became?'

Gregor licked Harry's hand.

'I know how Anna Bethsen was killed,' Harry said. He studied her back, but no reaction was discernible. The cigarette caught light at the second attempt. 'Yesterday afternoon I got the results of an analysis *Krimteknisk* were doing on four glasses which had been in the sink at Anna Bethsen's flat. They were my fingerprints. I had apparently been drinking Coke. I would never have dreamed of drinking it with wine. One wineglass had not been used. The interesting part, however, is that traces of morphine hydrochloride were found in the dregs of the Coke. In other words, morphine. You know the effect of large doses, don't you, fru Albu?'

She scoured his face. Shook her head slowly.

'No?' Harry said. 'Collapse and amnesia from the moment you ingest the drug followed by severe nausea and a headache when you come to. Easily confused with the effects of going on the bottle. It's a good date-rape drug, much like Rohypnol. And we *have* been raped. All of us. Haven't we, fru Albu?'

A seagull screamed with laughter above them.

'You again,' Astrid Monsen said with a brief, nervous laugh and let him in. They sat in the kitchen. She scuttled about, made some tea, put out a cake she had bought at Hansen's bakery 'in case anyone dropped by'. Harry mumbled trivialities about yesterday's snow and how the world they all thought would cave in, along with the twin towers on TV, hadn't changed much by and large. It was only when she had poured out the tea and sat down, that he asked her what she had thought of Anna.

She was open-mouthed.

'You hated her, didn't you.'

In the ensuing silence a tiny electronic ping was audible in another room.

'No. I didn't hate her.' Astrid hugged an enormous cup of green tea. 'She was just . . . different.'

'Different in what way?'

'The life she led. The way she was. She was lucky to be the way . . . she was.'

'And you didn't like that?'

'I . . . don't know. No, perhaps I didn't.'

'Why not?'

Astrid Monsen looked at him. For a long time. The smile flickered in and out of her eyes like an unsettled butterfly.

'It's not what you think,' she said. 'I envied Anna. I admired her. There were days when I wished I were her. She was the opposite of me. I sit inside here while she . . .'

Her eyes went to the window. 'She wore barely anything and stepped out into life, Anna did. Men came and went, she knew she couldn't have them, but she loved them, anyway. She couldn't paint, but she exhibited her pictures so the rest of the world could see for themselves. She talked to everyone as if she were justified in thinking they liked her. To me, too. There were days when I felt Anna had stolen the real me, that there was not enough room for the two of us and I would have to wait my turn.' She emitted the same nervous titter. 'But then she died. And I discovered it wasn't like that. I can't be her. Now no one can. Isn't that sad?' She directed her gaze at Harry. 'No, I didn't hate her. I loved her.'

Harry could feel his neck prickle. 'Can you tell me what happened the evening you found me in the corridor?'

The smile appeared and disappeared like an ailing neon light. As though a happy person occasionally appeared and peeped out of her eyes. Harry had a feeling a dam was about to burst.

'You were ugly,' she whispered. 'But in an attractive way.'

Harry raised an eyebrow. 'Mm. When you lifted me up, did you notice if I smelt of alcohol?'

She looked surprised. As though she hadn't thought of that before. 'No. Not really. You smelt . . . of nothing.'

'Nothing?'

She blushed a deep red. 'Nothing . . . in particular.'

'Did I lose anything on the stairs?'

'Like what, for example?'

'A mobile phone. Keys.'

'What keys?'

'You have to answer me.'

She shook her head. 'No mobile phone. And I put the keys back in your pocket. Why are you asking about all this?'

'Because I know who killed Anna. I just wanted to double-check the details first.'

44

Patrin

THE NEXT DAY THE LAST REMNANTS OF THE TWO-DAY-OLD snow were gone. At the morning meeting in the Robberies Unit, Ivarsson said if they were going to make any headway in the Expeditor case their best hope was another bank raid, but he added that unfortunately Beate's prediction that the Expeditor would strike sooner or later was incorrect. To everyone's surprise, Beate didn't seem to take this indirect criticism to heart. She shrugged and repeated confidently that it was just a question of time before the Expeditor cracked.

The same evening a police car slid into the car park in front of the Munch Museum and came to a halt. Four men stepped out, two uniformed officers plus two plain-clothes men who from a distance looked as if they were walking hand in hand.

'Apologies for the security precautions,' Harry said, jerking his head towards the handcuffs. 'It was the only way I could get permission to do this.'

Raskol hunched his shoulders. 'I think it irks you more than me that we're cuffed together, Harry.'

The group crossed the car park towards the football pitch and the caravans. Harry signalled to the officers to wait outside while he and Raskol entered the small caravan.

Simon was waiting inside. He had put out a bottle of Calvados and three glasses. Harry shook his head, unlocked the cuffs and crawled onto the sofa.

'Nice to be back?' Harry asked.

Raskol didn't answer, and Harry waited while Raskol's black eyes examined the caravan. Harry saw them stop by the photograph of the two brothers over the bed. He thought he detected a tiny twist of the gentle mouth.

'I've promised we'll be back in Botsen by twelve, so we have to get down to brass tacks,' Harry said. 'Alf Gunnerud did not kill Anna Bethsen.'

Simon looked across at Raskol, who was staring at Harry.

'And neither did Arne Albu.'

In the silence, the roar of the traffic in Finnmarkgata seemed to increase. Did Raskol miss the traffic noise when he lay in his cell at night? Did he miss the voice from the other bed, the smell, the sound of his brother's regular breathing? Harry turned to Simon: 'Would you mind leaving us alone?'

Simon turned to Raskol, who gave a brief nod. He closed the door after leaving. Harry folded his hands and raised his eyes. Raskol's eyes were shiny, as though he had a temperature.

'You've known for some time, haven't you,' Harry said in a low voice.

Raskol pressed his palms together, on the surface a sign of inner calm, but the white fingertips told a different story.

'Perhaps Anna had read Sun Tzu,' Harry said. 'And knew the first rule of all war was deception. Nevertheless she gave me the solution. I just couldn't crack the code. S^{2}MN. She even gave me a clue; she said the retina inverted things, so I would have to look in the mirror to see what they were.'

Raskol had closed his eyes. He seemed to be praying. 'Her mother was beautiful and crazy,' he whispered. 'Anna inherited both elements.'

'You solved the code ages ago, I know,' Harry said. 'Her signature was S²MN. The two stands for a second S and there are three vowels missing. From left to right it reads S-S-M-N, but in the mirror it becomes N-M-S-S, or with the vowels NeMeSiS. The goddess of vengeance. *She* told me. It was her masterpiece. What she wanted to be remembered for.'

Harry said it without a hint of triumph in his voice. It was a statement of fact. The cramped caravan seemed to shrink around them.

'Tell me the rest,' Raskol breathed.

'I suppose you can work it out.'

'Tell me!' he hissed.

Harry looked at the small, round window over the table, which had already misted up. A porthole. A spaceship. He fantasised that if he wiped away the condensation they would discover they were in outer space, two lonely astronauts in the Horsehead Nebula on board a flying caravan. That wouldn't be very much more fantastic than what he was about to tell now.

45

The Art of War

Raskol straightened up and Harry began:

'This summer my neighbour, Ali Niazi, received a letter from someone purporting to owe rent from the time he lived in the building several years ago. Ali couldn't find his name in the list of occupants, so he wrote to him telling him to forget it. The name was Eriksen. I rang Ali yesterday and asked him to dig up the letter he had received. It turned out the address was Sorgenfrigata 17. Astrid Monsen told me that Anna's letter box had had another name sticker on it for a few days this summer. Name of Eriksen. What was the point of the letter? I rang the locksmith. They had, in fact, received an order for a key to my flat. I had the papers faxed over. The first thing I noticed was that the order was made a week before Anna's death. The order was signed by Ali, chairman and key-man of our housing co-op. The forged signature on the order form was no more than passable. Done by a no more than passable painter, imitating the signature on a letter she had received, for instance. But it was good enough for the locksmith, who promptly ordered a key for Harry Hole's flat from Trioving. And Harry Hole had to appear personally, show ID and sign for the key, believing he was signing for a spare key for Anna. You could kill yourself laughing, couldn't you?'

Raskol didn't seem to have any problems restraining himself.

'Between our meeting and the evening meal she rigged all this up. Arranged an e-mail account via a server in Egypt and wrote the e-mails on the laptop, pre-programming their delivery dates. During the day she unlocked the door to our cellar and found my storeroom. She used the same key to get into my flat to look for an easily recognisable personal item which she could plant at Alf Gunnerud's. She chose the photo of Sis and me. Next item on the agenda was a visit to her ex-lover and dealer. Alf Gunnerud must have been a little surprised to see her again. What did she want? Buy or borrow a gun maybe? Because she knew he had one of the weapons Oslo appears to be full of right now, with the manufacturer's serial number filed off. He found her a gun, a Beretta M92F, while she went to the toilet. He thought she was in there for a long time. And when she eventually came out, she was suddenly in a hurry and had to leave. At least we can imagine that was how it might have happened.'

Raskol's jaws were clenched so hard Harry could see his lips narrow. Harry leaned backwards. 'The next job was to break into Albu's chalet and plant the key to her flat. That was child's play; she knew the chalet key was in the outside lamp. While she was there she unstuck the photograph of Vigdis and the children from the photo album and took it with her. And so everything was ready. She only had to wait now. For Harry to come to the meal. The menu was tom yam with japone chilli, Coke and morphine hydrochloride. The latter ingredient is particularly popular as a date-rape drug, as it is liquid and relatively tasteless, the dosage simple and the effect unpredictable. The victim will wake up with a big hole in their memory, which they think is caused by alcohol since they have all the symptoms of a hangover. And in many ways you could say I was raped. I was so befuddled she had no problem taking my mobile out of my jacket pocket before shoving me out of the door. After I had gone, she left as well and went to my room in the cellar, where she connected the mobile to the laptop. When she came home, she sneaked up the stairs. Astrid Monsen heard her, but thought it was fru Gundersen from the third floor. Then she prepared herself for the last performance before leaving the rest of the action to take care of itself. Of course, she knew I would investigate the case, officially or otherwise, so she left me two *patrins*. She held the gun in her right hand, knowing I knew she was left-handed. And she placed the photo in the shoe.'

Raskol's lips moved, but not a sound passed them.

Harry ran a hand across his face. 'The last brushstroke of the masterpiece was to pull the trigger of a gun.'

'But why?' whispered Raskol.

Harry shrugged. 'Anna was a person of extremes. She wanted to avenge herself on the people she thought had taken from her what she lived for. Love. The guilty parties were Albu, Gunnerud and I. And your family. In short: hatred won.'

'Bullshit,' Raskol said.

Harry turned and took down the photograph of Raskol and Stefan from the wall and placed it on the table between them. 'Hasn't hatred always won in your family, Raskol?'

Raskol knocked back his head and drained the glass. Then he beamed.

Harry recollected the seconds afterwards as a video on fast forward. When they were over, he was lying on the floor, held in a neck lock by Raskol, with alcohol in his eyes, the smell of Calvados in his nose and the jagged edge of the broken bottle against his neck.

'There's only one thing more dangerous than excessively high blood pressure, *Spiuni*,' Raskol whispered. 'And that's excessively low blood pressure. So keep still.'

Harry swallowed and tried to speak, but Raskol squeezed harder and it turned into a groan.

'Sun Tzu is absolutely clear on love and hatred, *Spiuni*. Both love and hatred win in wars. They're inseparable like Siamese twins. Rage and compassion are the losers.'

'Then we're both about to lose,' Harry groaned.

Raskol tightened his grip again. 'My Anna would never have chosen death.' His voice quivered. 'She loved life.'

Harry wheezed the words: 'Like – you – love – freedom?'

Raskol loosened his grip and with a whine Harry drank air down into his aching lungs. His heart hammered in his head, but the traffic noise outside returned.

'You made your choice,' Harry wheezed. 'You gave yourself up in order to do penance. Incomprehensible to others, but it was your decision. Anna did the same.'

Raskol pressed the bottle against Harry's neck as he tried to move. 'I had my reasons.'

'I know,' Harry said. 'Doing penance is almost as strong an instinct as taking revenge.'

Raskol didn't answer.

'Did you know Beate Lønn also made a decision? She realised nothing would bring her father back. There is no rage left. She asked me to pay her respects and tell you she forgives you.' A spike of glass scraped against his skin. It sounded like a fountain-pen nib writing on rough paper. Hesitantly writing the last word. Only the full stop was missing. Harry swallowed. 'Now it's your turn to choose, Raskol.'

'Choose between what, *Spiuni*? Whether you live or die?'

Harry breathed in, trying to keep his panic at a distance. 'Whether you want to set Beate Lønn free or not. Whether you will tell her what happened on the day you shot her father. Whether you will set yourself free.'

'Me?' Raskol laughed his soft laughter.

'I've found him,' Harry said. 'That is, Beate Lønn found him.'

'Found whom?'

'He lives in Gothenburg.'

Raskol's laughter stopped abruptly.

'He's lived there for nineteen years,' Harry went on. 'Ever since he discovered you were Anna's real father.'

'You're lying,' Raskol yelled and raised the bottle over his head.

Harry felt his mouth go dry and closed his eyes. On opening them again, he saw Raskol's glassy eyes. They breathed in unison; their chests rose and fell together.

Raskol whispered. 'And . . . Maria?'

Harry had to try twice before he got a sound from his vocal cords. 'No one has heard from her. Someone told Stefan they'd seen her with an itinerant group in Normandy several years ago.'

'Stefan? Have you spoken to him?'

Harry nodded.

'Why did he want to speak to a *Spiuni* like you?'

Harry tried to shrug, but was unable to move. 'Ask him yourself . . .'

'Ask . . .' Raskol stared at Harry in disbelief.

'Simon went to fetch him yesterday. He's sitting in the caravan next door. The police have a couple of issues outstanding, but the officers have been warned not to touch him. He wants to talk to you. The rest is up to you.'

Harry put his hand between the bottle and his neck. Raskol made no attempt to stop him as he stood up. He only asked: 'Why have you done this, *Spiuni*?'

Harry shrugged. 'You made sure the judges in Moscow allowed Rakel to keep Oleg. I'm giving you a chance to hold onto the only person you have left.' He took the handcuffs out of his jacket pocket and put them on the table. 'Whatever you decide, I consider we're quits now.'

'Quits?'

'You saw to it that mine returned. I have done the same for you.'

'I hear what you say, Harry, but what does it mean?'

'It means I'm going to tell everything I know about Arne Albu's murder. And we'll be after you with everything we possess.'

Raskol raised an eyebrow. 'It would be easier for you if you let it drop, *Spiuni*. You know you won't get anything on me, so why try?'

'Because we're the police,' Harry said. 'And not giggling concubines.'

Raskol's eyes didn't let go. Then he made a brief bow.

Harry turned in the doorway. The thin man sat bent over the plastic table with the shadows hiding his face.

'You've got until midnight, Raskol. Then the officers will take you back.'

An ambulance siren cut through the traffic noise in Finnmarkgata, rose and sank as if seeking a pure tone.

46

Medea

HARRY CAREFULLY PUSHED OPEN THE BEDROOM DOOR. HE thought he could still smell her perfume, but the fragrance was so diffuse he wasn't sure if it came from the room or his memory. The large bed in the middle of the room imposed like a Roman galley. He sat on the mattress, placed his fingers on the cold, white bedsheet, closed his eyes and felt it pitch and roll. A slow, heavy ground swell. Was it here – like this – Anna had waited for him that evening? An angry buzz. Harry looked at his watch. Seven sharp. It was Beate. Aune rang a few minutes later and his double chins were flushed as he came up the stairs. He said a breathless 'Hello' to Beate and all three of them went into the sitting room.

'So you can say who these three portraits represent?' Aune said.

'Arne Albu,' Beate said, pointing to the picture on the left. 'Harry in the middle and Alf Gunnerud on the right.'

'Impressive,' Aune said.

'Well,' Beate said. 'An ant can distinguish between millions of other ant faces in an anthill. Proportionate to body weight, it has a much larger *fusiform gyrus* than I have.'

'I'm afraid then my own is extremely under-developed,' Aune said. 'Can you see anything, Harry?'

'I can certainly see a little more than when Anna first showed me. Now I know it's these three who have been indicted, by her.' Harry motioned towards the female figure holding the three lamps. 'Nemesis, the goddess of justice and vengeance.'

'Which the Romans pinched off the Greeks,' Aune said. 'They kept the scales, changed the whip for a sword, bound her eyes and called her Justitia.' He went to the lamp. 'When, in 600 BC, they began to think the system of blood revenge didn't work and decided to exact revenge from the individual and make it a public affair, it was precisely this woman who became the symbol of the modern consti-tutional state.' He stroked the cold, bronze woman. 'Blind justice. Cold-blooded vengeance. Our civilisation rests in her hands. Isn't she beautiful?'

'As beautiful as an electric chair,' Harry said. 'Anna's revenge wasn't exactly cold-blooded.'

'It was both cold-blooded and hot-blooded,' Aune said. 'Premeditated and impassioned at the same time. She must have been very sensitive. Psychologically damaged of course, but then we all are. Basically, it is just a question of the degree of damage.'

'And how was Anna damaged?'

'I never met her, so it will have to be a pure guess.'

'Go on then,' Harry said.

'On the subject of ancient gods, I assume you have heard of Narkissos, the Greek god who became so enamoured of his own reflection that he couldn't tear himself away? Freud introduced the concept of a narcissist to psychology, a person with an exaggerated sense of uniqueness, obsessed by the dream of boundless success. For the narcissist the need for revenge against those who have affronted him or her is often greater than all other needs. It is called the "narcissist's rage". The American psychoanalyst Heinz Kohut has described how such a person would seek to avenge the affront – which may seem a mere bagatelle to us – with whatever means they

435

have at their disposal. For instance, what would seem on the surface to be a standard rejection might result in the narcissist working tirelessly, with a compulsive determination, to redress the balance, causing death if necessary.'

'Death to whom?' Harry asked.

'To all.'

'That's insane,' Beate burst out.

'In fact, that's what I'm saying,' Aune said drily.

They went into the dining room. Aune tested one of the old, upright chairs at the long, narrow oak table. 'They don't make them like this any more.'

Beate groaned. 'But why should she take her *own* life . . . just to get even? There must be other ways.'

'Of course,' Aune said. 'But suicide is often an act of revenge in itself. You want to inflict a sense of guilt on those who have failed you. Anna just ratcheted it up a few notches. Besides, there was every reason to suspect that she didn't want to live any longer. She was lonely, rejected by her lovers and her own family. She had failed as an artist and resorted to drugs, but that didn't help. She was, in sum, a deeply disappointed, unhappy person who chose premeditated suicide. And vengeance.'

'Without any moral scruples?' Harry asked.

'The morality angle is interesting, of course.' Aune crossed his arms. 'Our society imposes on us a moral duty to live and, hence, to condemn suicide. However, with her apparent admiration for antiquity, Anna may have found her prop in the Greek philosophers, who thought every person should choose for themselves when they die. Nietzsche also considered that the individual had a full moral right to take his own life. He used the word *freitod* or voluntary death.' Aune raised a pointed index finger. 'But she had to confront another moral dilemma. Revenge. Insofar as she professed to be a Christian, Christian ethics demand that you should not take revenge. The paradox is, naturally, that Christians worship a God who is the greatest avenger of them all. Defy him and you burn in eternal hell,

436

an act of revenge which is completely out of proportion to the crime, almost a case for Amnesty International, if you ask me. And if—'

'Perhaps she just hated?'

Aune and Harry both turned towards Beate. She looked up at them in fear, as if the words had slipped out by mistake.

'Morality,' she whispered. 'Love of life. Love. And yet hatred is strongest.'

47

Phosphorescence

HARRY STOOD BY THE OPEN WINDOW LISTENING TO THE distant ambulance siren slowly fading in the rumble of noise from the urban cauldron. The house Rakel had inherited from her father lay high above everything happening in the carpet of light he could glimpse between the tall pine trees in the garden. He liked to stand looking at the trees, wondering how long they had been there and feeling the thought calm him. And at the lights from the town so reminiscent of marine phosphorescence. He had seen it only once, one night when his grandfather had taken him out in a rowing boat to shine a light on the crabs by Svartholmen. It was only the one night, but he would never forget it. It was one of those things that become brighter and more real with every year that passes. Not everything is like that. How many nights had he spent with Anna? How many times had they set off in the Danish skipper's boat and sailed wherever their whim took them? He couldn't remember. Soon all the rest would be forgotten too. Sad? Yes. Sad and necessary.

Nevertheless, there were two Anna moments he knew would never quite be erased. Two almost identical images, both with her thick hair spread across the pillow like a black fan, eyes wide open and one hand clutching the white, white sheet. The difference was the other hand. In one image, her fingers were interlaced with his; in the other they held a pistol.

'Could you close the window?' Rakel said behind him. She was sitting on the sofa, her legs tucked beneath her, a glass of red wine in hand. Oleg had just gone to bed happy, after smashing Harry at Tetris for the first time, and Harry was frightened an era had just passed irrevocably.

The news had nothing new to say. Old refrains: the military crusade against the East, reprisals against the West. They had switched off the TV and put on the Stone Roses, which to Harry's surprise and joy had been in Rakel's record collection. Youth. That was a time when nothing pleased him more than to see arrogant English kids with guitars and attitude. Now he liked the Kings of Convenience because they sang with precision and sounded only a touch less stupid than Donovan. And the Stone Roses on low volume. Sad but true. Maybe necessary. Things went in circles. He closed the window and promised himself he would take Oleg out to an island and shine a torch on crabs as soon as the opportunity presented itself.

'Down, down, down,' mumbled the Stone Roses from the loudspeakers. Rakel bent forward and took a sip of wine. 'It's a story as old as the hills,' she whispered. 'Two brothers who love the same woman, the very recipe for a tragedy.'

They fell silent, entwined their fingers and listened to each other's breathing.

'Did you love her?' she asked.

Harry considered the question carefully before answering: 'I don't remember. It was a time in my life which was very . . . muddled.'

She stroked his chin. 'Do you know what I think is such an odd thought? This woman I have never seen or met entered your flat, walked around and saw the photo of the three of us in Frognerseteren on your mirror. Knowing she would spoil everything. And you two perhaps loved each other after all.'

'Mm. She had planned all the details long before she knew about you and Oleg. She got hold of Ali's signature this summer.'

'Imagine the trouble she must have had forging his signature, being left-handed.'

'I hadn't thought about that.' He twisted his head in her lap and looked up at her. 'Shall we talk about something else? What would you say if I rang my father and asked if we could use the house in Åndalsnes next summer? The weather's usually crap, but there's a boat-house and my grandfather's rowing boat.'

Rakel laughed. Harry closed his eyes. He loved her laughter. If he was careful not to put a foot wrong, he thought, perhaps he might be allowed to listen to that laugh for a long time to come.

Harry awoke with a start. Scrambled up into a sitting position and gasped for breath. He had been dreaming, but he couldn't recall what. His heart was beating like a bass drum gone wild. Had he been under water in the swimming pool in Bangkok again? Or facing the killer in the suite at the SAS hotel? His head ached.

'What's the matter?' Rakel mumbled in the dark.

'Nothing,' Harry whispered. 'Go back to sleep.'

He got up, went to the bathroom and drank a glass of water. The drawn, ashen face in the mirror peered back at him. There was a gale blowing outside. The branches of the great oak in the garden scraped against the wall. Poked him in the shoulder. Tickled his neck and made the hairs stand on end. Harry filled his glass again and drank slowly. He remembered now. What he had been dreaming. A boy sitting on the school roof, dangling his legs. Who wouldn't go in to the lesson. Whose little brother wrote his essays. Who showed his brother's new love all the places they had played when they were young. Harry had dreamed a recipe for tragedy.

When he crept back under the duvet, Rakel was asleep. He stared at the ceiling and began to wait for first light.

The clock on the bedside table showed 05.03 when he could stand it no longer, got up, rang directory enquiries and wrote down Jean Hue's private telephone number.

48

Heinrich Schirmer

BEATE AWOKE WHEN THE DOORBELL RANG FOR THE THIRD time.

She rolled over and looked at the clock. A quarter past five. She lay wondering what the wisest move would be – tell him to go to hell or pretend she wasn't at home. Another ring, of a kind which made it clear he wasn't going to give up.

She sighed, got up and wrapped her dressing gown around her. She took the intercom phone.

'Yes?'

'Sorry to be stopping by so late, Beate. Or so early.'

'Go to hell, Tom.'

There was a long silence.

'This isn't Tom,' the voice said. 'It's me, Harry.'

Beate swore softly and pressed the OPEN button.

'I couldn't lie awake any longer,' Harry said as he came in. 'It's about the Expeditor.'

He slumped on the sofa as Beate slipped into the bedroom.

'As I said, what you do with Waaler's none of my business . . .' he shouted towards the open bedroom door.

'As you said, it's none of your business,' she shouted back. 'And, besides, he's been suspended.'

'I know. I was called to appear at the SEFO tribunal to talk about my meeting with Alf Gunnerud.'

She reappeared wearing a white T-shirt and jeans and stood opposite him. Harry looked up at her.

'I meant suspended by me,' she said.

'Oh?'

'He's a bastard. That doesn't mean you can say what you like to whom you like, though.'

Harry tilted his head and screwed up one eye.

'Should I repeat?' she asked.

'No,' he said. 'I think I've got the message now. What about if it isn't just anyone, but a friend?'

'Coffee?' But Beate didn't quite make it to the kitchen before a blush suffused her face. Harry got to his feet and followed her. There was just one chair by the small table. On the wall was a rose-painted wooden plaque with an old Hávamál poem:

> *At every door-way,*
> *ere one enters,*
> *one should spy round,*
> *one should pry round*
> *for uncertain is the witting*
> *that there be no foeman sitting,*
> *within, before one on the floor.*

'There were two things Rakel said last night which made me think,' Harry said, leaning against the sink. 'The first was that two brothers loving the same woman was a recipe for tragedy. The second was that Anna must have had a hard time imitating Ali's signature as she was left-handed.'

'Oh, yes?' She put a scoopful of coffee in the filter machine.

'Lev's schoolbooks. You got them from Trond Grette, to compare with the handwriting in the suicide letter. Do you remember which subject it was?'

'I didn't look that carefully. I just remember checking it was his.' She poured water into the machine.

'It was Norwegian,' Harry said.

'Could have been,' she said, facing him.

'It was,' Harry said. 'I've just come from Jean Hue, from *Kripos*.'

'The handwriting expert? Now, in the middle of the night?'

'He has an office at home and was very understanding. He checked the notebook and the suicide letter against this.' Harry unfolded a sheet of paper and placed it on the draining board. 'Will the coffee be long?'

'What's so urgent?' Beate asked, leaning over the sheet.

'Everything,' Harry said. 'The first thing you have to do is re-check all the bank accounts.'

Else Lund, the office manager in the travel agency Brastour and one of two employees, was occasionally phoned in the middle of the night by a customer in Brazil who had been robbed, or had lost their passport and tickets, and in their desperation they had rung her mobile phone without thinking about the time difference. Consequently she switched it off when she went to sleep. That was why she was furious when her landline rang at half past five and the voice at the other end asked whether she could get in to the office as soon as possible. She was only marginally less infuriated when the voice added it was the police.

'I hope this is a matter of life and death,' Else Lund said.

'It is,' the voice said. 'Mostly death.'

Rune Ivarsson was, as usual, the first to arrive at work. He stared out of the window. He liked the tranquillity, having the whole floor to himself, but that wasn't the reason. When the others arrived,

Ivarsson had already read all the faxes, the reports from the previous evening and all the newspapers, and had the head start he needed. If you are the boss, it is all about being one step ahead – establishing a bridgehead to give you a perspective. When his subordinates in the division expressed sporadic frustration that management was holding back information, it was because they didn't understand that knowledge is power and that any management team must have power if it is to plot the course which will ultimately bring a case to fruition. Indeed, it was simply for their own good that management possessed greater knowledge. When he had instructed everyone working on the Expeditor case to report directly to him, it was for exactly that reason, to keep the information where it belonged instead of wasting time on endless plenary discussions, which were only intended to give subordinates the feeling they were participants in the process. Right now it was more important that he, as Unit Head, got a grip, showed initiative and acted. Even though he had done his best to make it look as if the revelations about Lev Grette were his work, he knew the way it had happened had weakened his authority. A Unit Head's authority was not a question of personal prestige, but a matter for the whole police force, he had told himself.

There was a knock at the door.

'Didn't know you were a morning person, Hole,' Ivarsson said to the pasty face in the doorway, continuing to read the fax in front of him. He had had some quotes sent over from a daily newspaper which had interviewed him about the hunt for the Expeditor. He didn't like the interview. Fair enough, he hadn't been misquoted, but they had still managed to make him sound evasive and helpless. Fortunately, the photographs were good. 'What do you want, Hole?'

'Merely to say that I've called a meeting on the sixth floor. I thought you might be interested in coming along. It's about the so-called bank raid in Bogstadveien. We're about to begin.'

Ivarsson stopped reading and looked up. 'So you've called a meeting? Interesting. Might I ask who authorised this meeting, Hole?'

'No one.'

'No one.' Ivarsson emitted a short rattle of seagull laughter. 'Then you'd better get up there and say the meeting is postponed until after lunch. You see, I have a pile of reports to work through right now. Got it?'

Harry nodded slowly, as if giving the matter due, careful consideration. 'Got it. This is Crime Squad business, though, and we're starting now. Good luck with the reports.'

He turned and at that moment Ivarsson's fist hammered down on the table.

'Hole! Don't turn your fucking back on me like that! *I* call the meetings in this department. Especially when it's a robbery. Understood?' A wet, red lower lip quivered in the centre of the PAS's face.

'As you heard, I said the *so-called* robbery in Bogstadveien, Ivarsson.'

'And what the hell do you mean by that?' The voice was a whine now.

'That the robbery in Bogstadveien was never a robbery,' Harry said. 'It was a meticulously planned murder.'

Harry stood by the window and looked across at Botsen prison. The day had reluctantly got under way, like a creaking cart. Rain clouds over Ekeberg and black umbrellas in Grønlandsleiret. They were assembled behind his back: Bjarne Møller, yawning and sunk into the chair; the smiling Chief Superintendent chatting with Ivarsson; Weber with crossed arms, silent and impatient; Halvorsen with his notebook at the ready; and Beate Lønn with nervously wandering eyes.

49

Stone Roses

THE RAIN SHOWERS PETERED OUT LATER IN THE DAY. THE SUN peeped out in between all the leaden grey, and then the clouds parted like curtains opening on the final act. It would turn out to be the last hours of a blue sky before the city of Oslo pulled the grey winter duvet over its head. Disengrenda lay bathed in sun as Harry pressed the bell for the third time.

He could hear the bell like a grumbling in the terraced house's abdomen. The neighbour's window opened with a bang.

'Trond's not here,' a voice trilled. Her face wore a different brown hue now, a kind of golden brown, which made Harry think of nicotine-stained skin. 'Poor boy,' she added.

'Where is he?' Harry asked.

She rolled her eyes in answer and pointed her thumb over her shoulder.

'The tennis court?'

Beate made to go, but Harry stayed put.

'I've been thinking about what we discussed last time,' Harry said. 'About the footbridge. You said everyone was surprised because he was such a quiet, polite boy.'

'I did?'

'But everyone here in Grenda knew he had done it?'

'We saw him cycling off in the morning.'

'Wearing the red jacket?'

'Yes.'

'Lev?'

'Lev?' She laughed and shook her head. 'I'm not talking about Lev. He did a lot of weird things, but he was never wicked.'

'Who was then?'

'Trond. I was talking about him the whole time. I did say he was completely ashen when he returned. Trond can't stand the sight of blood.'

The wind was picking up. In the west, black popcorn clouds were beginning to gobble up the blue sky. The gusts gave the puddles on the red clay court goose pimples and erased the reflected image of Trond Grette, who tossed the ball up for another serve.

'Hello,' Trond said, hitting a ball which gently spun through the air. A little cloud of white chalk puffed up at the back of the server's box and was immediately blown away as the ball bounced, high and unreturnable, past the imaginary opponent on the other side of the net.

Trond faced Harry and Beate standing outside the wire fence. He was wearing a white tennis shirt, white tennis shorts, white socks and white shoes.

'Perfect, wasn't it.' He smiled.

'Almost,' said Harry.

Trond beamed even wider, shaded his eyes and scanned the sky. 'Looks like it's clouding over. How can I help you?'

'You can come with us to Police HQ,' Harry said.

'Police HQ?' He eyed them in surprise. That is, he seemed to be *trying* to appear surprised. His widening eyes were a touch too theatrical and there was something affected about his voice they hadn't heard before when they questioned him. The intonation was too low and gave a little jump at the end: *Police H-Q*? Harry could feel his hackles rising.

'Right now,' Beate said.

'Right.' Trond nodded as if something had just clicked into place and smiled again. 'Of course.' He made for the bench where a couple of tennis racquets peered out from underneath a grey coat. His shoes shuffled along in the shale.

'He's lost it,' Beate whispered. 'I'll cuff him.'

'Don't . . .' Harry began and grabbed her arm, but she had already shoved open the door and stepped in. Time expanded, inflated like an airbag and trapped Harry, immobilised him. Through the wire netting he saw Beate go for the handcuffs she had attached to her belt. He heard the sound of Trond's shoes on the shale. Small steps. Like an astronaut. Harry's hand automatically moved towards the gun in his shoulder holster under his jacket.

'Grette, I'm sorry . . .' was all Beate managed to say before Trond reached the bench and put his hand under the coat. Time had begun to breathe now, it shrank and expanded in one movement. Harry felt his hand close around the butt of his gun, knowing there was an eternity between this second and getting the weapon out, loading, releasing the safety catch and aiming. Beneath Beate's raised arm he caught a flash of reflected sunlight.

'Me, too,' Trond said, lifting the steel-grey and olive-green AG3 to his shoulder. She took a step back.

'My dear,' Trond said softly. 'Stand quite, quite still if you want to stay alive for a few more seconds.'

'We've made a mistake,' Harry said, turning away from the window and addressing the assembled detectives. 'Stine Grette was not killed by Lev but by her own husband, Trond Grette.'

The conversation between the Chief Superintendent and Ivarsson stopped, Møller sat up in his chair, Halvorsen forgot to take notes and even Weber's face lost its lethargic expression.

Møller, it was, who finally broke the silence. 'The accountant guy?'

Harry nodded to the disbelieving faces.

'It's not possible,' Weber said. 'We have the video from the 7-Eleven, and we have the fingerprint on the Coke bottle. There is no doubt that Lev Grette was the killer.'

'We have the handwriting on the suicide letter,' Ivarsson said.

'And unless I'm much mistaken, the robber was identified as Lev Grette by Raskol himself,' the Chief Superintendent said.

'The case looks pretty cut and dried,' Møller said.

'Let me explain,' Harry said.

'Yes, would you be so kind?' said the Chief Superintendent.

The clouds had gathered pace now and sailed in over Aker hospital like a black armada.

'Don't do anything stupid, Harry,' Trond said. The muzzle of the gun was pressed against Beate's forehead. 'Drop the gun I know you're holding.'

'Or what?' Harry asked, pulling out his gun.

Trond gave a low chuckle. 'Elementary. I'll shoot your colleague.'

'Like you shot your wife?'

'She deserved it.'

'Oh? Because she liked Lev more than you?'

'Because she was *my* wife!'

Harry breathed in. Beate stood between Trond and him, but with her back to Harry so he was unable to read any of her facial expressions. There were several possible routes to take. Option number 1 was to tell Trond he was being stupid and hasty, and hope he would see that. Against that: a man who took a loaded AG3 with him onto the tennis court had already worked out what he was going to use it for. Option number 2 was to do what Trond said, put down his gun and wait to be slaughtered. Option number 3 was to put pressure on Trond, make something happen, something which would make him change his plans. Or explode and pull the trigger. The first option was hopeless, the second the worst possible outcome and the third, well, if the same happened to Beate as happened to Ellen, Harry knew he would never be able to live with himself – if he survived.

'Perhaps she didn't want to be your wife any longer,' Harry said. 'Was that what happened?'

Trond's finger tightened round the trigger and his eyes met Harry's above Beate's shoulder. Inside, Harry instinctively began to count. 'One-thousand-and-one, one-thousand-and-two . . .'

'She thought she could just leave me,' Trond said in a low voice. 'Me – who had given her everything.' He laughed. 'For a guy who had never done anything for anyone, who thought life was a birthday party and all the presents were for him. Lev didn't steal. He was just confused by the prepositions *from* and *to*.' Trond's laughter was carried away on the wind like the crumbs of alphabet biscuits.

'Like from Stine to Trond,' Harry said.

Trond blinked hard with both eyes. 'She said she loved him. *Loved*. She didn't even use those words on the day we married. *Fond of*, she said. She was *fond of* me. Because I was so good to her. But she loved the boy who dangled his legs from a roof and waited for applause. That was what it was about for him. Applause.'

There were fewer than six metres between them and Harry could see the knuckles on Trond's left hand whiten as he held the gun barrel.

'But not for you, Trond. You didn't need any applause, did you. You enjoyed your triumphs in silence. Alone. Like that time by the bridge.'

Trond pushed out his lower lip. 'Own up, you believed me, didn't you.'

'Yes, we believed you, Trond. We believed every word you said.'

'So where did I slip up?'

'Beate has checked Trond and Stine Grette's bank accounts for the last two quarters,' Harry said.

Beate held up a pile of papers for the others in the room. 'They've both transferred money to Brastour, the travel agency,' she said. 'The agency has confirmed that in March of this year Stine Grette booked a trip to São Paulo for June, and Trond Grette followed a week later.'

'So far, that tallies with what Trond Grette told us,' Harry said. 'The strange thing is that Stine told Klementsen, the branch manager, she was going on holiday to Greece. Also that Trond Grette booked and bought his ticket the same day he left. Pretty bad planning if you're going on holiday together to celebrate ten years of marriage, isn't it?'

The room was so quiet they could hear the refrigerator motor on the other side of the corridor switch itself on.

'Suspiciously reminiscent of a wife who has lied to everyone about where she's going, and an already sceptical husband who has checked her bank statement and been unable to make Brastour square with a trip to Greece. Who then rang Brastour, found the name of the hotel where his wife was staying and followed her to bring her back.'

'And so?' Ivarsson said. 'Did he find her with a darkie?'

Harry shook his head. 'I don't think he found her at all.'

'We've checked and she didn't stay at the hotel she booked,' Beate said. 'Trond returned on an earlier flight.'

'Furthermore, Trond took out thirty thousand kroner on his bank card in São Paulo. At first, he said he'd bought a diamond ring, then that he'd met Lev and given him the money because he was broke. I'm fairly sure, though, that neither is true. I believe the money was for a service for which São Paulo is even more famous than jewellery.'

'And that is?' Ivarsson asked, clearly irritated by the silence, which had become unbearable.

'Contract murder.'

Harry had felt like dragging it out even longer, but a glance from Beate told him he was already being melodramatic. 'When Lev came back to Oslo this autumn, it was for his own money. He wasn't broke at all and had no intention of robbing any bank. He had returned to take Stine with him to Brazil.'

'Stine?' Møller exclaimed. 'His brother's wife?'

Harry nodded. The detectives present exchanged glances.

'And Stine was supposed to move to Brazil without telling any-one?' Møller continued. 'Not her parents, not her friends? Without even giving notice to her employers?'

'Well,' Harry said, 'when you've decided to spend your life with a bank robber wanted by both the police and your colleagues you don't announce your plans and leave a forwarding address. There was only one person she had told, and that was Trond.'

'The last person she should have told,' Beate added.

'She probably thought she knew him, after being with him for thirteen years.' Harry walked over to the window. 'The sensitive but kind, safe accountant who loved her so dearly. Let me speculate a little about what happened afterwards.'

Ivarsson sniffed. 'And what do you call what you've been doing so far?'

'When Lev comes to Oslo, Trond gets in touch. Says they're adults and brothers so they should be able to talk about things. Lev is relieved and happy. But he doesn't show his face around town, it's too risky, so they agree to meet in Disengrenda while Stine's at work. Lev goes and is well received by Trond, who says he had been sad at first, but now he was basically over that and happy for them. He opens a bottle of Coke for each of them and they drink and talk about practical details. Trond has Lev's secret address in d'Ajuda so he can forward post, back-payments and so on to Stine. Lev doesn't realise he has just given Trond the final details he needs to implement a plan which Trond had initiated when he was in São Paulo.'

Harry saw Weber slowly nodding his head.

'Friday morning. D-day. In the afternoon Stine is flying to London with Lev and from there to Brazil the following morning. The trip has been booked through Brastours. The suitcases are packed and ready at home, but she and Trond go to work as usual. At two Trond leaves work and goes to Focus in Sporveisgata. He arrives, pays for the squash court he has booked, but says he hasn't found a partner.

452

That's the first alibi in place: a registered payment at 14.34. Then he says he'll do some training in the fitness room instead and goes into the changing room. There are lots of people moving in and out at that time. He locks himself in the toilet with the bag, changes into the boiler suit with something over it, probably a long coat, waits until he can be sure the people he saw in the toilet have gone, puts on his sunglasses, takes the bag and passes quickly and unnoticed out of the changing room through the reception area. I would guess he walks towards Stenspark and then up Pilestredet by the building site where they clock off at three. He nips in, tears off his coat, puts on a folded balaclava he has hidden under his cap. Then he walks up the hill and turns left down Industrigata. At the Bogstadveien crossroads he goes into the 7-Eleven. He'd been there a couple of weeks earlier to check the camera angles. And the skip he ordered is in position. The scene is set for the diligent police officers he obviously knows will check all the video footage in the shops and petrol stations around. So he puts on this little show for us: we don't see his face but we do see *very* clearly a bottle of Coke he's holding in his bare hand and drinking from. He puts it in a plastic bag, so we're all convinced the fingerprints have not been wiped off by the rain and places it in the green skip he knows won't be collected for a good while. He must have had a fairly high opinion of our efficiency, and we nearly lost the evidence, but he got lucky – Beate drove like crazy and we managed it: to give Trond Grette a watertight alibi by acquiring the final, incontrovertible piece of evidence against Lev.'

Harry broke off. The faces in front of him expressed mild perplexity.

'The bottle of Coke was the one Lev had drunk from in Disengrenda,' Harry said. 'Or somewhere. Trond had taken it for precisely this purpose.'

'I'm afraid you've forgotten something, Hole,' Ivarsson whinnied. 'You saw yourself that the bank robber was holding the bottle in his bare hands. If it was Trond Grette, it must be his prints on the bottle.'

Harry motioned towards Weber.

'Glue,' said the experienced detective.

'I beg your pardon?' The Chief Superintendent turned to Weber.

'An old trick used by bank robbers. You spread a little glue over your fingertips, let it harden and, bingo, no prints.'

The Chief Superintendent shook his head. 'But where has this accountant, as you call him, learned these tricks?'

'He was the little brother of one of the most professional bank robbers Norway has seen,' Beate said. 'He knew Lev's methods and style inside out. Amongst other things, Lev kept video recordings of his raids at his home in Disengrenda. Trond had taught himself his brother's techniques so well that even Raskol was deceived into thinking he recognised Lev Grette. On top of that, there is the physical similarity of the two brothers, which meant that computer manipulation of the videos showed the robber *could* have been Lev.'

'Shit!' Halvorsen exclaimed involuntarily. He ducked and sent a fearful glance at Bjarne Møller, but Møller was sitting with mouth wide open, staring blankly in front of him as if a bullet had passed through his head.

'You haven't put down the gun, Harry. Can you explain?'

Harry attempted to breathe regularly even though his heart was running amok. Oxygen to the brain, that was crucial. He tried not to look at Beate. The wind puffed up thin, blonde strands of her hair. Muscles in the thin neck were straining and her shoulders had begun to tremble.

'Elementary,' Harry said. 'You'll shoot us both. You have to give me a better deal than that, Trond.'

Trond laughed and rested his cheek against the green butt of the gun. 'What do you say to this deal, Harry? You've got twenty-five seconds to think through the alternatives and put down the weapon.'

'The usual twenty-five?'

'Correct. I suppose you recall how quickly the time went. Think fast, Harry.'

'Do you know what put the idea in my head about Stine knowing the robber?' Harry shouted. 'They were standing too close. Much closer than you and Beate now. It's odd, but, even in life-and-death situations, people respect others' intimate spaces if they can. Isn't that strange?'

Trond placed the barrel under Beate's chin and raised her face. 'Beate, would you be so kind as to count for us?' He was using the theatrical tone again. 'From one to twenty-five. Not too fast and not too slow.'

'I was wondering about something,' Harry said. 'What did she say before you shot her?'

'Would you really like to know, Harry?'

'Yes, I would.'

'Beate has two seconds to start counting. One . . .'

'Count, Beate!'

'One.' Her voice was a dry whisper. 'Two.'

'Stine pronounced the final death sentence for herself and Lev,' Trond said.

'Three.'

'She said I could shoot her, but I should spare him.'

Harry felt his throat constrict and his grip on the gun weaken.

'Four.'

'In other words, he would have shot Stine however long the branch manager took to put the money in the bag?' Halvorsen asked.

Harry nodded gloomily.

'Since you seem to know everything, I take it you also know his escape route,' Ivarsson said. The tone was intended to be sarcastic and amusing, but the irritation shone through all too clearly.

'No, but I assume he took the same route back. Up Industrigata, down Pilestredet, into the building site where he took off the balaclava and stuck the POLITI label on the back of the boiler suit. When he was back in Focus, he was wearing a cap and sunglasses, and failed to attract the attention of the centre staff since they didn't recognise the photos of him. He went into the changing room and put on the sports gear he had been wearing when he arrived from work, then joined the general hubbub in the fitness rooms, did a bit of cycling, maybe lifted a few weights. Then he showered, went to the reception desk and reported his squash racquet missing. The girl who took his details gave the exact time as 16.02. The alibi was cemented and he went into the street, heard the sirens and drove home. Possibly.'

'I don't know if I understand the purpose of the police labels,' the Chief Inspector said. 'We don't even have boiler suits in the force.'

'Elementary psychology,' Beate said and her cheeks glowed when she saw the Chief Superintendent's raised eyebrow. 'I mean . . . not elementary in the sense that it's . . . erm, obvious.'

'Go on,' the Chief Superintendent said.

'Trond Grette knew, of course, that the police would search for anyone wearing a boiler suit observed in the area. He, therefore, had to have something on his boiler suit which would cause all the police swarming around to pay little attention to this unidentified person in Focus. The public always shies away from the police.'

'Interesting theory,' Ivarsson said with a sour smile and the tips of two fingers under his chin.

'She's right,' the Chief Superintendent said. 'Everyone has a fear of authority. Go on.'

'But, to be absolutely sure, he pretended to be a witness and volunteer information about a man he had seen walking past the fitness room wearing a boiler suit with POLITI on.'

'Which was a stroke of genius in itself,' Harry said. 'Grette told us this as if he was unaware that the police strip ruled the man out of our inquiries. Of course, it also strengthened Trond Grette's credibility in our eyes that he volunteered information which – seen from his point of view – might place him on the murderer's escape route.'

'Eh?' said Møller. 'Repeat that one more time, Harry. Slowly.'

Harry took a deep breath.

'Oh, never mind,' Møller said. 'I've got a headache.'

'Seven.'

'But you didn't do what she asked,' Harry said. 'You didn't spare your brother.'

'Of course not,' Trond said.

'Did he know you had killed her?'

'I had the pleasure of telling him myself. On the mobile. He was waiting in Gardemoen airport. I told him if he didn't get on the plane, I would go after him too.'

'And he believed you when you said you'd killed Stine?'

Trond laughed. 'Lev knew me. He didn't doubt it for a second. While I was giving him the details, he was reading about the raid on teletext in the business lounge. He switched off his phone when I heard them call his flight. His and Stine's. Hey, you!' He put the gun to Beate's head.

'Eight.'

'He must have thought he had a safe passage home,' Harry said. 'Didn't know about the contract in São Paulo, though, did he.'

'Lev was a thief, but a naive thief. He should never have given me the secret address in d'Ajuda.'

'Nine.'

Harry tried to ignore Beate's robotic monotones. 'Then you sent instructions to the hired killer, and the suicide letter. Which you wrote with the same handwriting style you used to do Lev's essays.'

'Bravo,' Trond said. 'Good work, Harry. Apart from the fact that they had been sent before the bank job.'

'Ten.'

'Well,' Harry said, 'the contract killer also did good work. It really did look as if Lev had hanged himself. Even though the missing little finger business was perplexing. Was that the receipt?'

'Let's put it this way. A little finger fits nicely in a standard envelope.'

'Didn't think you could stand the sight of blood, Trond?'

'Eleven.'

Harry heard a distant rumble of thunder over the whistling, roaring wind. The field and the paths around them were deserted. Everyone had taken shelter from the looming storm.

'Twelve.'

'Why don't you just give yourself up?' Harry said. 'You know it's hopeless.'

Trond chuckled. 'Of course it's hopeless. That's the point, isn't it. No hope. Nothing to lose.'

'Thirteen.'

'So what's the plan, Trond?'

'The plan? I have two million kroner from the bank job and I'm planning a long – if not happy – life in exile. The travel plans have had to be put forward, but I was prepared for that. The car has been packed and ready ever since the robbery. You can choose between being shot or handcuffed to the fence.'

'Fourteen.'

'You know it won't work,' Harry said.

'Believe me, I know a lot about disappearing. Lev did nothing but. Twenty minutes' head start is all I need. I'll have changed transport and identity twice. I have four cars and four passports en route, and I have good contacts. In São Paulo, for example. Twenty million inhabitants. You can start the search there.'

'Fifteen.'

'Your colleague will die soon, Harry. What's it going to be?'

'You've said too much,' Harry said. 'You're going to kill us anyway.'

'You'll have to take a risk and find out. What options have you got?'

'That you die before me,' Harry said, loading his gun.

'Sixteen,' whispered Beate.

Harry had finished.

'Amusing theory, Hole,' Ivarsson said. 'Especially the one about the contract killer in Brazil. Extremely . . .' He bared his small teeth into a thin smile: 'Exotic. There's no more? Proof, for example?'

'Handwriting. The suicide letter,' Harry said.

'You've just said it doesn't match Trond Grette's writing.'

'Not his usual writing, no. But the essays . . .'

'Have you got a witness to swear he wrote them?'

'No,' Harry said.

Ivarsson groaned: 'In other words, you don't have one single shred of incriminating evidence in this robbery case.'

'Murder case,' Harry said softly, eyeing Ivarsson. At the edge of his vision he could see Møller staring at the floor, ashamed, and Beate wringing her hands in despair. The Chief Superintendent cleared his throat.

Harry released the safety catch.

'What are you doing?' Trond scrunched up his eyes and shoved the gun barrel into Beate's head so hard he forced it backwards.

'Twenty-one,' she groaned.

'Isn't it liberating?' Harry said. 'When you finally realise you have nothing to lose. That makes all decisions so much easier.'

'You're bluffing.'

'Am I?' Harry placed the gun against his left forearm and fired. The crack was loud and sharp. A few tenths of a second passed before the echo from the tall blocks came crashing back. Trond stared. A jagged edge stood up around the hole in the policeman's leather jacket and a white tuft of wool lining swirled away in the wind. The blood trickled through. Heavy, red droplets hit the ground with a muffled tick-tick clock-like sound, vanished in the mixture of shale and rotting grass to be absorbed by the soil. 'Twenty-two.'

The droplets grew and fell faster and faster, sounding like an accelerating metronome. Harry raised his gun, poked the barrel through a gap in the wire netting fence and took aim. 'That's what my blood looks like, Trond,' he said in a voice so low it was barely audible. 'Shall we have a peek at yours?'

At that moment the clouds covered the sun.

'Twenty-three.'

A dark shadow fell like a wall from the west, firstly across the fields, then across the terraced houses, the blocks, the red shale and the three people. The temperature fell, too. Like a stone, as though the obstruction in front of the light not only cut off the heat but also radiated cold. But Trond didn't notice. All he sensed and saw was the policewoman's brief, hurried gulps of air, her wan, expressionless face and the muzzle of the policeman's gun staring at him like a black eye which had finally found what it was seeking and was already boring through him, dissecting him and stretching him out. The distant thunder rumbled. But all he heard was the sound of blood. The policeman's flesh was open and the contents were spilling out. The blood, his insides, his life dripped loudly onto the grass. It wasn't being devoured; it did the devouring, burned its way into the ground. Trond knew that even if he closed his eyes and covered his ears, he would still hear his own blood rushing in his ears, singing and throbbing to get out.

He felt the nausea like a kind of mild labour pain, a foetus which would be born through his mouth. He swallowed, but the water was running from all his glands, greasing his insides, preparing him. The fields, the blocks and the tennis court began to revolve. He huddled up, tried to hide behind the policewoman, but she was too small, too transparent, just a gossamer veil of life trembling in the squalls. He clung to the gun as though it was holding him up and not the opposite, tightened his finger on the trigger, then waited. Had to wait. What for? For the fear to release its grip? For things to recover their equilibrium? But they wouldn't, they just whirled around and would not come to rest until they had smashed on the bottom. Everything had been in free fall from the moment Stine had said she was leaving, and the blood rushing in his ears had been a constant reminder that the pace was gathering. He had woken every morning thinking that now he must have got used to falling, now the horror must have let go, the end was in sight, he had been through the pain barrier. But it wasn't true. Then he had begun to long to hit rock bottom, the day he would stop being frightened. And now he could see the bottom he was even more frightened. The ground on the other side of the wire fence rushed towards him.

'Twenty-four.'

The countdown was nearing the end. Beate had the sun in her eyes, she was standing inside in a bank in Ryen and the light outside was dazzling, making everything white and harsh. Her father stood beside her, as silent as ever. Her mother was shouting from somewhere, but she was far away, she always had been. Beate counted the images, the summers, the kisses and the defeats. There were a lot, she was surprised how many there were. She recalled faces, Paris, Prague, a smile from under a black fringe, a clumsily expressed declaration of love, a breathless, fearful: Does it hurt? And a restaurant she hadn't been able to afford in San Sebastian, but where she had reserved a table anyway. Perhaps she should be grateful after all?

She had woken from these thoughts when the gun nudged her forehead. The images disappeared and there was only a white, crackling snowstorm on the screen. She wondered: Why did Father only stand beside me? Why didn't he ask me for something? He had never done that. And she hated him for it. Didn't he know it was the only thing she desired, to do something for him, anything at all? She had walked where he had walked, but when she found the bank raider, the killer, the widow-maker and wanted to give her father his vengeance, their vengeance, he had stood beside her, as silent as ever, and refused.

Now she was standing where he had stood. All the people she had watched on the bank videos from all over the world at night in the House of Pain, wondering what they were thinking. Now it was her turn and still she didn't know.

Then someone had turned off the light, the sun disappeared and she was immersed in the cold. She had awoken again in the cold. As if the first awakening had only been part of a new dream. And she had started counting again. But now she was counting places she had never been, people she had never met, tears she had never cried, words she had never heard said as yet.

'Yes, I do,' Harry said. 'I have this piece of evidence.' He produced a sheet of paper and set it on the long table.

Ivarsson and Møller leaned forward together, clunking heads.

'What is this?' Ivarsson barked. ' "A Wonderful Day".'

'Scribbles,' Harry said. 'Written on a notepad at Gaustad hospital. Two witnesses, Lønn and myself, were present and can testify that the writer was Trond Grette.'

'So?'

Harry looked at them. He turned his back and walked slowly to the window. 'Have you examined your own scribbles when you imagine you're thinking about something else? They can be quite revealing. That was why I took the piece of paper, to see if it made any sense. At first, it didn't. I mean when your wife has just been killed and you're sitting in a closed psychiatric ward writing "A Wonderful Day" again and again, then you're absolutely barking mad or you're writing the opposite of what you think. Then I discovered something.'

Oslo was pale grey, like the face of a tired old man, but today in the sun the few colours still remaining shone. Like a final smile before saying goodbye, Harry mused.

' "A Wonderful Day",' he said. 'It's not a thought, a comment or an assertion. It's a title. Of the kind of essay you write at primary school.'

A hedge sparrow flew past the window.

'Trond Grette wasn't thinking, he was just scribbling on automatic pilot. As he had done from his school days when he sat practising the new handwriting style. Jean Hue, the handwriting expert at *Kripos*, has already confirmed the same person wrote the suicide letter and the school essays.'

The film seemed to be stuck, the image frozen, not a movement, not a word, only the repeated actions of a photocopier outside in the corridor.

Finally, Harry turned around and broke the silence: 'Seems like the mood is for Lønn and me to bring Trond Grette in for a little bit of questioning.'

Fuck, fuck, fuck! Harry tried to hold the gun steady, but the pain was making him giddy and the blasts of wind were pulling and pushing at his body. Trond had reacted to the blood as Harry had hoped, and for a moment Harry had a clear line of fire. But Harry had hesitated and now Trond had Beate in front of him so that Harry could only see part of his head and his shoulder. She was similar, he could see that now, my God she was so similar. Harry blinked hard to get them in focus. The next blast of wind was so strong it caught hold of the grey coat on the bench and for a moment it seemed as if an invisible man clad only in a coat was running across the tennis court. Harry knew a downpour was on its way; this was the air mass the wall of rain was pushing forward as the final warning. Then it went as dark as night, the two bodies in front of him merged and then the rain was overhead; large, heavy drops hammered down.

'Twenty-five.' Beate's voice was suddenly loud and clear.

In the flash of light Harry could see their bodies casting shadows on the red shale. The crack which followed was so loud it attached itself to their ears like a lining. One body slipped away from the other and fell to the ground.

Harry sank to his knees and heard his voice roar: 'Ellen!'

He saw the figure still standing turn and begin to walk towards him, gun in hand. Harry took aim, but the rain was streaming down his face and blinding him. He blinked and aimed. He no longer felt anything, neither pain nor cold, sorrow nor triumph, only a huge void. Things were not meant to make sense; they just repeated themselves in an eternal, self-explanatory mantra – living, dying, being reborn, living, dying. He squeezed the trigger halfway. Took aim.

'Beate?' he whispered.

She kicked open the door and passed the AG3 to Harry, who grabbed it.

'What . . . happened?'

'The Setesdal Twitch,' she said.

'The Setesdal Twitch?'

'He went down like a pile of bricks, poor thing.' She showed him her right hand. The rain washed and rinsed away the blood from the two wounds on her knuckles. 'I was just waiting for something to distract him. And the clap of thunder scared the living daylights out of him. You too, it seems.'

They looked at the motionless body in the left-hand service box.

'Will you help me with the handcuffs, Harry?' Her blonde hair was stuck to her face, but she didn't seem to notice. She smiled.

Harry raised his face into the rain and closed his eyes. 'God in heaven above,' he mumbled. 'This poor soul will not be set free until 12 July 2022. Have mercy.'

'Harry?'

He opened his eyes. 'Yes?'

'If he's not to be set free before 2022 we'd better get him to Police HQ right now.'

'Not him,' Harry said, getting up. 'Me. That's when I retire.'

He put his arm around her shoulders and smiled. 'You Setesdal Twitch, you . . .'

50

Ekeberg Ridge

IT BEGAN TO SNOW AGAIN IN DECEMBER. AND THIS TIME IT was for real. The snow drifted against the walls of the houses and more snow was forecast. The confession came on Wednesday afternoon. Trond Grette, in consultation with his solicitor, told how he had planned and later carried out the murder of his wife.

It snowed right through the night, and the next day he also confessed to being behind the murder of his brother. The man he had paid for the job was called El Ojo, The Eye, of no fixed abode. He changed his professional name and mobile telephone number every week. Trond had only met him once, in a car park in São Paulo, where they had agreed on the details. El Ojo had received 1,500 dollars in advance; Trond had placed the rest in a paper bag in a left-luggage locker at Tietê airport terminal. The agreement was that he would send the suicide letter to a post office in Campos Belos, a suburb in the south of the city, and the key when he had received Lev's little finger.

The only thing remotely approaching amusement during the long hours of questioning was when Trond was asked how, as a tourist, he had managed to contact a professional contract killer. He replied that it had been a great deal easier than trying to get hold of a Norwegian builder. The analogy was not entirely by chance.

'Lev told me about it once,' Trond said. 'They advertise themselves as *plomeros* next to chat-line ads in the newspaper *Folha de São Paulo*.'

'Plum-whats?'

'*Plomeros*. Plumbers.'

Halvorsen faxed the scanty information to the Brazilian embassy, who refrained from making a sarcastic comment and promised to pursue the case.

The AG3 Trond had used in the raid was Lev's and had been in the loft in Disengrenda for several years. The gun was impossible to trace as the manufacturer's serial number had been filed off.

Christmas came early for Nordea's consortium of insurance companies since the money from the Bogstadveien robbery was found in the boot of Trond's car and not a krone had been touched.

The days passed, the snow came and the questioning continued. One Friday afternoon, when everyone was exhausted, Harry asked Trond why he hadn't thrown up when he shot his wife through the head – after all he couldn't stand the sight of blood. The room went quiet. Trond stared at the video camera in the corner. Then he merely shook his head.

But when they had finished and they were walking through the Culvert back to the detention cells, he had suddenly turned to Harry: 'It depends on whose blood it is.'

At the weekend Harry sat in a chair by the window watching Oleg and local boys building snow forts in the garden outside the timber house. Rakel asked him what he was thinking about and it almost slipped out. Instead he suggested going for a little walk. She fetched hats and gloves. They walked past the Holmenkollen ski jump and Rakel asked whether they should invite Harry's father and sister over to hers on Christmas Eve.

'We're the only family left,' she said and squeezed his hand.

On Monday Harry and Halvorsen started work on the Ellen case. Right from scratch. Questioned witnesses who had been in before, read old reports and checked tip-offs that had not been followed up and old leads. Cold leads, it turned out.

'Have you got the address of the guy who said he'd seen Sverre Olsen with a man in a red car in Grünerløkka?' Harry asked.

'Kvinsvik. His address is given as his parents' place, but I doubt we'll find him there.'

Harry didn't expect much cooperation when he walked into Herbert's Pizza asking for Roy Kvinsvik. But after buying a beer for a young guy with the *Nasjonalallianse* logo on his T-shirt, he learned that Roy no longer had to maintain an oath of silence since he had recently cut ties with his former friends. Apparently Roy had met a Christian girl and lost his faith in Nazism. No one knew who she was or where Roy lived now, but someone had seen him singing outside the Philadelphian church.

The snow lay in deep drifts as the snow ploughs shuttled to and fro down the streets of Oslo city centre.

The woman who had been shot in the Grensen branch of the Den norske Bank was discharged from hospital. In *Dagbladet* she showed where the bullet had entered with one finger and how close it had been to hitting her heart with two fingers. Now she was going home to take care of her husband and children over Christmas, the paper said.

On Wednesday morning at ten o'clock the same week Harry stamped the snow off his boots outside Room 3, Police HQ, before knocking.

'Come in, Hole,' came the roar of Judge Valderhaug's voice. He was leading the internal SEFO inquiry into the shooting incident in the container terminal. Harry was led to a chair in front of a five-person tribunal. Apart from Valderhaug, there was a Public Prosecutor, one female detective, one male and Defence Counsel Ola Lunde whom Harry knew as tough but competent and genuine.

'We would like to have our findings tied up before we break for Christmas,' Valderhaug opened. 'Can you tell us as concisely as possible about your role in this case?'

To the clatter of the male detective's computer keyboard, Harry talked about his brief meeting with Alf Gunnerud. When he had finished, Valderhaug thanked him and rustled his papers for a while before finding what he was looking for. He peered at Harry over his glasses.

'We would like to know if from your brief meeting with Gunnerud you were surprised when you heard he had pulled a gun on a policeman.'

Harry remembered what he had thought when he saw Gunnerud on the staircase. A young man who was afraid of further beatings. Not a hardened killer. Harry met the judge's gaze and said: 'No.'

Valderhaug took off his glasses. 'But when Gunnerud met you, he chose to run off. Why this change of tactics when he met Waaler, I wonder.'

'I don't know,' Harry said. 'I wasn't there.'

'But you don't think it strange?'

'Yes, I do.'

'But you just answered you weren't surprised.'

Harry tipped his chair back. 'I've been a policeman for a long time, sir. It no longer surprises me when people do strange things. Not even murderers.'

Valderhaug replaced his glasses and Harry thought he detected a smile playing around the mouth of the lined face.

Ola Lunde cleared his throat. 'As you know, Inspector Tom Waaler was suspended for a brief period in connection with a similar incident last year while arresting a young neo-Nazi.'

'Sverre Olsen,' Harry said.

'At that time SEFO concluded that there were insufficient grounds for the Public Prosecutor to bring a charge.'

'You only sat for a week,' Harry said.

Ola Lunde raised an eyebrow at Valderhaug, who nodded. 'Nonetheless,' Lunde continued, 'it is naturally conspicuous that the same man is in the same situation once again. We know that there is a strong sense of solidarity in the police force and officers are reluctant to put a colleague in a difficult spot by er . . . um . . . er . . .'

'Grassing,' Harry said.

'I beg your pardon?'

'I think the word you're looking for is "grassing".'

Lunde exchanged glances with Valderhaug again. 'I know what you mean, but we prefer to call it presenting relevant information to ensure rules are enforced. Do you agree, Hole?'

Harry's chair landed back on its front legs with a bang. 'Yes, in fact, I do. I'm just not as good with words as you.'

Valderhaug could no longer conceal his smile.

'I'm not so sure about that, Hole,' Lunde said, who had himself begun to smile. 'It's good we agree, and since you and Waaler have worked together for many years, we would like to use you as a character witness. We have had other officers in here who have alluded to Waaler's uncompromising style when dealing with criminals and sometimes non-criminals. Could you imagine that Tom Waaler may have shot Alf Gunnerud in a moment of rashness?'

Harry cast lingering looks out of the window. He could barely see the outline of Ekeberg Ridge through the snow showers. But he knew it was there. Year in, year out, he had sat behind his desk at Police HQ and Ekeberg had always been there, and always would be, green in the summer, black and white in the winter, it couldn't be shifted, it was a fact. The great thing about facts is that you don't have to ponder whether they're desirable or not.

'No,' Harry said. 'I cannot imagine that Tom Waaler would have shot Alf Gunnerud in a moment of rashness.'

If anyone on the SEFO panel had noticed the tiny extra stress Harry had given to "rashness", they didn't say anything.

In the corridor outside, Weber got up as soon as Harry came out.

'Next please,' Harry said. 'What's that you've got?'

Weber lifted up a plastic bag. 'Gunnerud's gun. I'll have to go in and get this over with.'

'Mm.' Harry flipped a cigarette out of the packet. 'Unusual gun.'

'Israeli,' Weber said. 'Jericho 941.'

Harry stood staring at the door as it slammed after Weber until Møller came past and called his attention to the unlit cigarette in his mouth.

It was strangely quiet in the Robberies Unit. At first the detectives had joked that the Expeditor had gone into hibernation, but now they said he had let himself be shot and buried in a secret place so as to achieve eternal legendary status. The snow lay on the roofs around town, slid down and new snow came while smoke rose peacefully from chimneys.

The three units at Police HQ arranged a Christmas party in the canteen. Seating was fixed and Bjarne Møller, Beate Lønn and Halvorsen ended up sitting next to each other. Between them, an empty chair and a plate with Harry's name card on.

'Where is he?' Møller asked, pouring wine for Beate.

'Out looking for one of Sverre Olsen's pals who says he saw Olsen and another guy on the night of the murder,' Halvorsen said, struggling to open a beer bottle with a disposable lighter.

'That's frustrating,' Møller said. 'Tell him not to work himself to death. A Christmas dinner doesn't take up much time after all.'

'You tell him,' Halvorsen said.

'Perhaps he just doesn't want to be here,' Beate said.

The two men looked at her and smiled.

'What's the matter?' She laughed. 'Don't you think I know Harry as well?'

They toasted. Halvorsen hadn't stopped smiling. He just watched. There was something – he couldn't quite put his finger on what – different about her. The last time he saw her was in the meeting

470

room, but she hadn't had this *life* in her eyes. The blood in her lips. The posture, the willowy back.

'Harry would rather go to prison than to affairs like these,' Møller said and told them about the time Linda from reception in POT had forced him to dance. Beate laughed so much she had to wipe the tears from her eyes. Then she turned to Halvorsen and tilted her head: 'Are you going to sit there gawping all night, Halvorsen?'

Halvorsen could feel his cheeks burning and managed to stammer out a puzzled 'Not at all' before Møller and Beate burst out laughing again.

Later that evening he plucked up the courage to ask her if she felt like a whirl on the dance floor. Møller sat alone until Ivarsson came over and sat on Beate's chair. He was drunk, slurring his speech, and he talked about the time he sat terrified out of his wits in front of a bank in Ryen.

'It's a long time ago, Rune,' Møller said. 'You were straight out of college. You couldn't have done anything anyway.'

Ivarsson leaned back and studied Møller. Then he got up and left. Møller guessed Ivarsson was a lonely person who didn't even know it himself.

When the DJs Li and Li finished by playing 'Purple Rain' Beate and Halvorsen bumped into one of the other couples dancing and Halvorsen noticed how Beate's body suddenly stiffened. He looked up at the other couple.

'Sorry,' said a deep voice. The strong white teeth in the David Hasselhoff face shone in the dark.

When the evening was over, it was impossible to get hold of a taxi and Halvorsen offered to accompany Beate home. They trudged eastwards in the snow and it took them over an hour before they were standing outside her door in Oppsal.

Beate smiled and faced Halvorsen. 'If you would like that, you're very welcome,' she said.

'I'd love it,' he said. 'Thank you.'

'Then it's a deal,' she said. 'I'll tell my mother tomorrow.'

He said goodnight, kissed her on the cheek and began the polar expedition westwards again.

The Norwegian Meteorological Institute announced that the twenty-year-old snowfall record for December was about to be broken.

The same day the SEFO wound up the Tom Waaler case.

The panel concluded that nothing contrary to regulations had been uncovered. Quite the contrary, Waaler was praised for having acted correctly and maintained his composure in an extremely tense situation. The Chief Superintendent called the Chief Constable to make a tentative enquiry about whether he thought they should recommend Waaler for an award. However, since Alf Gunnerud's family was one of the more distinguished in Oslo – his uncle was on the City Council – they felt it might be perceived as inappropriate.

It was Christmas Eve and Christmas peace and goodwill settled over, well, at least, little Norway.

Rakel had chased Harry and Oleg out of the house and made Christmas lunch. When they returned, the whole house smelt of ribs. Olav Hole, Harry's father, arrived with Sis in a taxi.

Sis was ecstatic about the house, the food, Oleg, everything. During the meal she and Rakel chatted away like best friends while old Olav and young Oleg sat opposite each other and exchanged monosyllables for the most part. But they thawed when it was time for presents and Oleg opened his large parcel with 'from Olav to Oleg' on. It was Jules Verne's collected works. Open-mouthed, Oleg flicked through one of the books.

'He was the one who wrote about the moon rocket that Harry read to you,' Rakel said.

'Those are the original illustrations,' Harry said, pointing to the drawing of Captain Nemo standing by the flag at the South Pole and he read aloud: ' "Farewell. My new empire begins with six months of darkness." '

'These books were in my father's bookcase,' Olav said, as excited as Oleg.

'That doesn't matter!' Oleg burst out.

Olav received the hug of thanks with a shy but warm smile.

When they had gone to bed and Rakel was asleep, Harry got up and went to the window. He thought of all the people who were no longer there: his mother, Birgitta, Rakel's father, Ellen and Anna. And those who were there. Øystein in Oppsal, to whom Harry had given a new pair of shoes for Christmas, Raskol in Botsen and the two women in Oppsal who had been so kind as to invite Halvorsen to a late Christmas dinner since he had been on duty and wasn't going home to Steinkjer this year.

Something had happened this evening, he wasn't exactly sure what, but something had changed. He stood watching the lights in the town before he realised it had stopped snowing. Tracks. Those walking along the Akerselva tonight would leave tracks.

'Was your wish granted?' Rakel whispered when he was back in bed.

'Wish?' He put his arms round her.

'It looked as if you were making a wish by the window. What was it?'

'I have everything I could wish for,' Harry said, kissing her on the forehead.

'Tell me,' she whispered, leaning back to see him properly. 'Tell me your wish, Harry.'

'Do you really want to know?'

'Yes.' She snuggled up closer to him.

He closed his eyes and the film began to roll, so slowly that he could see every image like a still. Tracks in the snow.

'Peace,' he lied.

51

Sans Souci

HARRY LOOKED AT THE PHOTOGRAPH, AT THE WARM, WHITE smile, the powerful jaws and the steel-blue eyes. Tom Waaler. Then he pushed the picture across the desk.

'Take your time,' he said. 'And look carefully.'

Roy Kvinsvik seemed nervous. Harry leaned back in his office chair and looked around him. Halvorsen had hung up an Advent calendar on the wall over the filing cabinet. Christmas Day. Harry almost had the whole floor to himself. That was the best thing about holidays. He doubted he would hear Kvinsvik speaking in tongues as he had when he found him in the front row in the Philadelphian church, but you lived in hope.

Kvinsvik cleared his throat and Harry sat up straight.

Outside the window snowflakes gently fluttered down onto the empty streets.